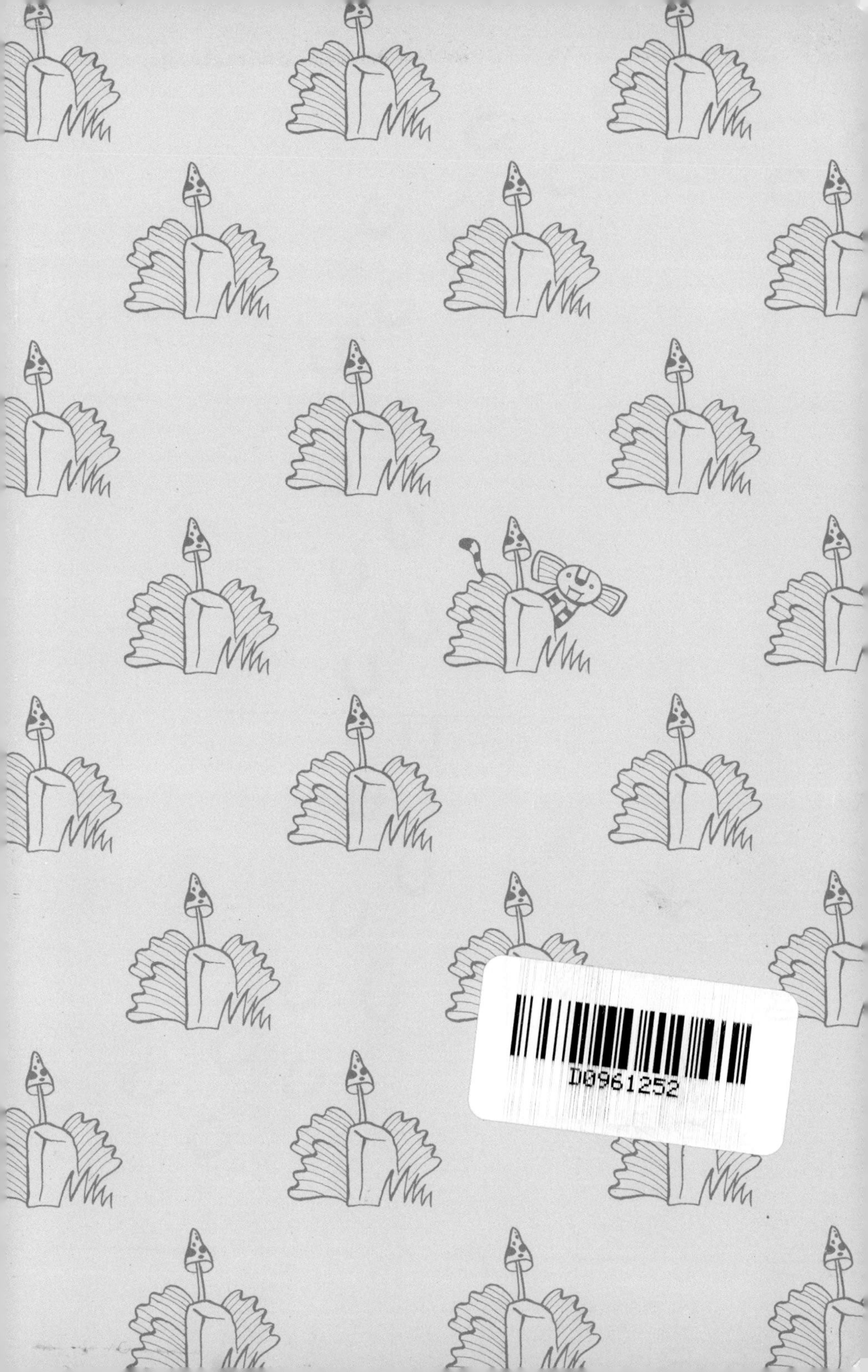

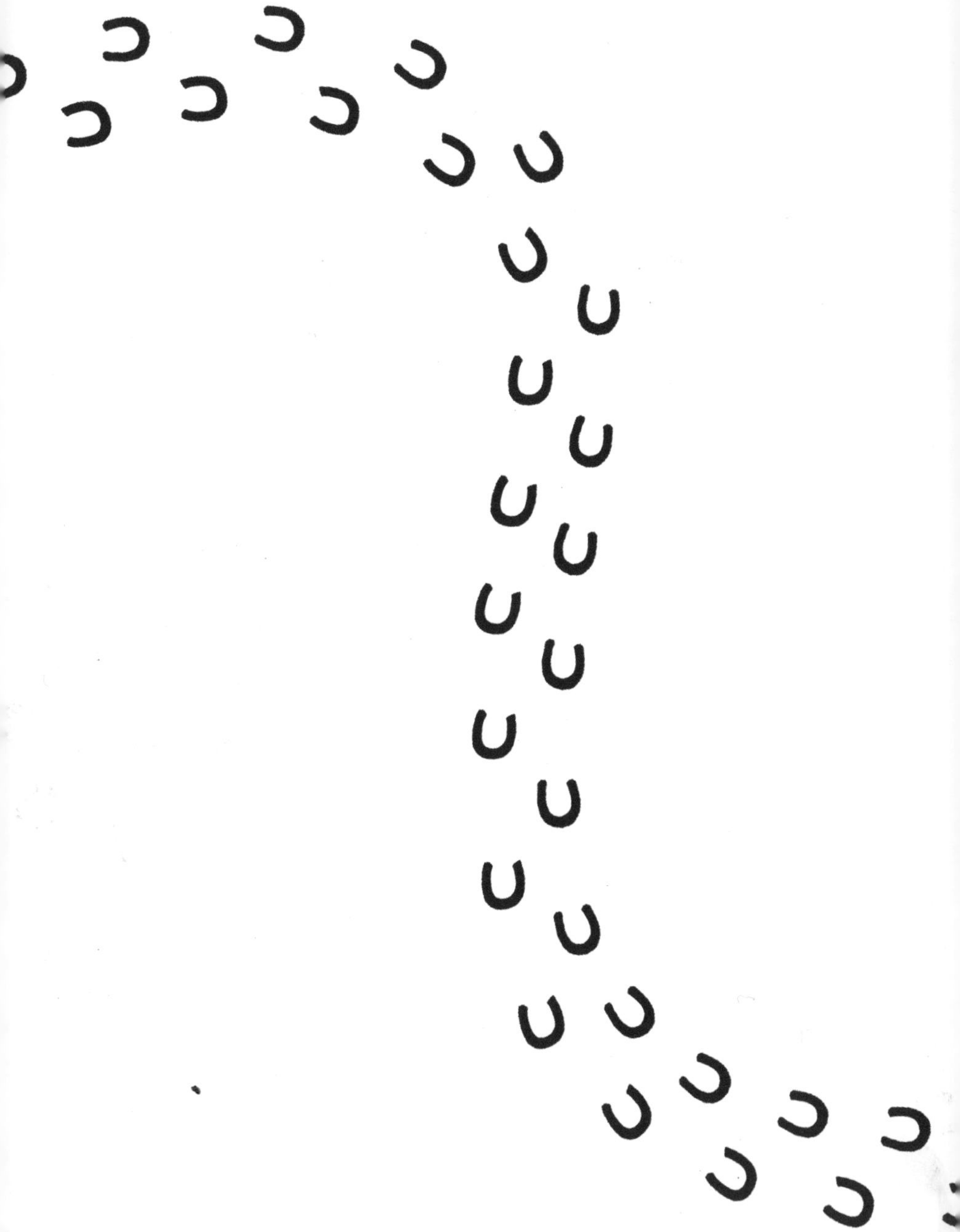

PACEY PACKER
UNICORN TRACKER

WITHDRAWN

J. C. PHILLIPPS

RANDOM HOUSE 🏠 NEW YORK

This is a work of fiction. Names, characters, places, and incidents either
are the product of the author's imagination or are used fictitiously. Any resemblance
to actual persons, living or dead, events, or locales is entirely coincidental.

Copyright © 2020 by J. C. Phillipps
All rights reserved. Published in the United States by Random House Children's Books,
a division of Penguin Random House LLC, New York.

Random House and the colophon are registered trademarks of Penguin Random House LLC.
Visit us on the Web! rhcbooks.com
Educators and librarians, for a variety of teaching tools,
visit us at RHTeachersLibrarians.com

Library of Congress Cataloging-in-Publication Data
Names: Phillipps, J. C. (Julie C.), author.
Title: Pacey Packer: unicorn tracker / J. C. Phillips.
Description: First Edition. | New York: Random House, [2020] | Series: Pacey Packer, unicorn tracker
Summary: Twelve-year-old Pacey travels through Rundalyn to rescue her
little sister, Mina, who was taken there by Slasher, her unicorn-turned-plush-toy,
who hopes to regain his rightful form and place in society.
Identifiers: LCCN 2019012007 (print) | LCCN 2019016460 (ebook) |
ISBN 978-1-9848-5054-6 (hardcover) | ISBN 978-1-9848-5055-3 (lib. bdg.) |
ISBN 978-1-9848-5056-0 (ebook)
Subjects: | CYAC: Adventure and adventurers—Fiction. | Unicorns—Fiction. |
Stuffed animals (Toys)—Fiction. | Sisters—Fiction. |
Kidnapping—Fiction. | Babysitters—Fiction.
Classification: LCC pZ7.P53725 (ebook) | LCC PZ7.P53725 Pac 2020 (print) | DDC [Fic]—dc23

MANUFACTURED IN CHINA
10 9 8 7 6 5 4 3 2 1
First Edition

Random House Children's Books supports the
First Amendment and celebrates the right to read.

For my husband,
who thought it was funny to tell
people that I loved unicorns

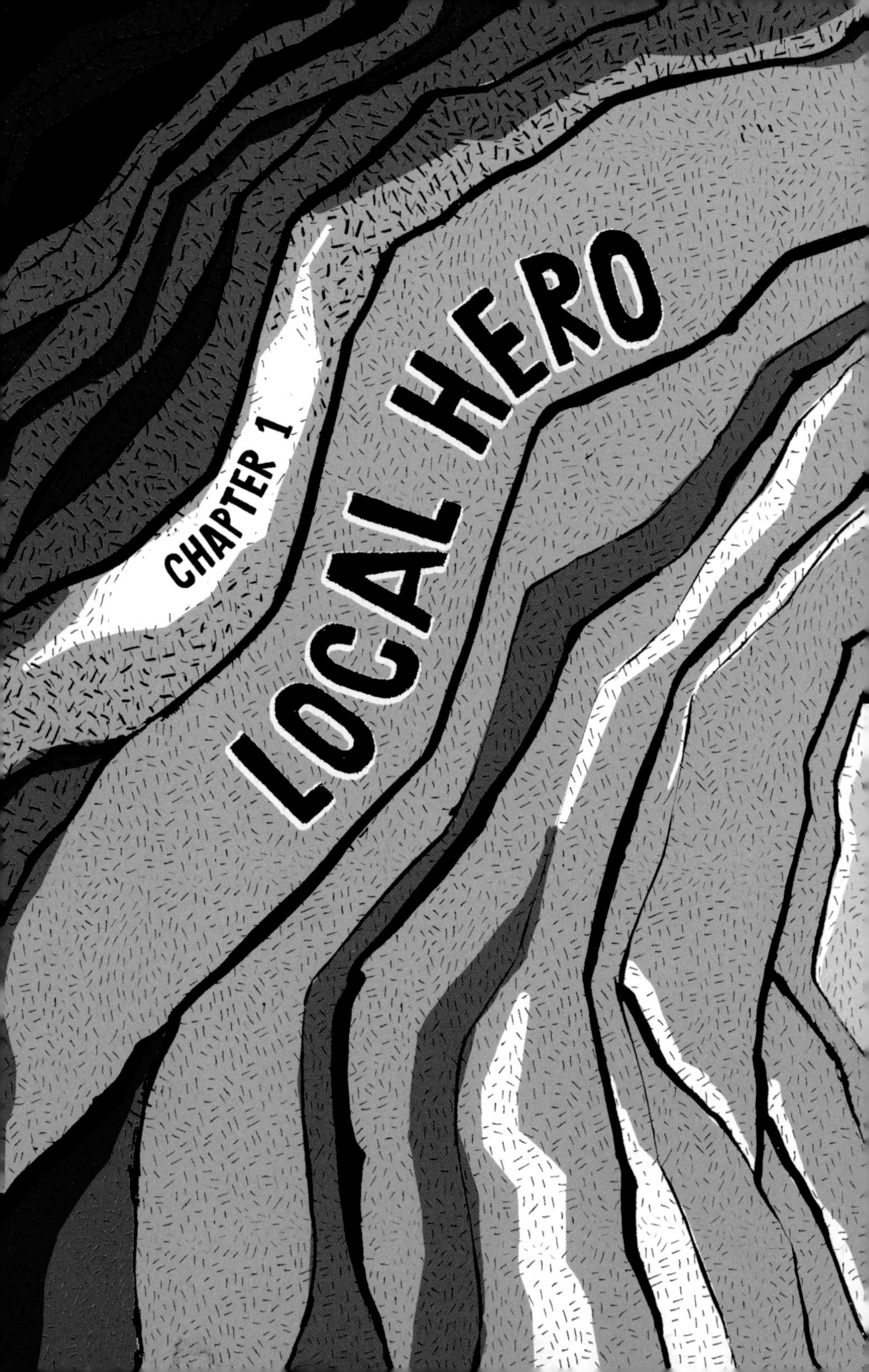
CHAPTER 1
LOCAL HERO

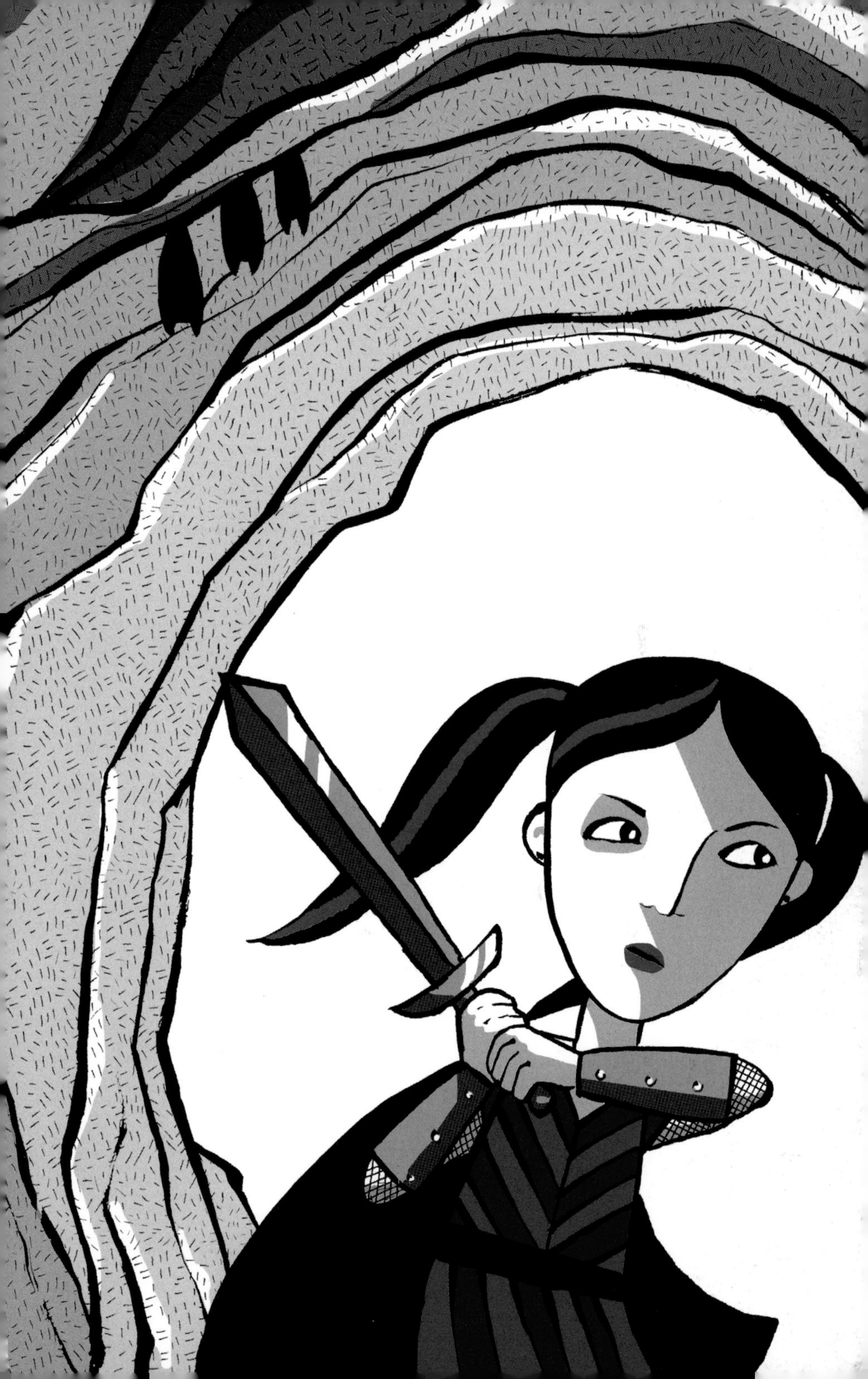

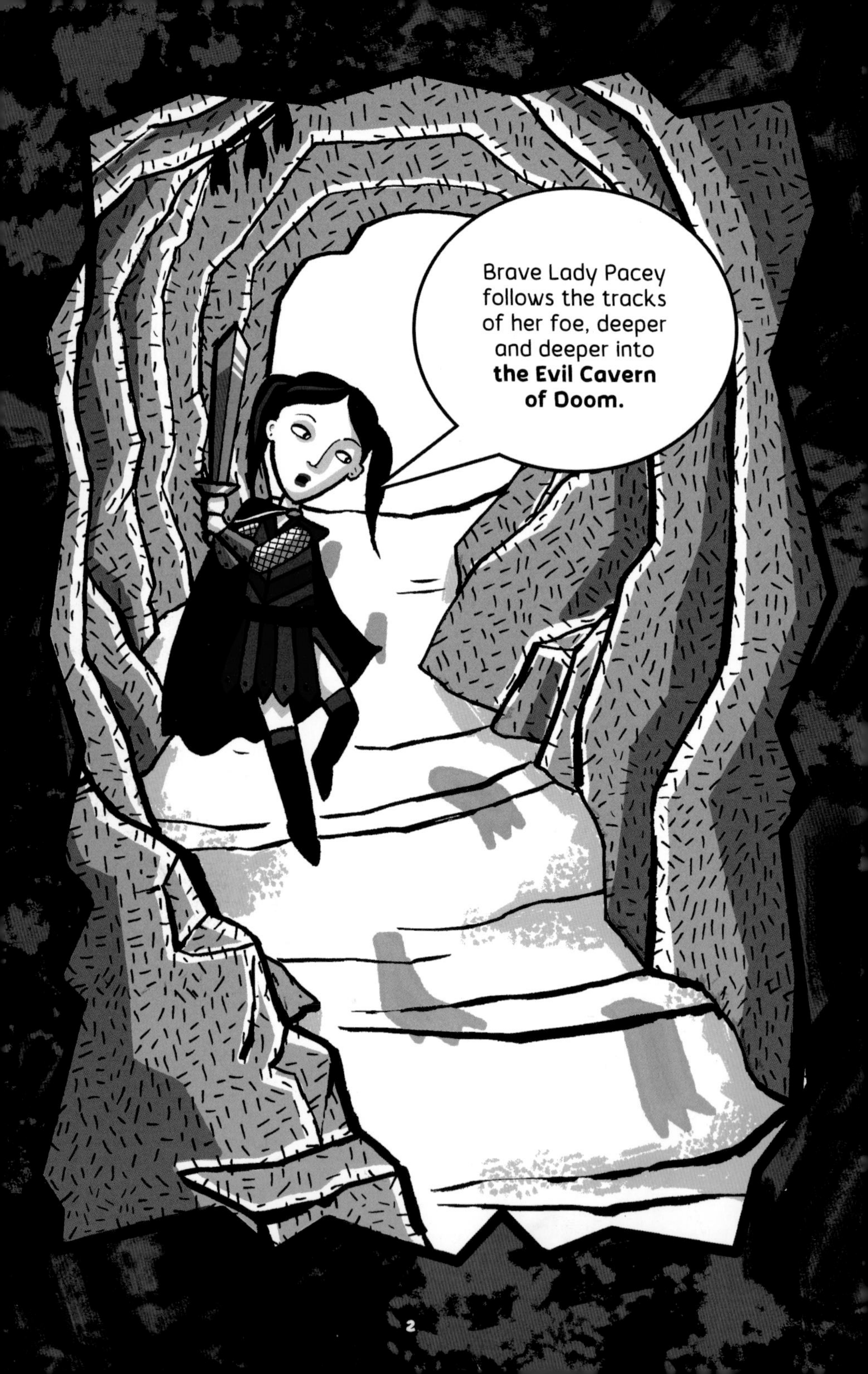
Brave Lady Pacey follows the tracks of her foe, deeper and deeper into **the Evil Cavern of Doom.**

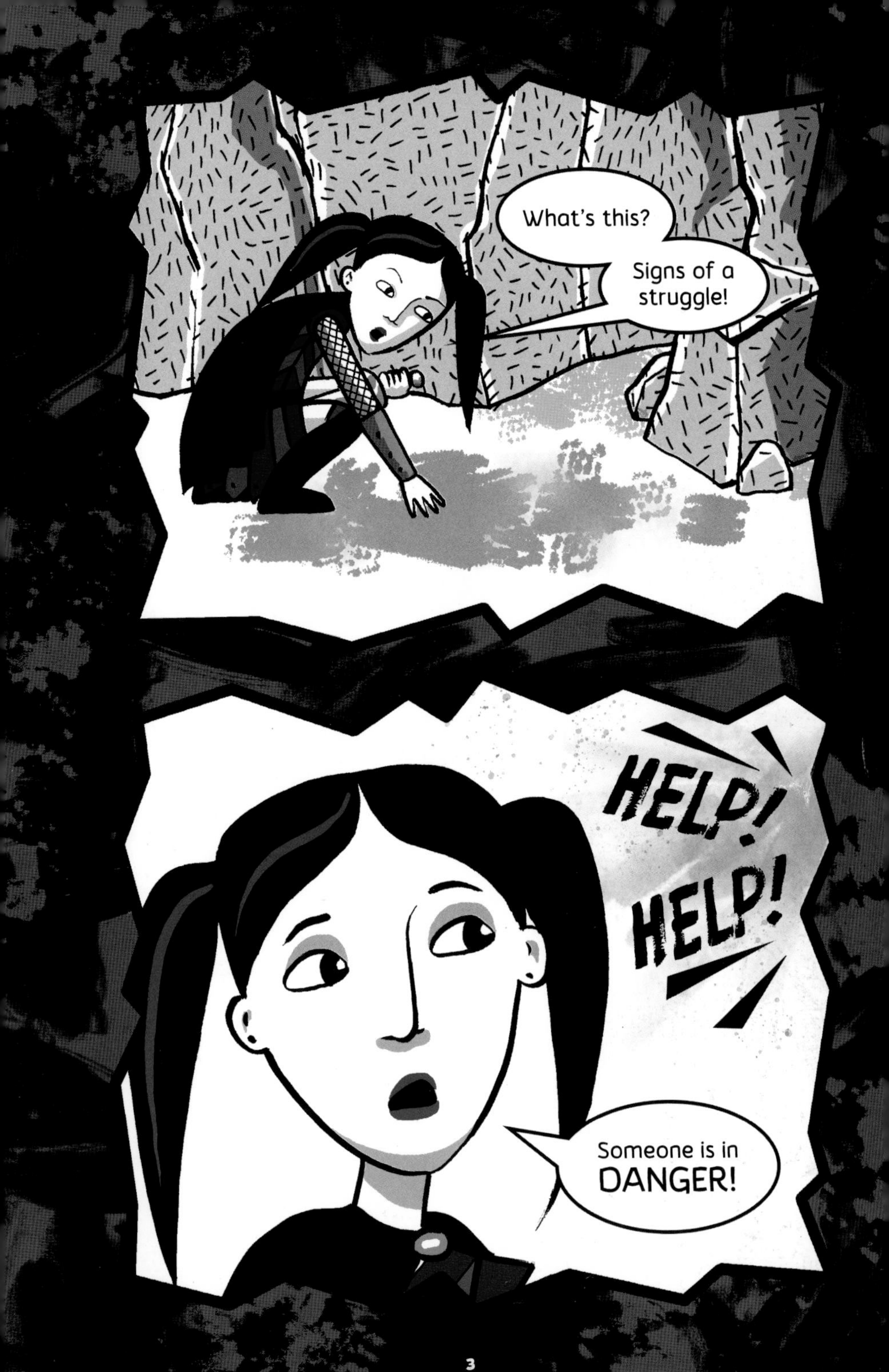
What's this?
Signs of a struggle!
HELP!
HELP!
Someone is in DANGER!

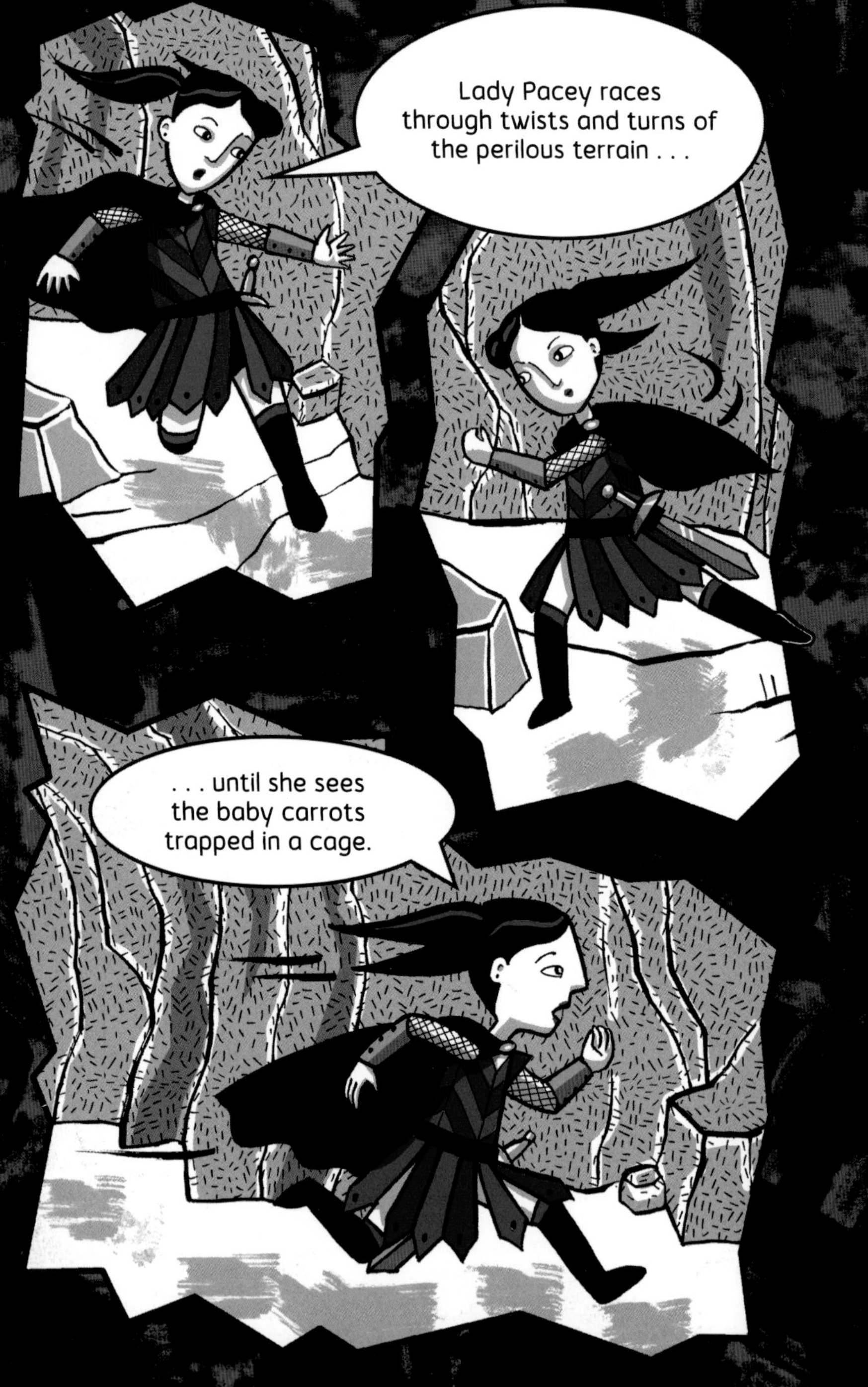
Lady Pacey races through twists and turns of the perilous terrain . . .
. . . until she sees the baby carrots trapped in a cage.

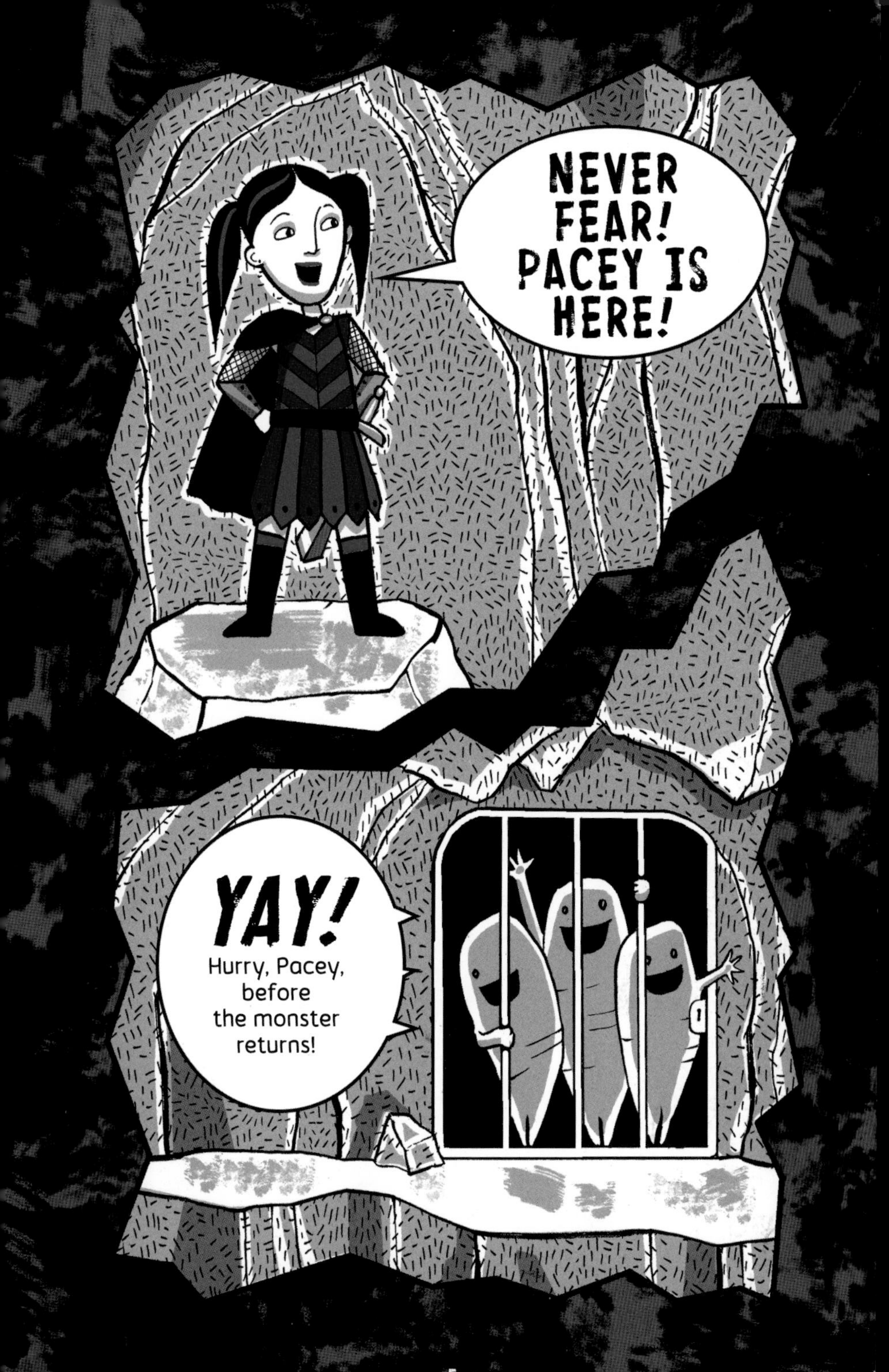
NEVER FEAR! PACEY IS HERE!
YAY!
Hurry, Pacey, before the monster returns!

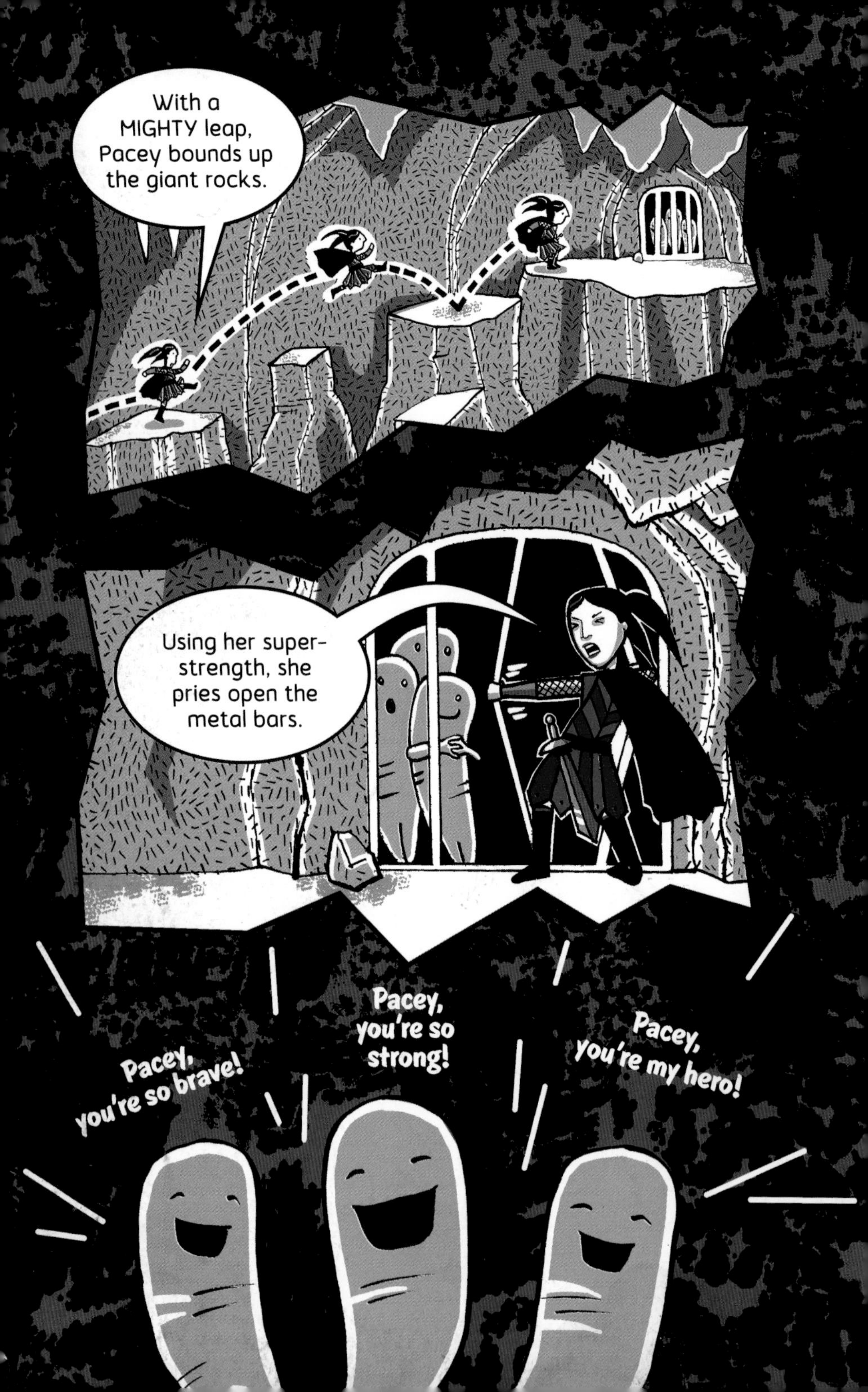
With a MIGHTY leap, Pacey bounds up the giant rocks.
Using her super-strength, she pries open the metal bars.
Pacey, you're so brave!
Pacey, you're so strong!
Pacey, you're my hero!

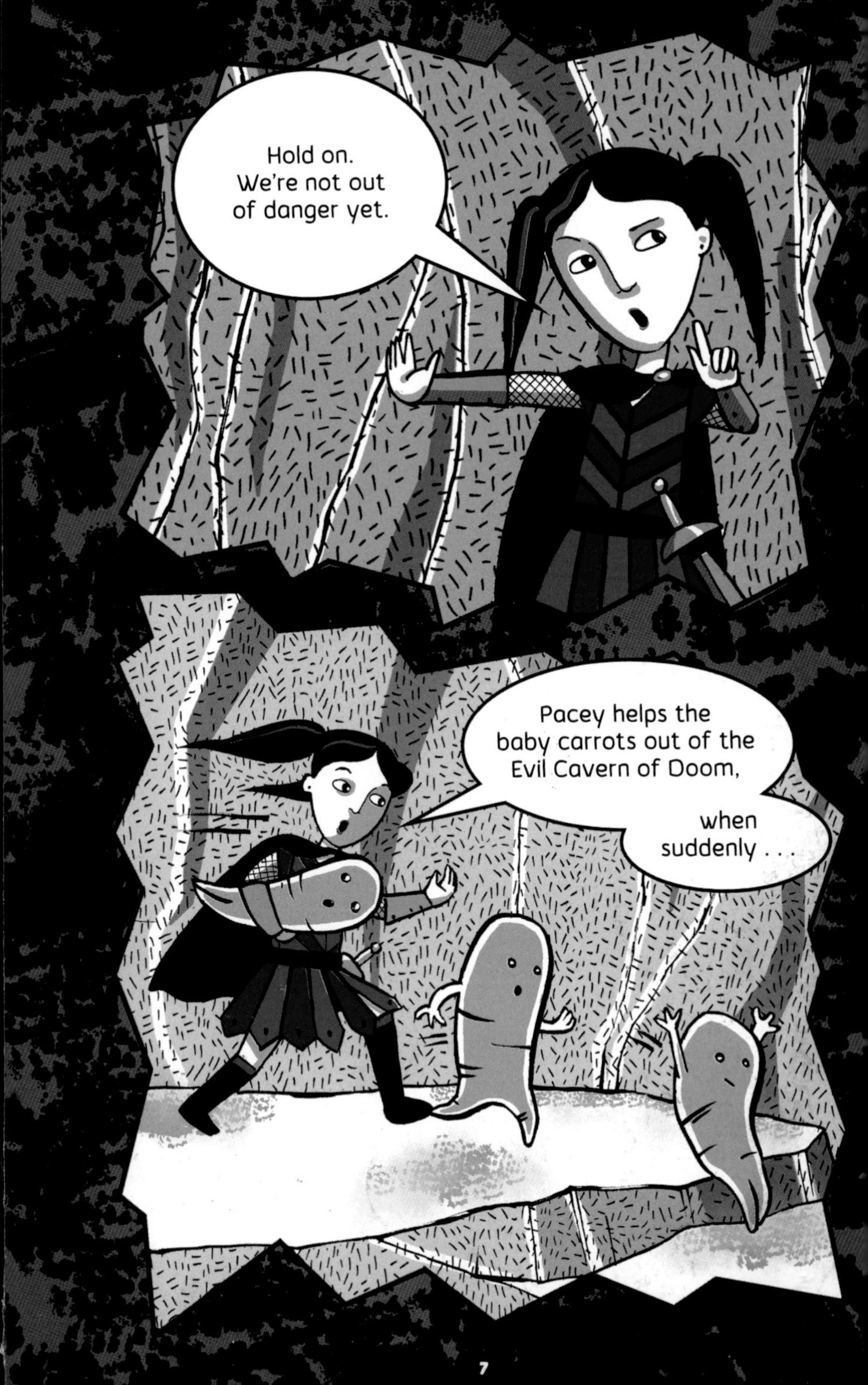
Hold on.
We're not out
of danger yet.
Pacey helps the
baby carrots out of the
Evil Cavern of Doom,
when
suddenly . . .

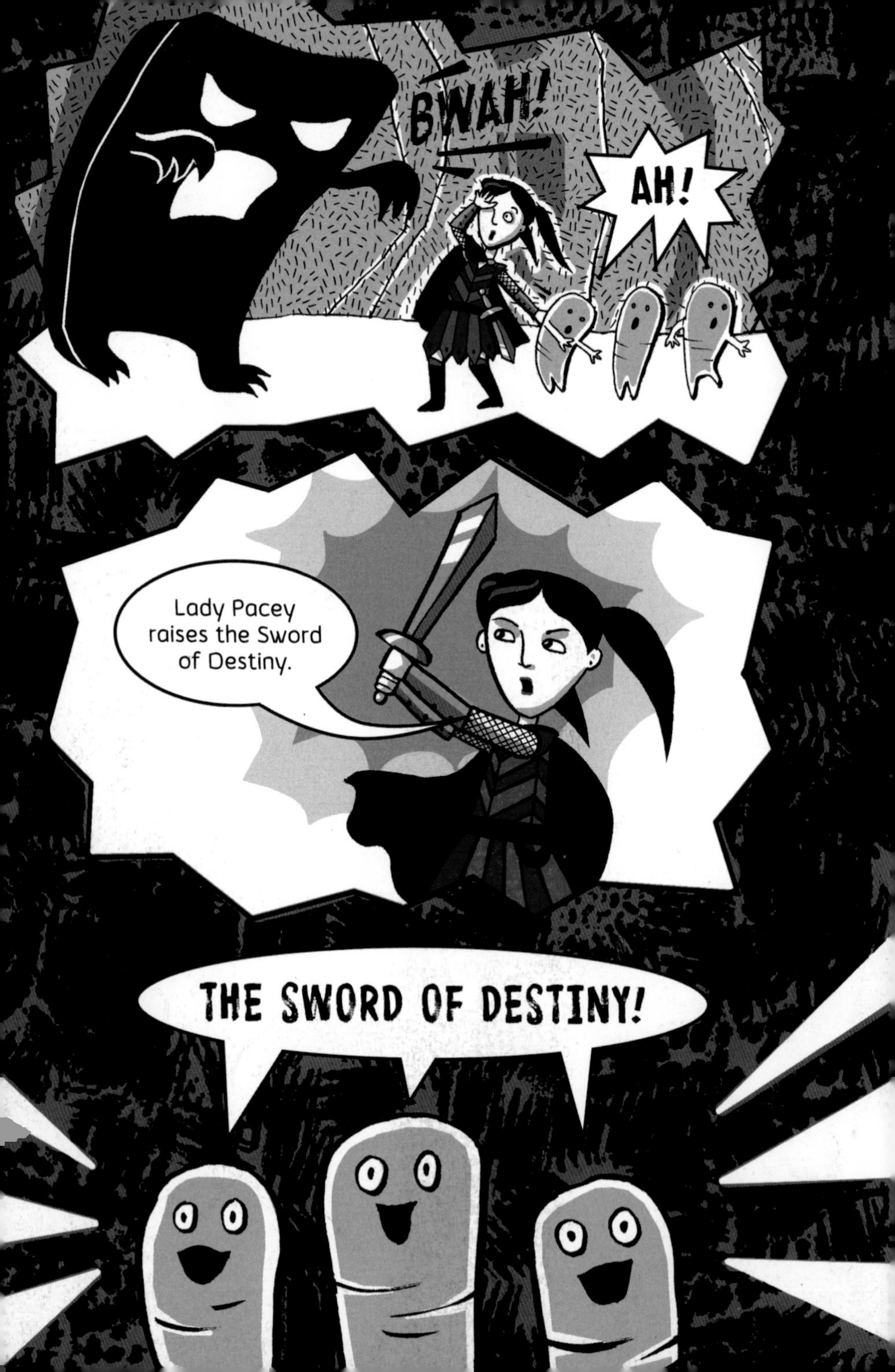
BWAH!
AH!
Lady Pacey raises the Sword of Destiny.
THE SWORD OF DESTINY!

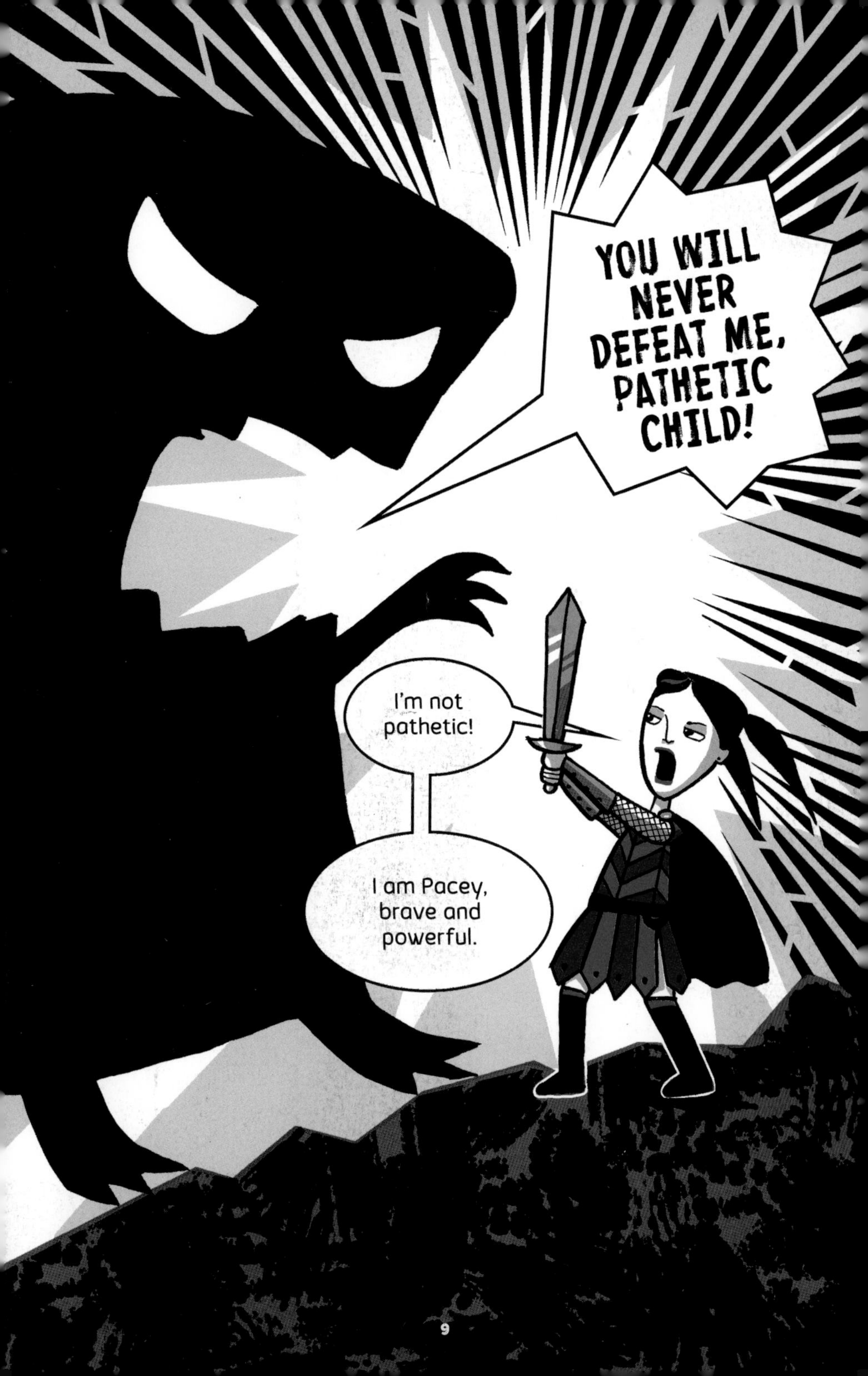
YOU WILL NEVER DEFEAT ME, PATHETIC CHILD!
I'm not pathetic!
I am Pacey, brave and powerful.

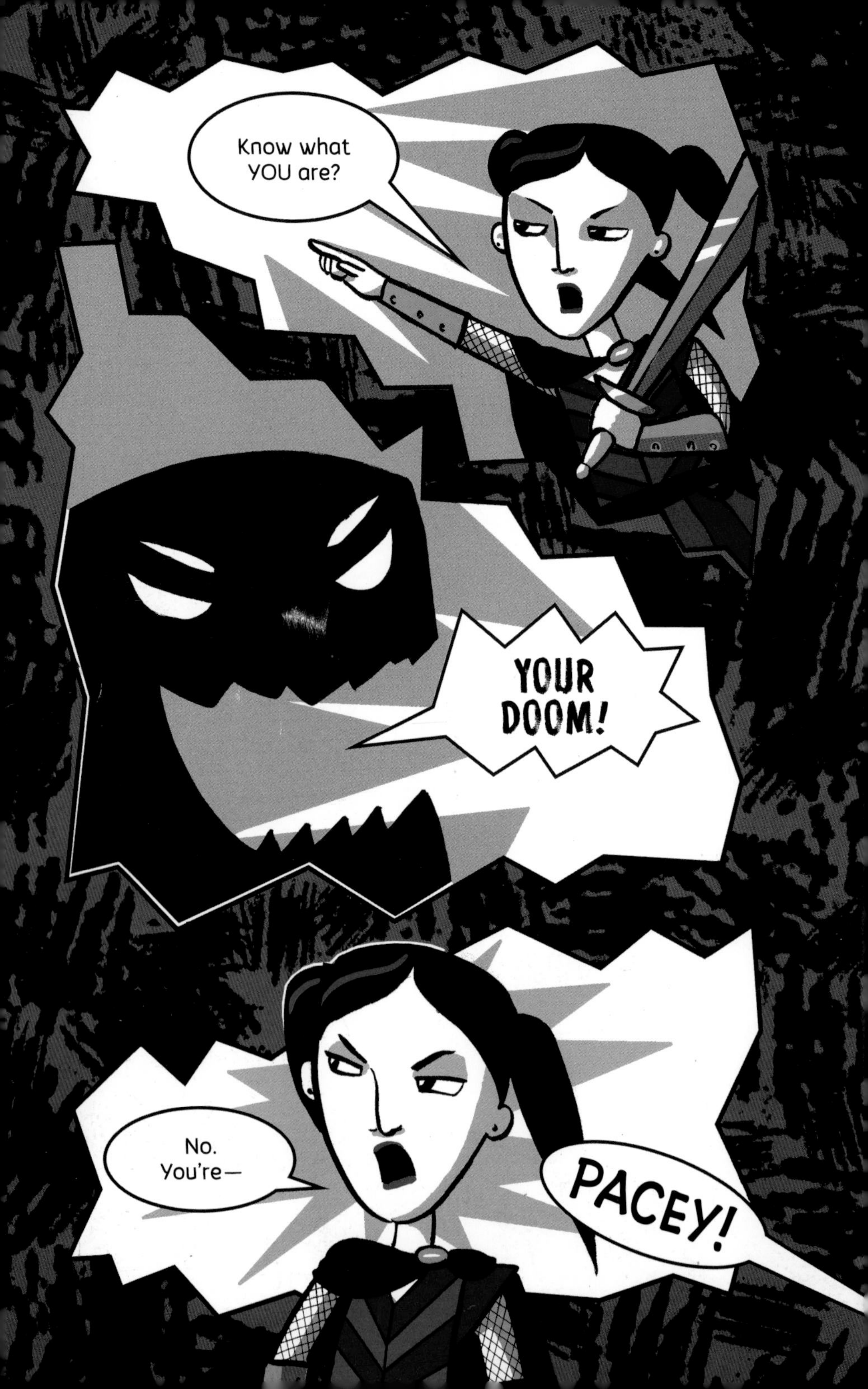
Know what YOU are?
YOUR DOOM!
No. You're—
PACEY!

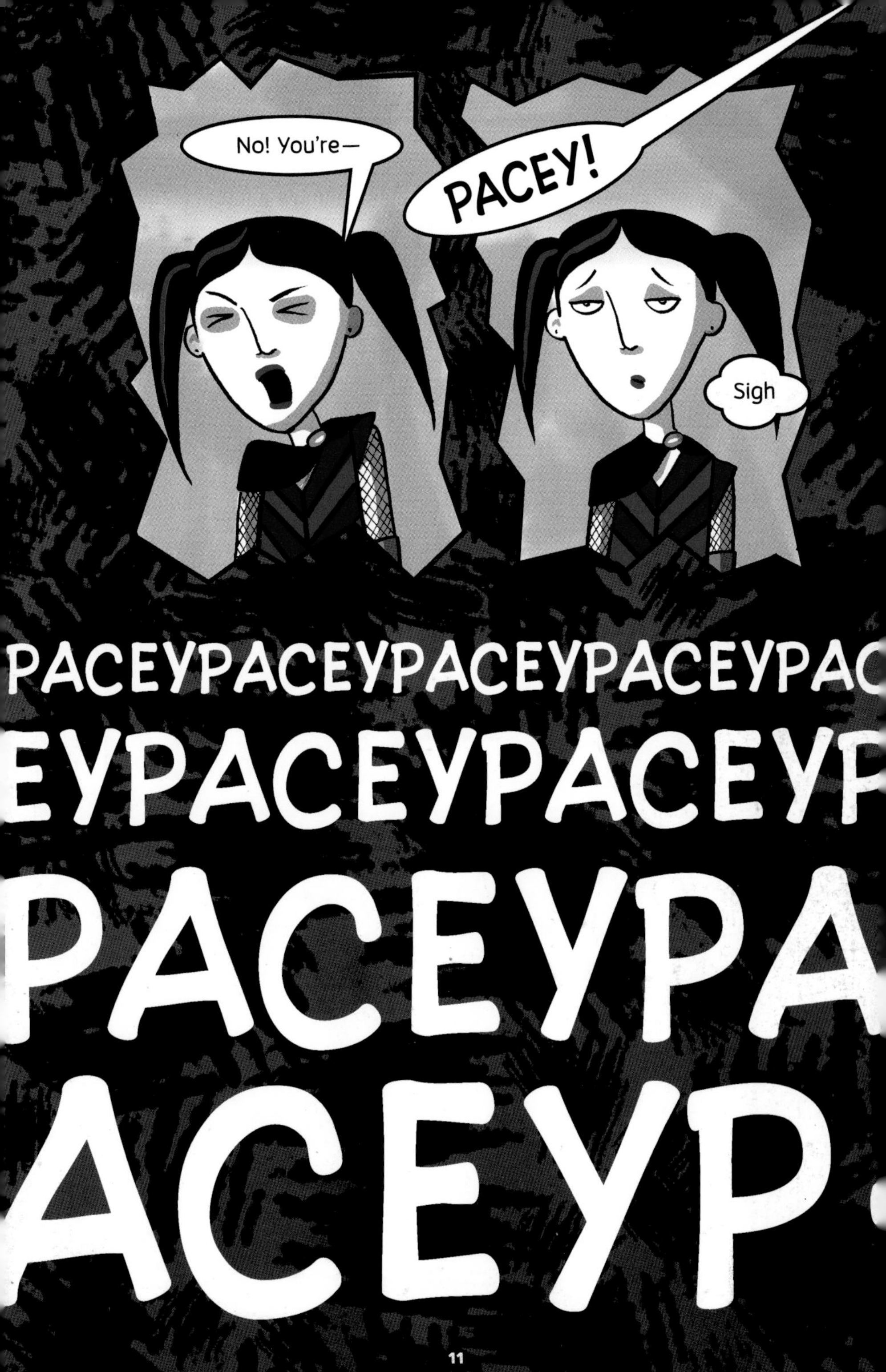
No! You're—
PACEY!
Sigh
PACEYPACEYPACEYPACEYPAC
EYPACEYPACEYP
PACEYPA
ACEYP

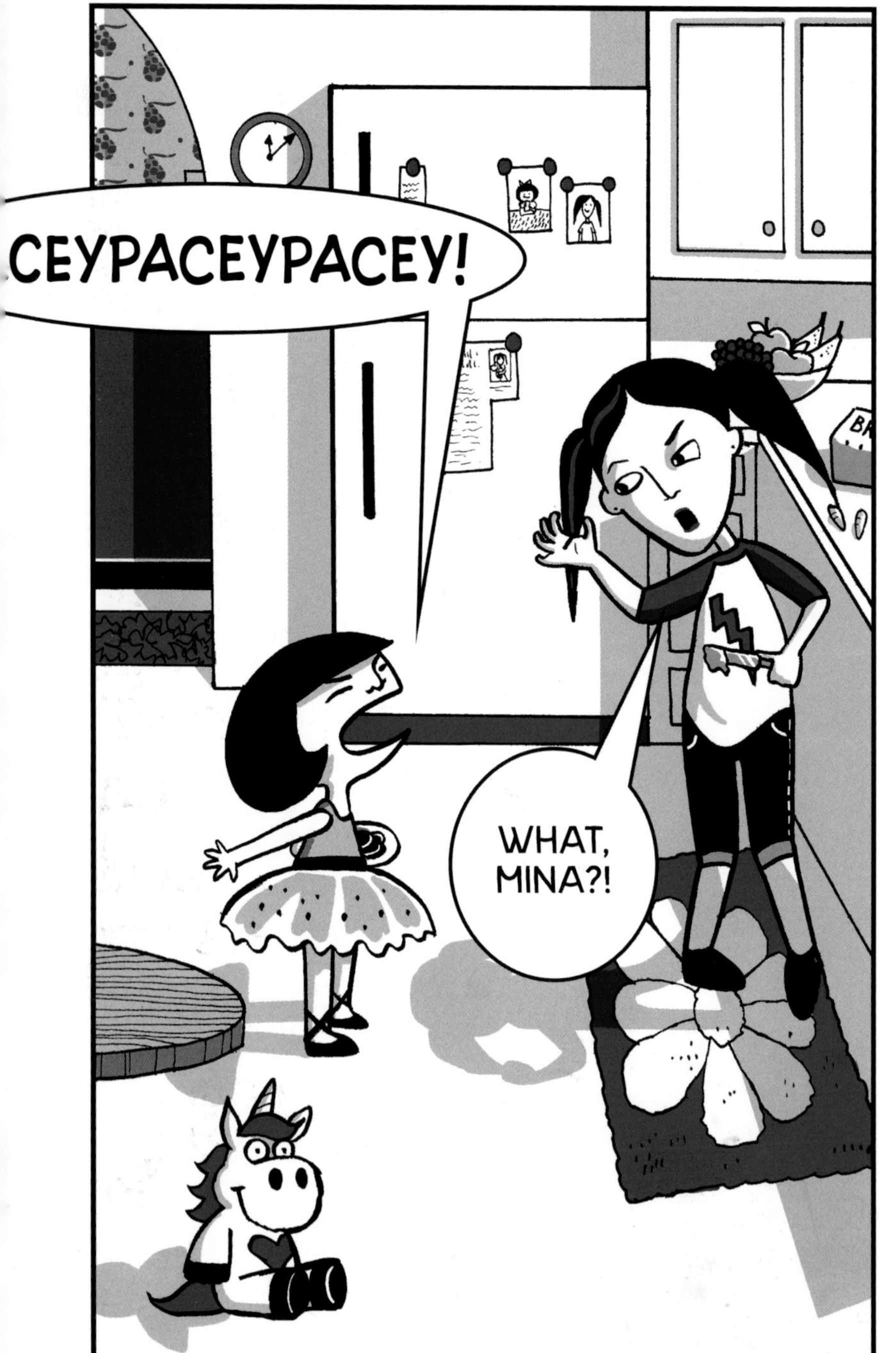
CEYPACEYPACEY!
WHAT, MINA?!

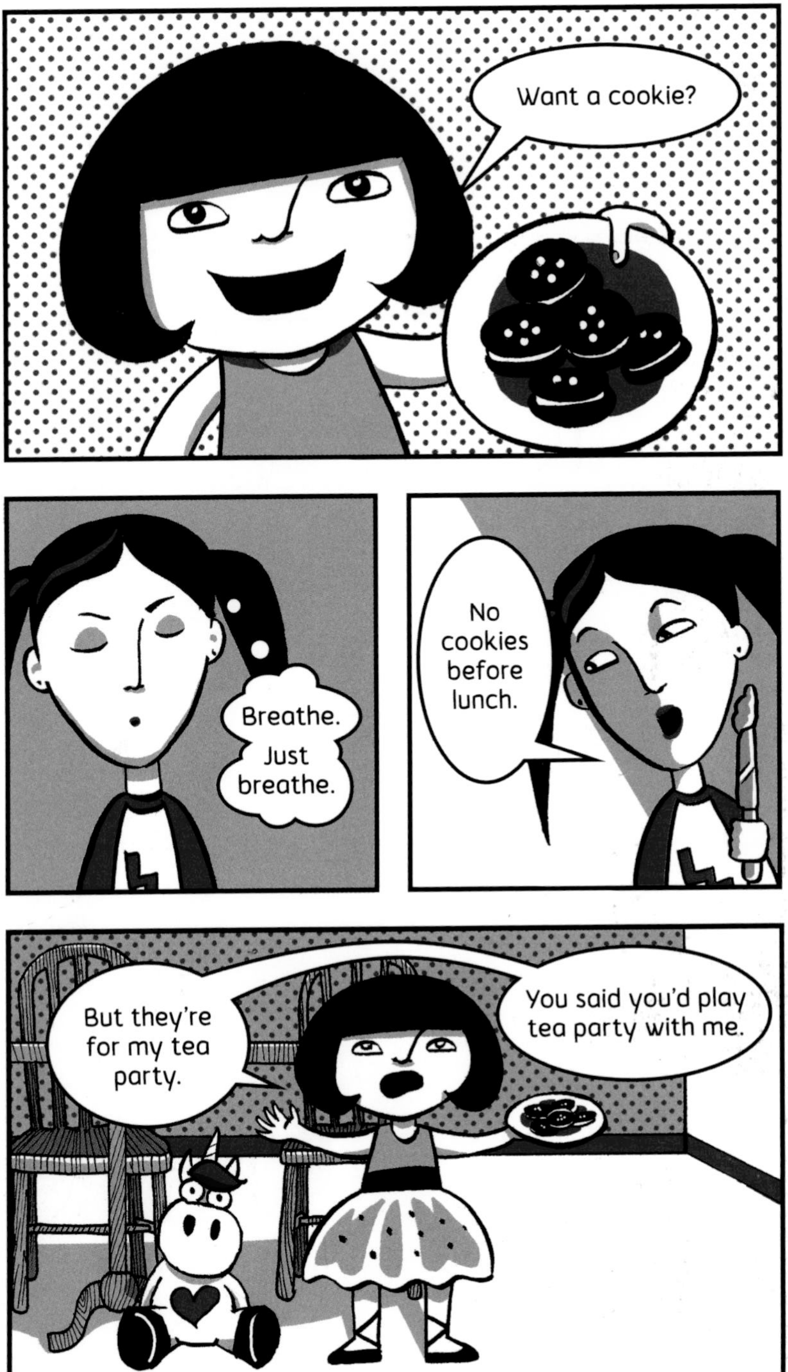
Want a cookie?
Breathe. Just breathe.
No cookies before lunch.
But they're for my tea party.
You said you'd play tea party with me.

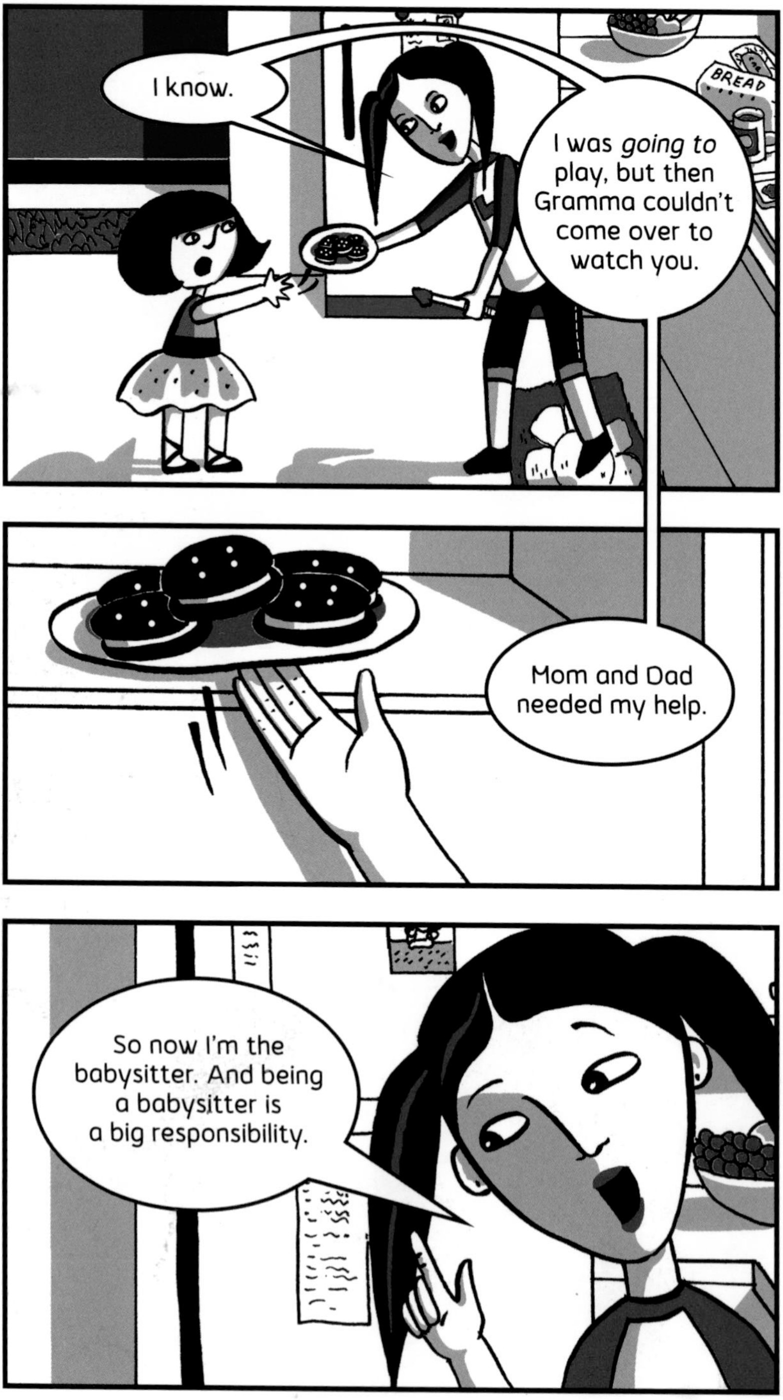
I know.
I was *going to* play, but then Gramma couldn't come over to watch you.
BREAD
Mom and Dad needed my help.
So now I'm the babysitter. And being a babysitter is a big responsibility.

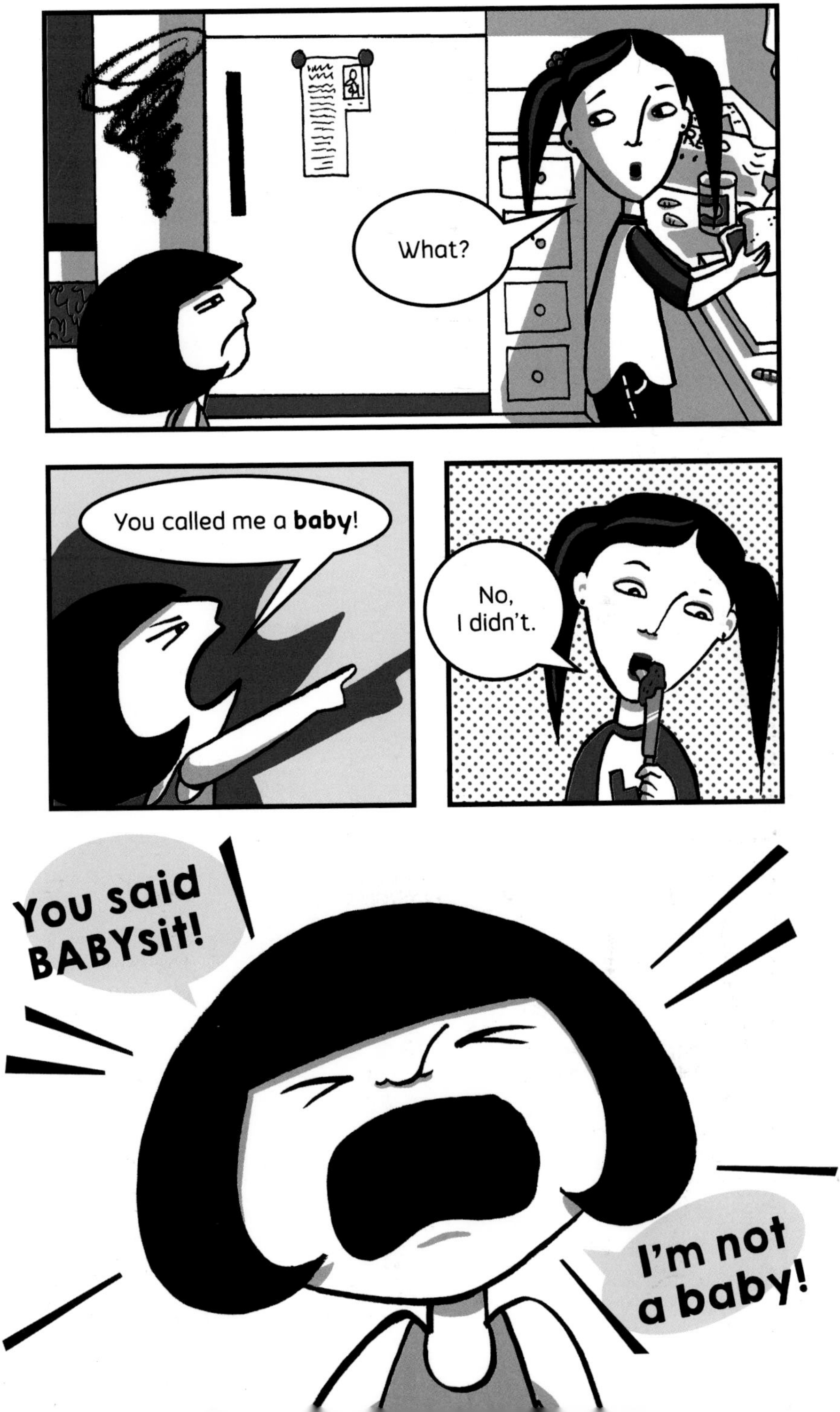
What?
You called me a **baby**!
No,
I didn't.
You said
BABYsit!
I'm not
a baby!

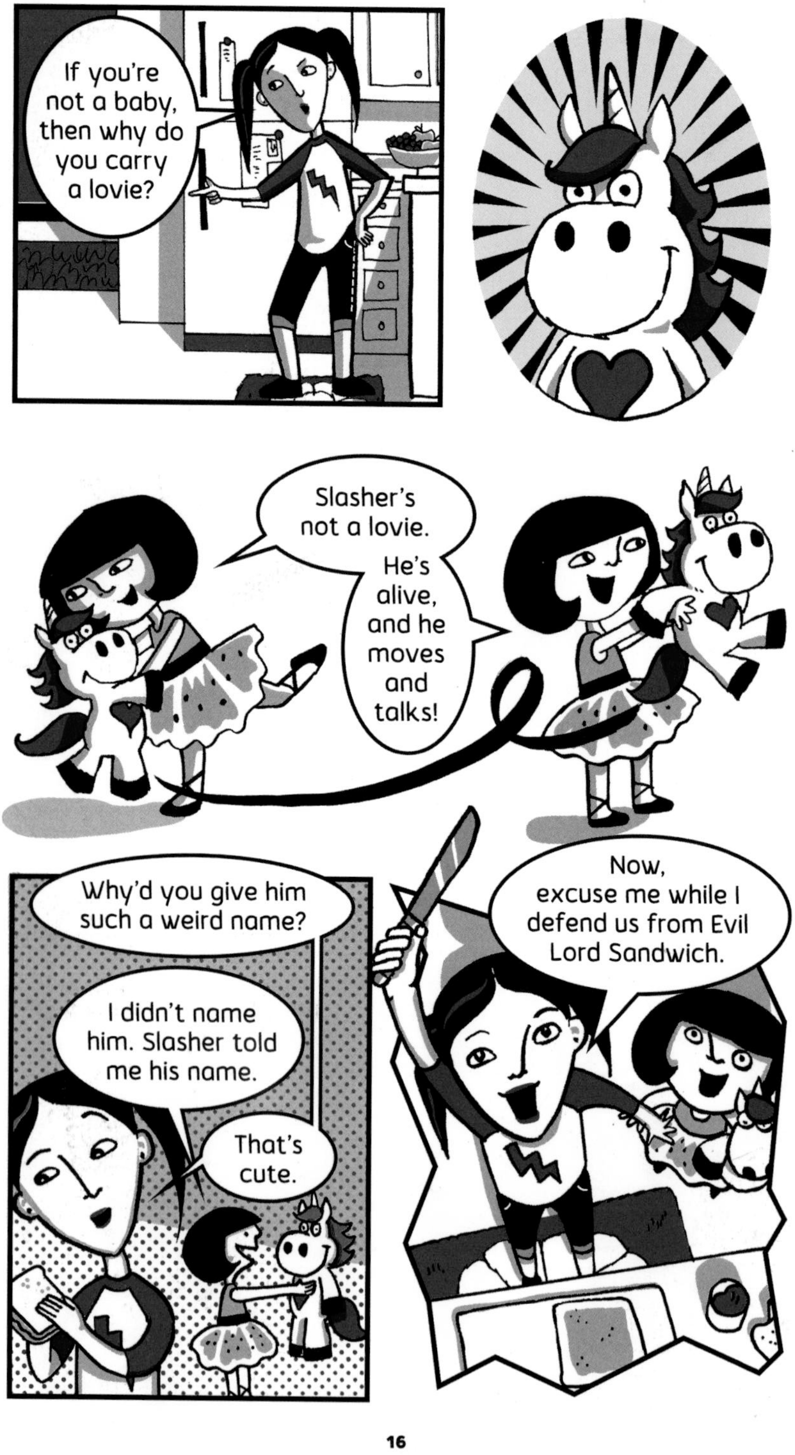
If you're not a baby, then why do you carry a lovie?
Slasher's not a lovie.
He's alive, and he moves and talks!
Why'd you give him such a weird name?
I didn't name him. Slasher told me his name.
That's cute.
Now, excuse me while I defend us from Evil Lord Sandwich.

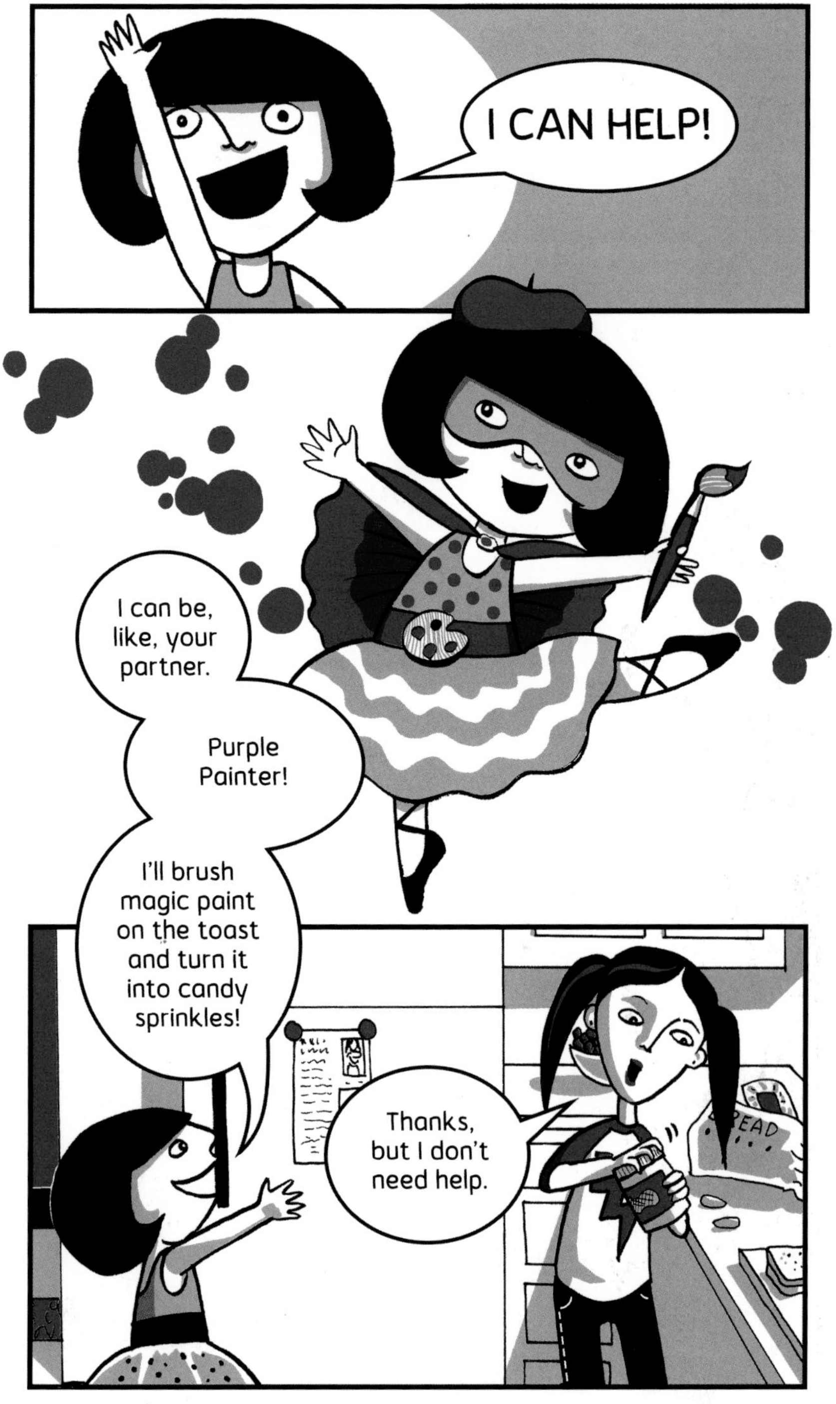
I CAN HELP!
I can be, like, your partner.
Purple Painter!
I'll brush magic paint on the toast and turn it into candy sprinkles!
Thanks, but I don't need help.
BREAD

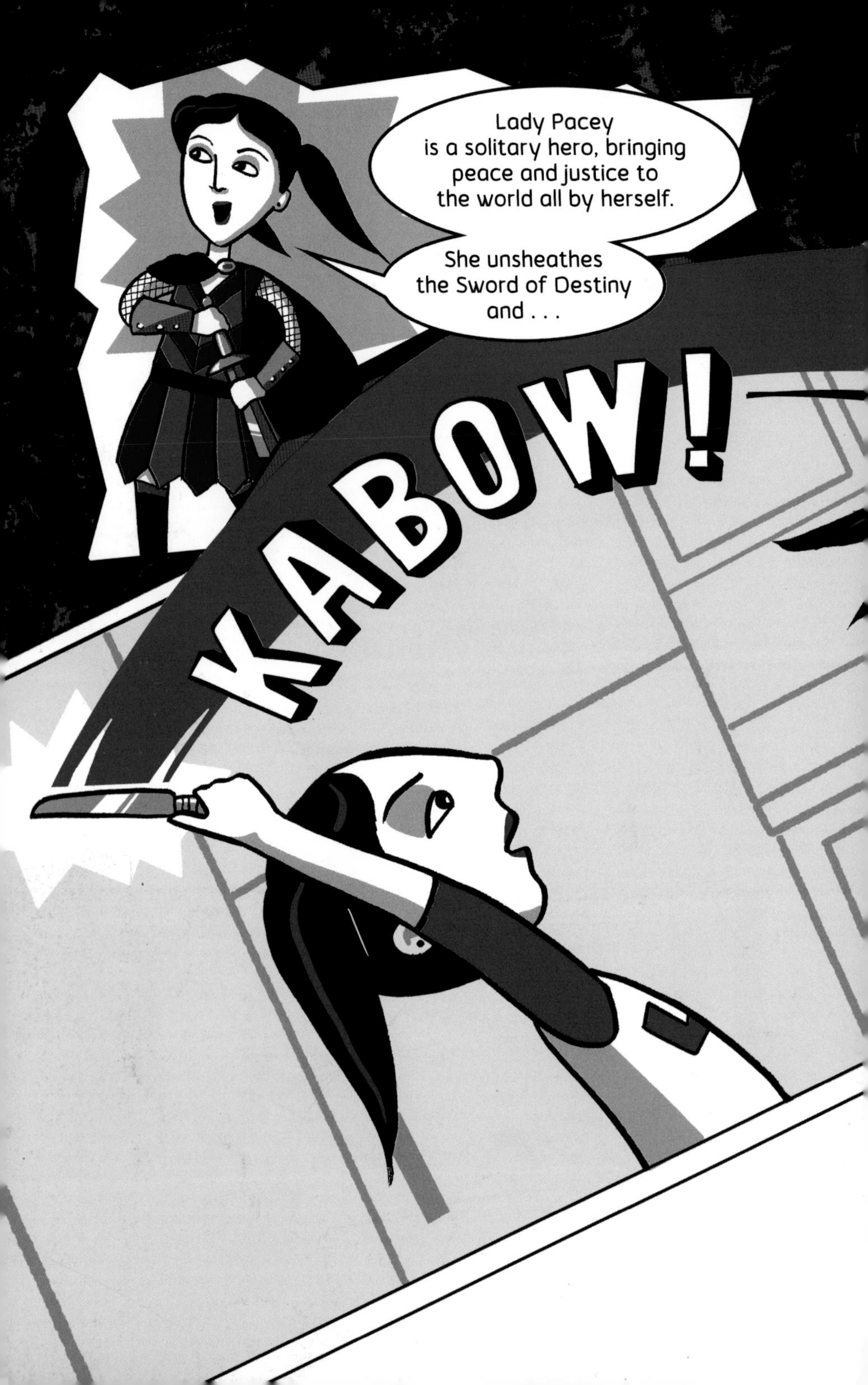
Lady Pacey is a solitary hero, bringing peace and justice to the world all by herself.
She unsheathes the Sword of Destiny and . . .
KABOW!

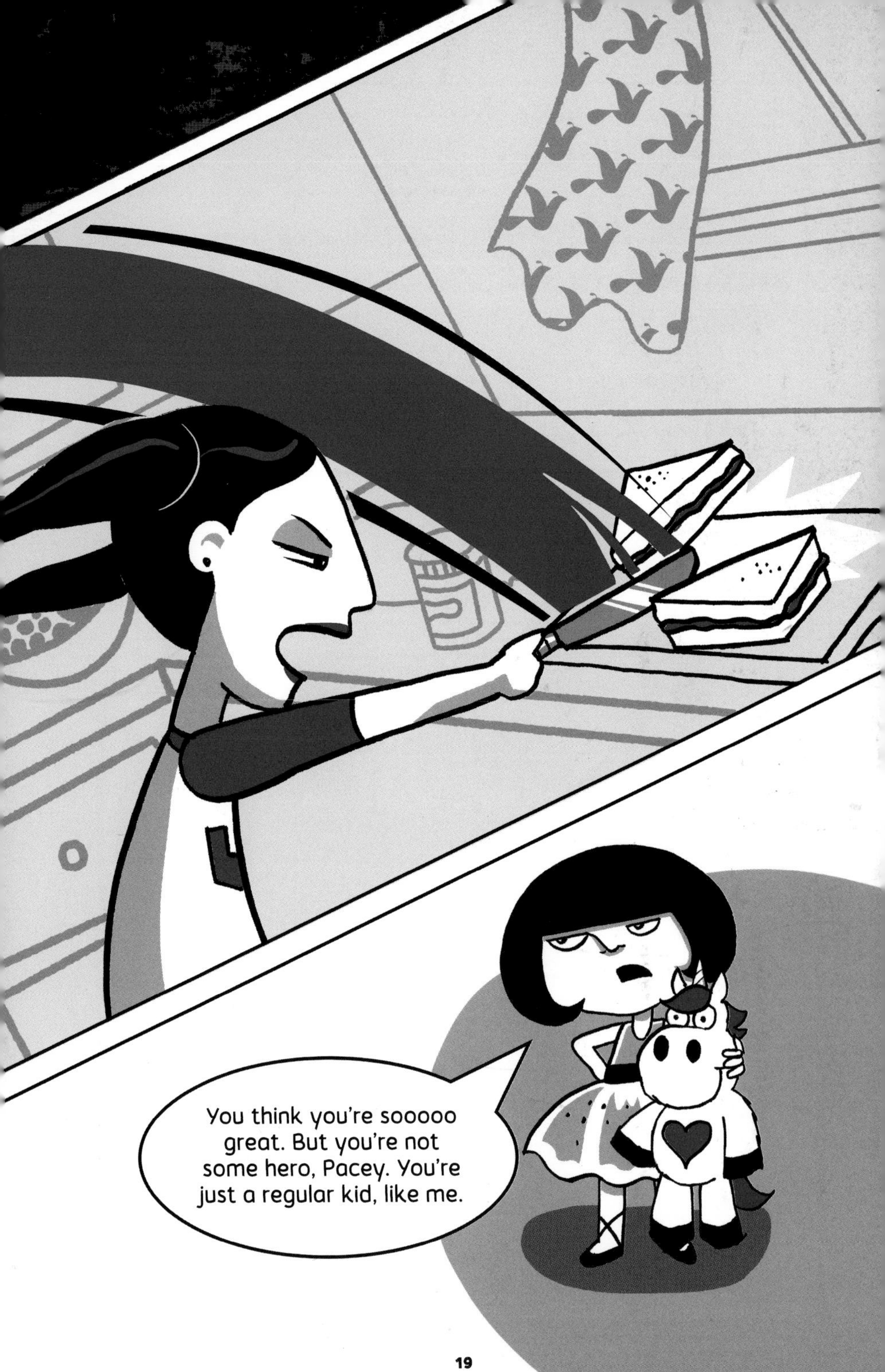
You think you're sooooo great. But you're not some hero, Pacey. You're just a regular kid, like me.

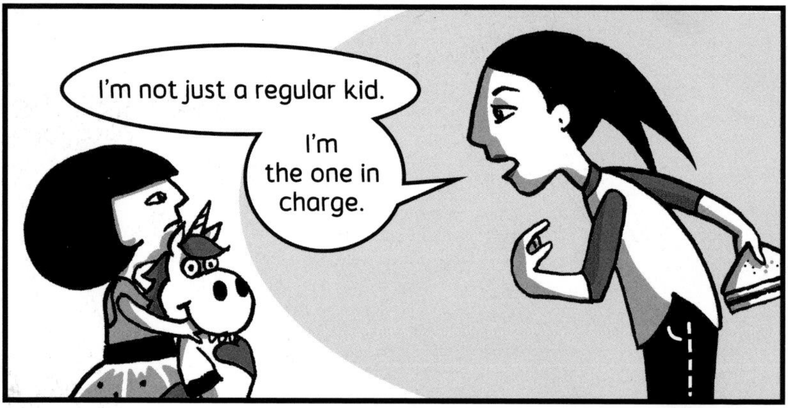
I'm not just a regular kid.
I'm the one in charge.

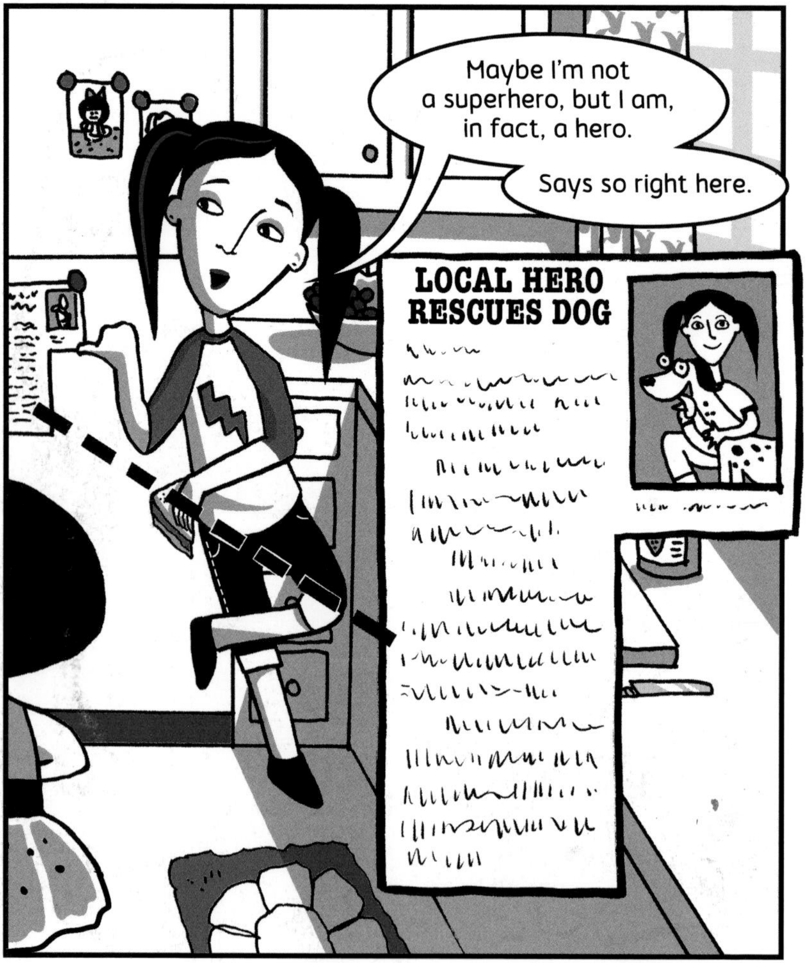
Maybe I'm not a superhero, but I am, in fact, a hero.
Says so right here.
LOCAL HERO RESCUES DOG

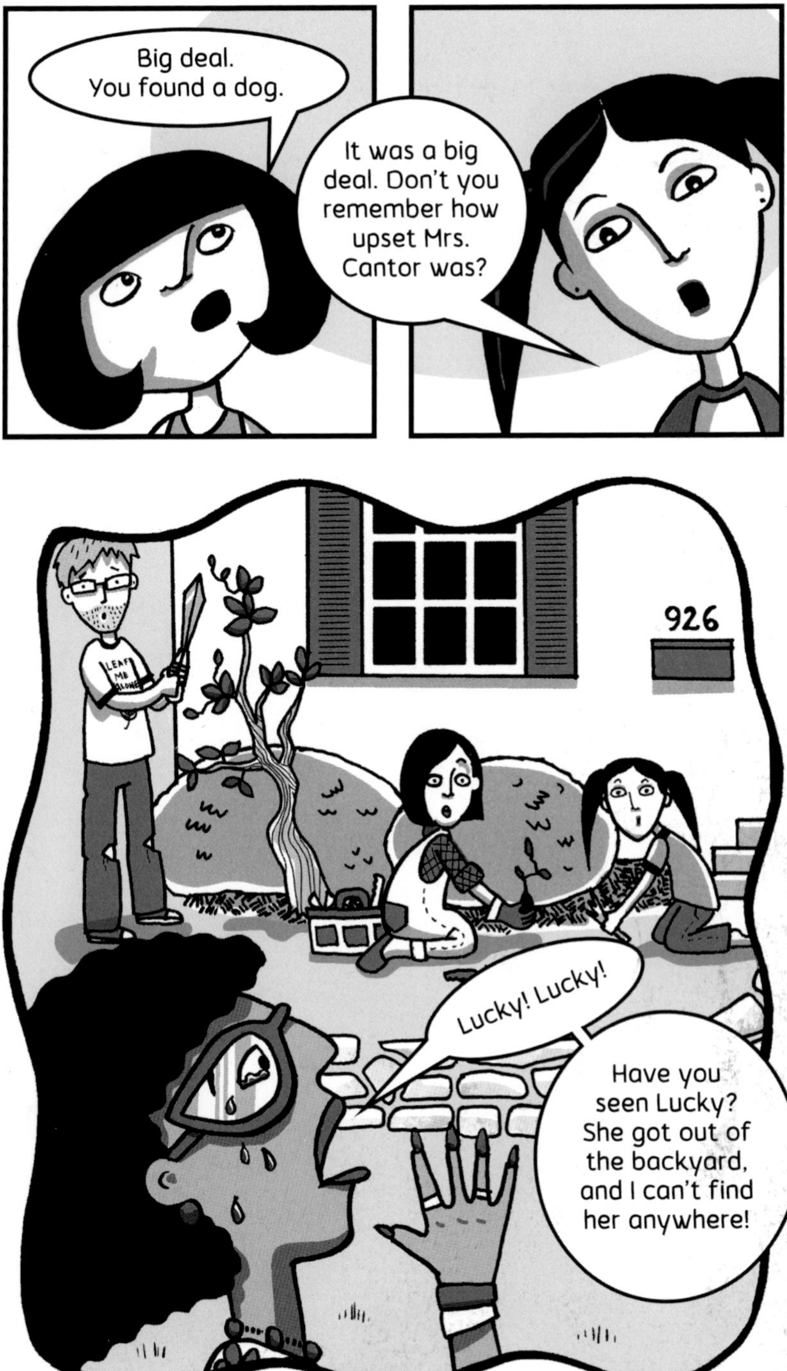
Big deal.
You found a dog.
It was a big deal. Don't you remember how upset Mrs. Cantor was?
926
LEAF ME ALONE
Lucky! Lucky!
Have you seen Lucky? She got out of the backyard, and I can't find her anywhere!

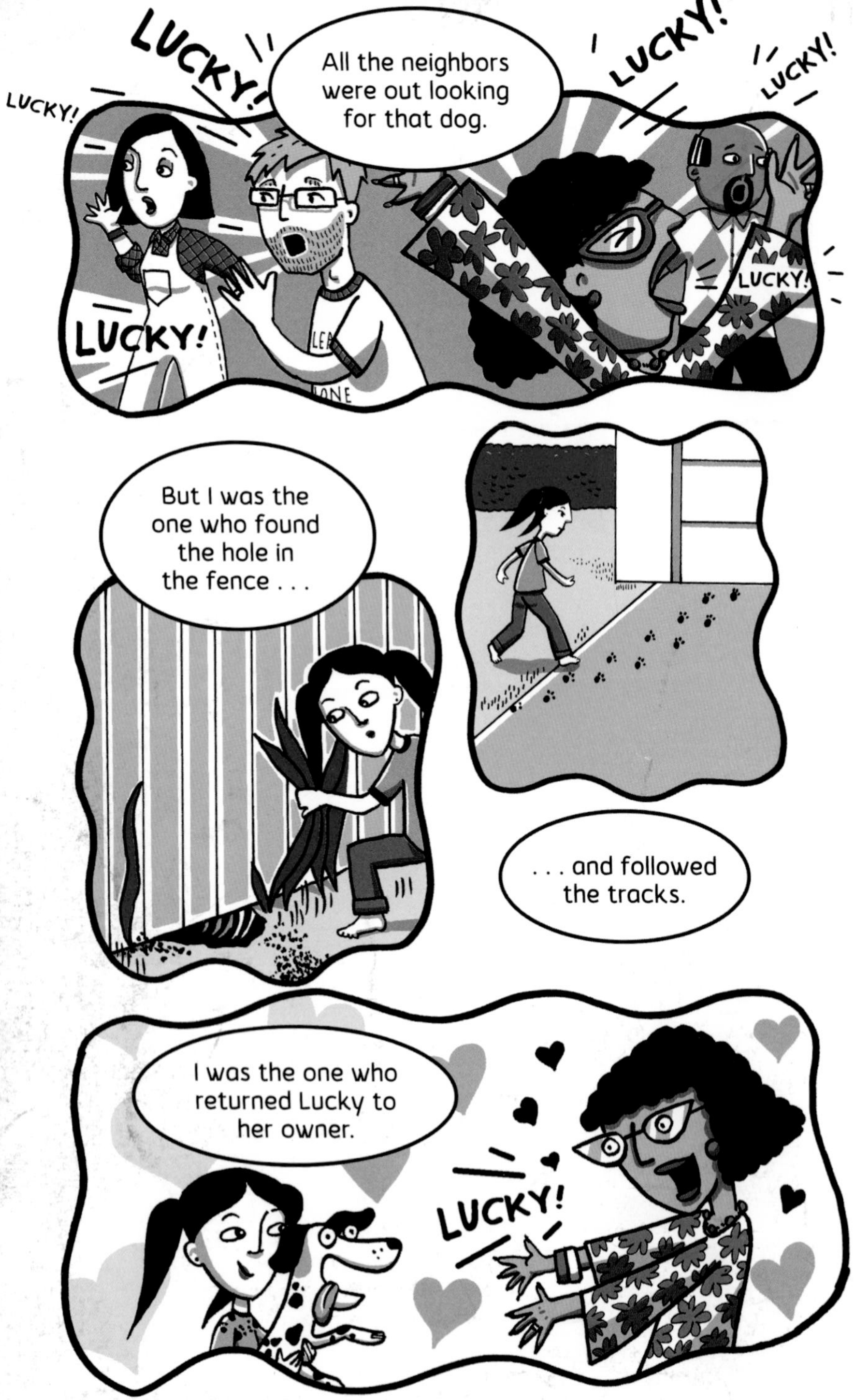
LUCKY!
LUCKY!
All the neighbors were out looking for that dog.
LUCKY!
LUCKY!
LUCKY!
LUCKY!
But I was the one who found the hole in the fence . . .
. . . and followed the tracks.
I was the one who returned Lucky to her owner.
LUCKY!

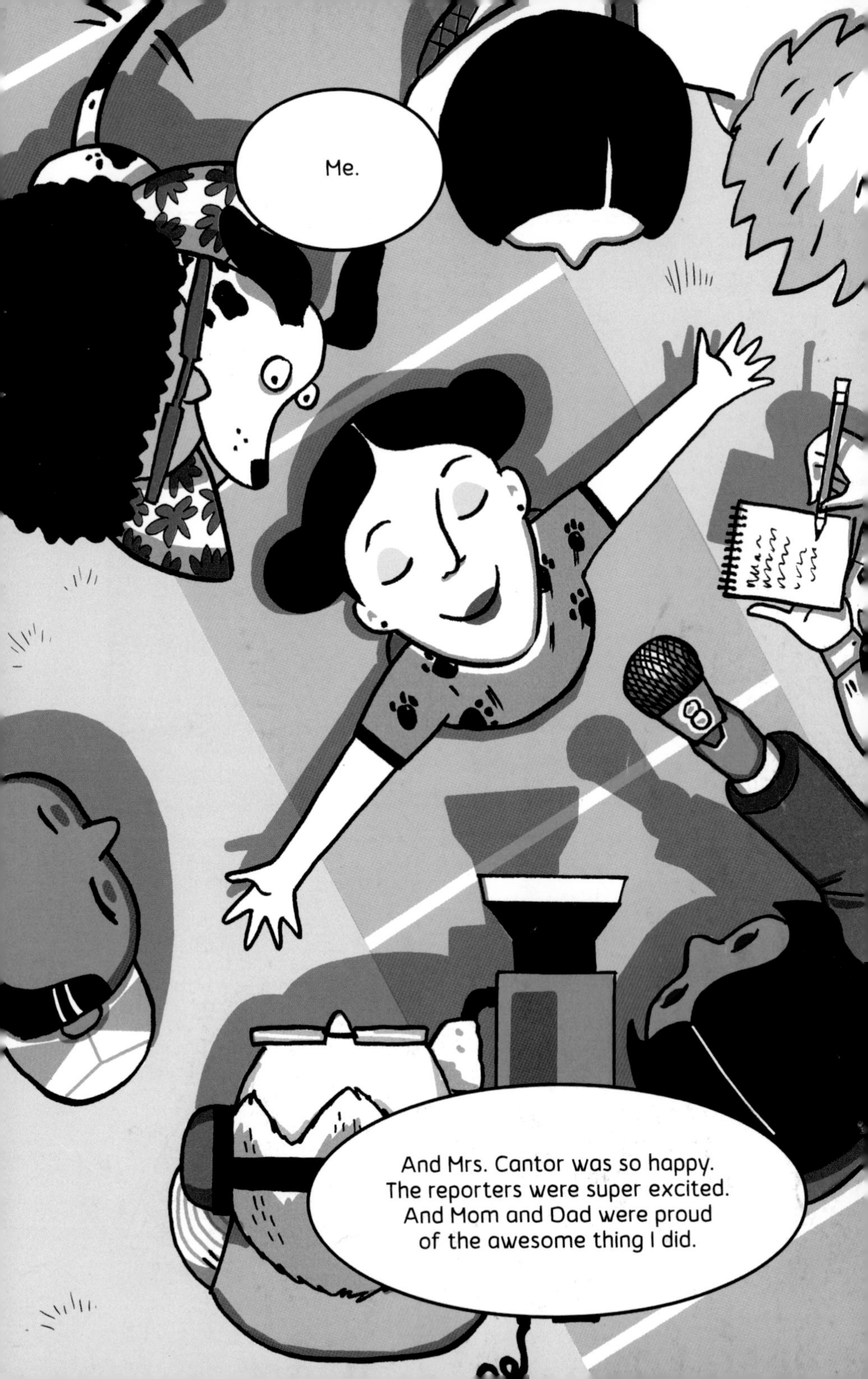
Me.
And Mrs. Cantor was so happy.
The reporters were super excited.
And Mom and Dad were proud
of the awesome thing I did.

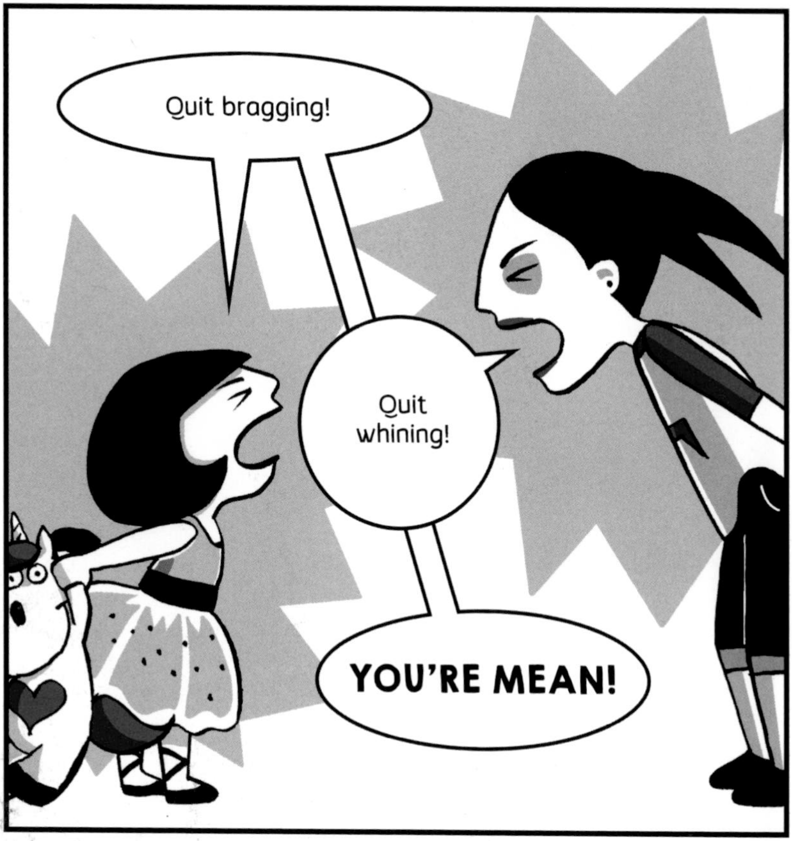
Quit bragging!
Quit whining!
YOU'RE MEAN!

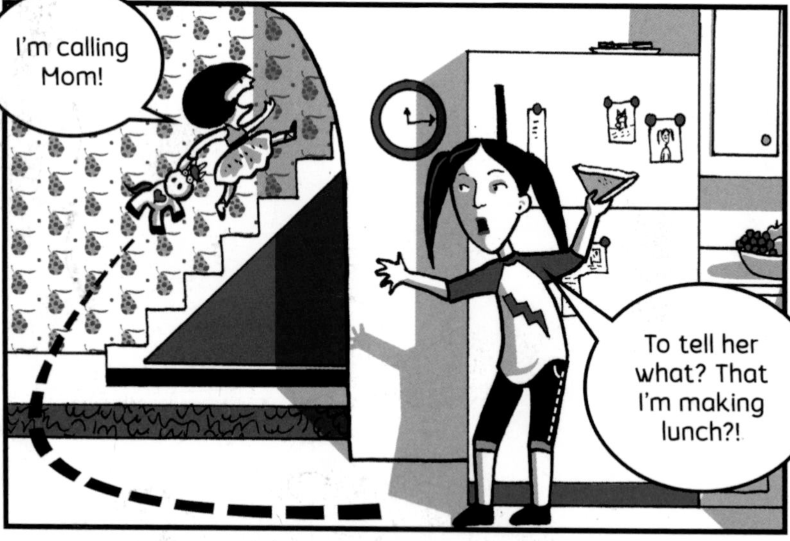
I'm calling Mom!
To tell her what? That I'm making lunch?!

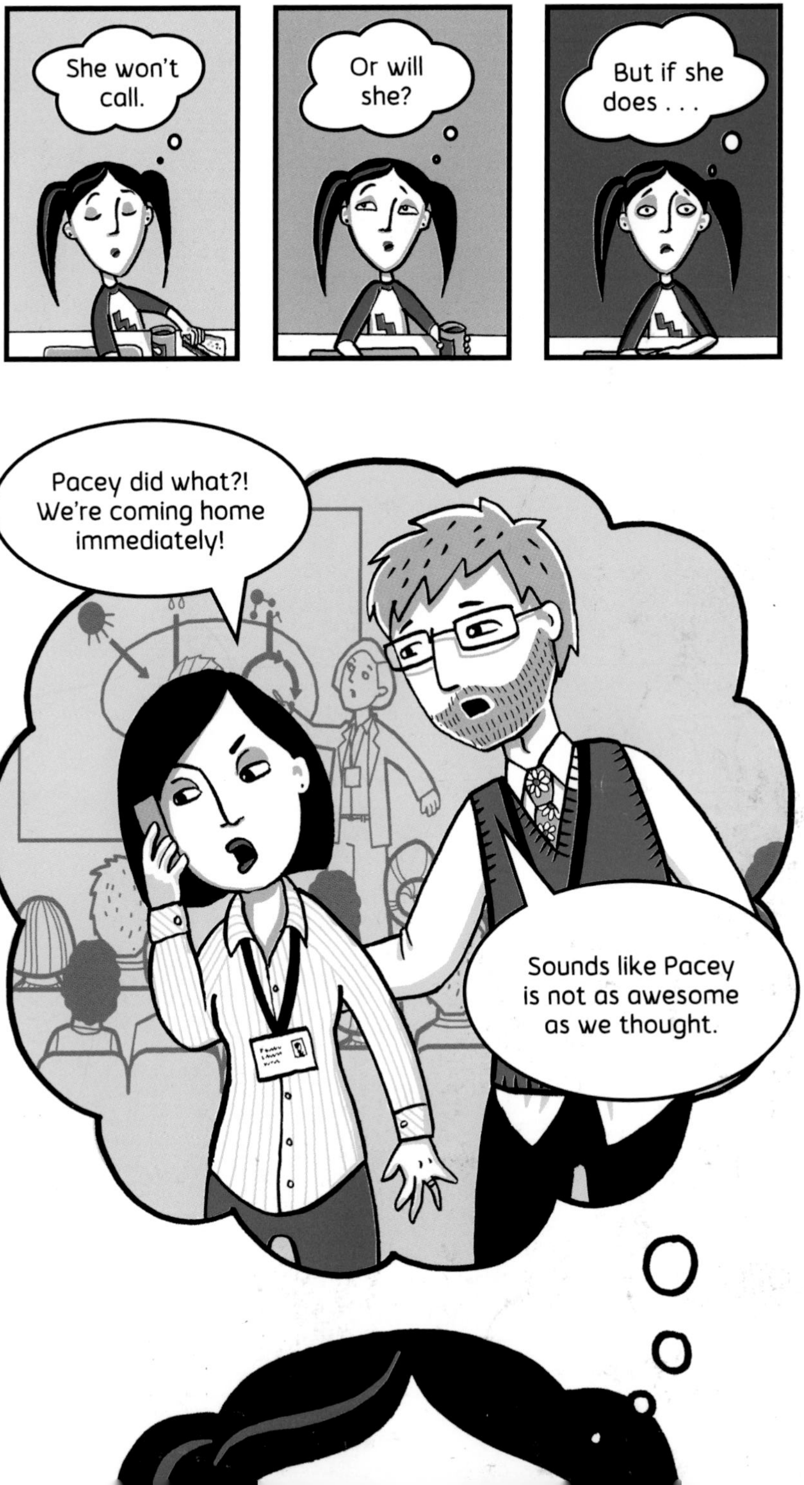
She won't call.
Or will she?
But if she does . . .
Pacey did what?! We're coming home immediately!
Sounds like Pacey is not as awesome as we thought.

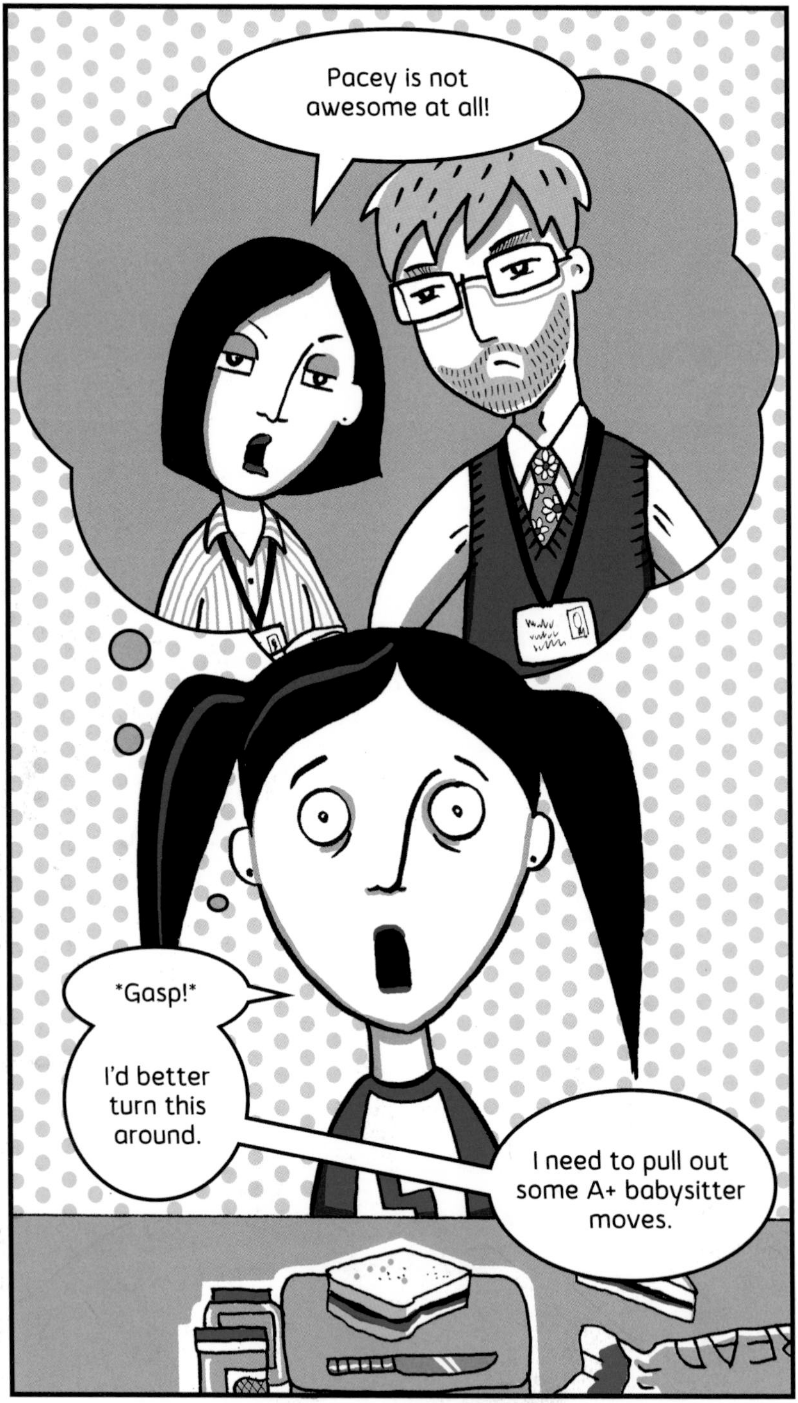
Pacey is not awesome at all!
Gasp!
I'd better turn this around.
I need to pull out some A+ babysitter moves.

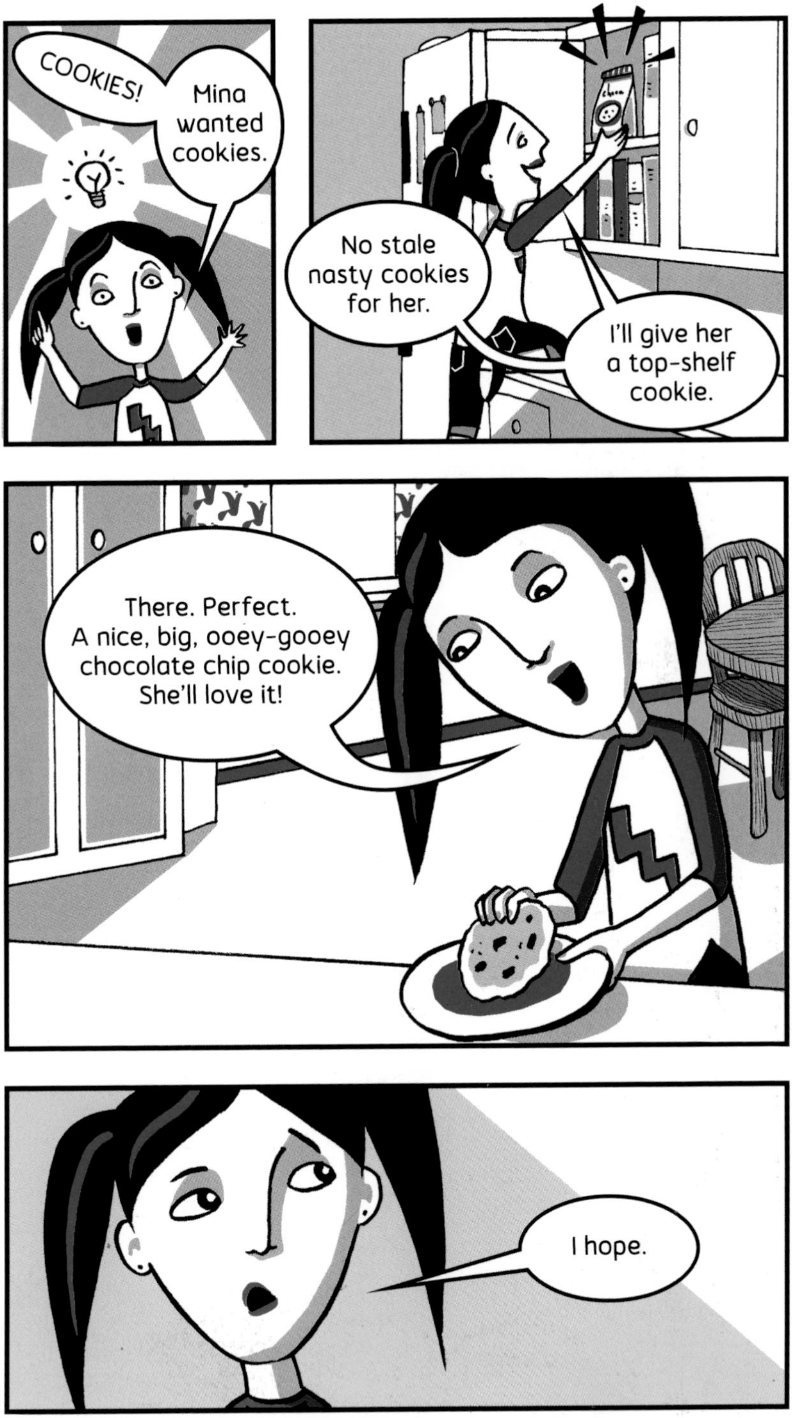
COOKIES!
Mina wanted cookies.
No stale nasty cookies for her.
I'll give her a top-shelf cookie.
There. Perfect. A nice, big, ooey-gooey chocolate chip cookie. She'll love it!
I hope.

CHAPTER 2

NOT IN KANSAS ANYMORE

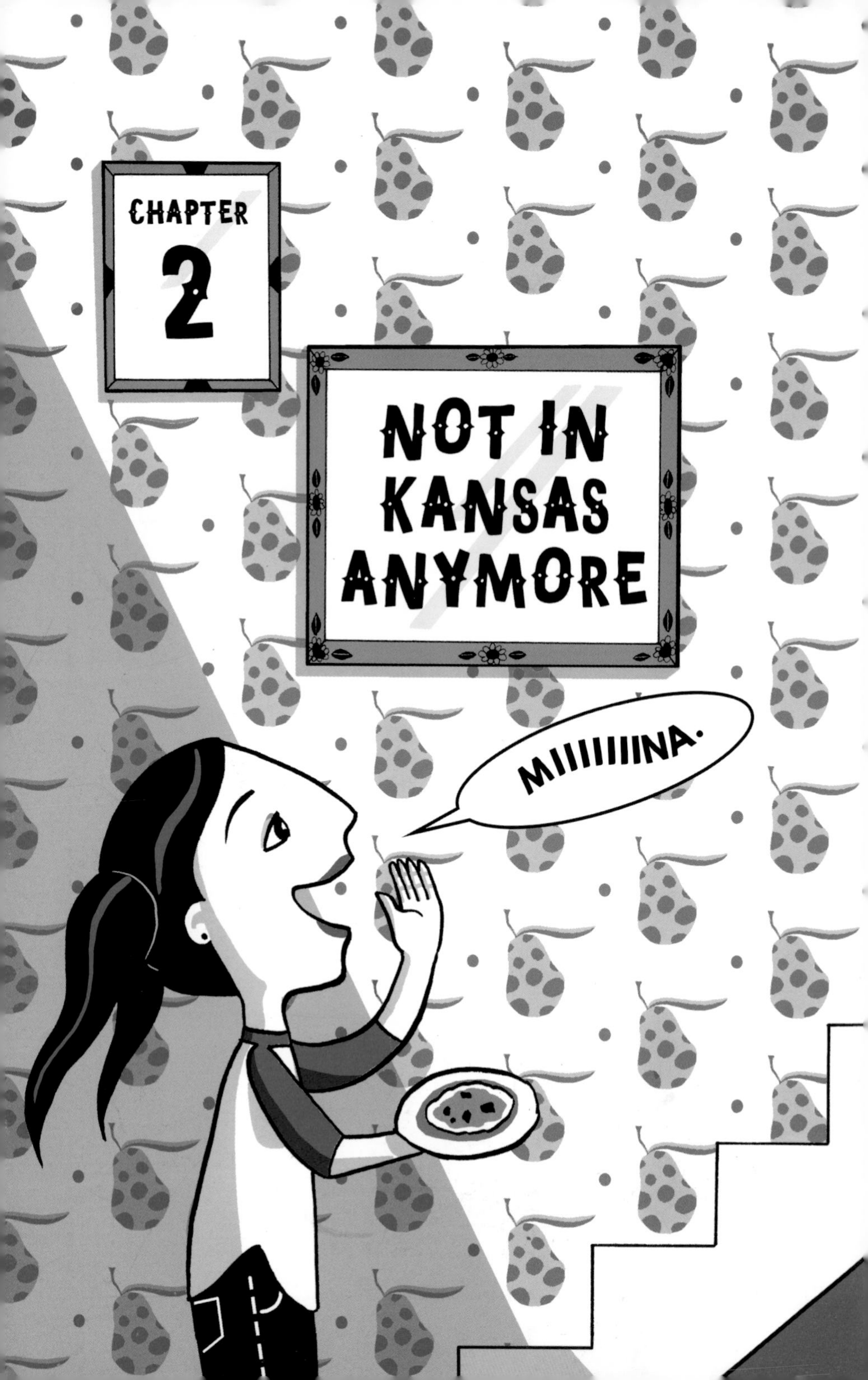
MIIIIIIINA.

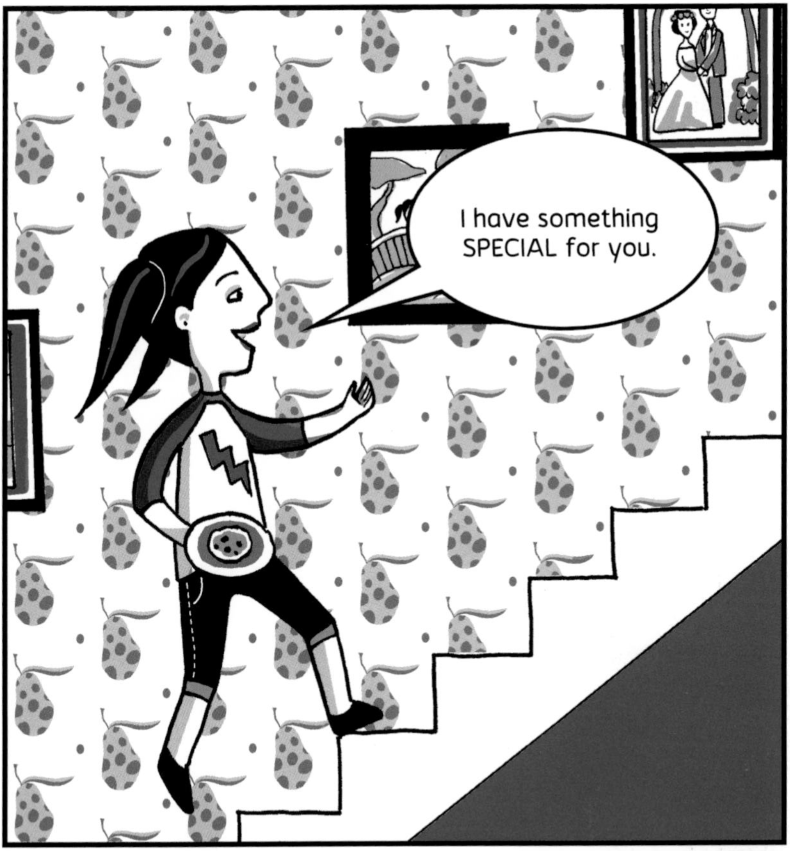
I have something SPECIAL for you.

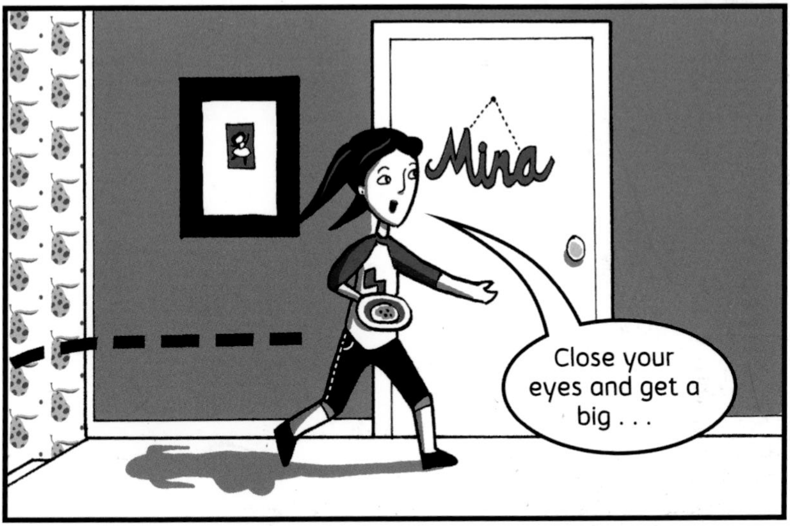
Mina
Close your eyes and get a big . . .

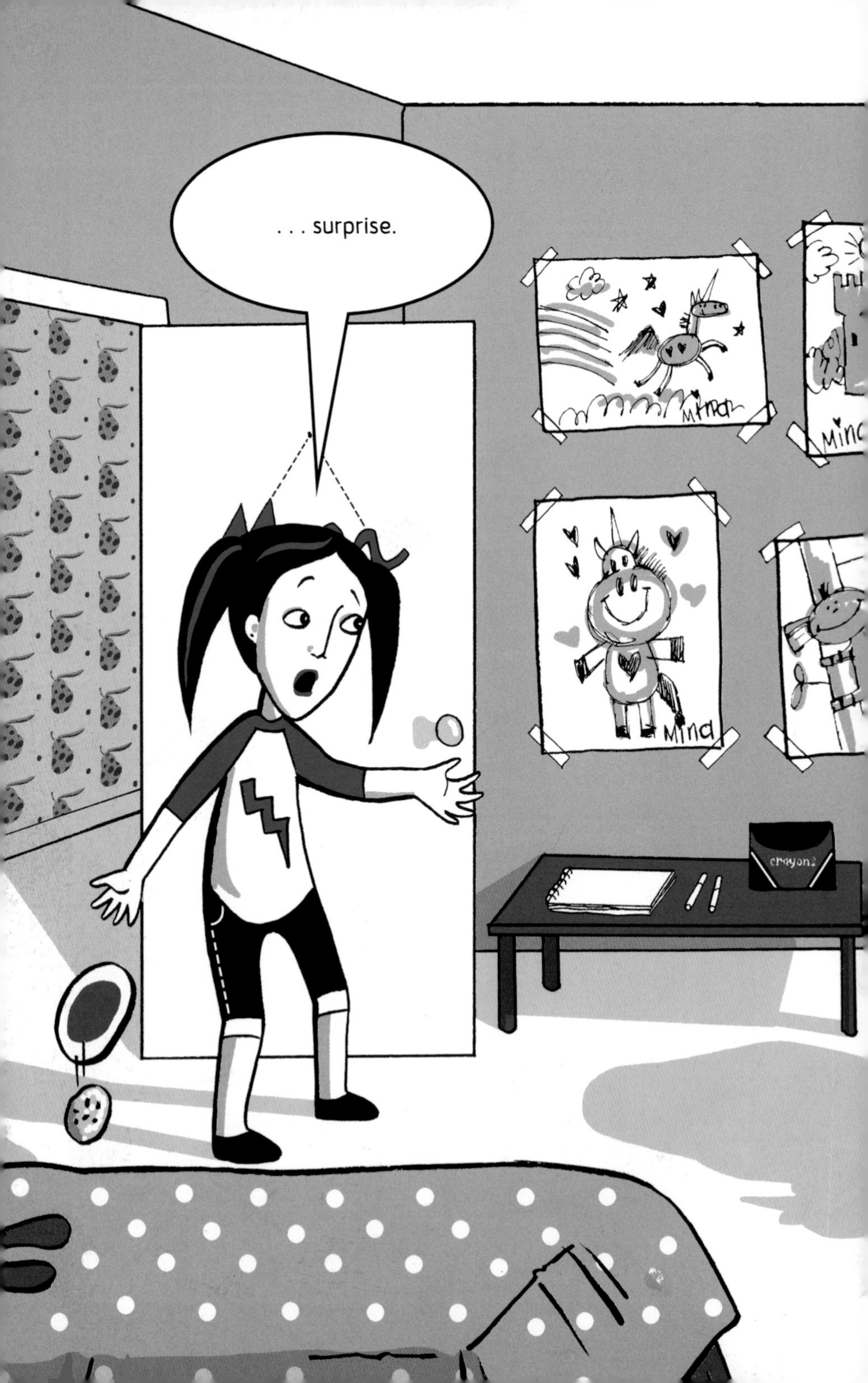
. . . surprise.
Mina
crayons

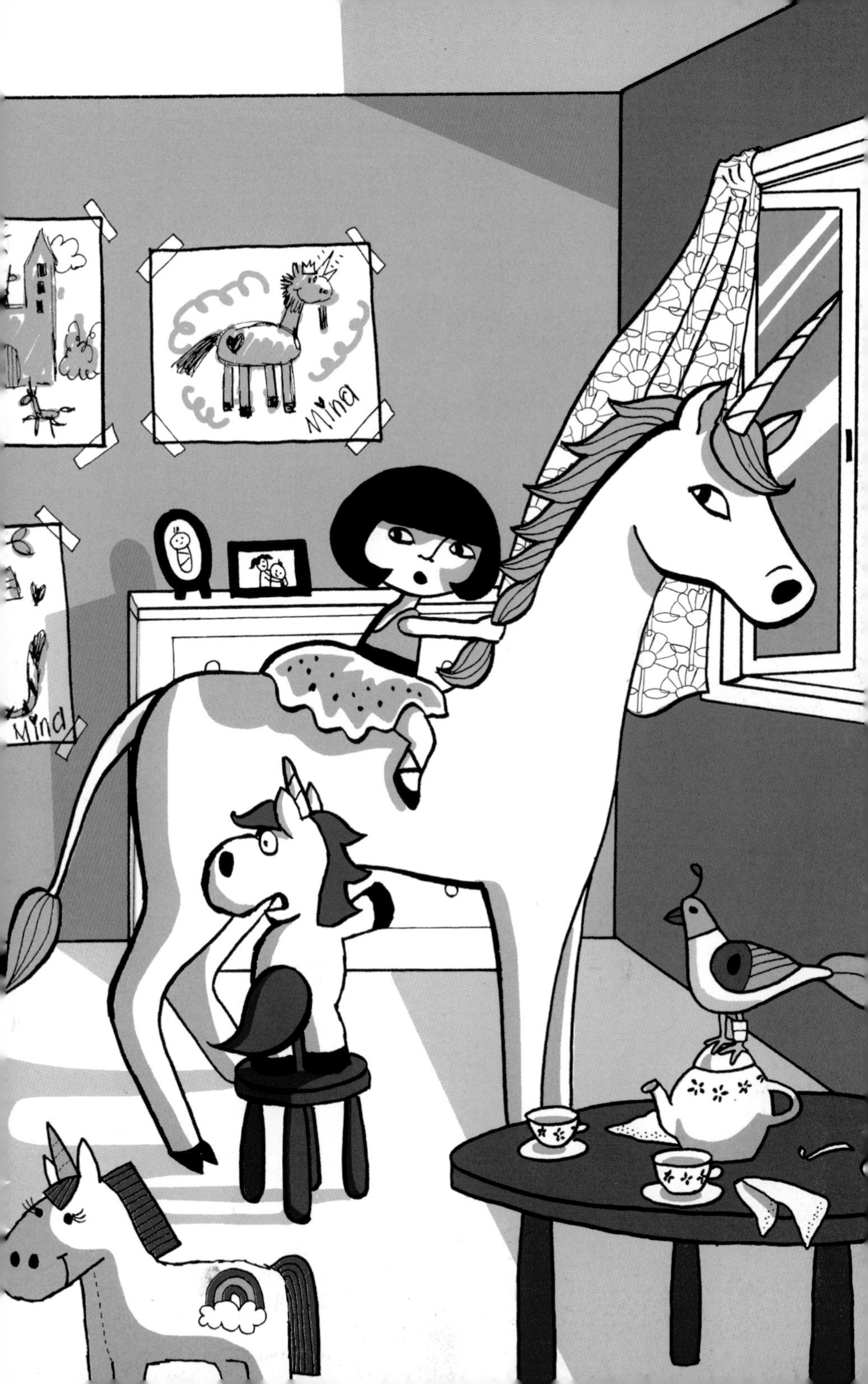
Mina
Mina

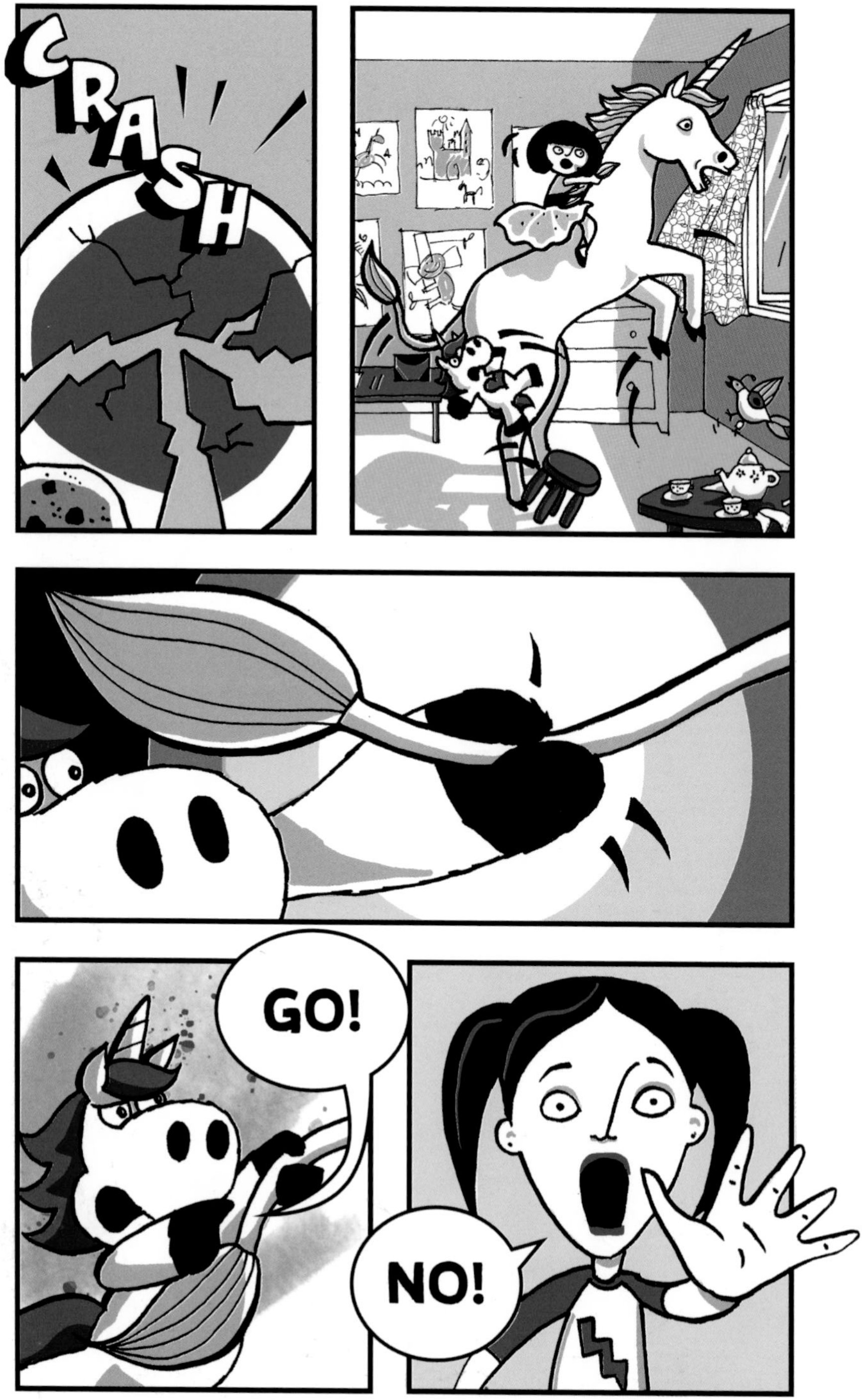
CRASH
GO!
NO!

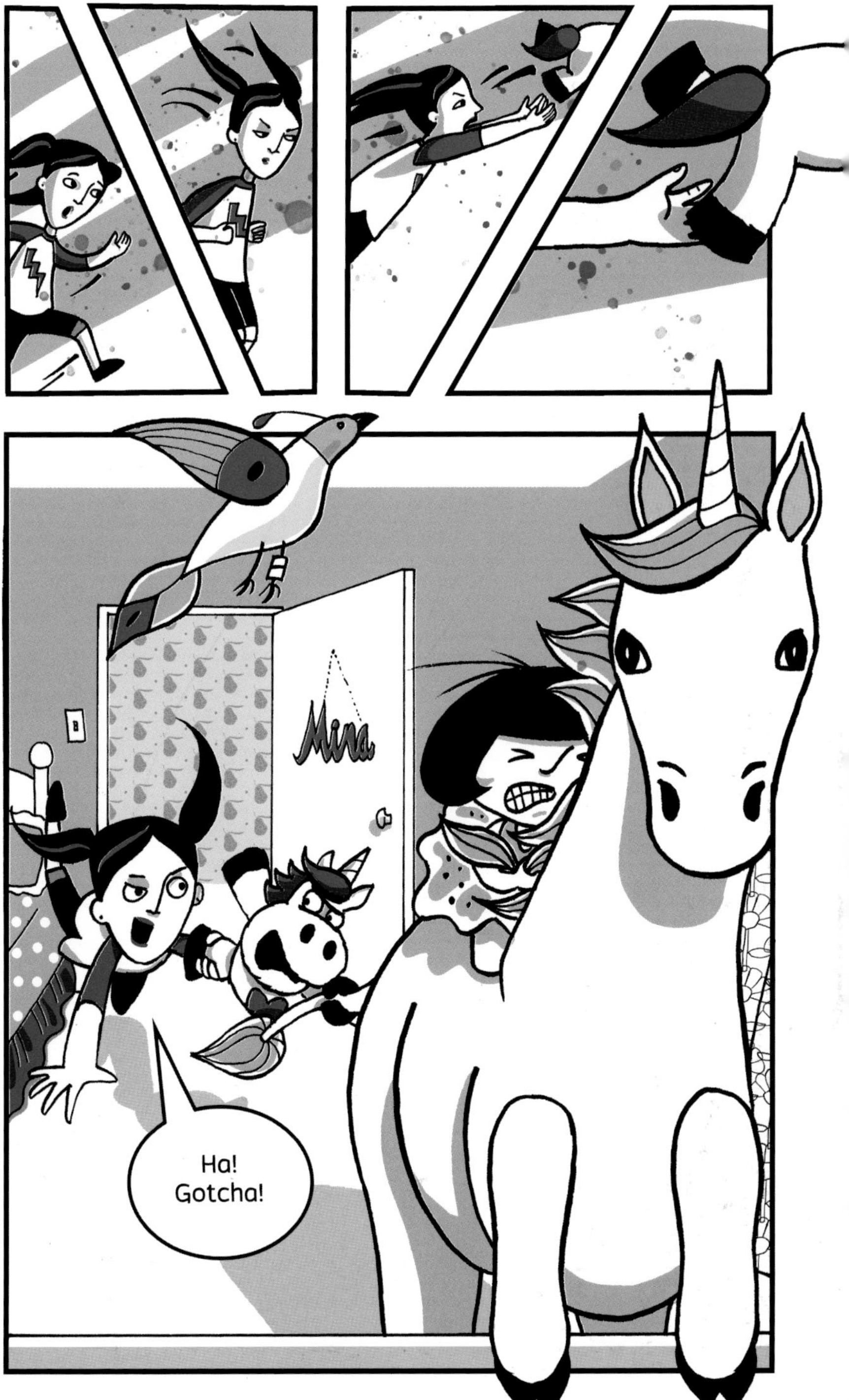
Mina
Ha!
Gotcha!

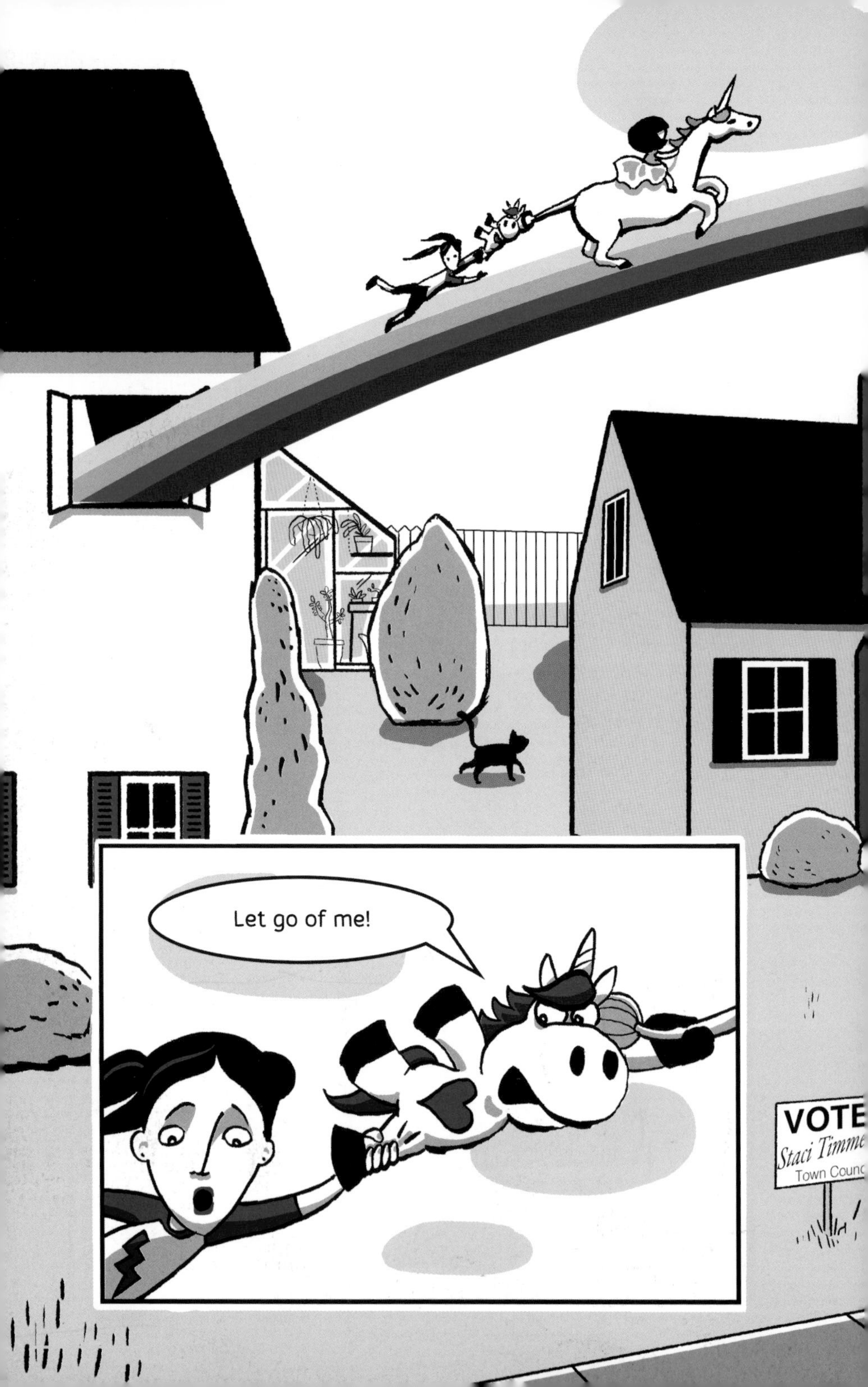
Let go of me!
VOTE
Staci Timme
Town Counc

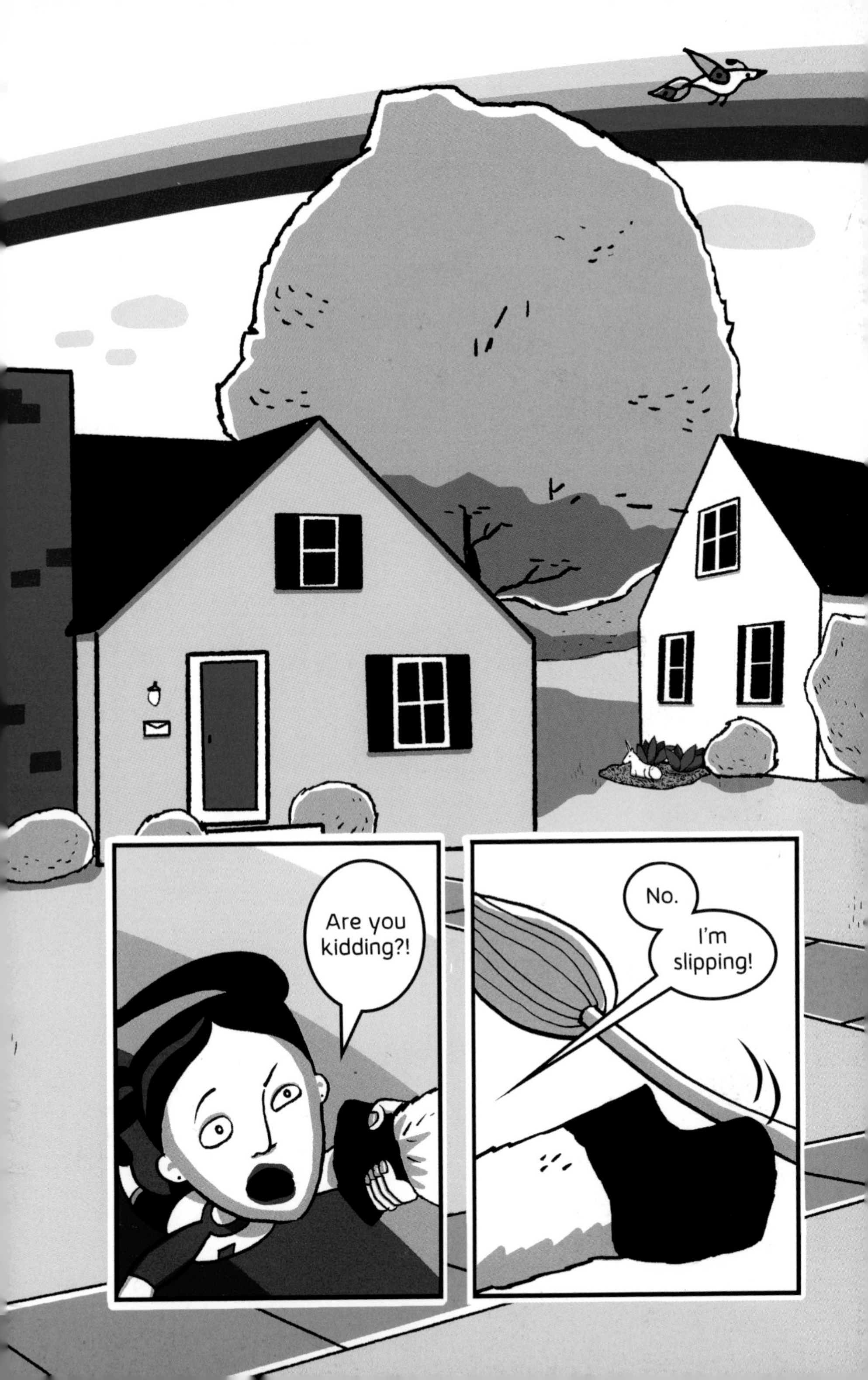
Are you kidding?!
No.
I'm slipping!

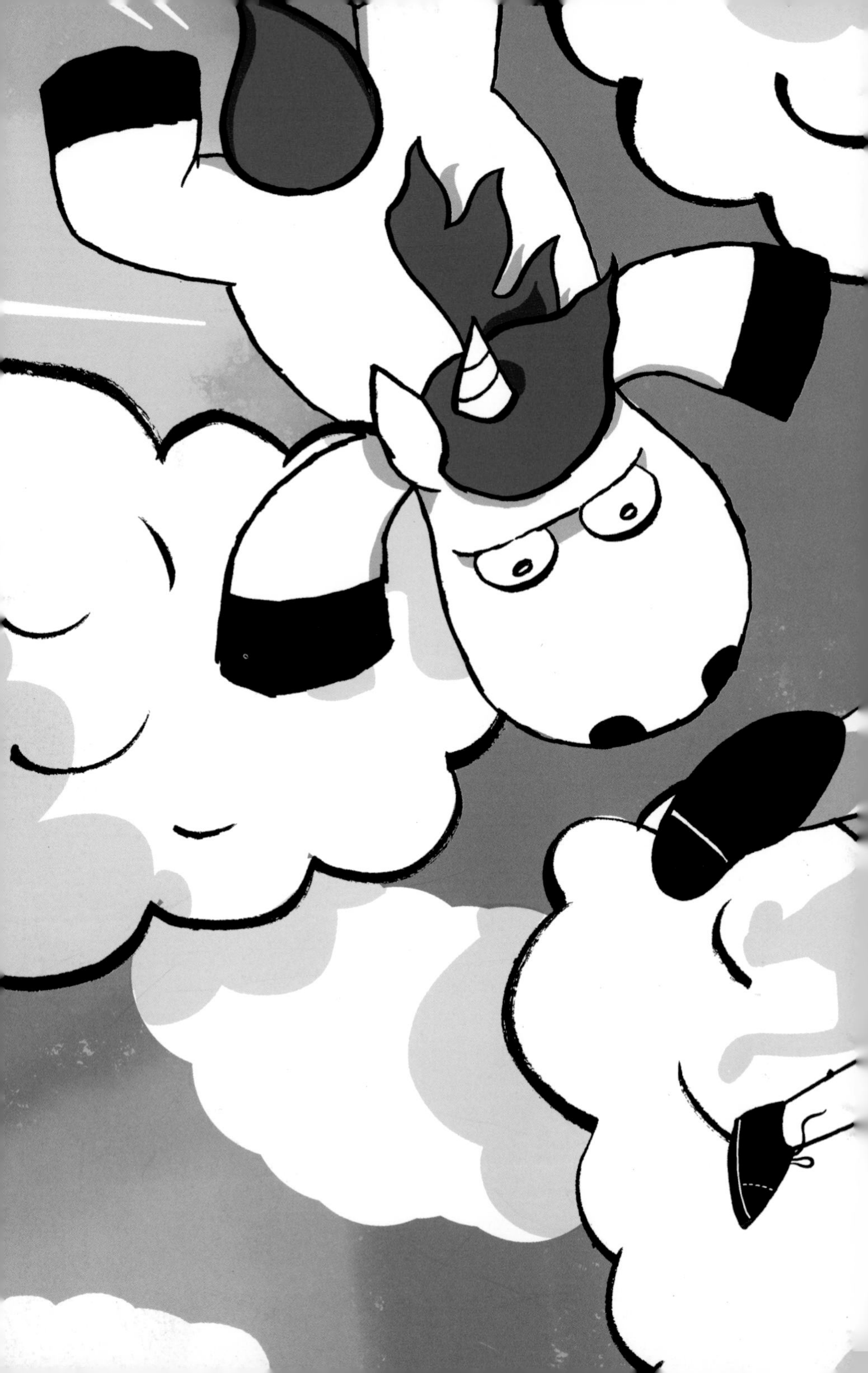

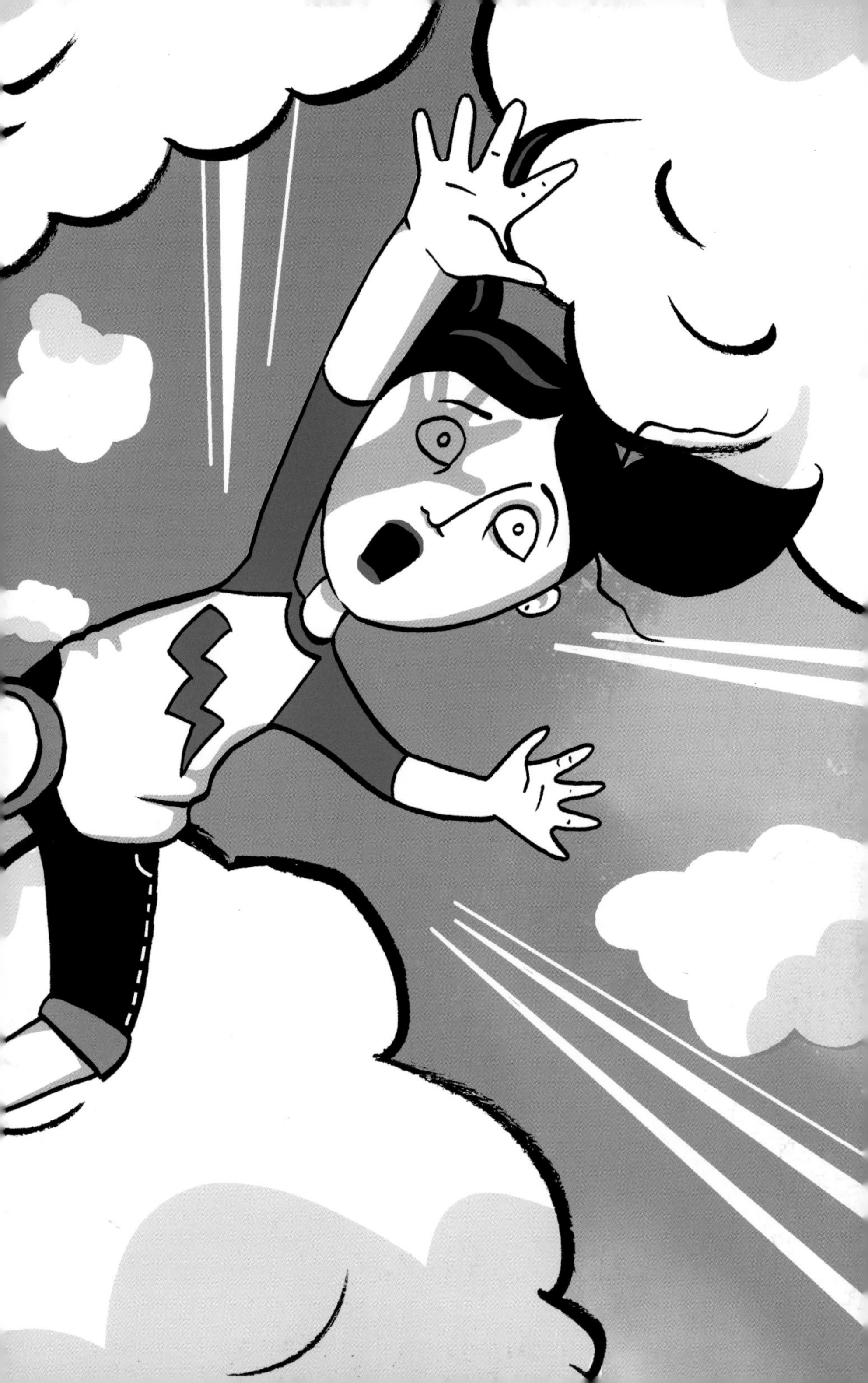

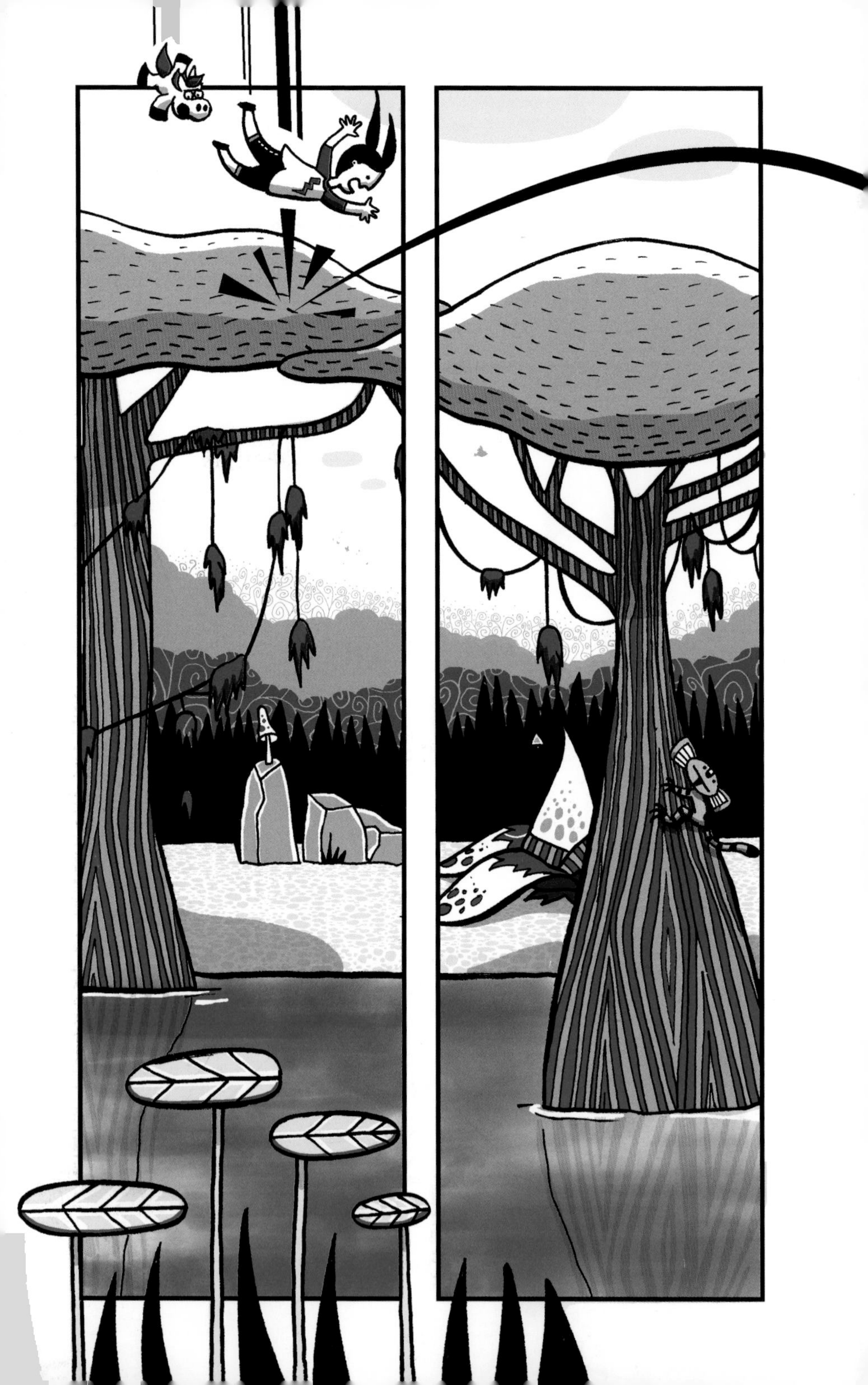

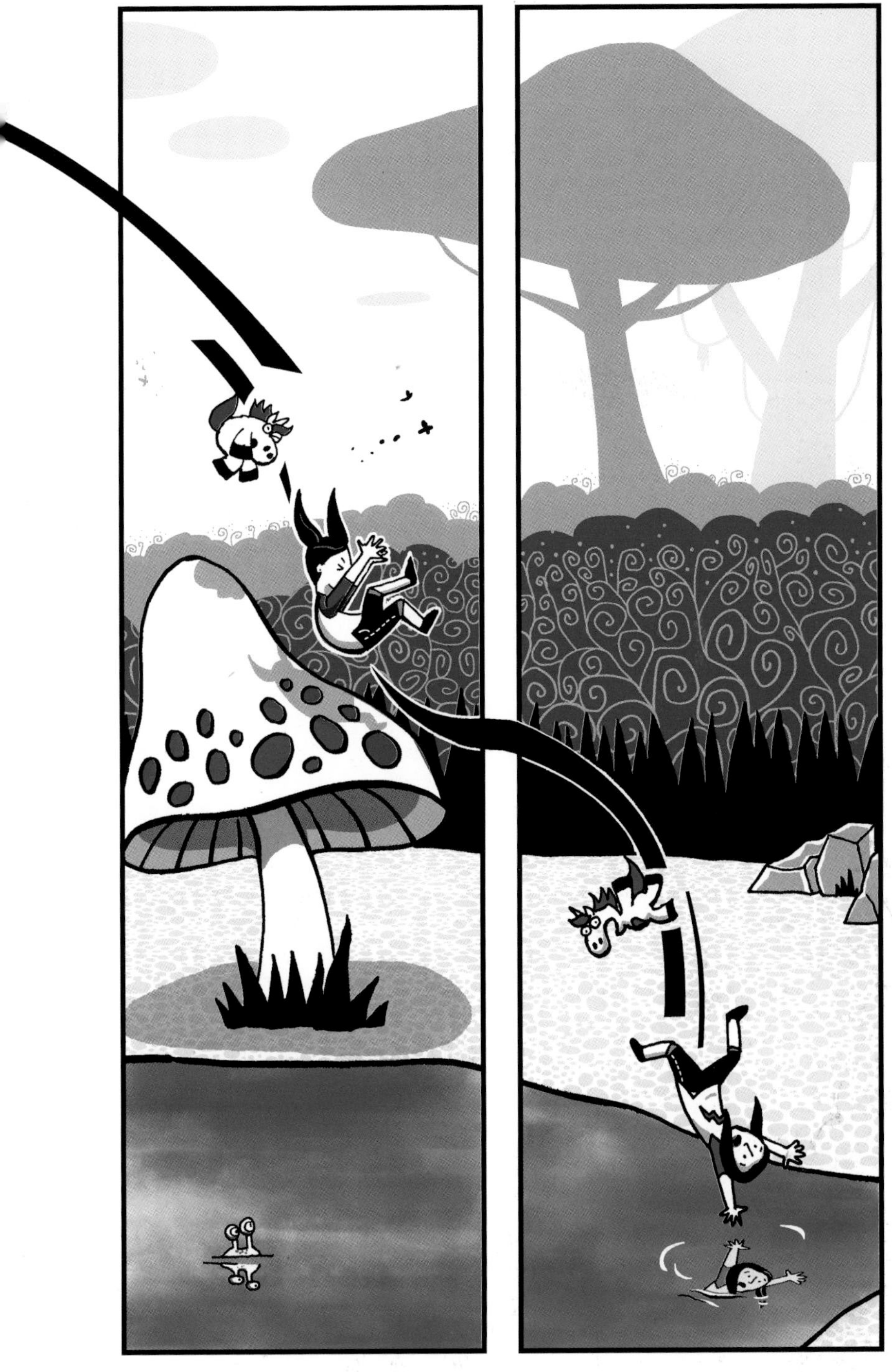

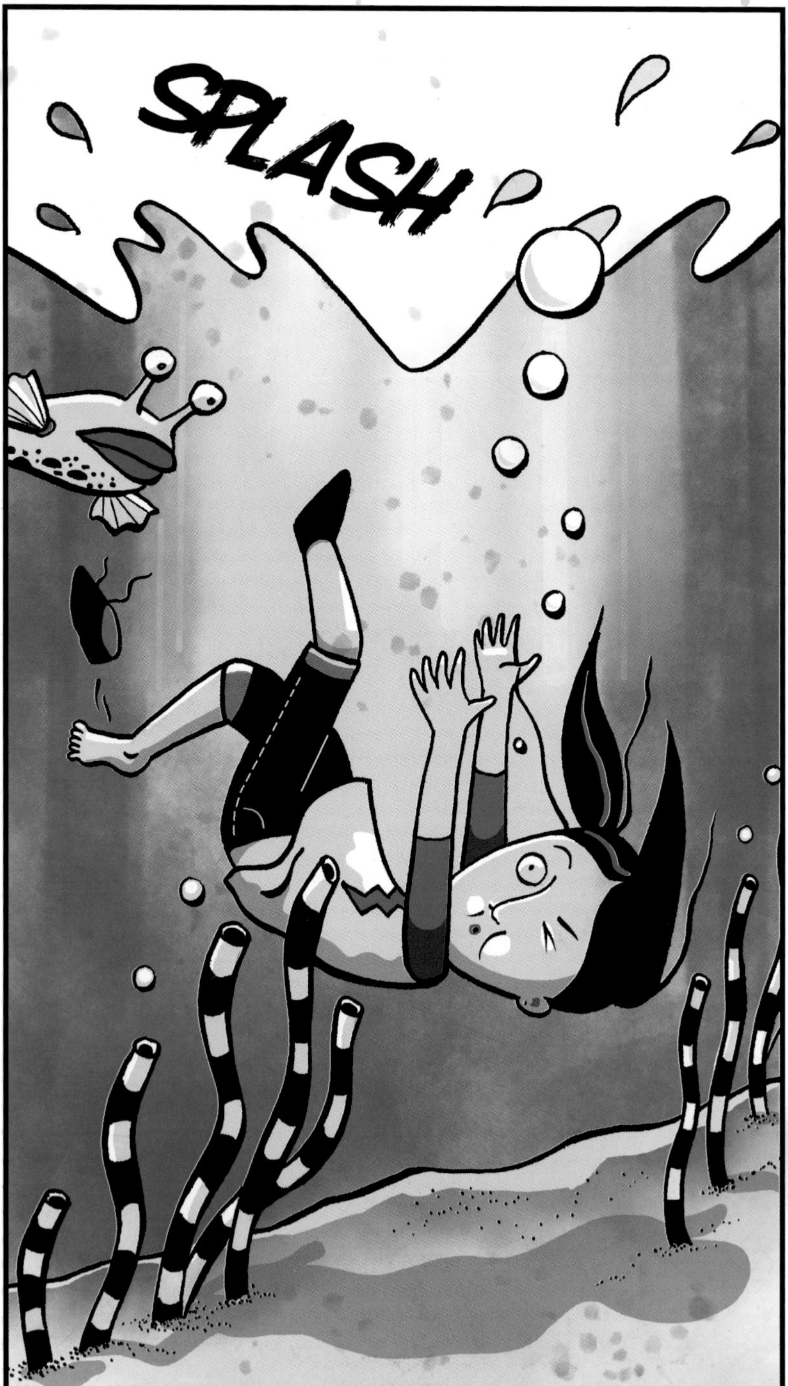
SPLASH

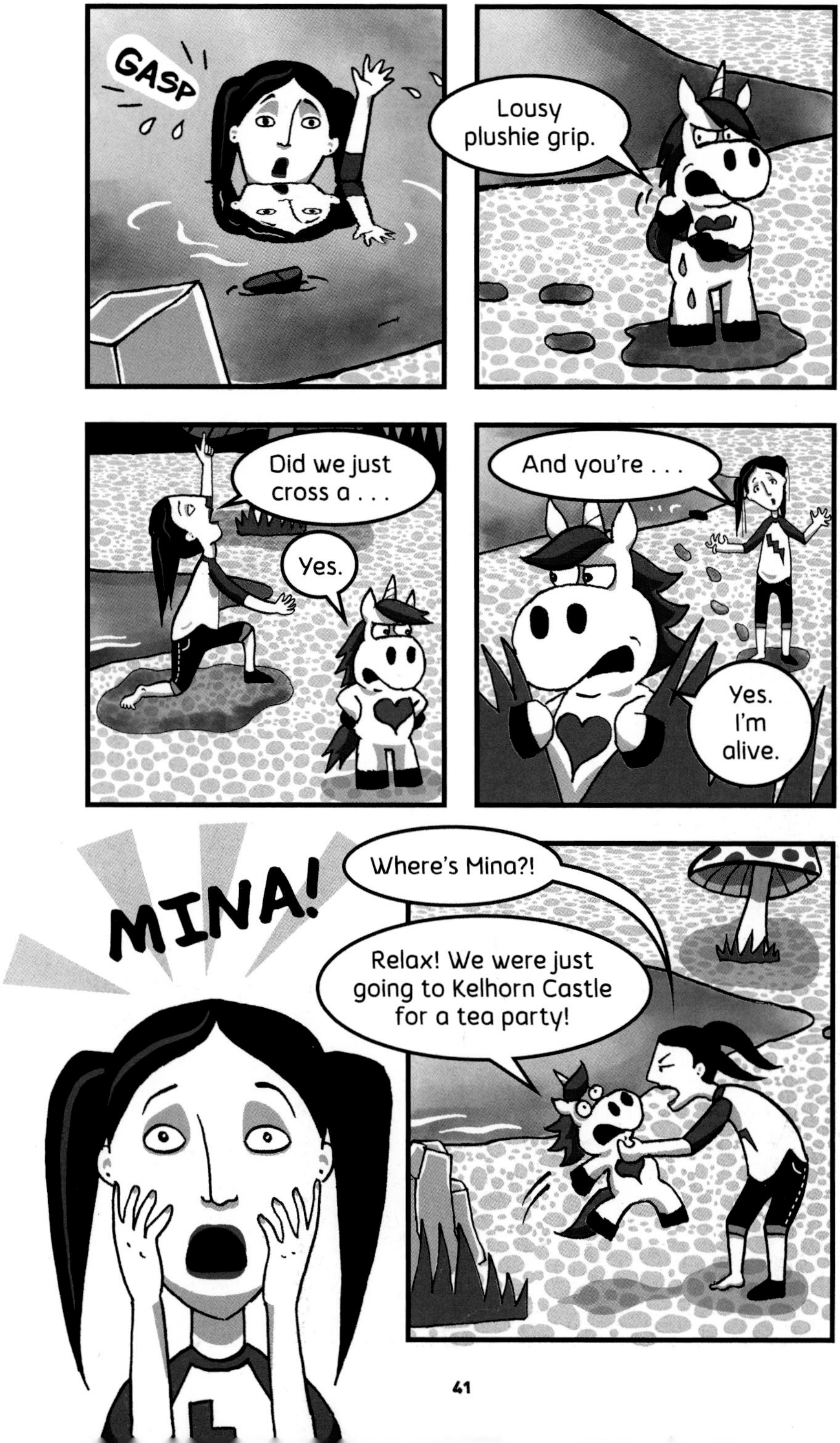
GASP
Lousy plushie grip.
Did we just cross a . . .
Yes.
And you're . . .
Yes. I'm alive.
MINA!
Where's Mina?!
Relax! We were just going to Kelhorn Castle for a tea party!

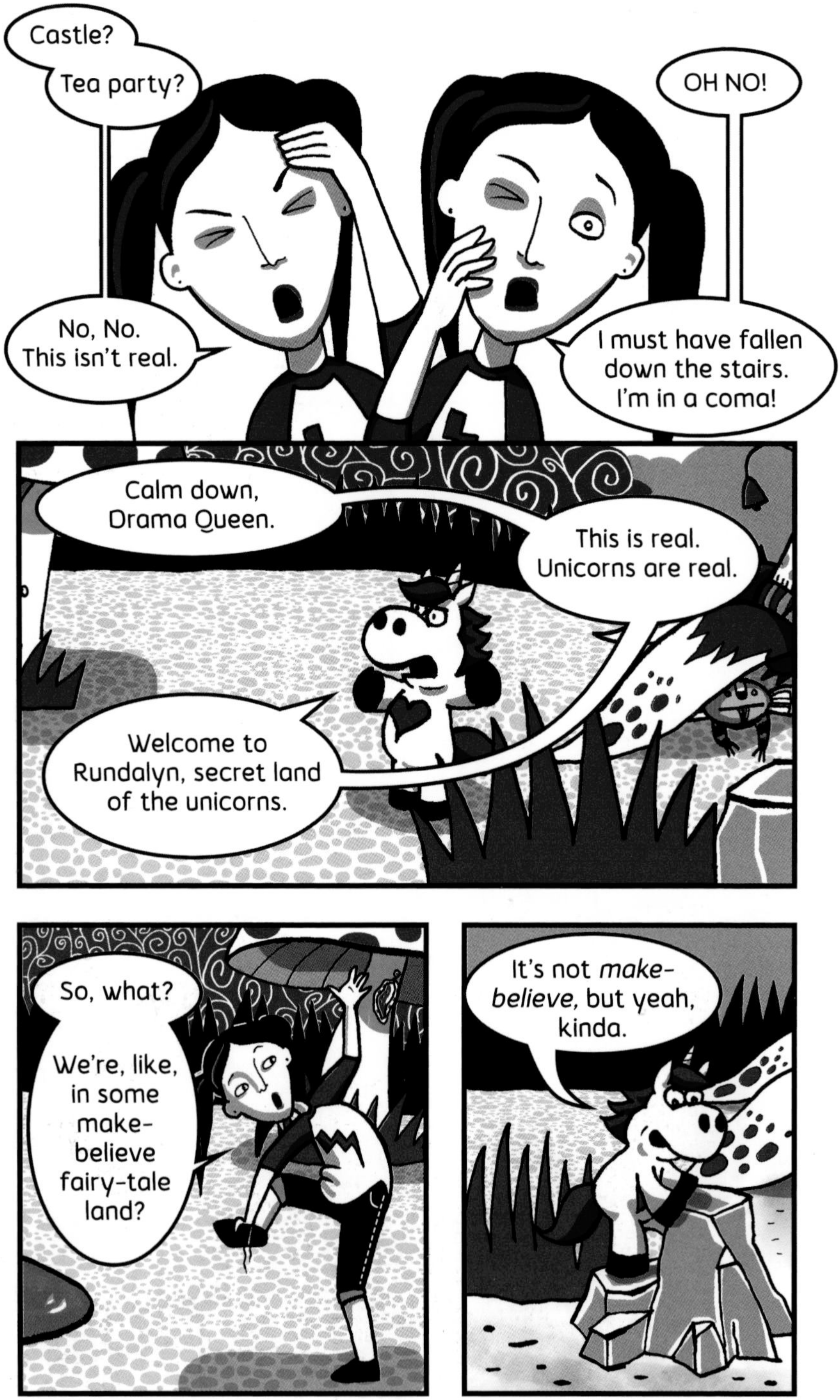
Castle?
Tea party?
No, No.
This isn't real.
OH NO!
I must have fallen down the stairs. I'm in a coma!
Calm down, Drama Queen.
This is real. Unicorns are real.
Welcome to Rundalyn, secret land of the unicorns.
So, what?
We're, like, in some make-believe fairy-tale land?
It's not *make-believe,* but yeah, kinda.

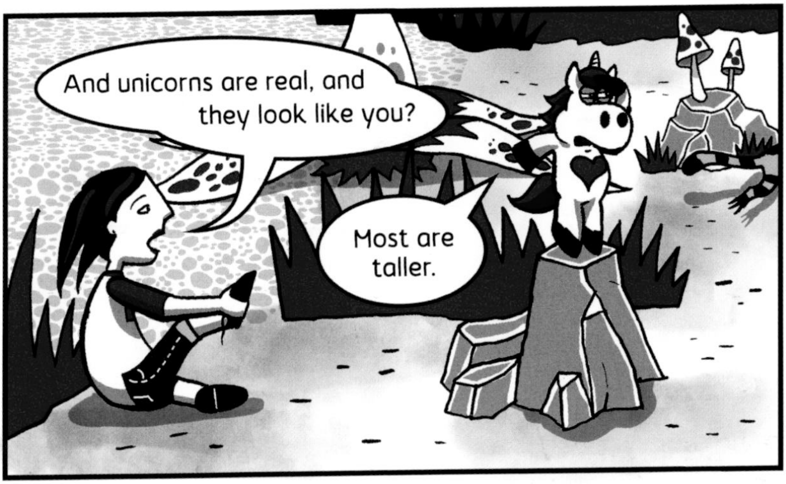
And unicorns are real, and they look like you?
Most are taller.

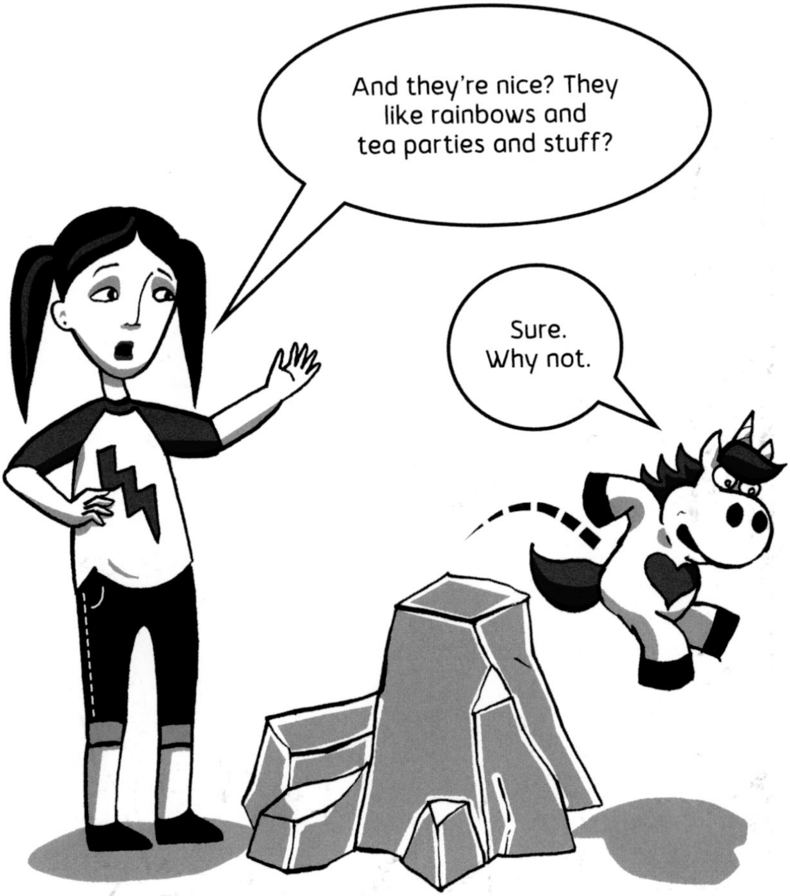
And they're nice? They like rainbows and tea parties and stuff?
Sure. Why not.

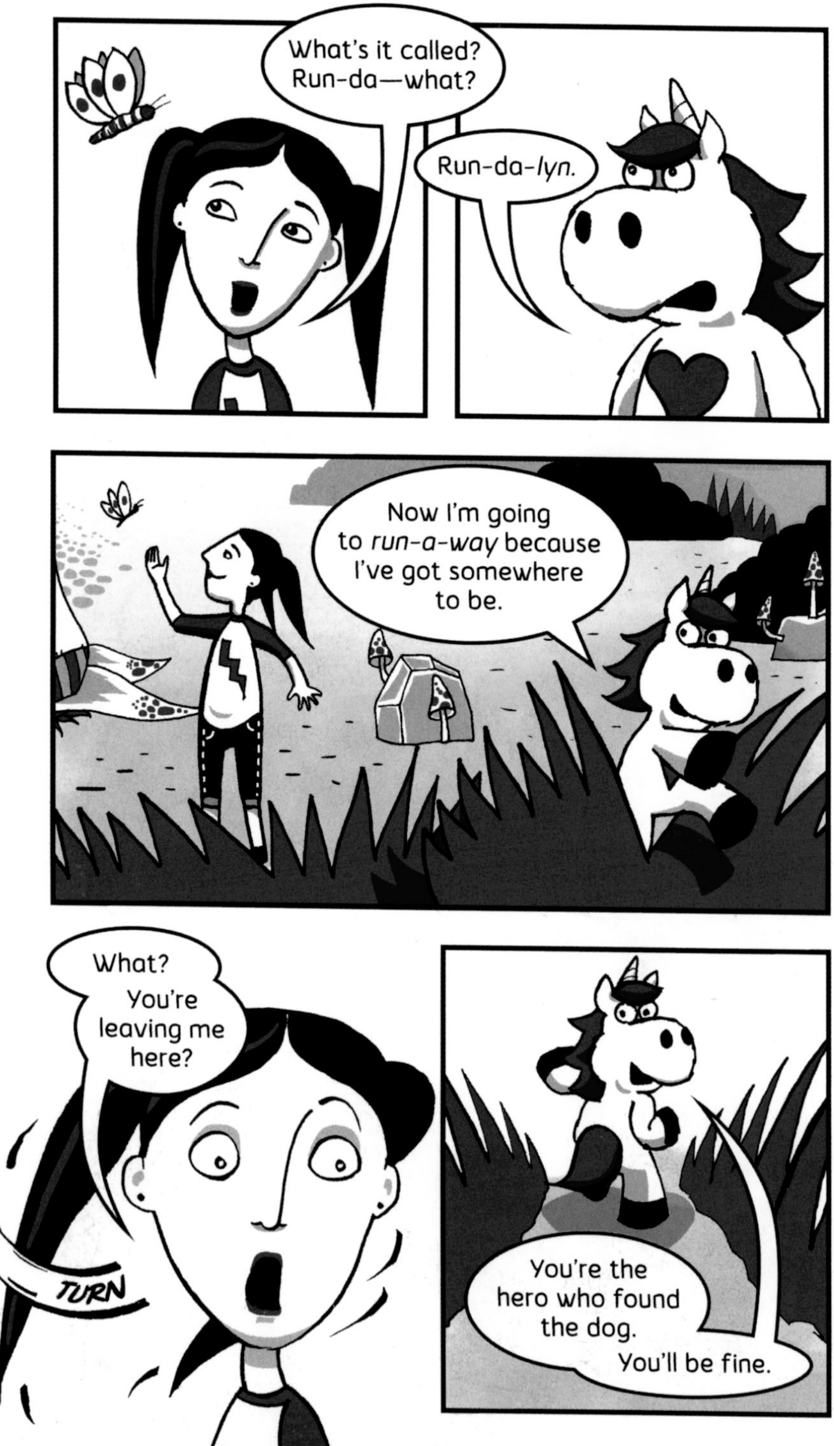
What's it called? Run-da—what?
Run-da-*lyn.*
Now I'm going to *run-a-way* because I've got somewhere to be.
What? You're leaving me here?
TURN
You're the hero who found the dog.
You'll be fine.

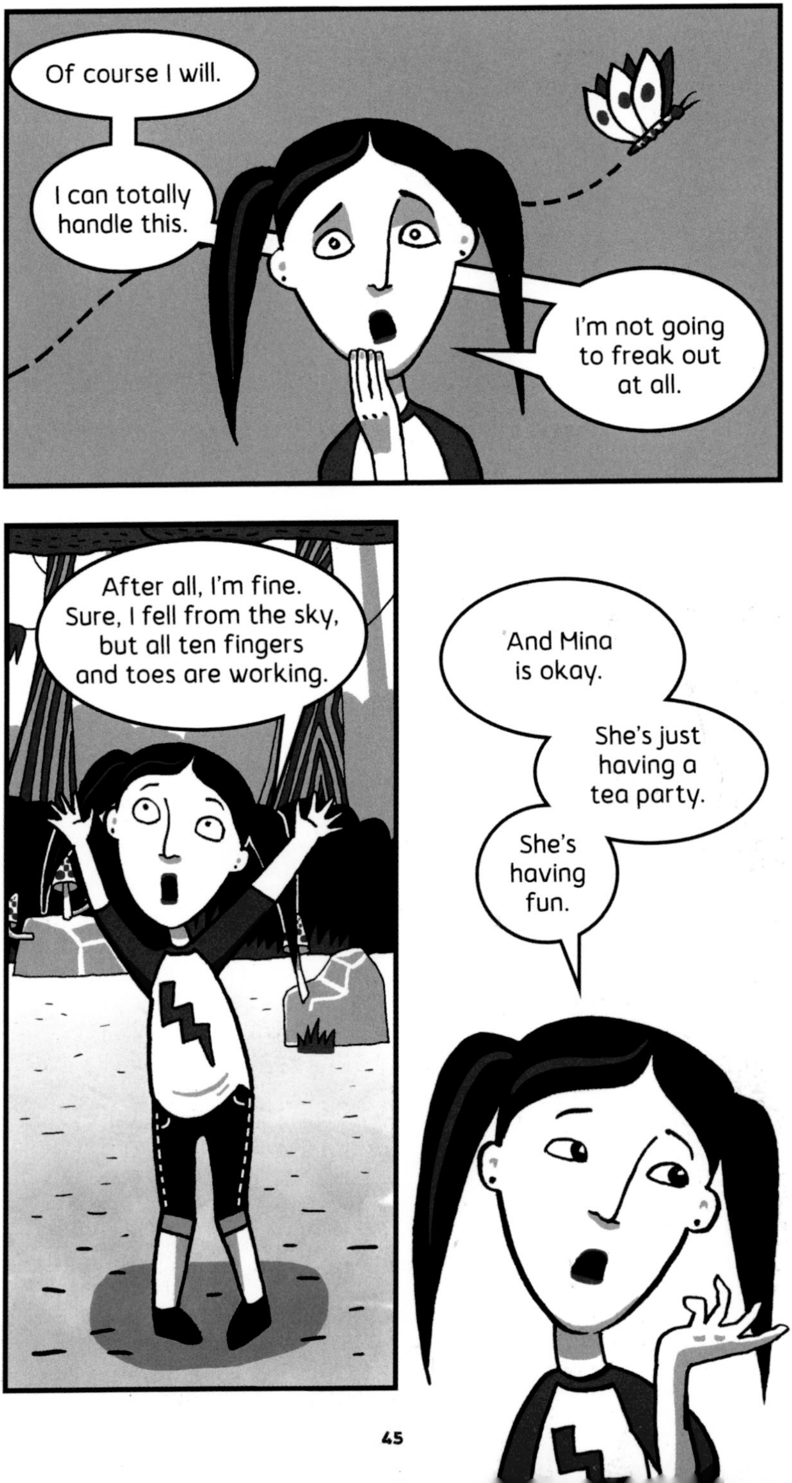
Of course I will.
I can totally handle this.
I'm not going to freak out at all.
After all, I'm fine. Sure, I fell from the sky, but all ten fingers and toes are working.
And Mina is okay.
She's just having a tea party.
She's having fun.

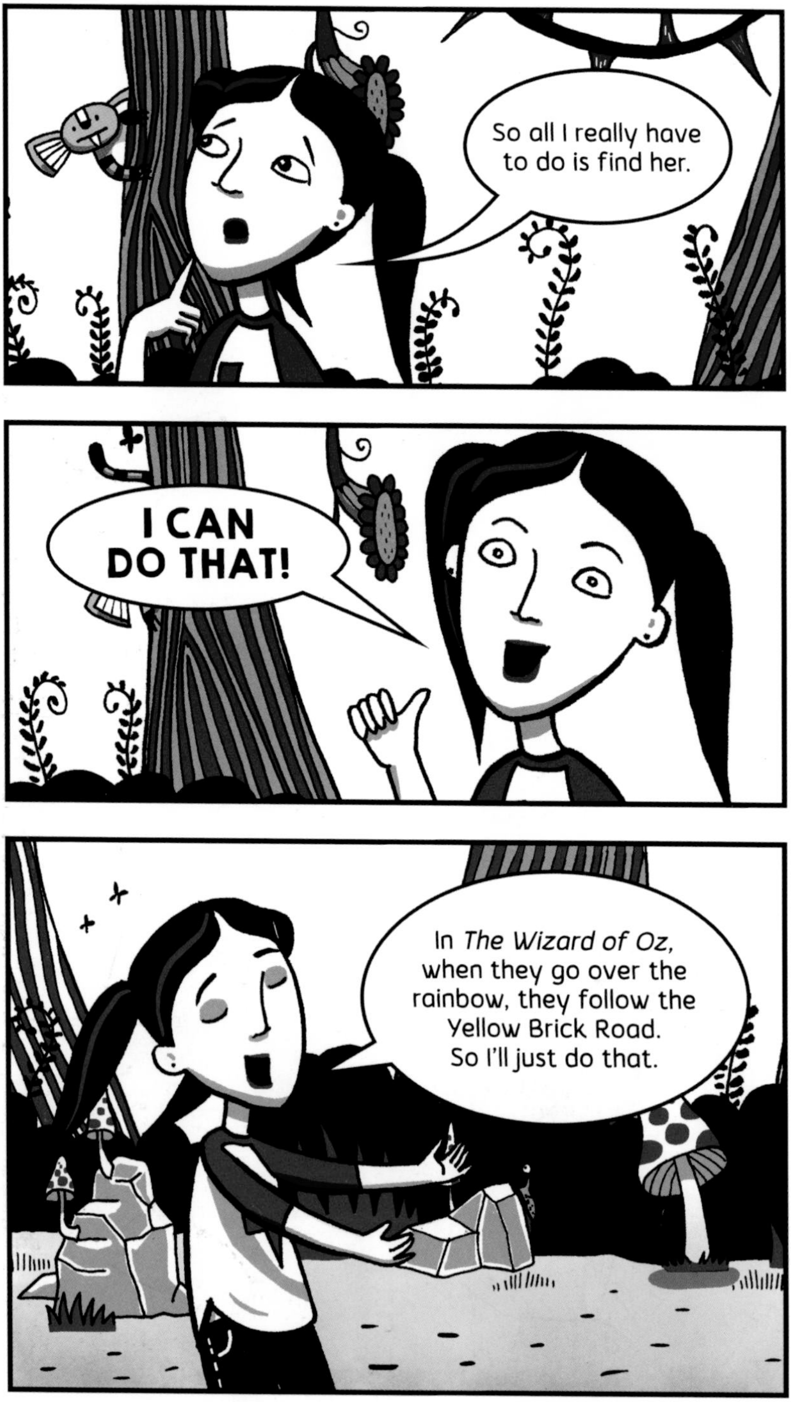
So all I really have to do is find her.
I CAN DO THAT!
In *The Wizard of Oz,* when they go over the rainbow, they follow the Yellow Brick Road. So I'll just do that.

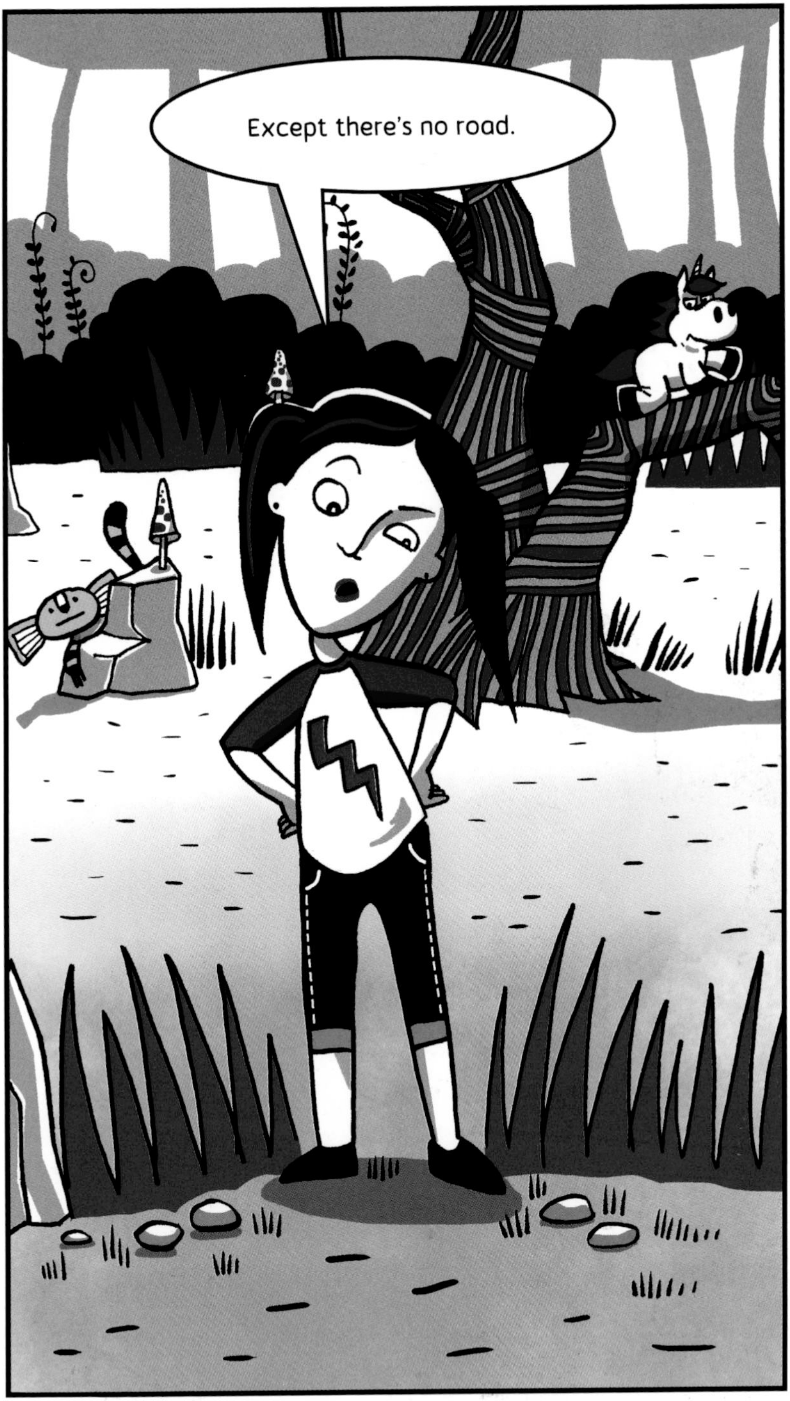
Except there's no road.

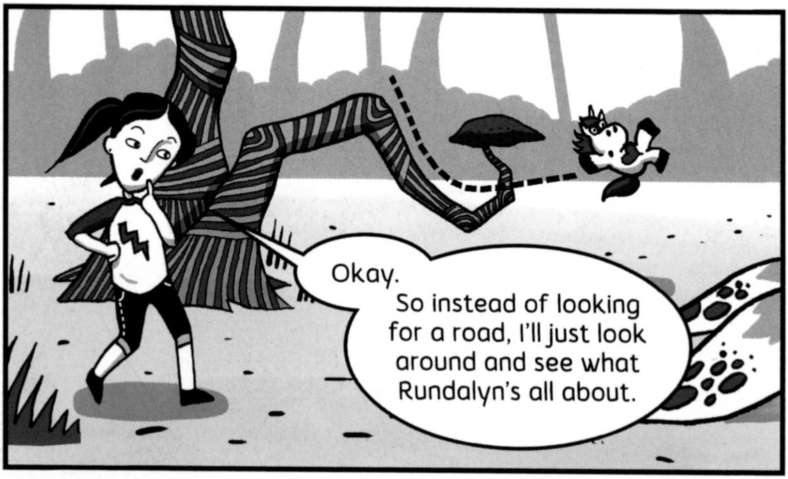
Okay.
So instead of looking for a road, I'll just look around and see what Rundalyn's all about.

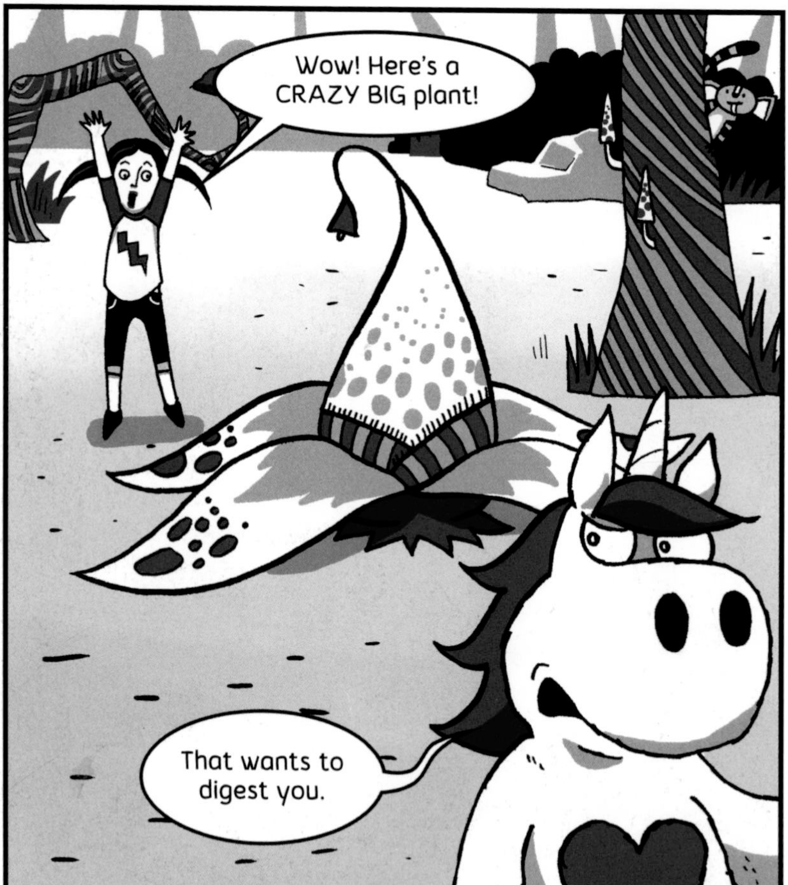
Wow! Here's a CRAZY BIG plant!
That wants to digest you.

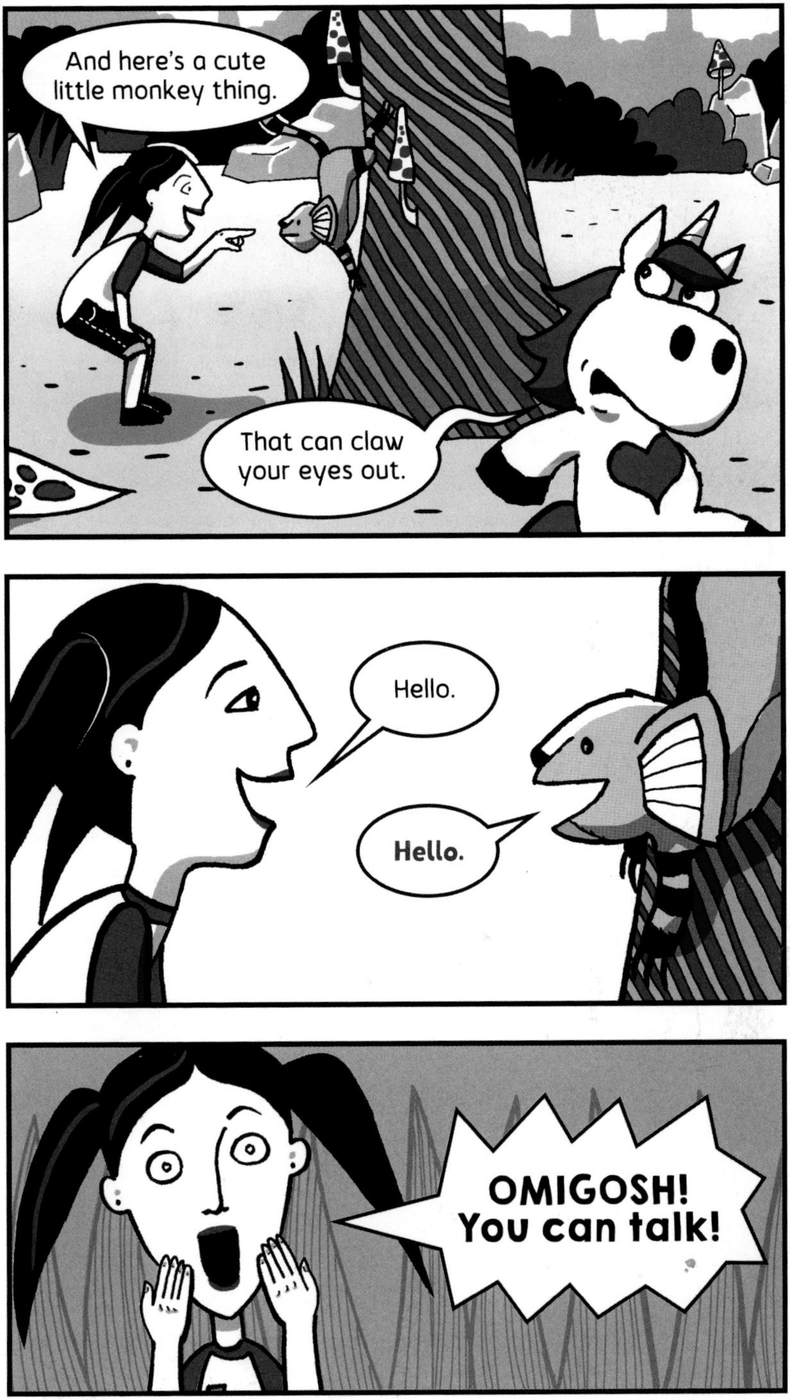
And here's a cute little monkey thing.
That can claw your eyes out.
Hello.
Hello.
OMIGOSH! You can talk!

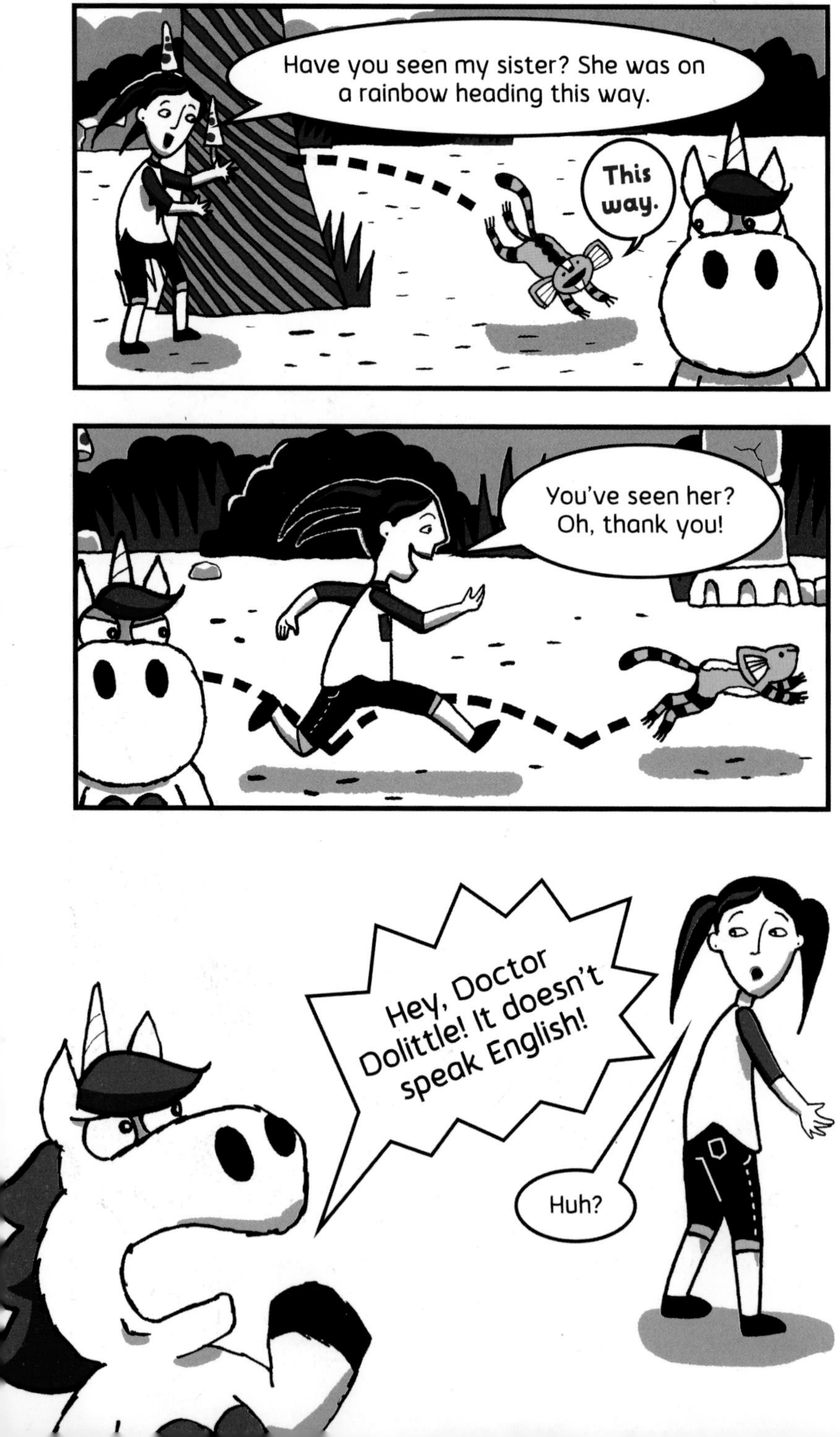
Have you seen my sister? She was on a rainbow heading this way.
This way.
You've seen her? Oh, thank you!
Hey, Doctor Dolittle! It doesn't speak English!
Huh?

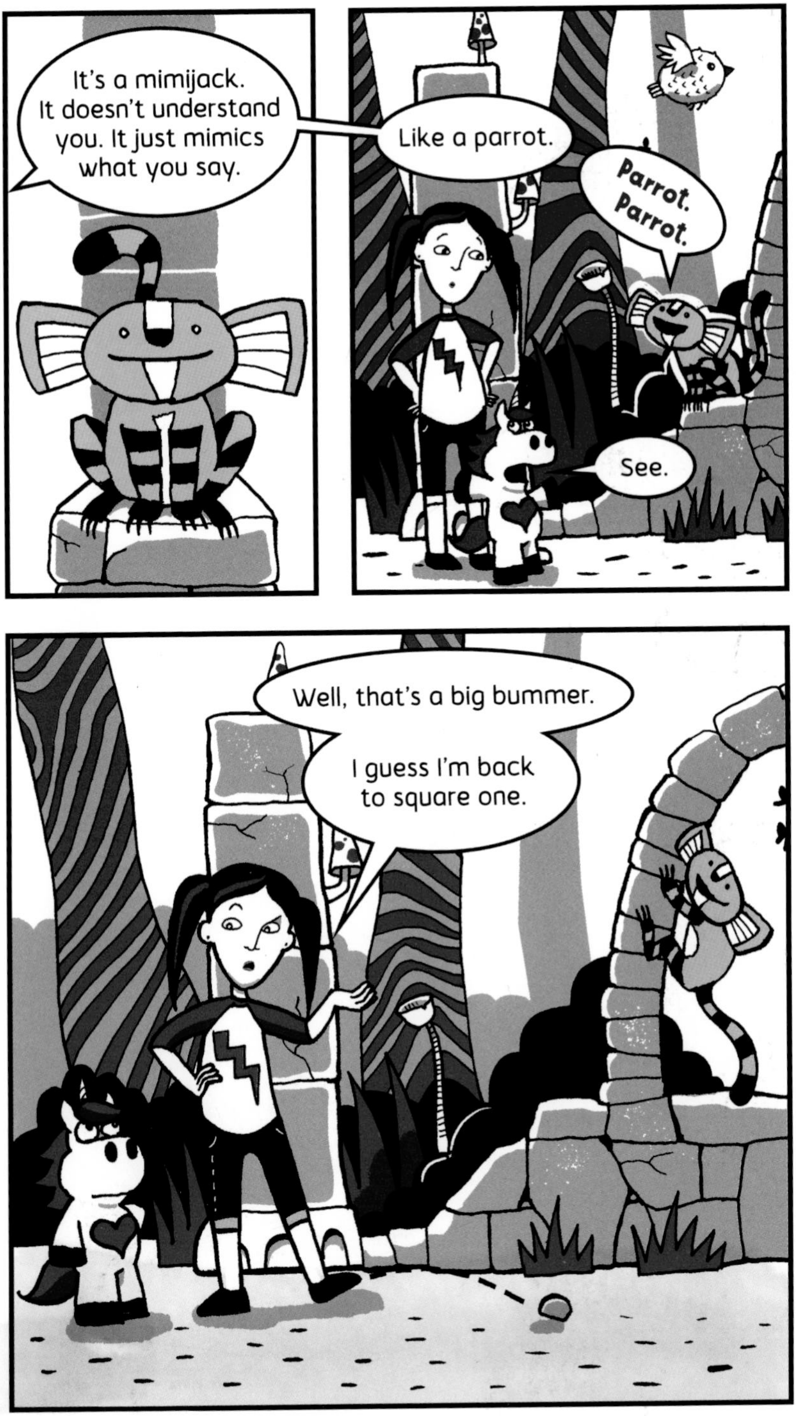
It's a mimijack. It doesn't understand you. It just mimics what you say.
Like a parrot.
Parrot. Parrot.
See.
Well, that's a big bummer.
I guess I'm back to square one.

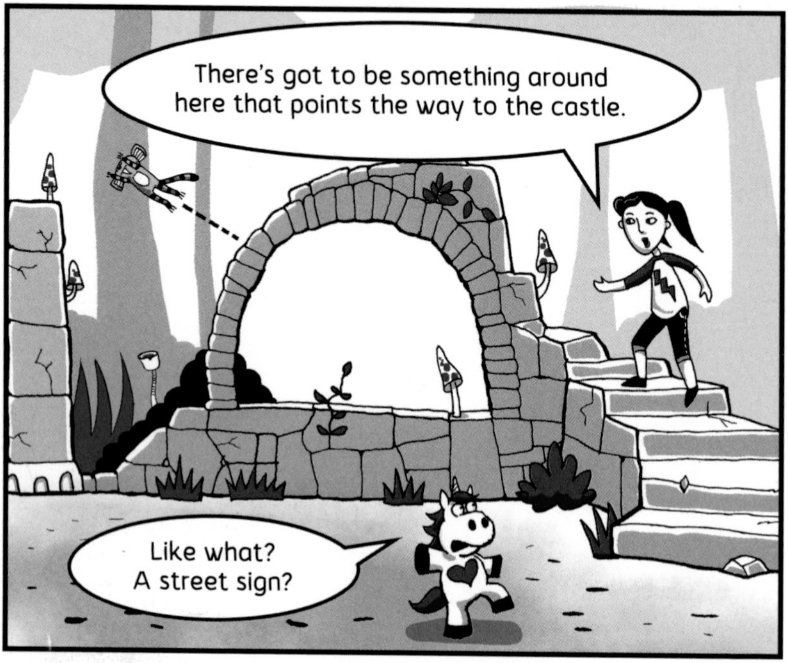
There's got to be something around here that points the way to the castle.
Like what? A street sign?

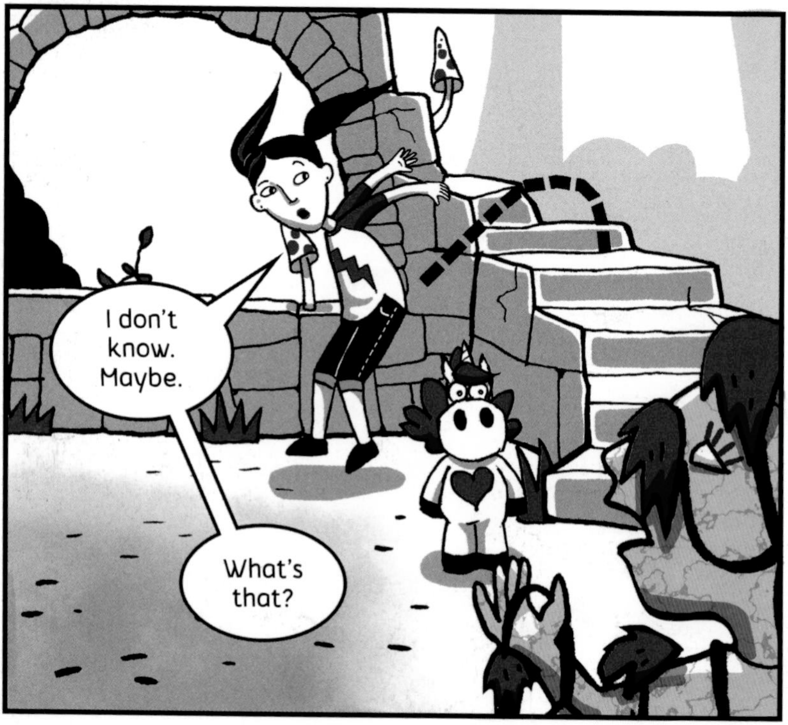
I don't know. Maybe.
What's that?

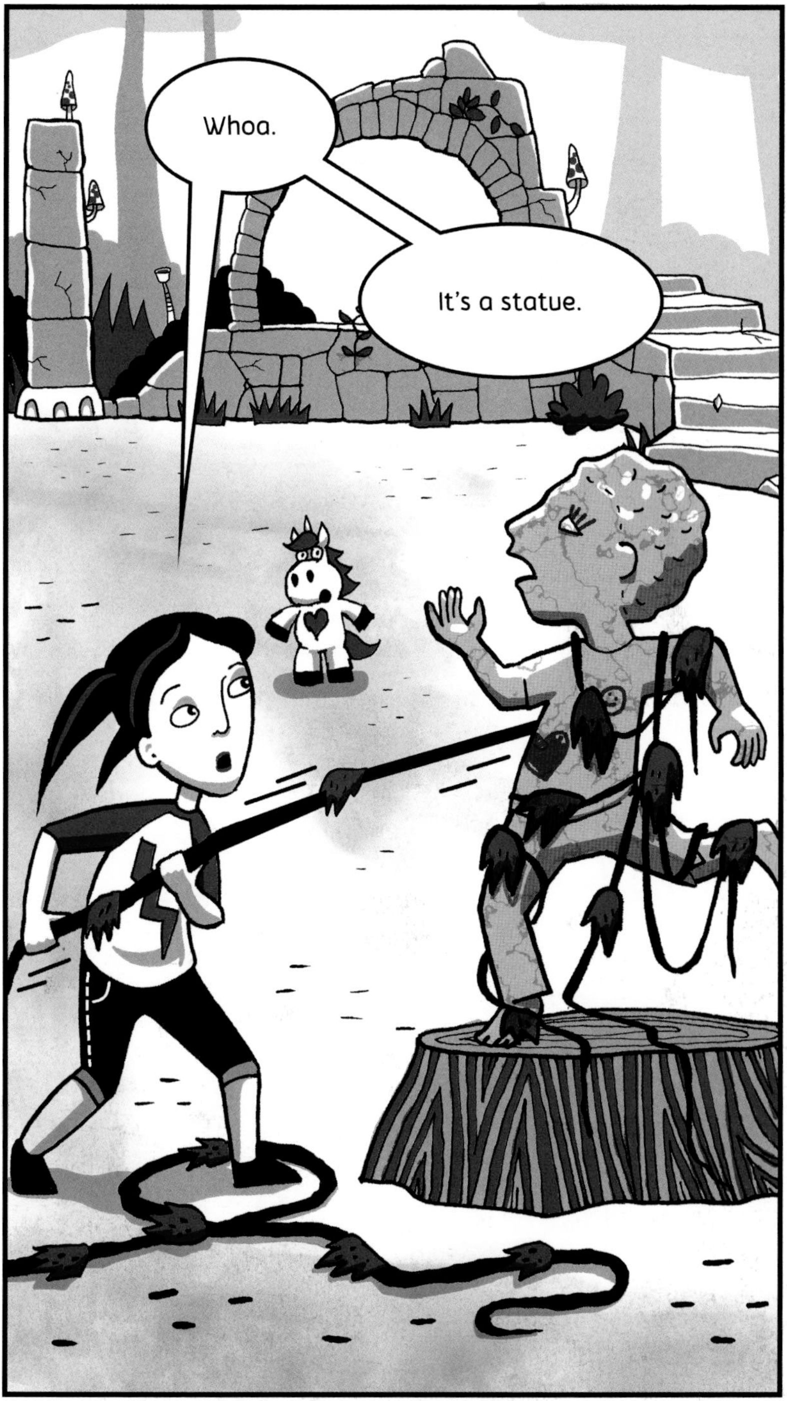
Whoa.
It's a statue.

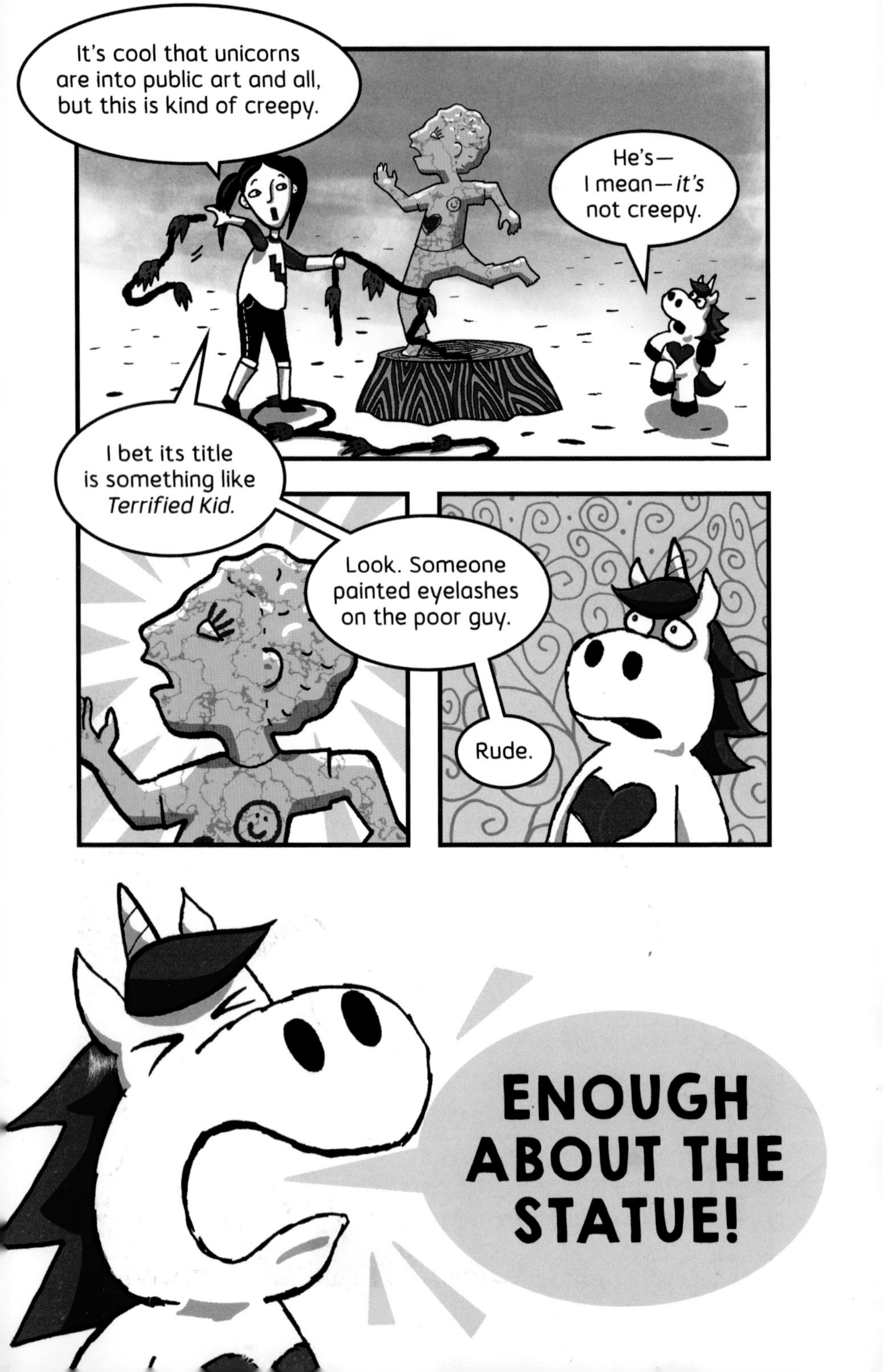
It's cool that unicorns are into public art and all, but this is kind of creepy.
He's— I mean—*it's* not creepy.
I bet its title is something like *Terrified Kid.*
Look. Someone painted eyelashes on the poor guy.
Rude.
ENOUGH ABOUT THE STATUE!

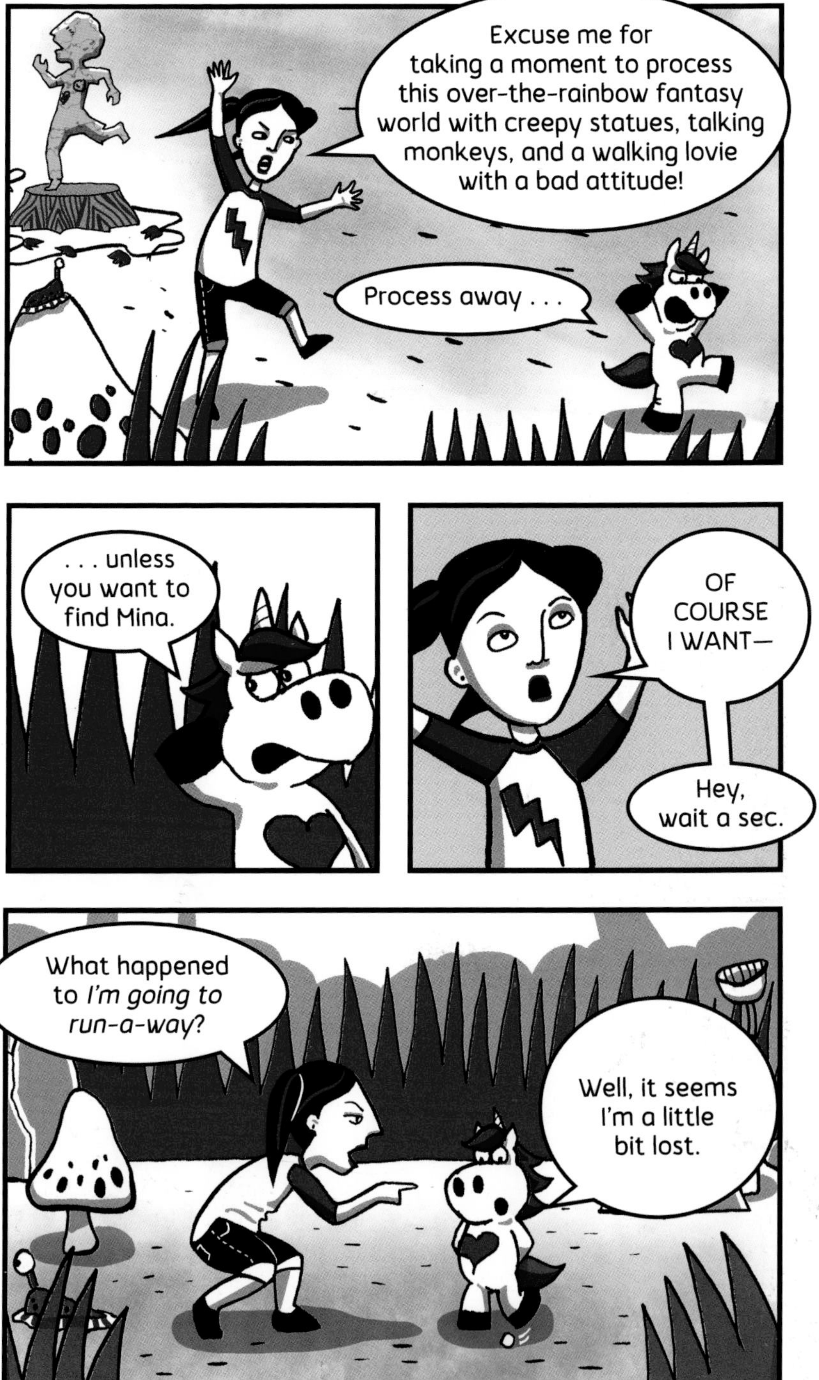
Excuse me for taking a moment to process this over-the-rainbow fantasy world with creepy statues, talking monkeys, and a walking lovie with a bad attitude!
Process away . . .
. . . unless you want to find Mina.
OF COURSE I WANT—
Hey, wait a sec.
What happened to *I'm going to run-a-way?*
Well, it seems I'm a little bit lost.

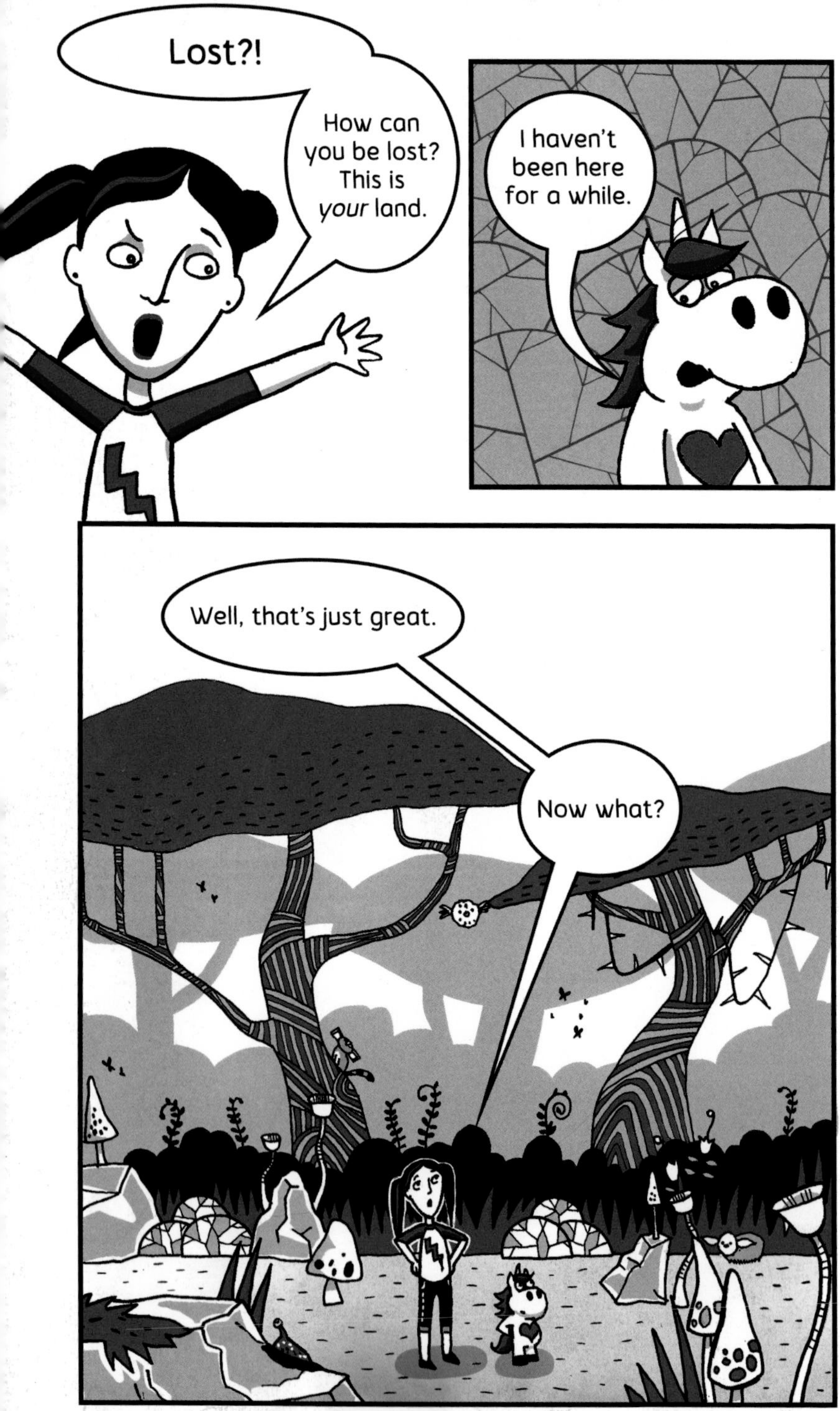
Lost?!
How can you be lost? This is *your* land.
I haven't been here for a while.
Well, that's just great.
Now what?

Chapter 3
SPRING FLING

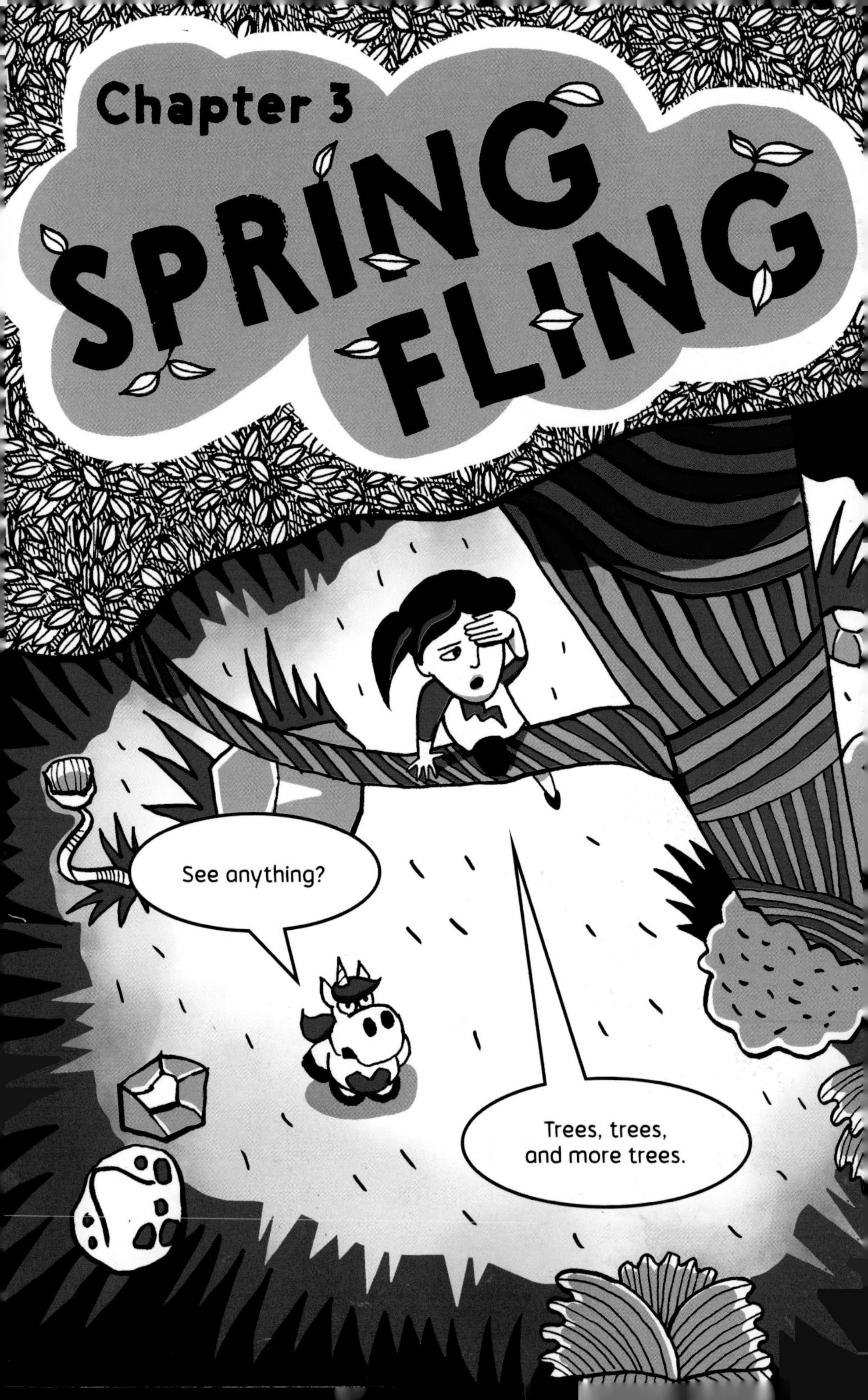
See anything?
Trees, trees, and more trees.

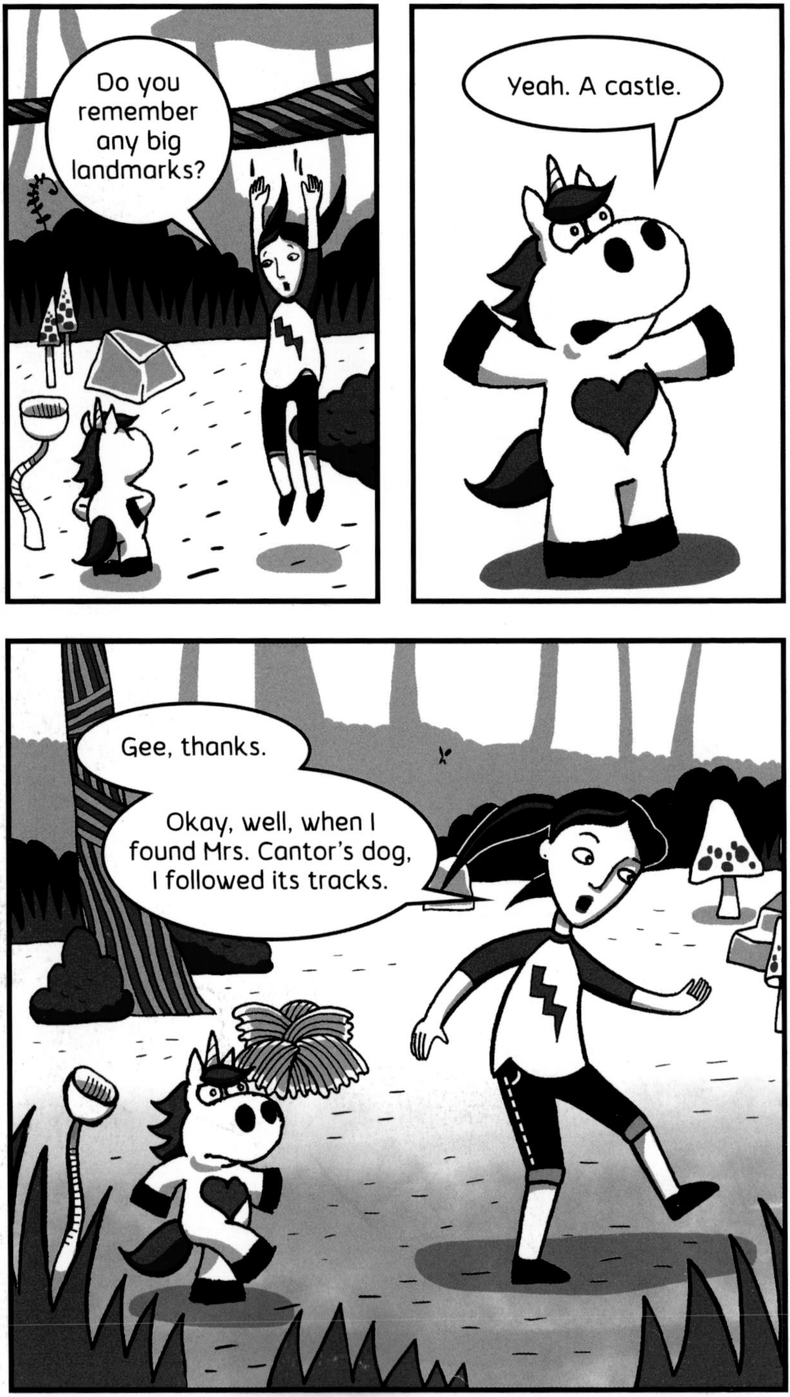
Do you remember any big landmarks?
Yeah. A castle.
Gee, thanks.
Okay, well, when I found Mrs. Cantor's dog, I followed its tracks.

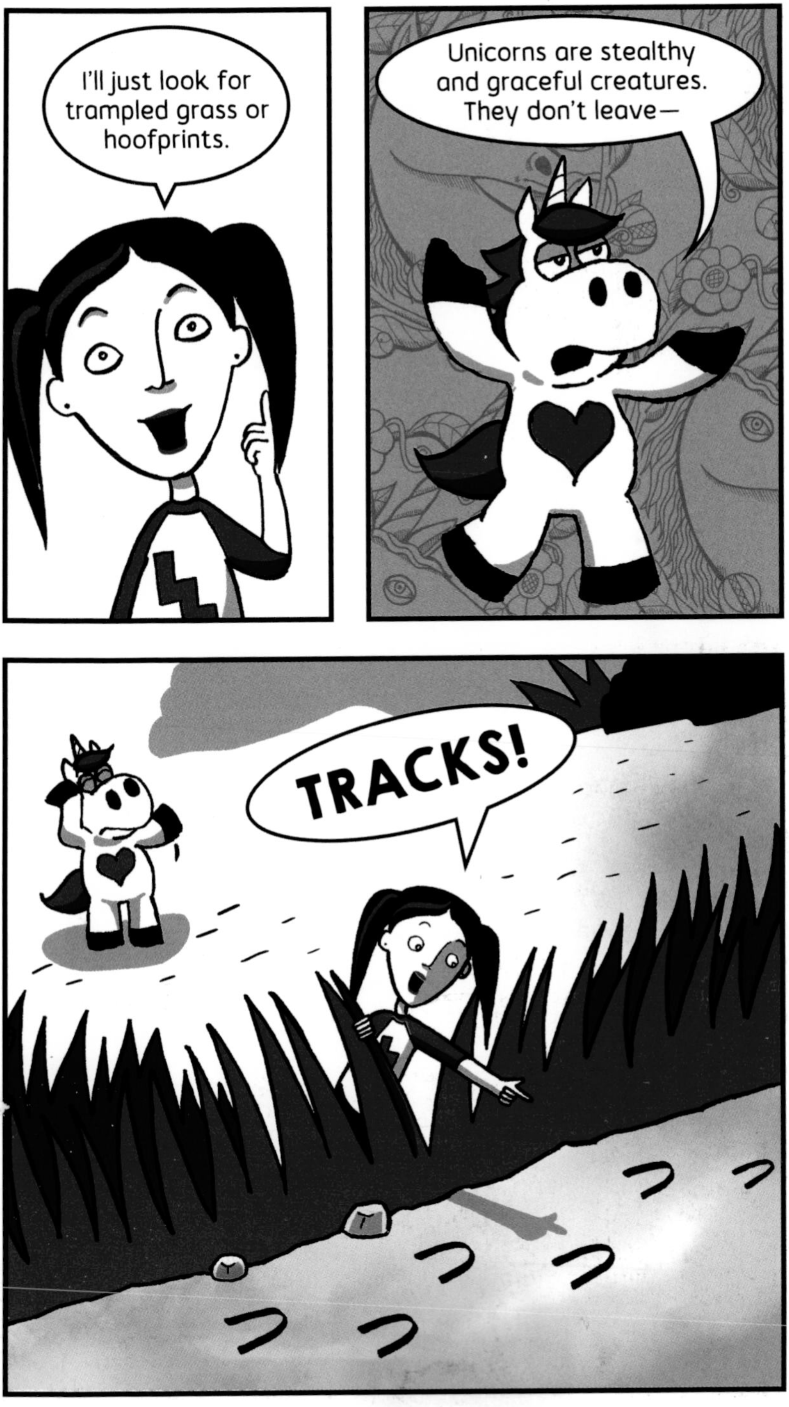

I'll just look for trampled grass or hoofprints.
Unicorns are stealthy and graceful creatures. They don't leave—
TRACKS!

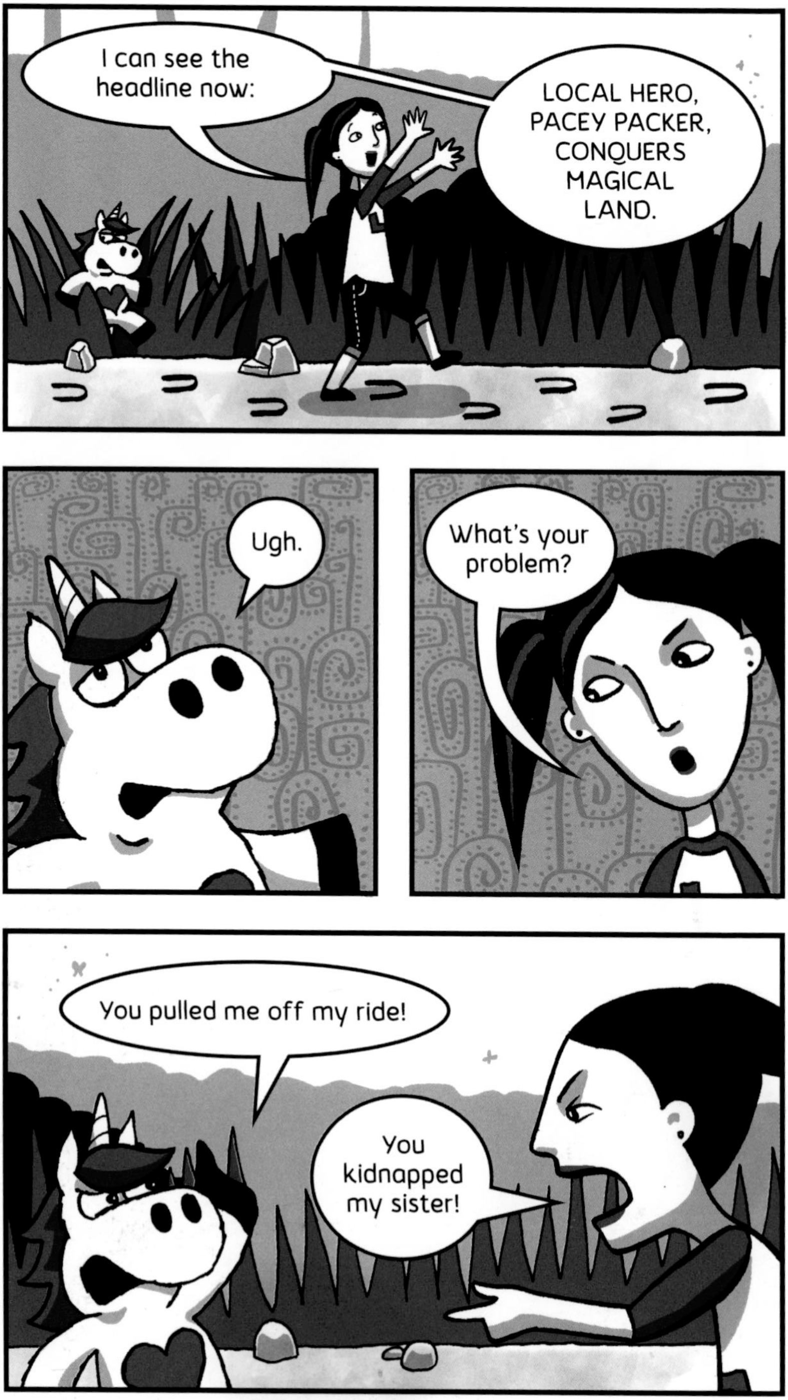
I can see the headline now:
LOCAL HERO, PACEY PACKER, CONQUERS MAGICAL LAND.
Ugh.
What's your problem?
You pulled me off my ride!
You kidnapped my sister!

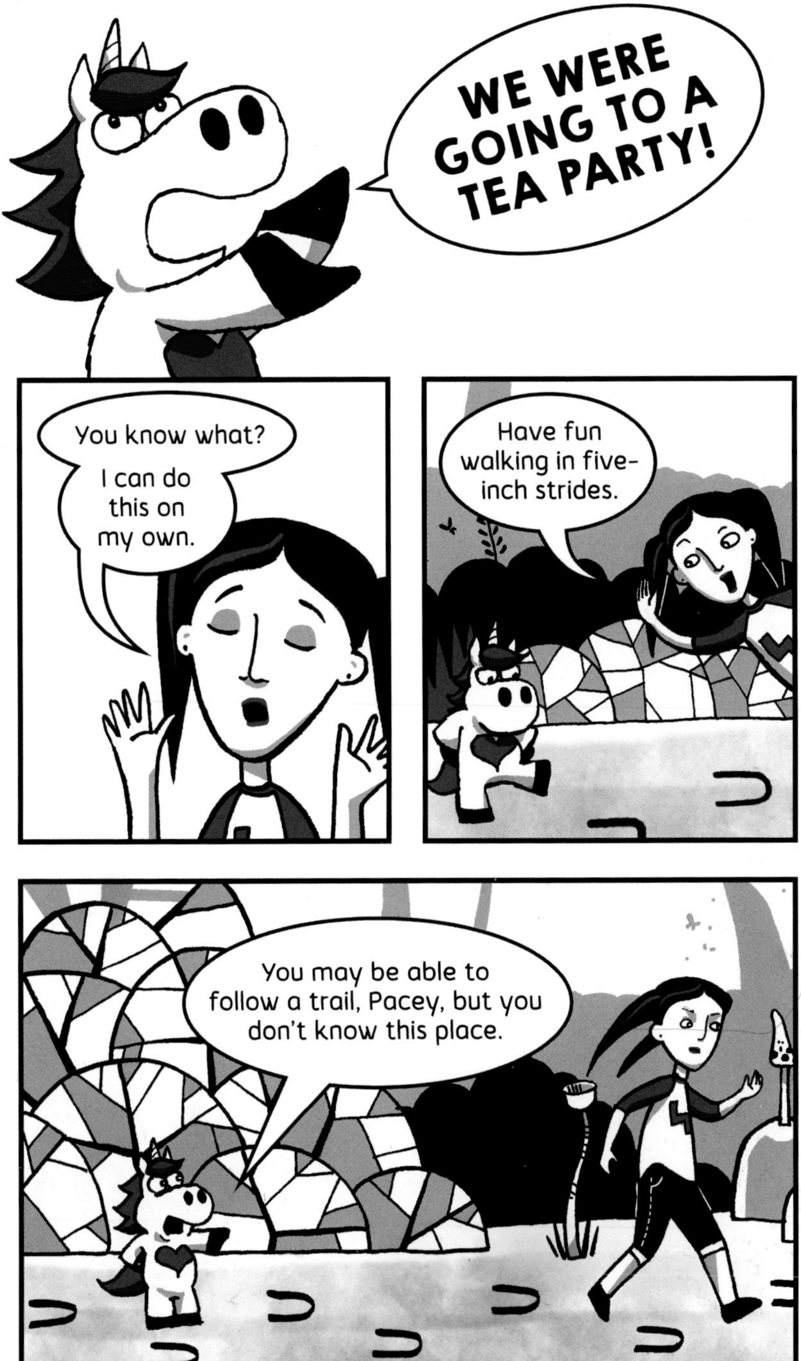
WE WERE GOING TO A TEA PARTY!
You know what?
I can do this on my own.
Have fun walking in five-inch strides.
You may be able to follow a trail, Pacey, but you don't know this place.

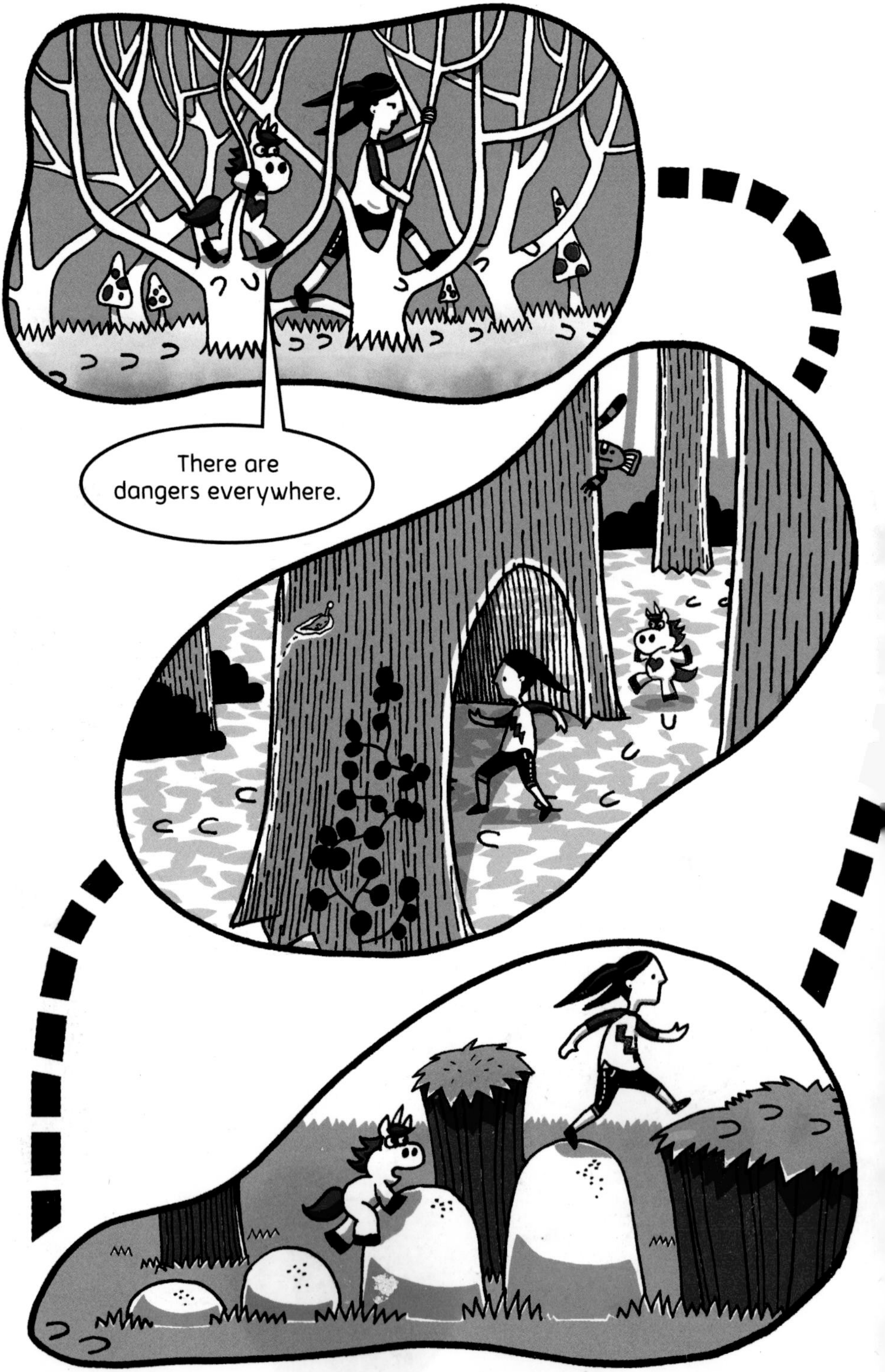
There are dangers everywhere.

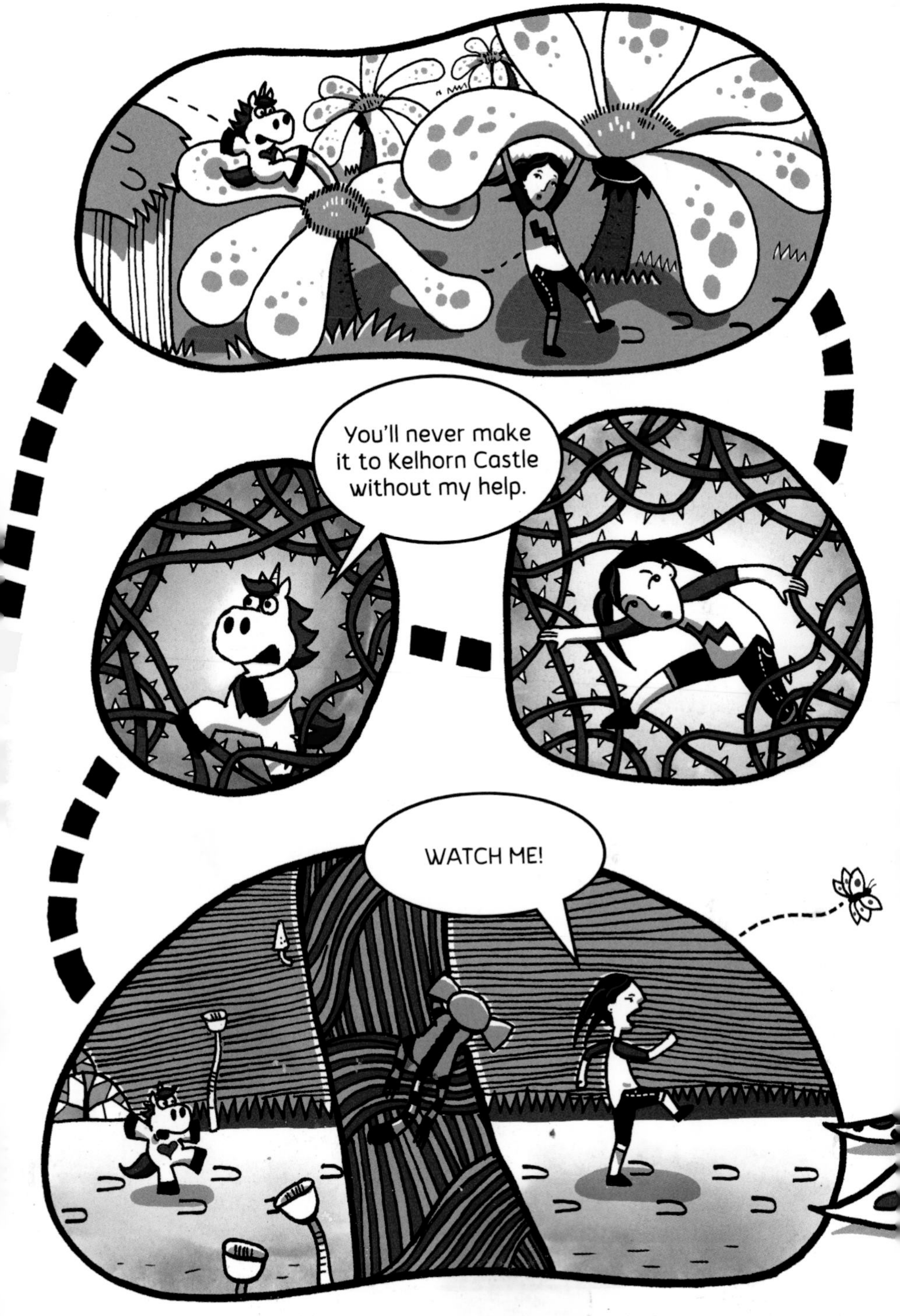
You'll never make it to Kelhorn Castle without my help.
WATCH ME!

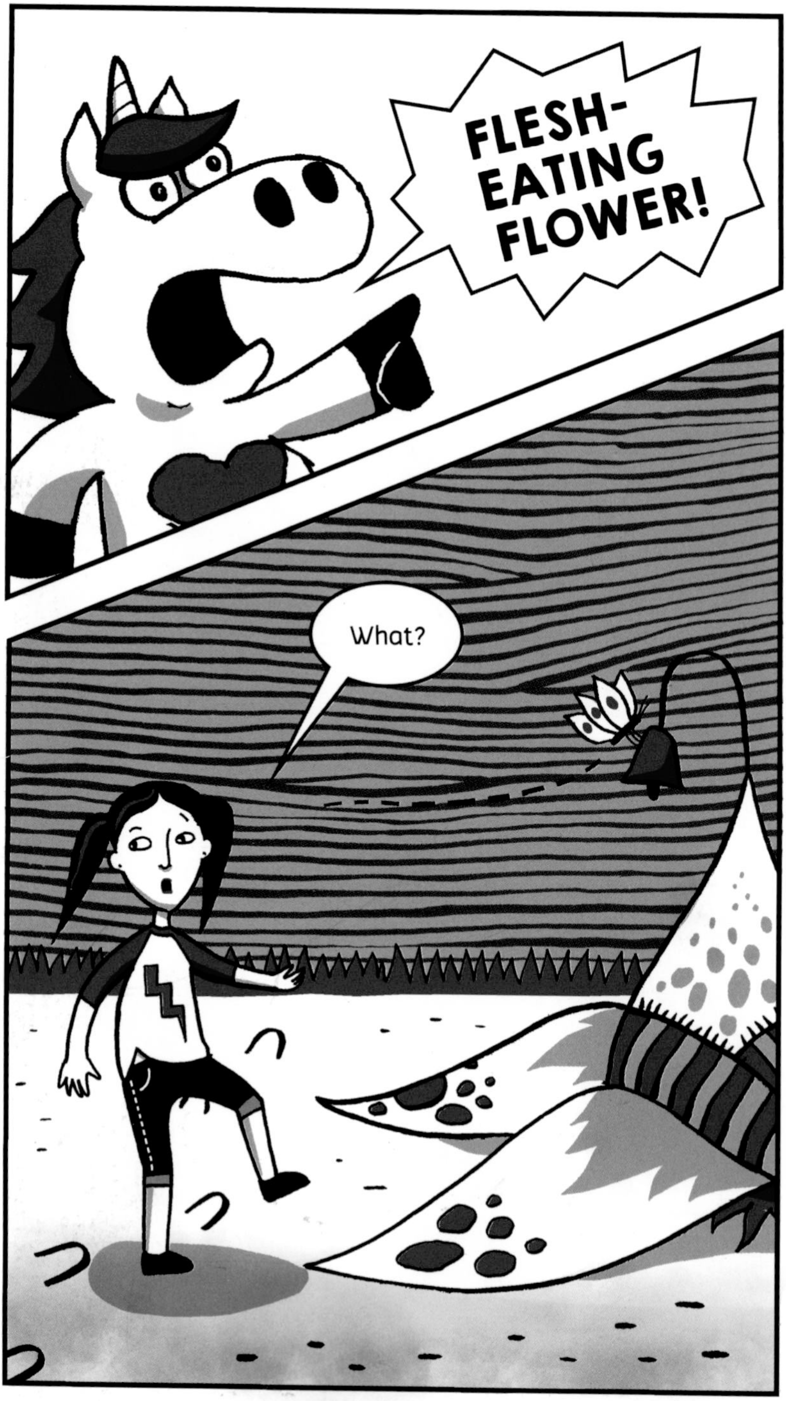
FLESH-EATING FLOWER!
What?

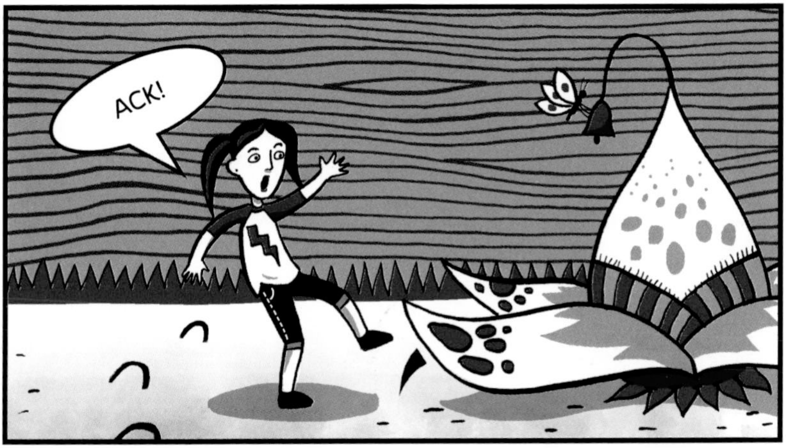
ACK!

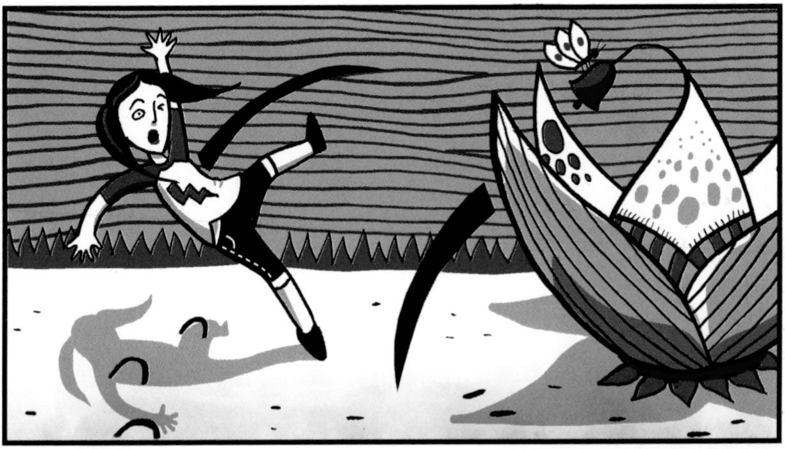

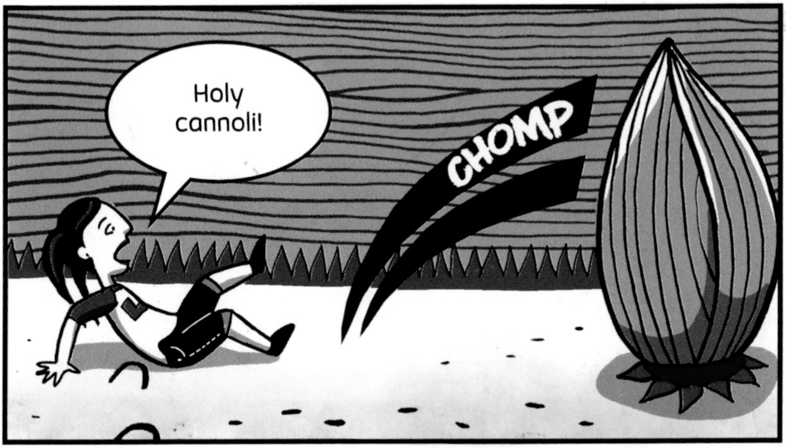
Holy cannoli!
CHOMP

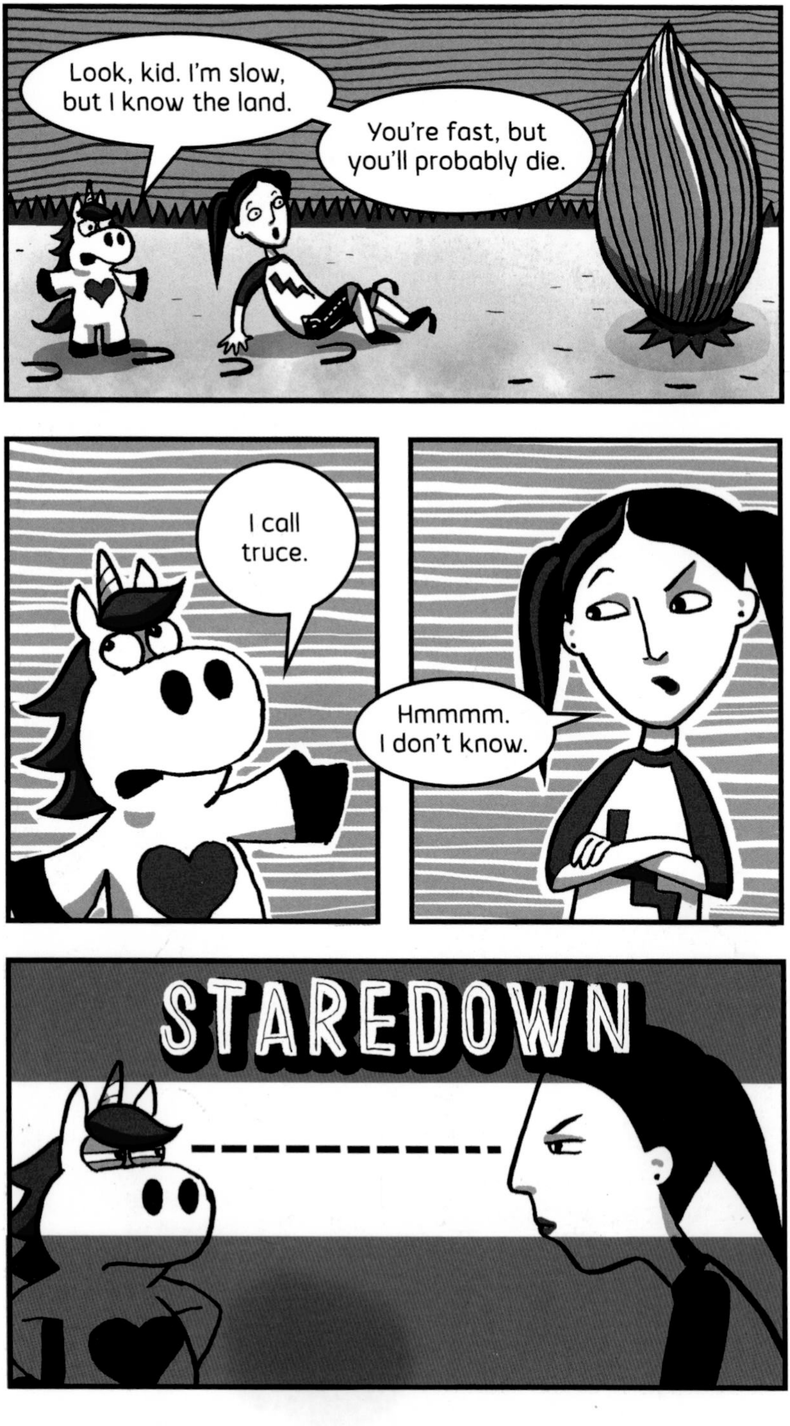
Look, kid. I'm slow, but I know the land.
You're fast, but you'll probably die.
I call truce.
Hmmmm. I don't know.
STAREDOWN

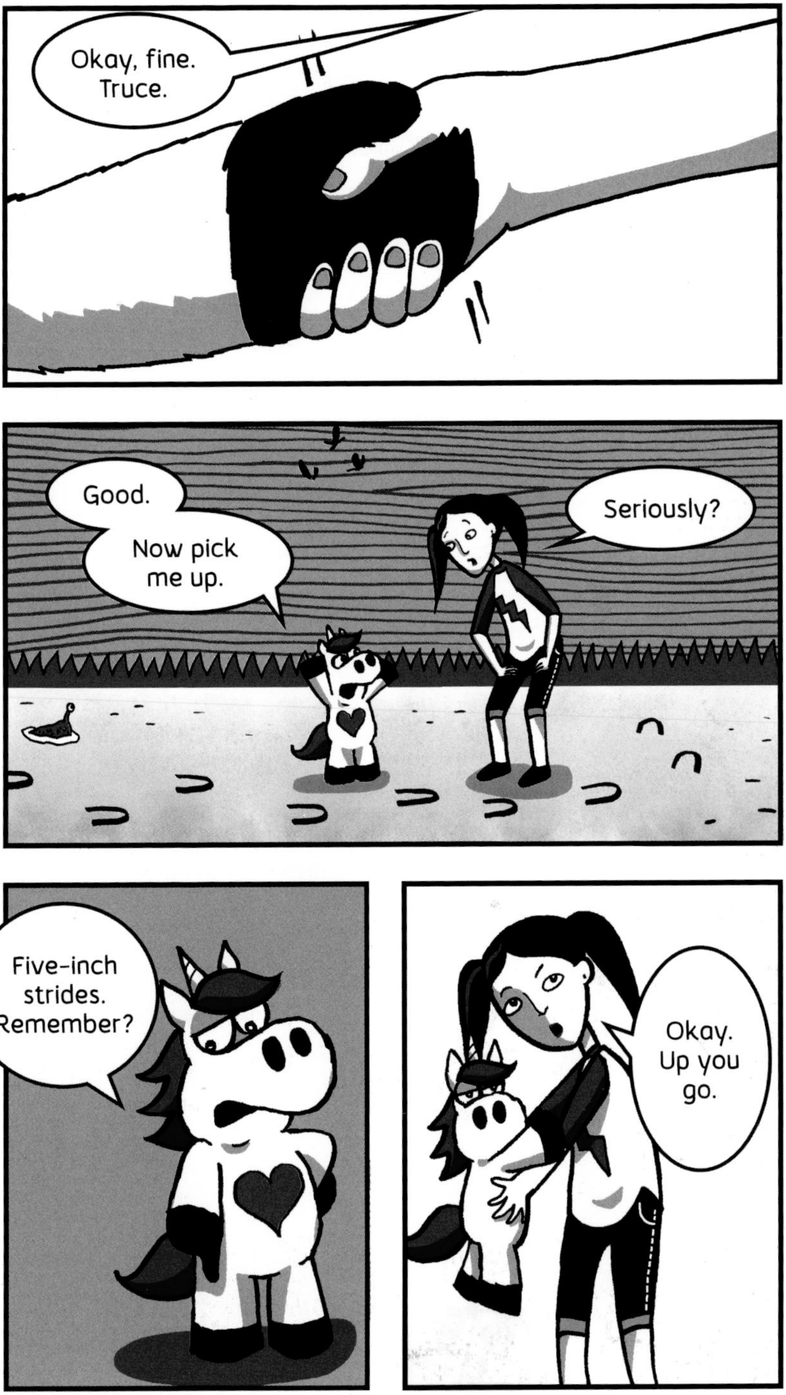

Okay, fine. Truce.
Good.
Now pick me up.
Seriously?
Five-inch strides. Remember?
Okay. Up you go.

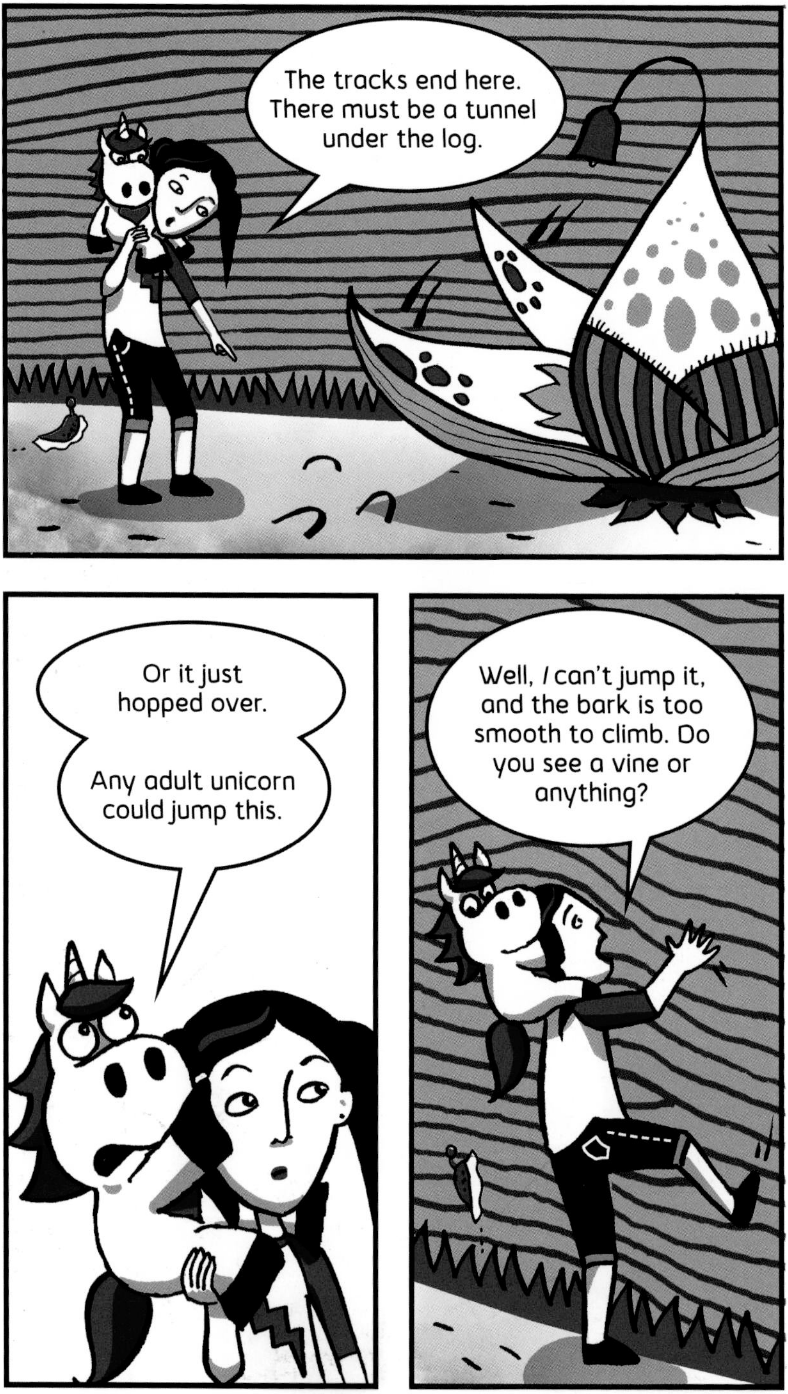
The tracks end here. There must be a tunnel under the log.
Or it just hopped over.
Any adult unicorn could jump this.
Well, *I* can't jump it, and the bark is too smooth to climb. Do you see a vine or anything?

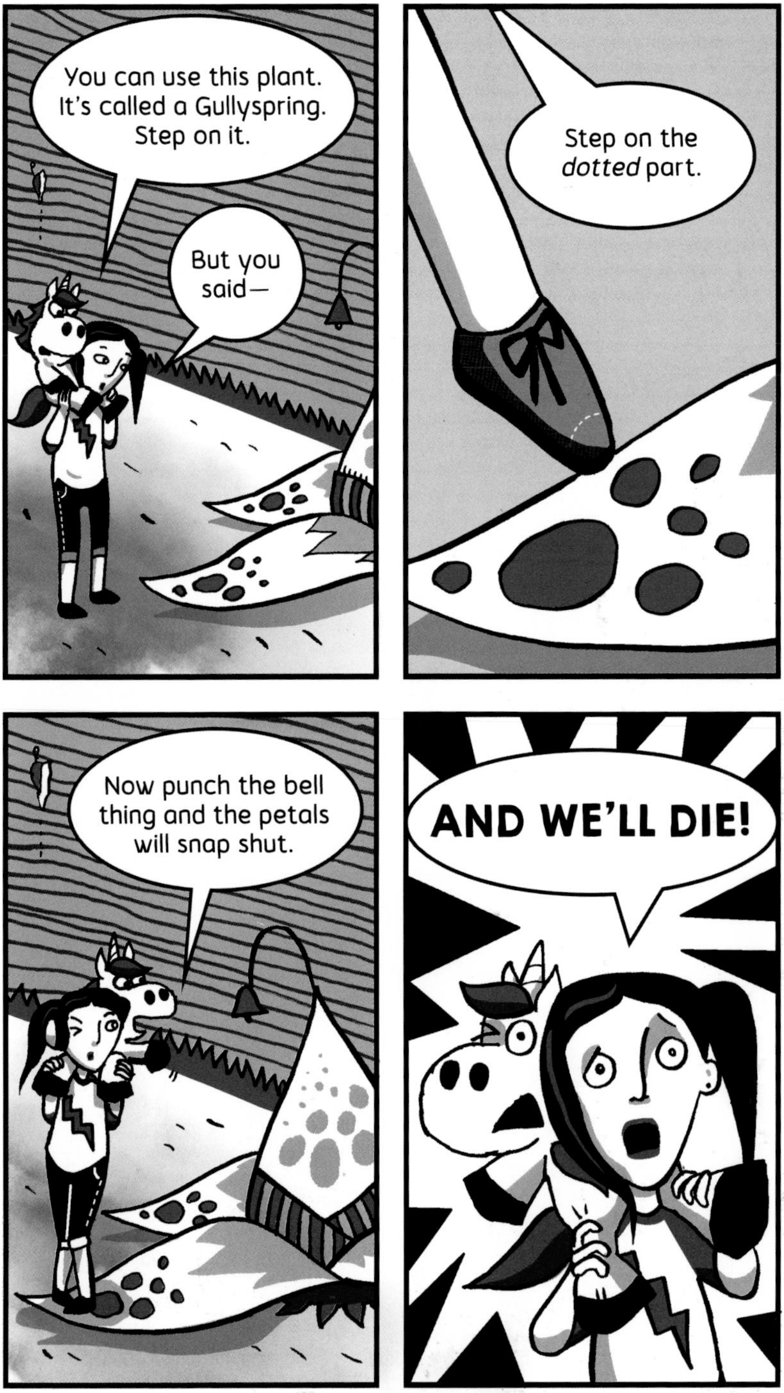
You can use this plant. It's called a Gullyspring. Step on it.
But you said—
Step on the *dotted* part.
Now punch the bell thing and the petals will snap shut.
AND WE'LL DIE!

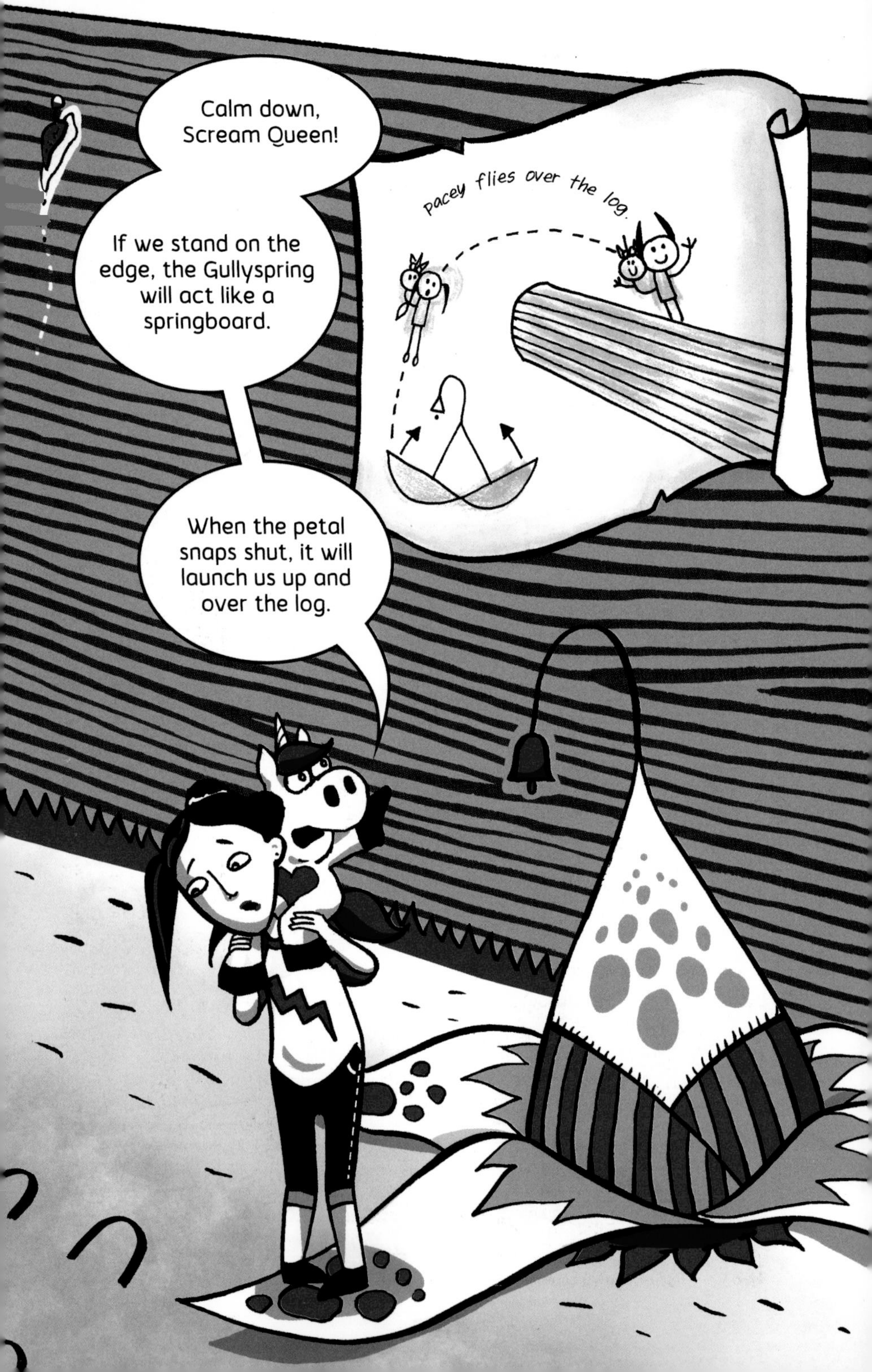
Calm down, Scream Queen!
If we stand on the edge, the Gullyspring will act like a springboard.
pacey flies over the log.
When the petal snaps shut, it will launch us up and over the log.

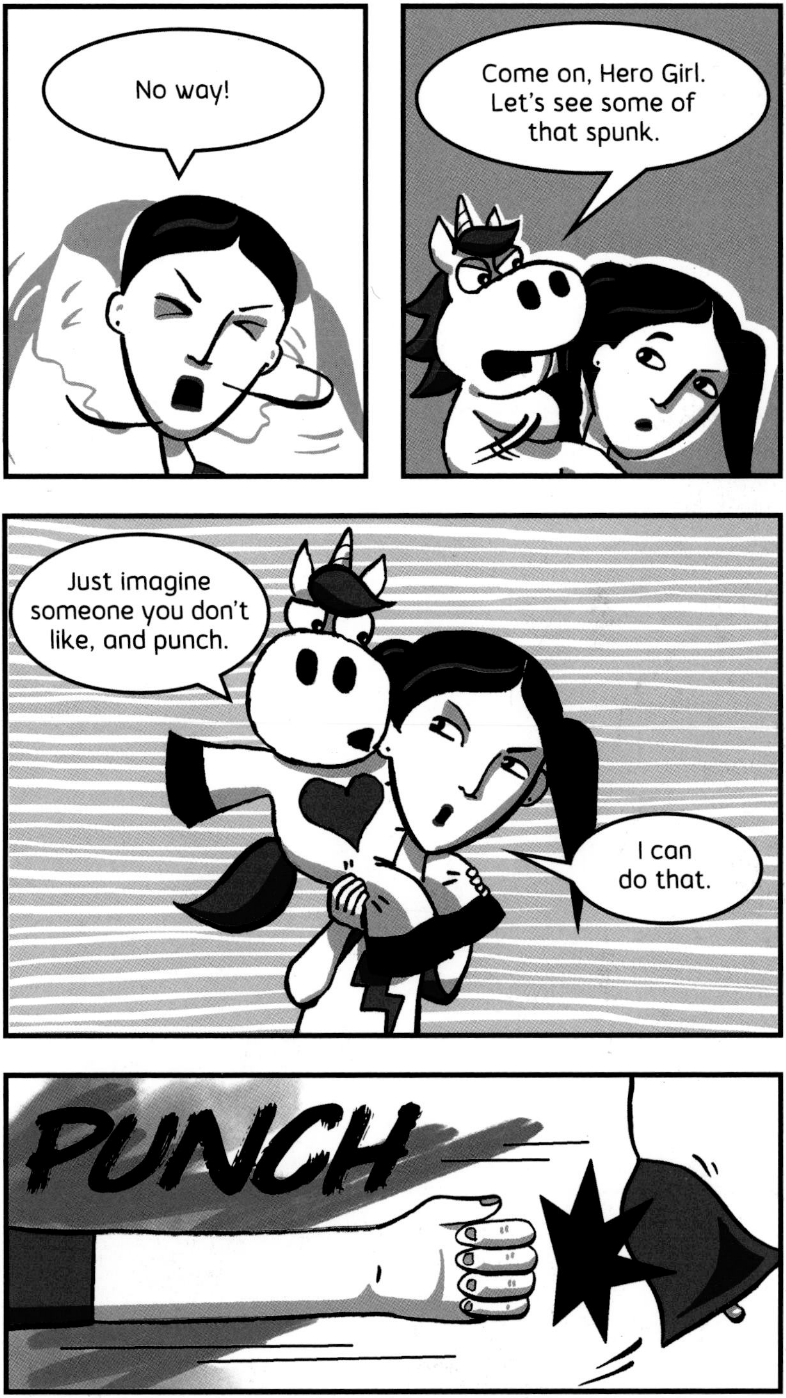
No way!
Come on, Hero Girl. Let's see some of that spunk.
Just imagine someone you don't like, and punch.
I can do that.
PUNCH

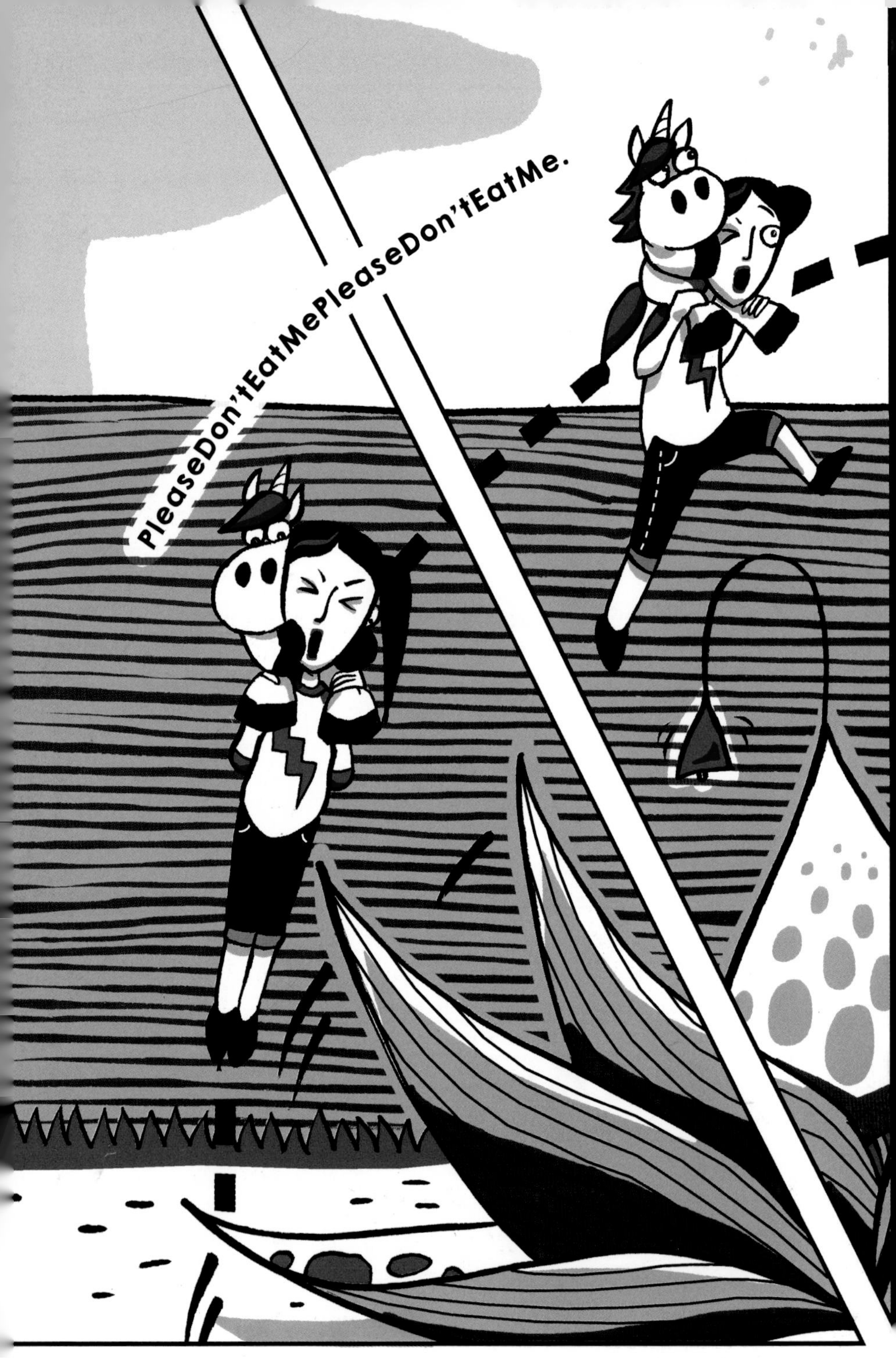
PleaseDon'tEatMePleaseDon'tEatMe.

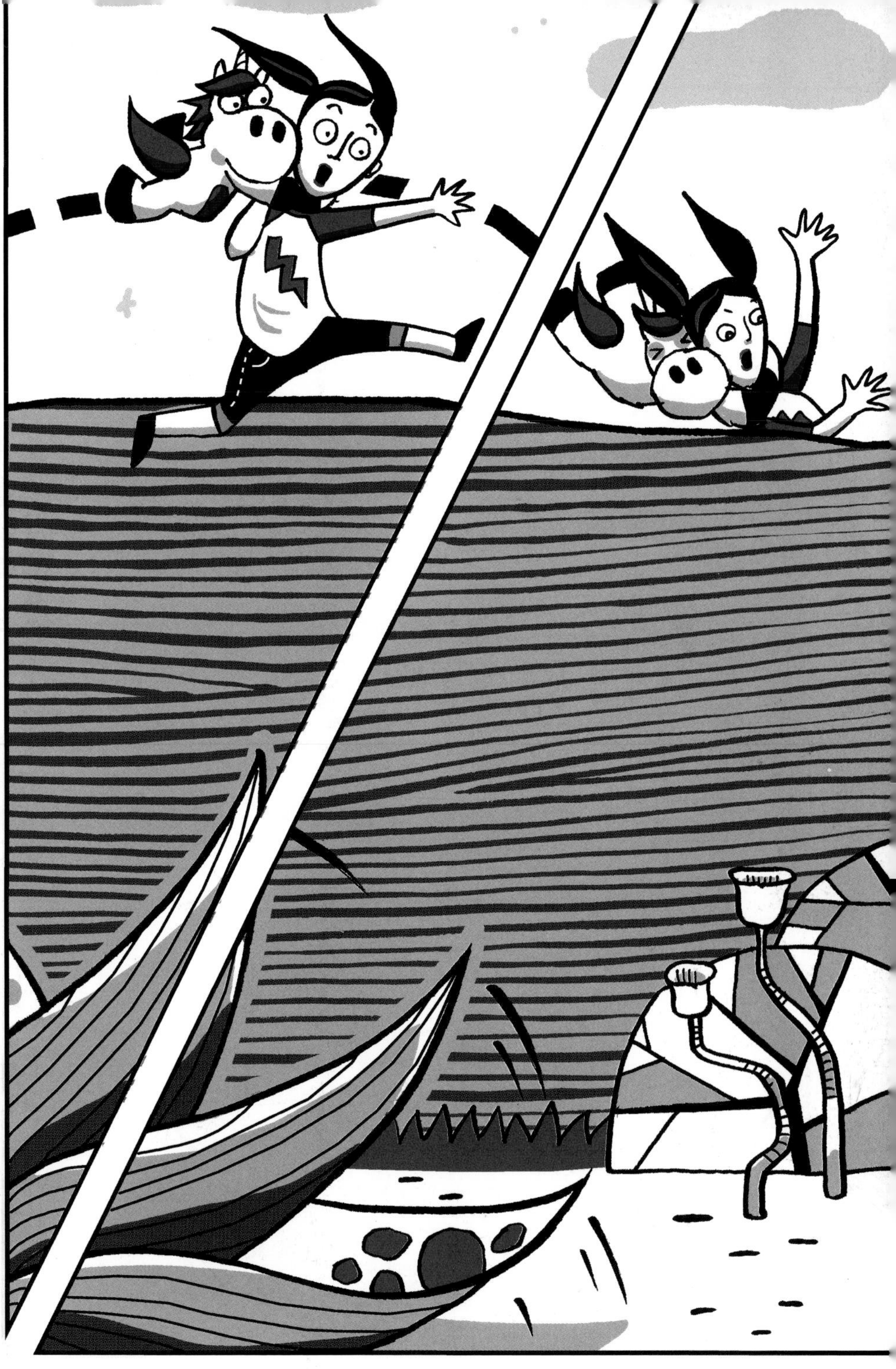

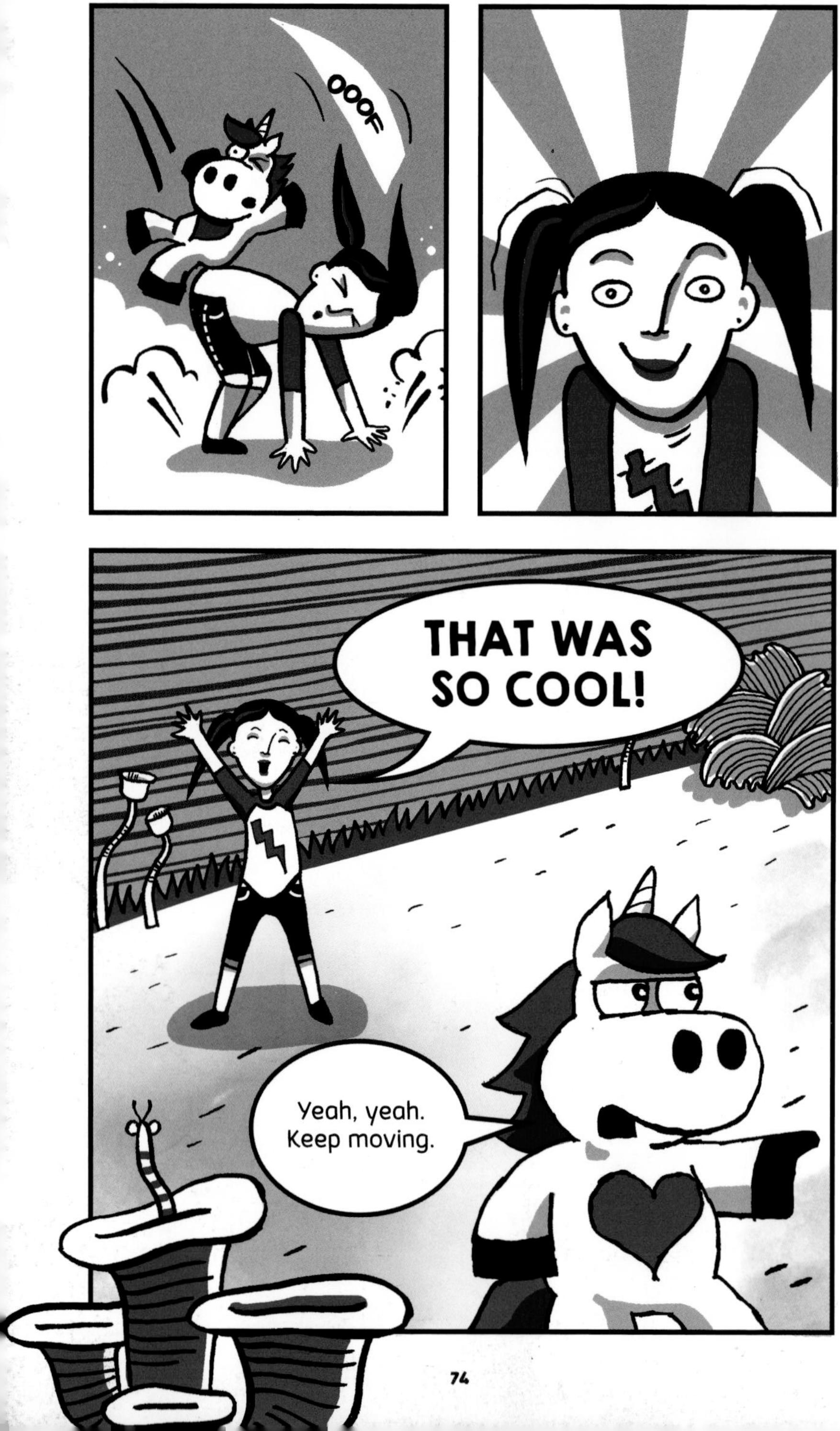
OOOF
THAT WAS SO COOL!
Yeah, yeah. Keep moving.

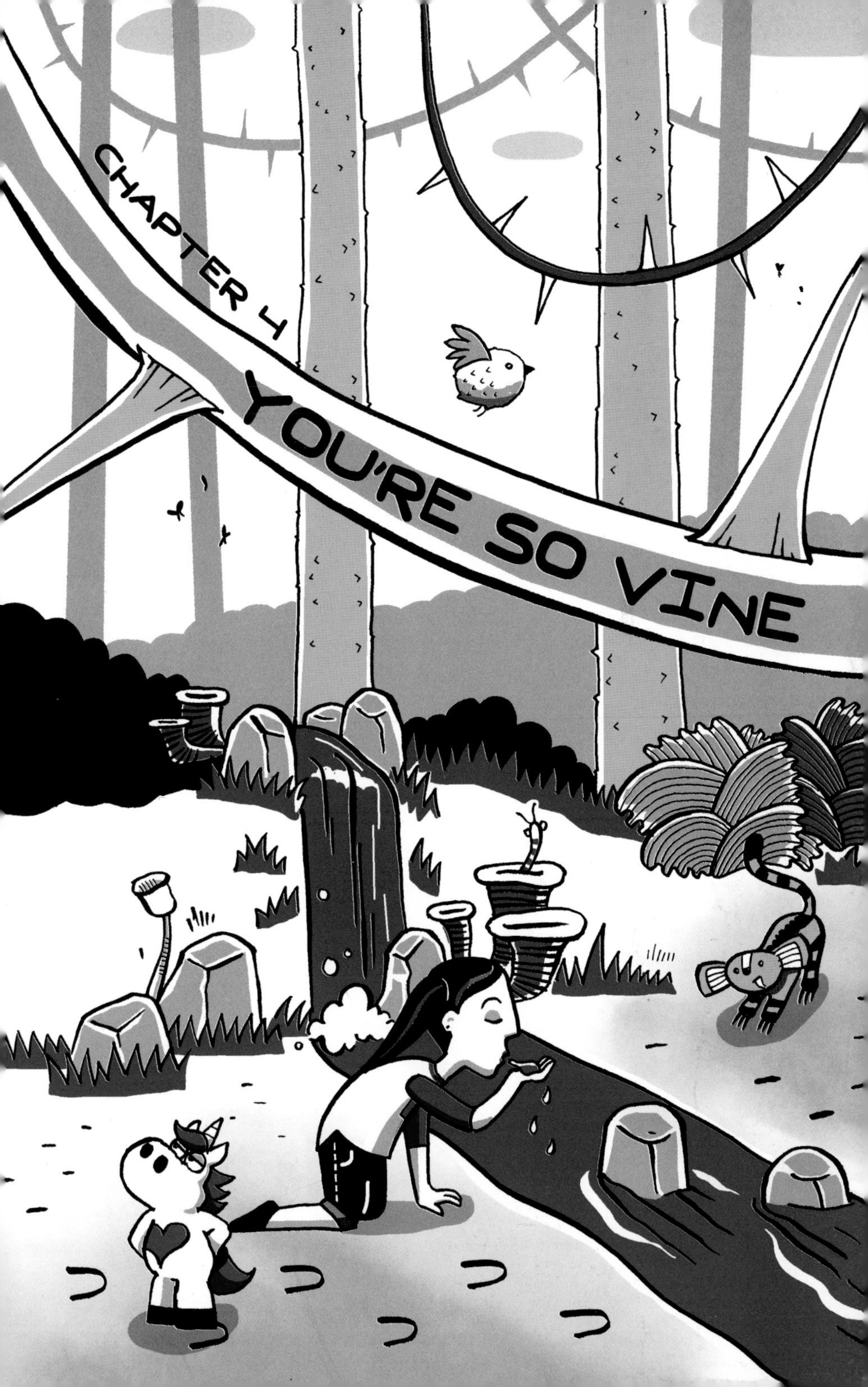
CHAPTER 4
YOU'RE SO VINE

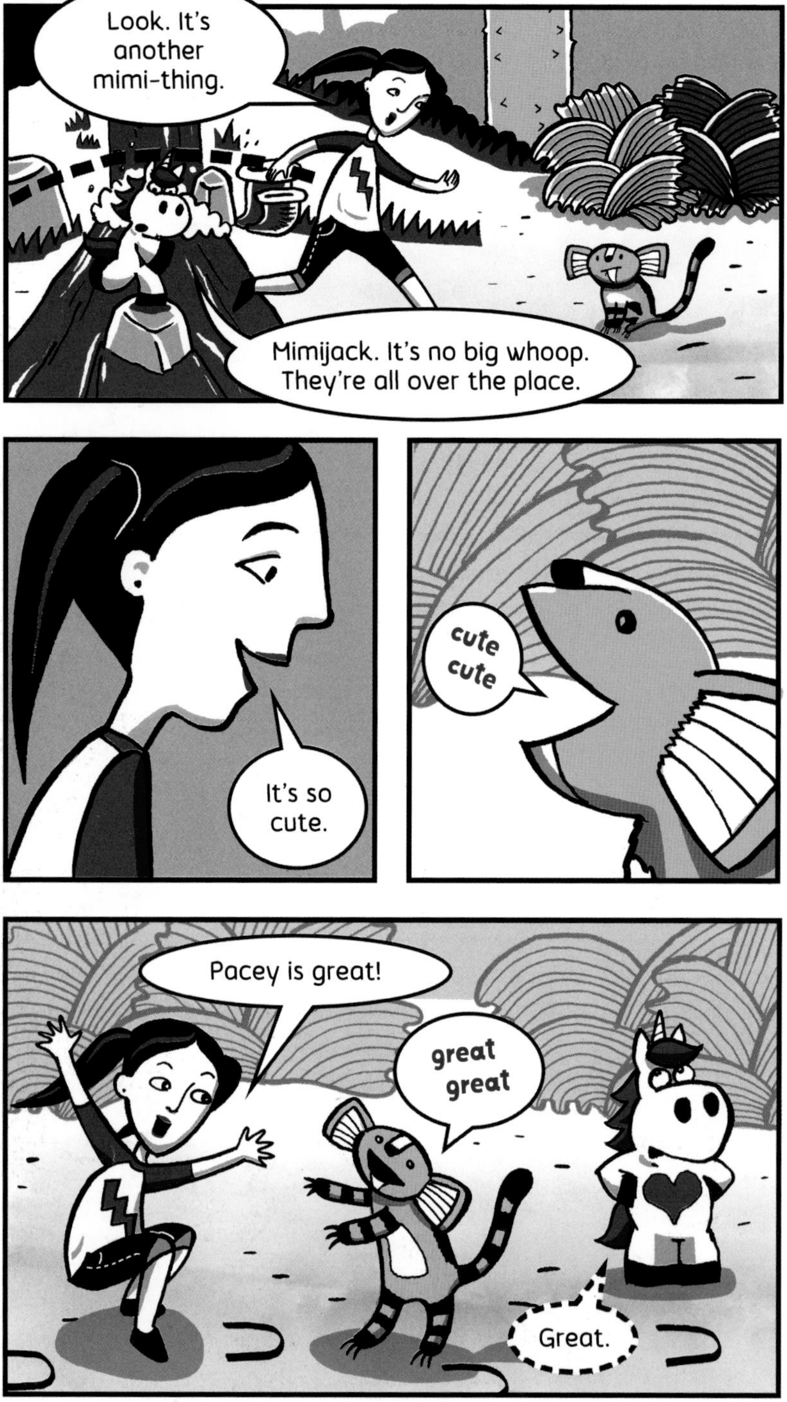
Look. It's another mimi-thing.
Mimijack. It's no big whoop. They're all over the place.
It's so cute.
cute cute
Pacey is great!
great great
Great.

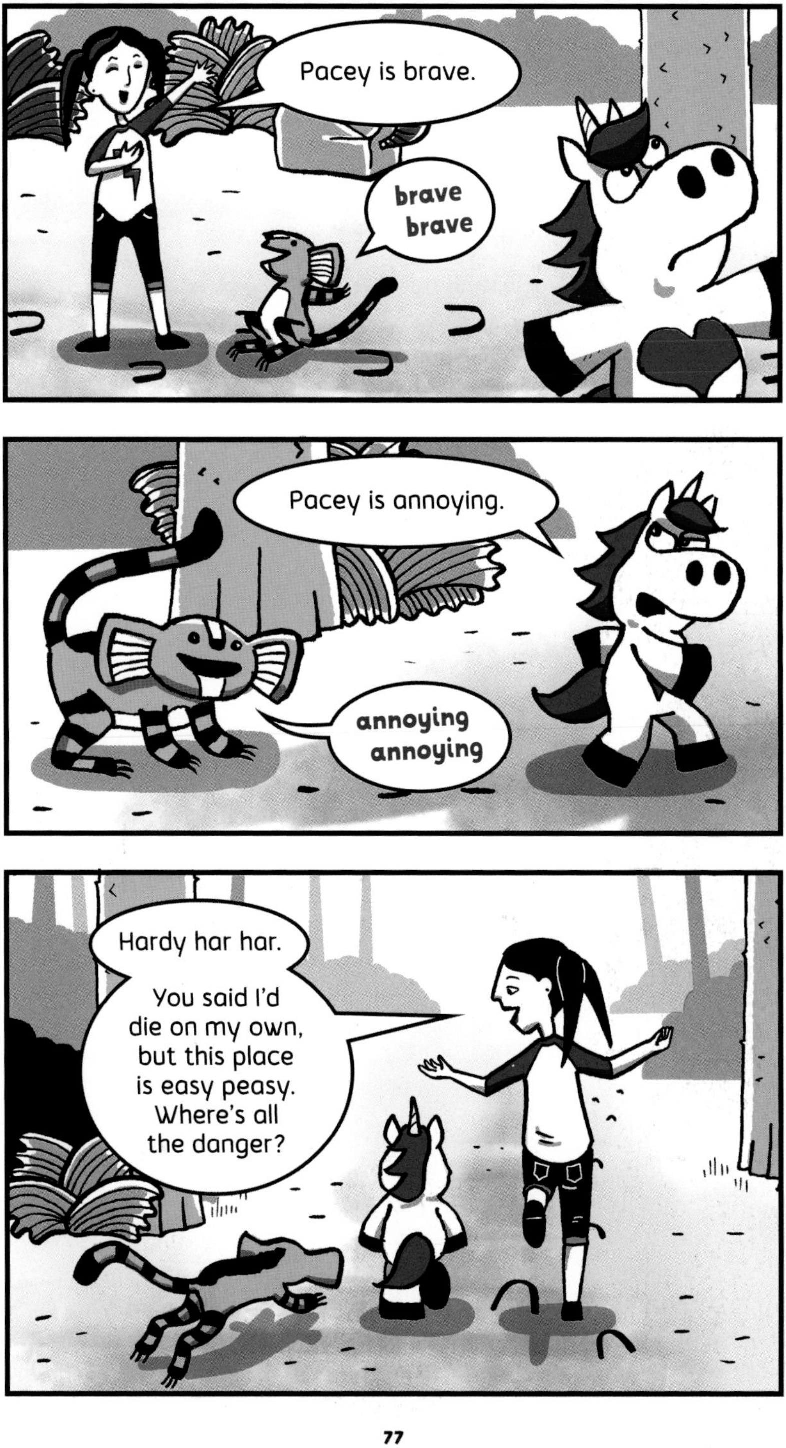
Pacey is brave.
brave brave
Pacey is annoying.
annoying annoying
Hardy har har.
You said I'd die on my own, but this place is easy peasy. Where's all the danger?

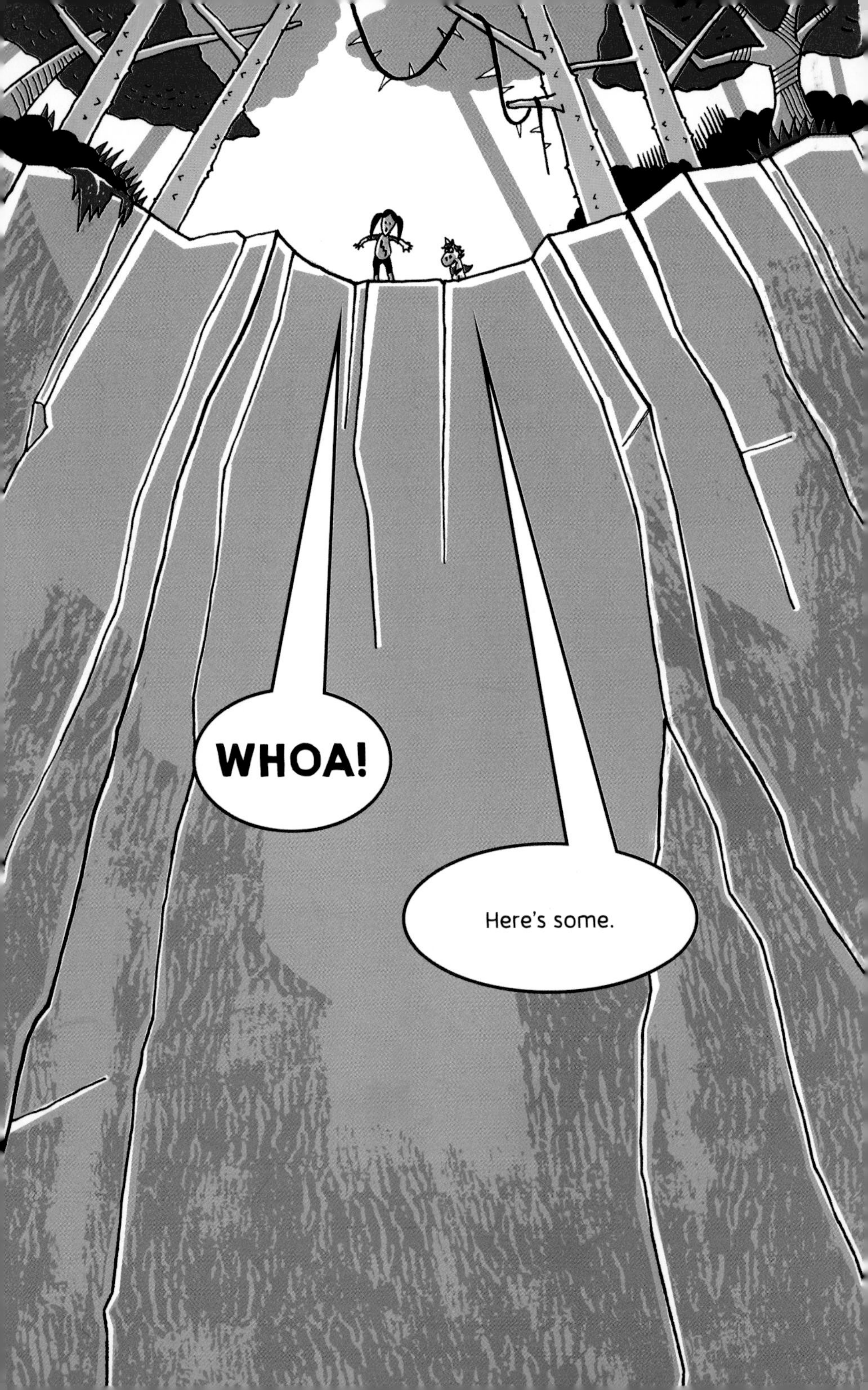
WHOA!
Here's some.

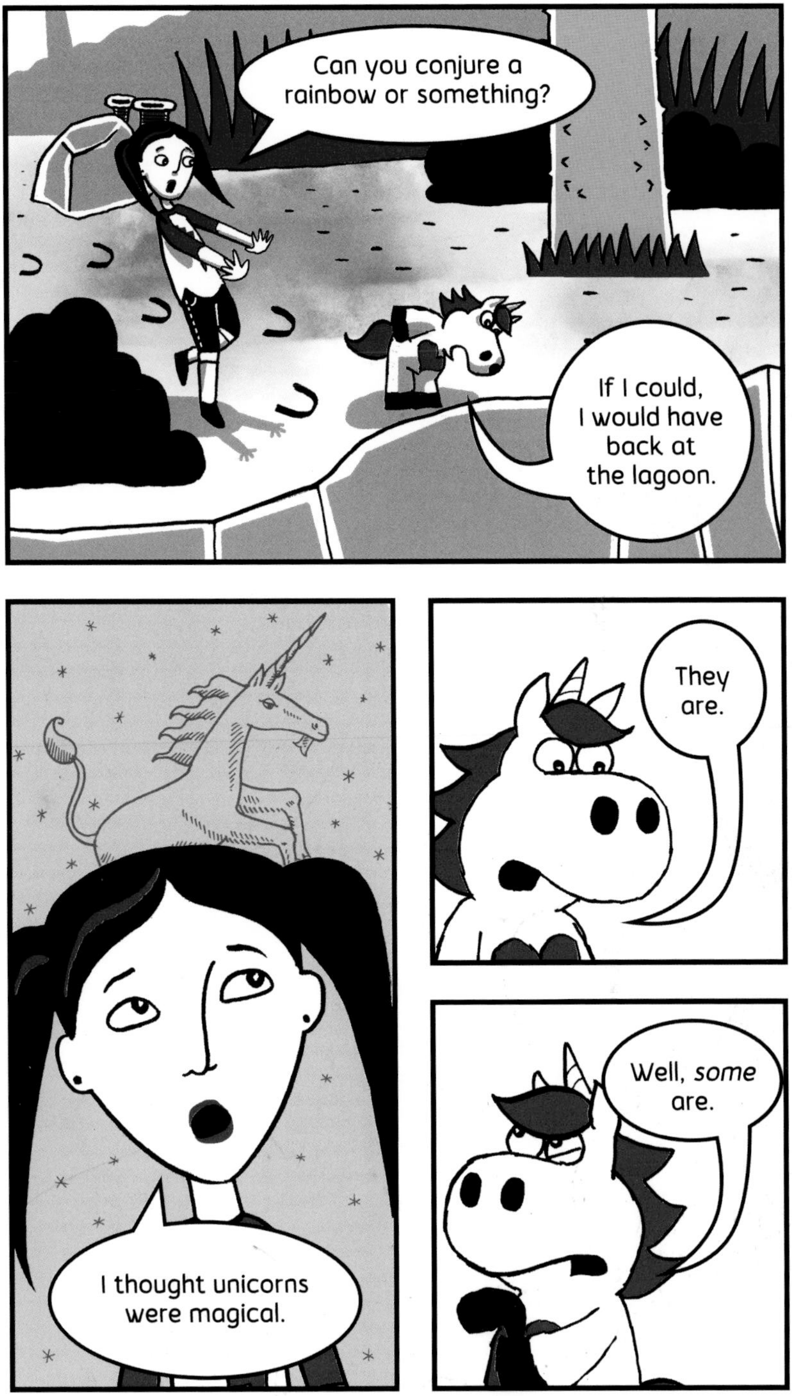
Can you conjure a rainbow or something?
If I could, I would have back at the lagoon.
I thought unicorns were magical.
They are.
Well, *some* are.

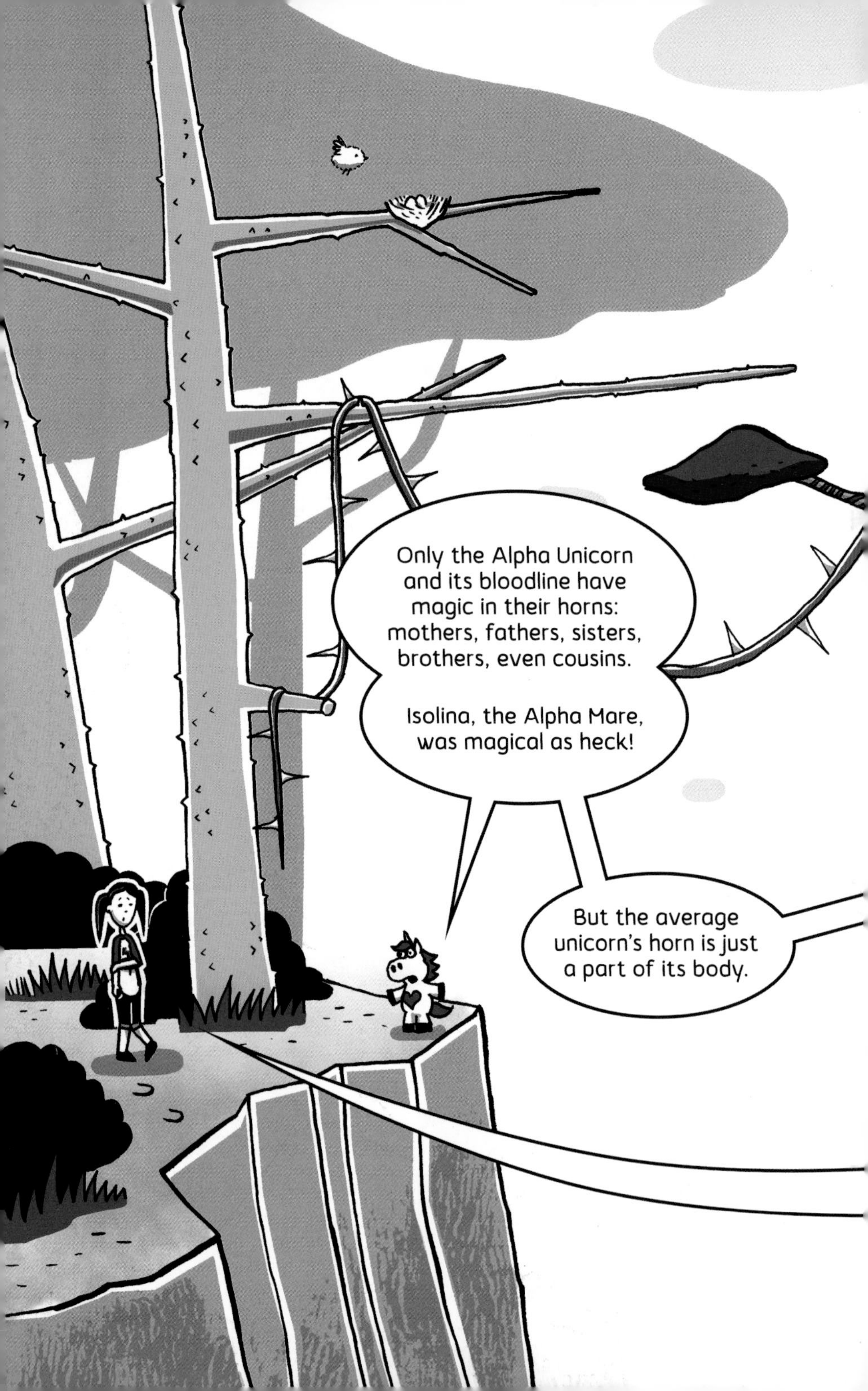
Only the Alpha Unicorn and its bloodline have magic in their horns: mothers, fathers, sisters, brothers, even cousins.
Isolina, the Alpha Mare, was magical as heck!
But the average unicorn's horn is just a part of its body.

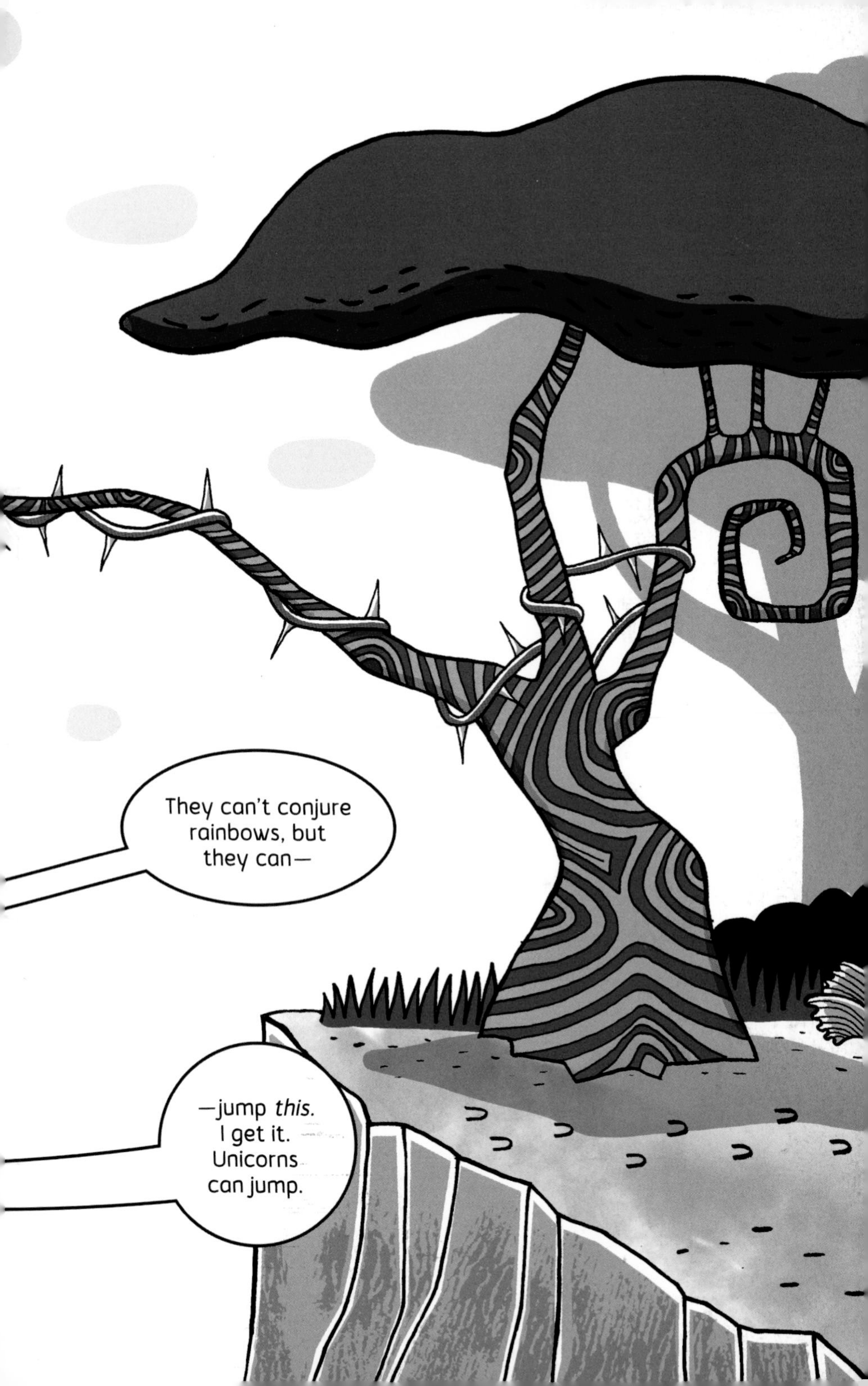
They can't conjure rainbows, but they can—
—jump *this.* I get it. Unicorns can jump.

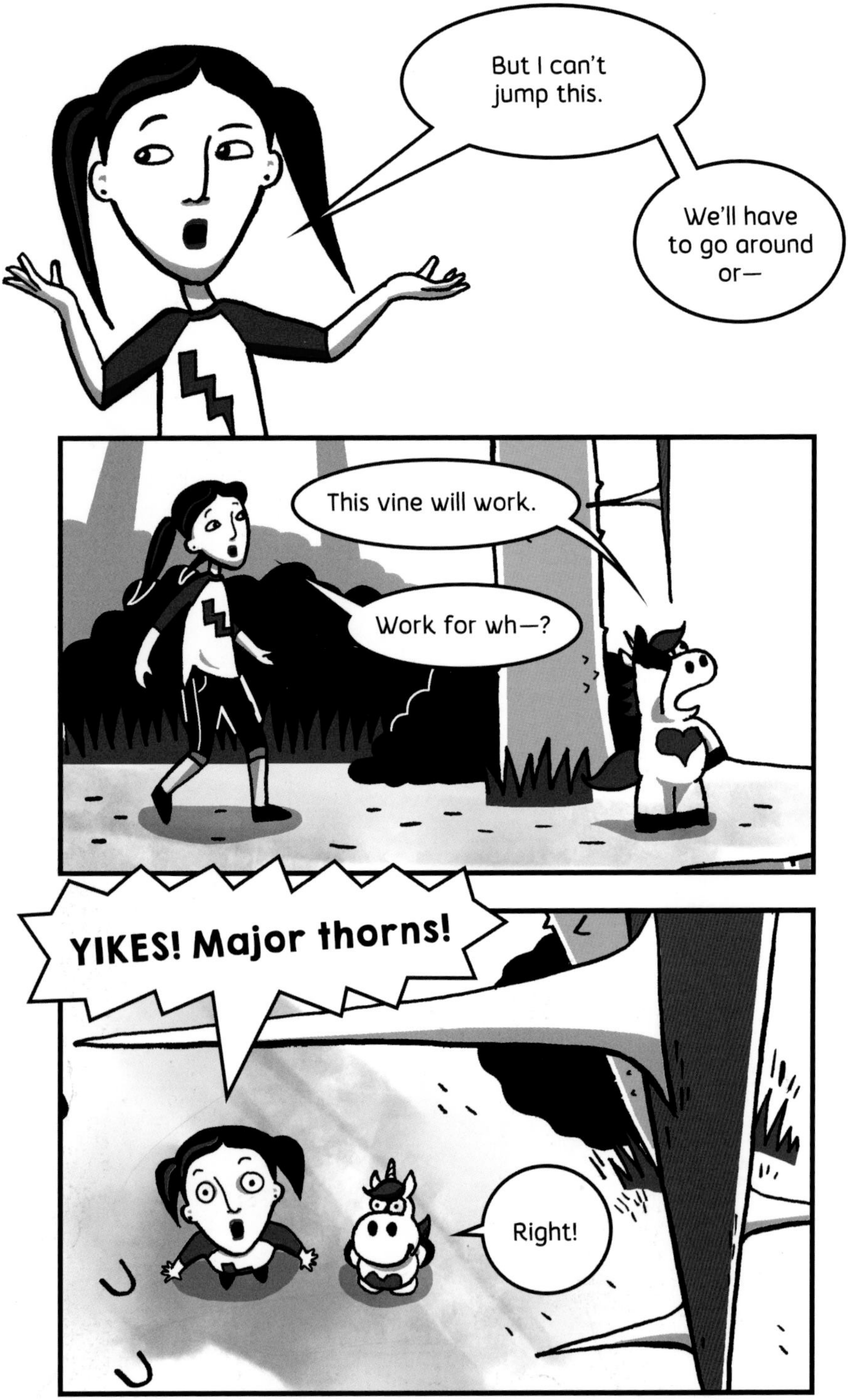
But I can't jump this.
We'll have to go around or—
This vine will work.
Work for wh—?
YIKES! Major thorns!
Right!

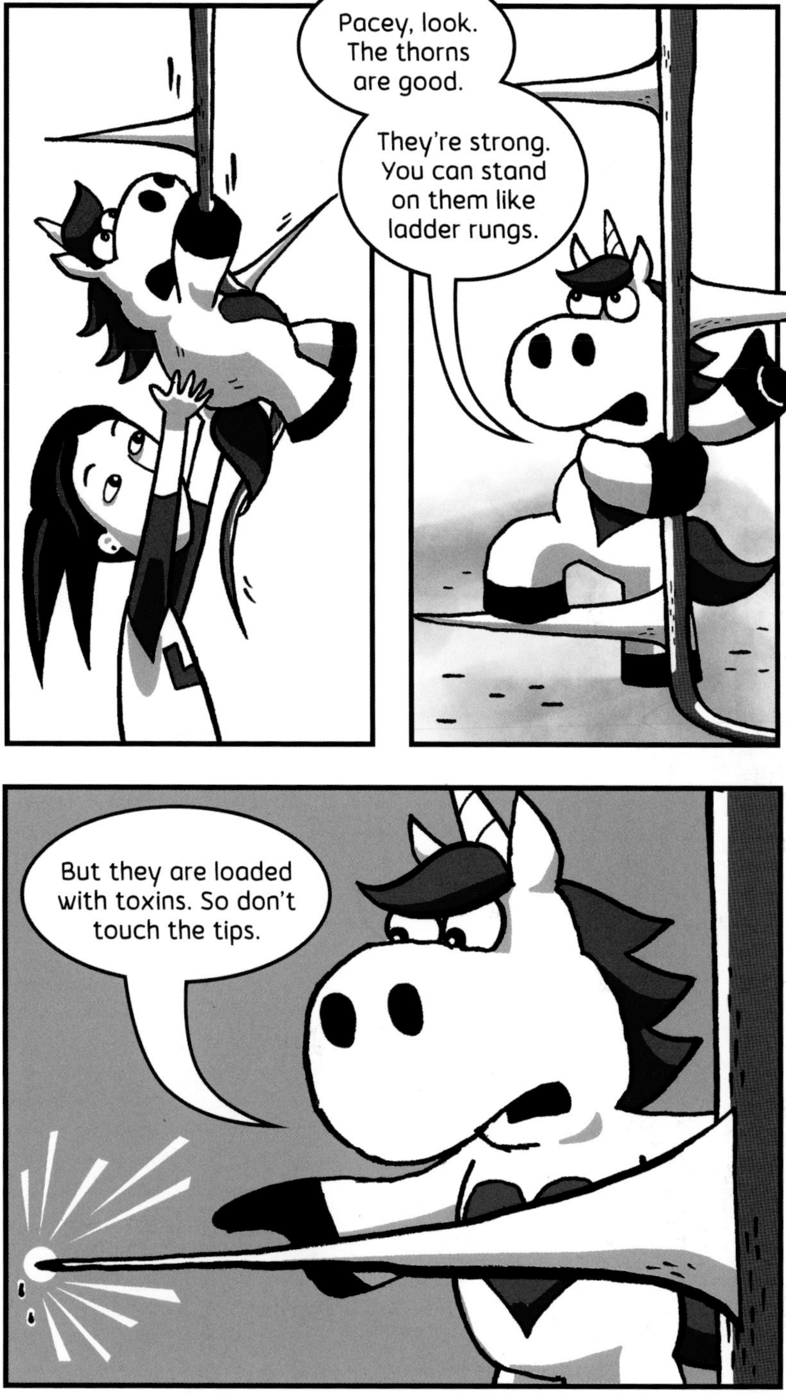
Pacey, look. The thorns are good.
They're strong. You can stand on them like ladder rungs.
But they are loaded with toxins. So don't touch the tips.

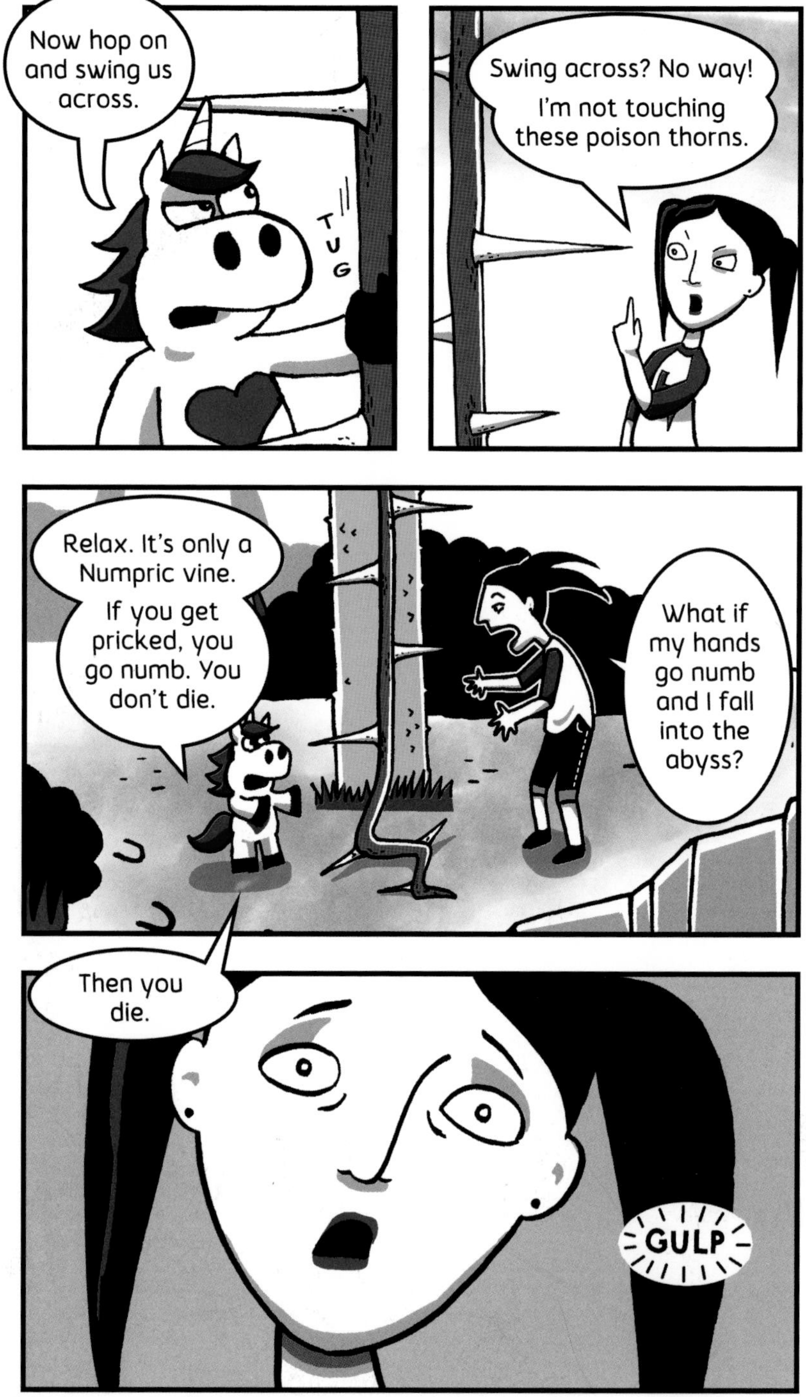
Now hop on and swing us across.
TUG
Swing across? No way!
I'm not touching these poison thorns.
Relax. It's only a Numpric vine.
If you get pricked, you go numb. You don't die.
What if my hands go numb and I fall into the abyss?
Then you die.
GULP

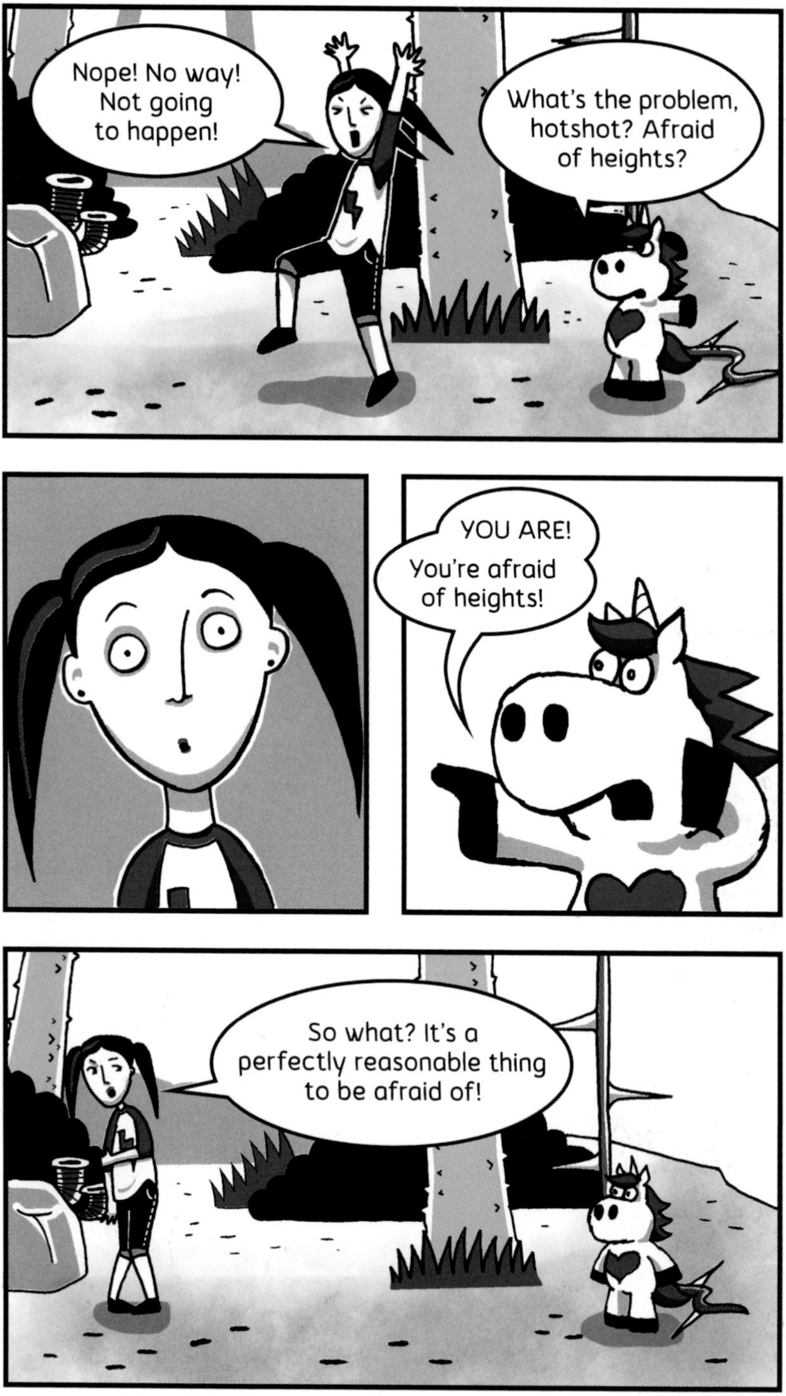
Nope! No way! Not going to happen!
What's the problem, hotshot? Afraid of heights?
YOU ARE!
You're afraid of heights!
So what? It's a perfectly reasonable thing to be afraid of!

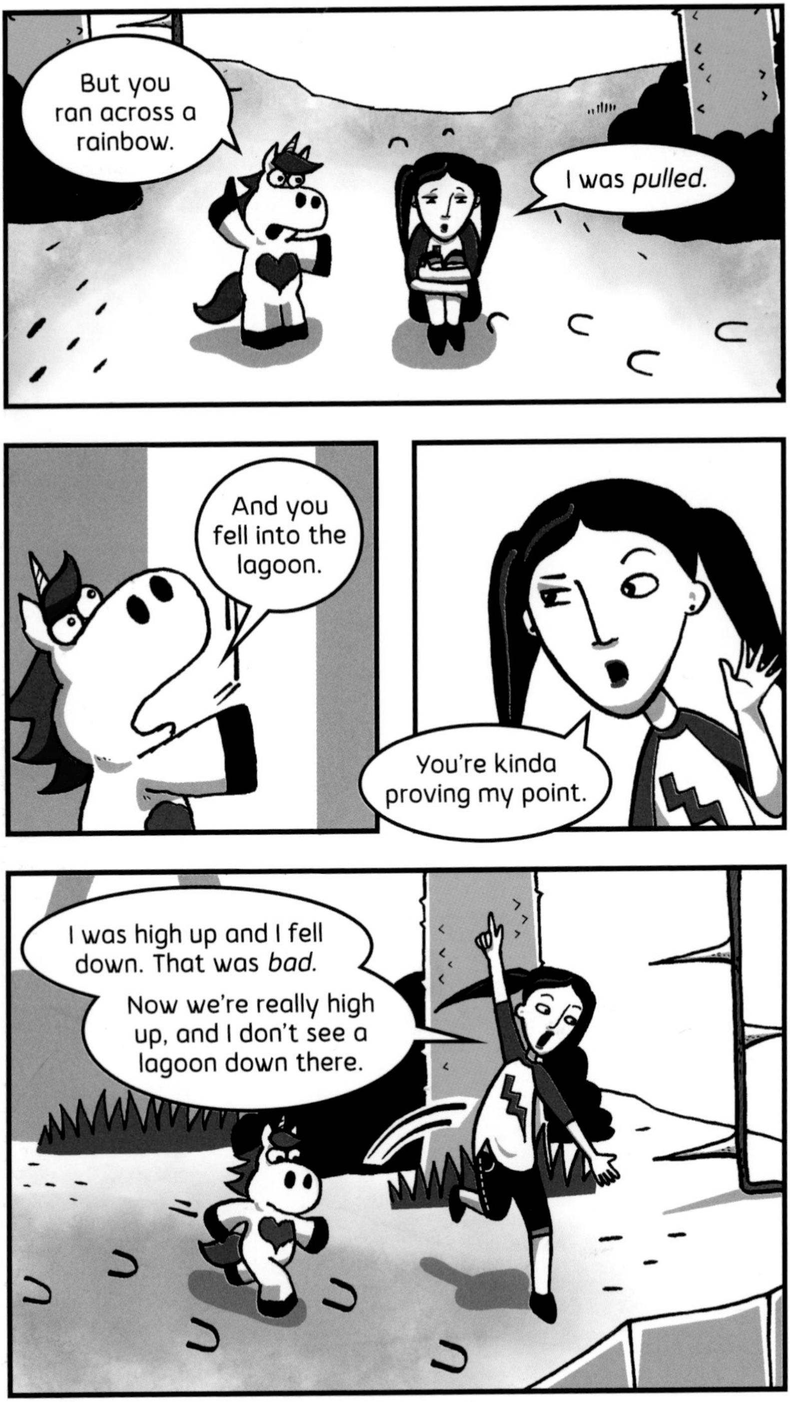
But you ran across a rainbow.
I was *pulled.*
And you fell into the lagoon.
You're kinda proving my point.
I was high up and I fell down. That was *bad.*
Now we're really high up, and I don't see a lagoon down there.

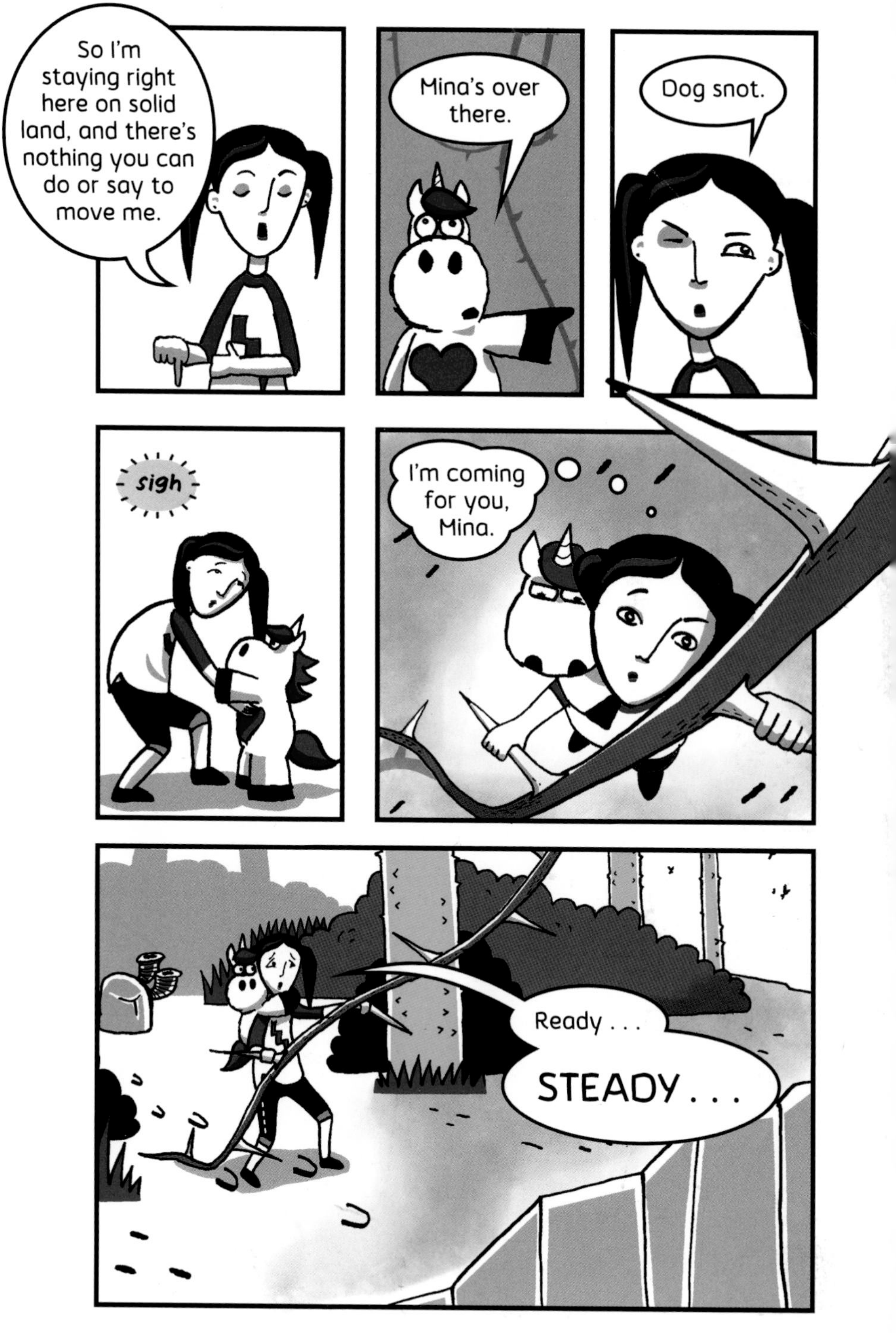
So I'm staying right here on solid land, and there's nothing you can do or say to move me.
Mina's over there.
Dog snot.
sigh
I'm coming for you, Mina.
Ready . . .
STEADY . . .

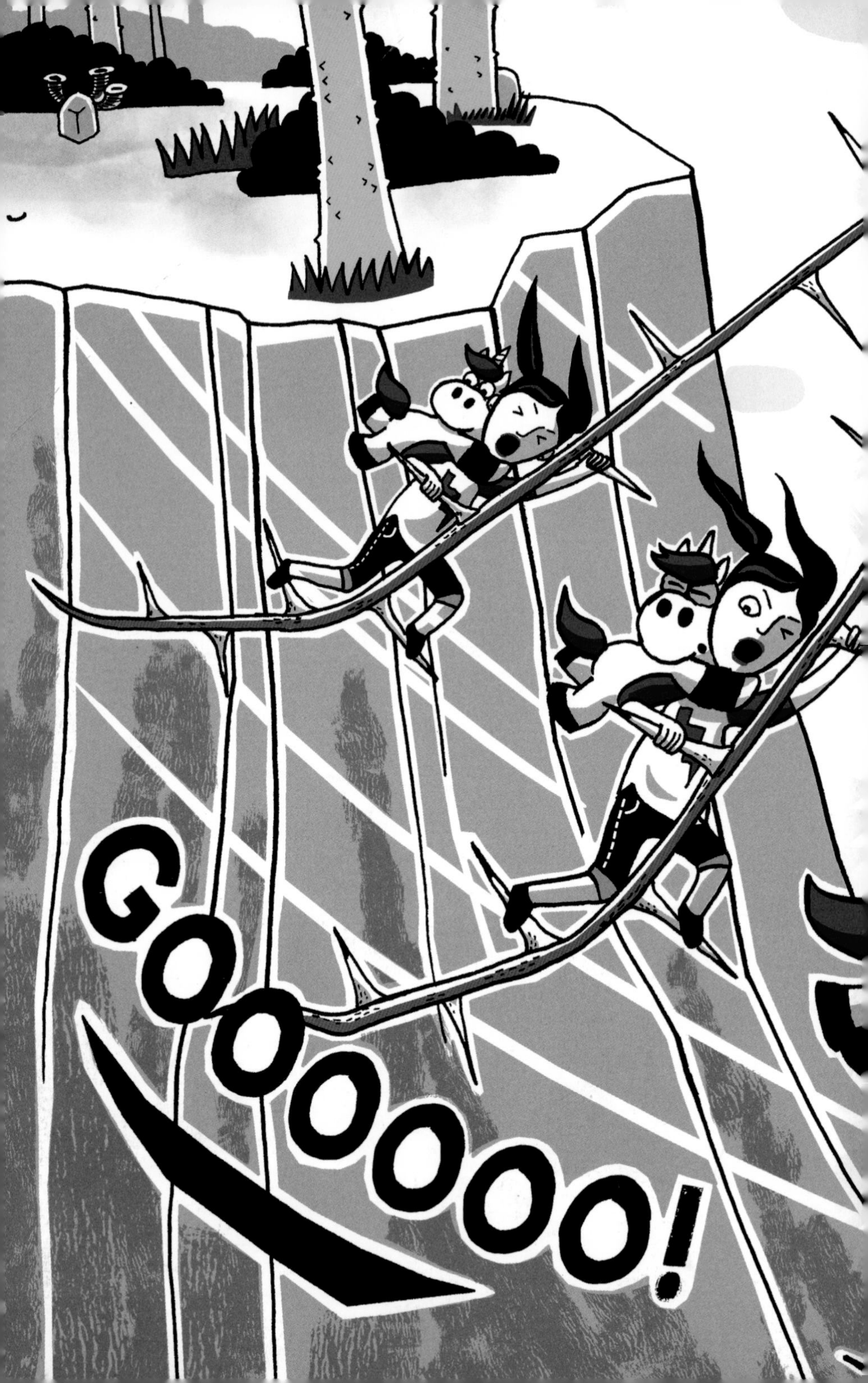
GOOOOOOO!

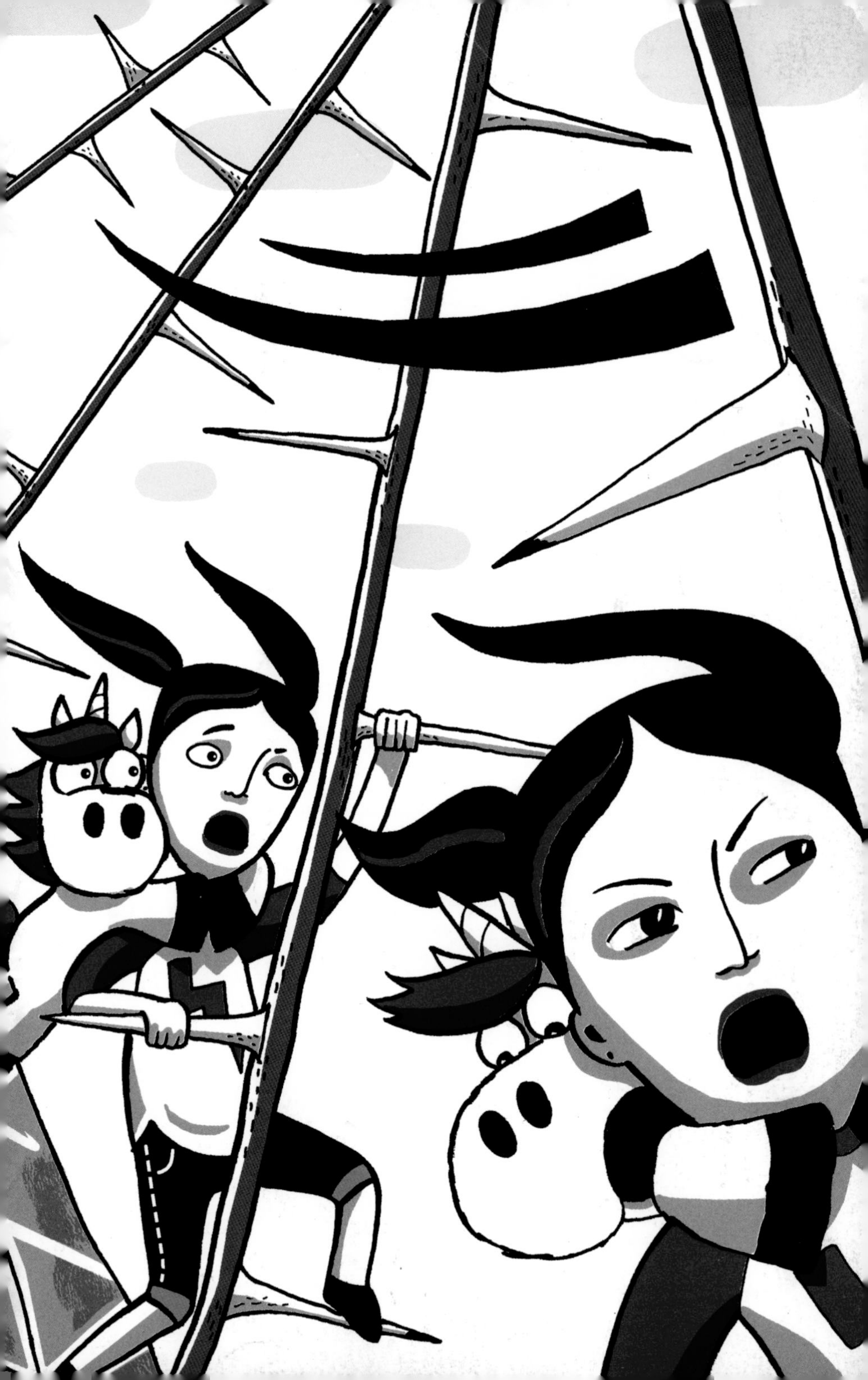

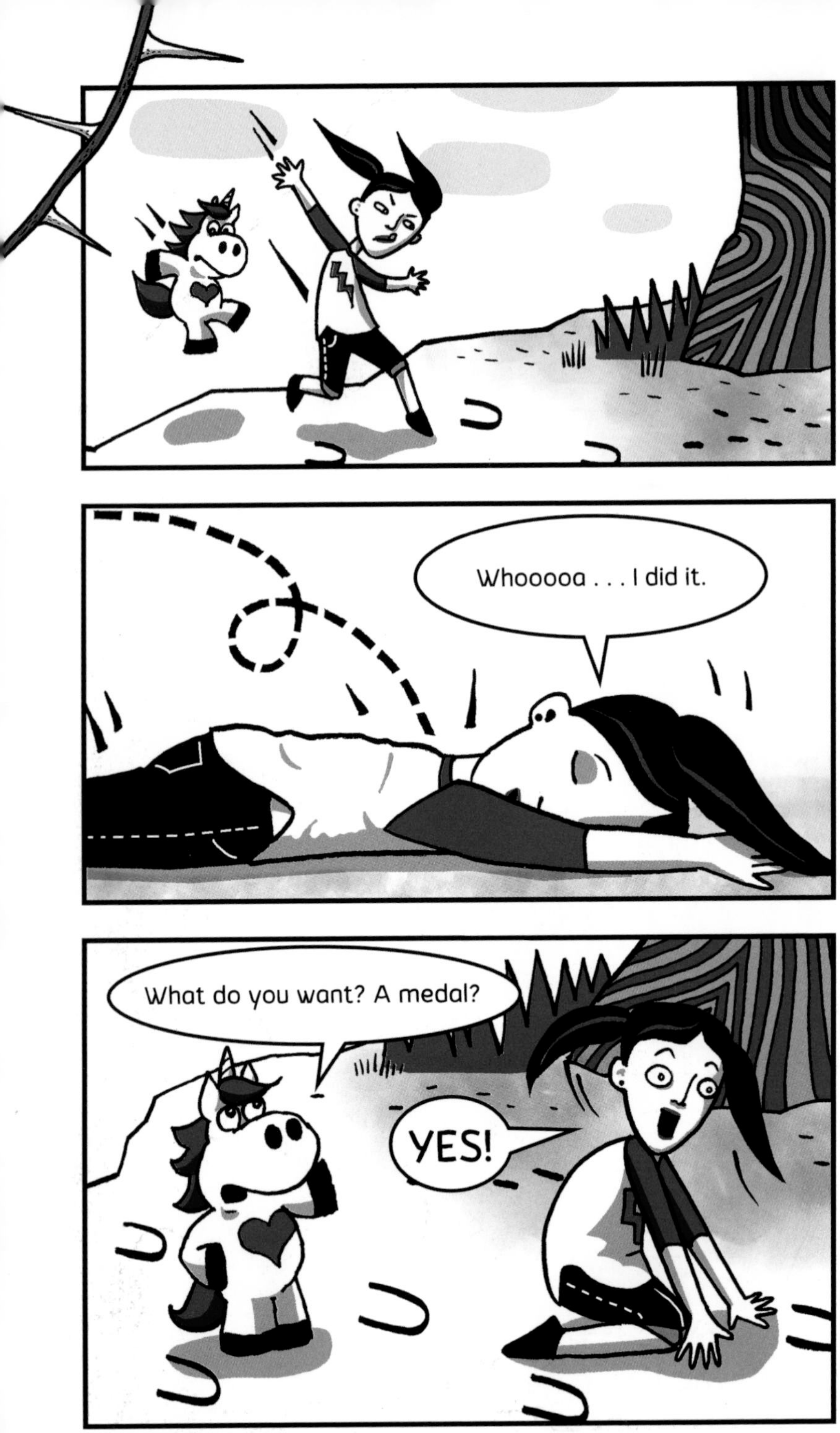
Whooooa . . . I did it.
What do you want? A medal?
YES!

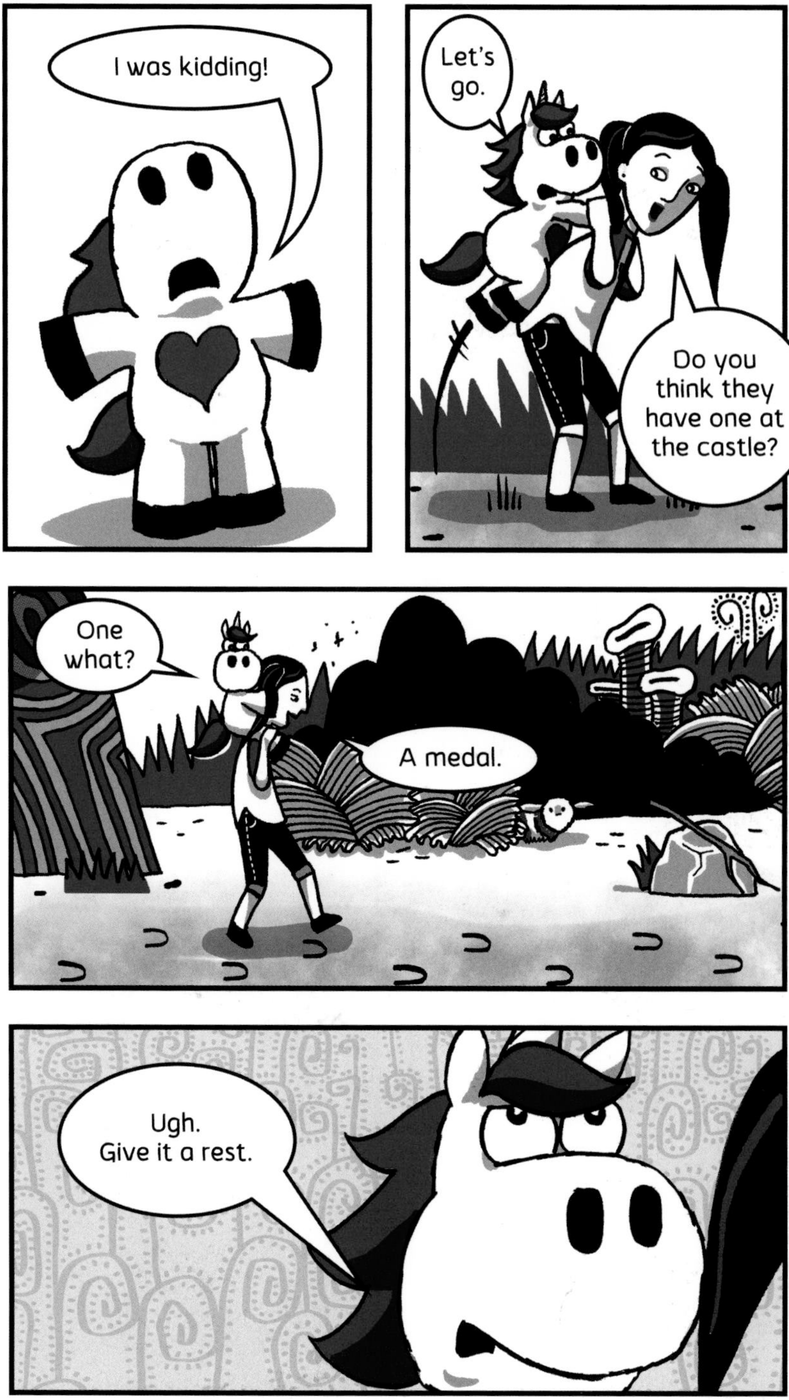
I was kidding!
Let's go.
Do you think they have one at the castle?
One what?
A medal.
Ugh. Give it a rest.

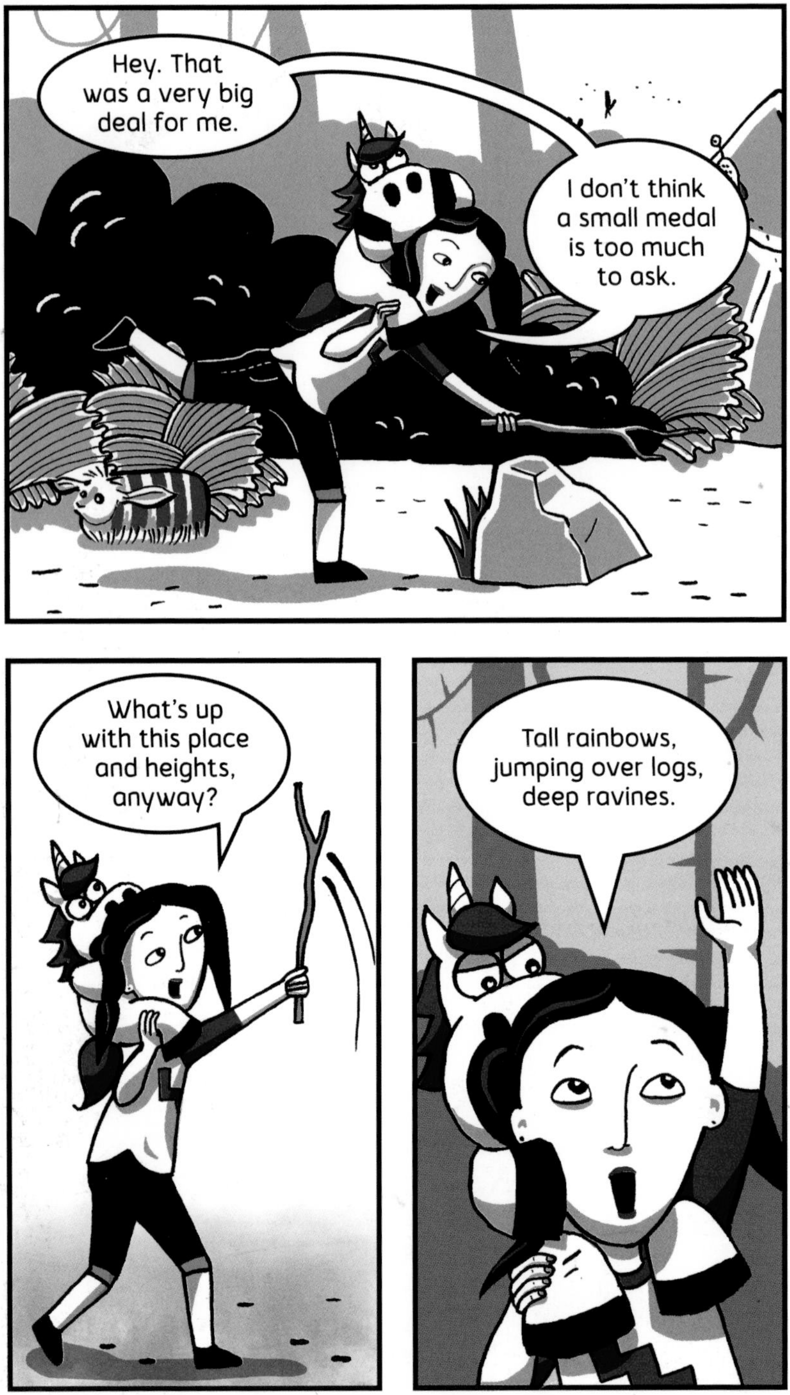
Hey. That was a very big deal for me.
I don't think a small medal is too much to ask.
What's up with this place and heights, anyway?
Tall rainbows, jumping over logs, deep ravines.

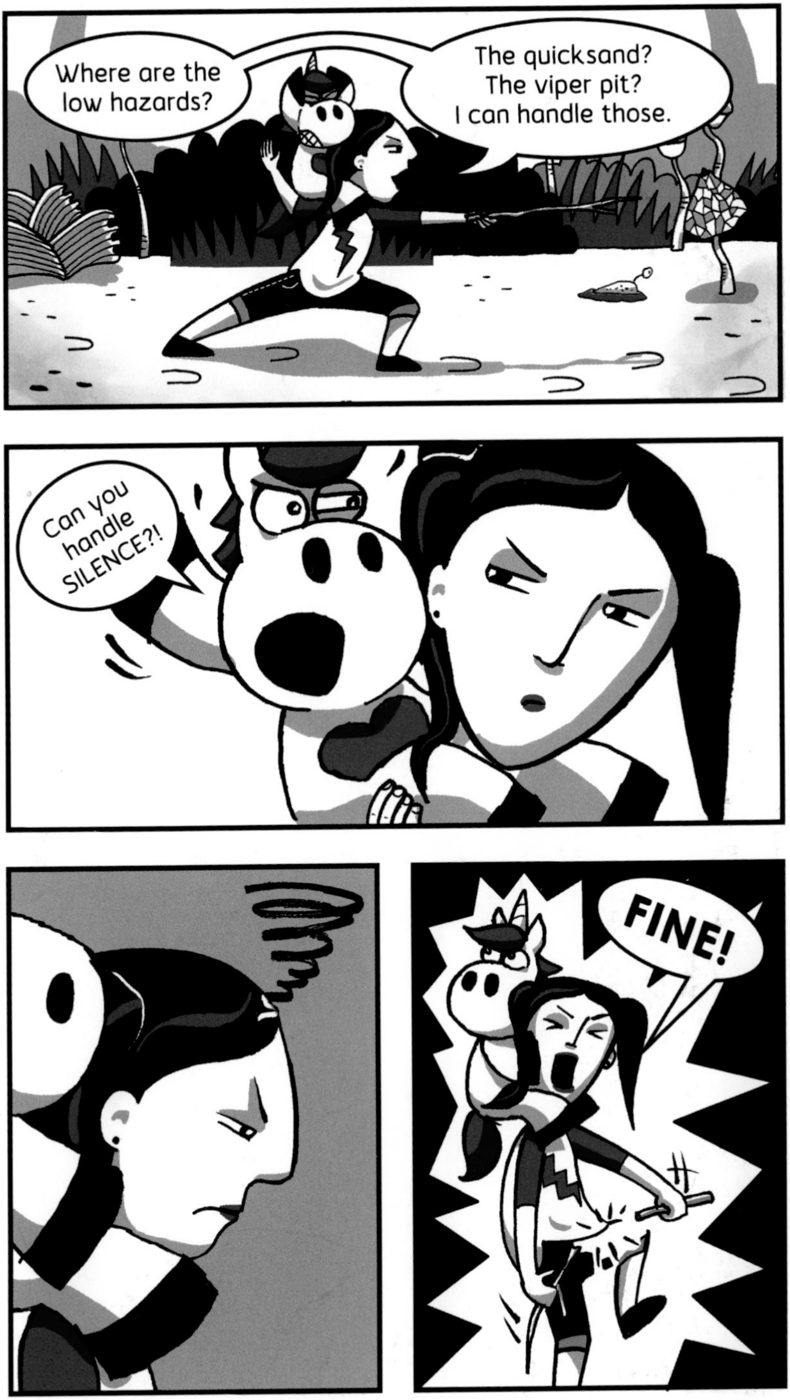
Where are the low hazards?
The quicksand? The viper pit? I can handle those.
Can you handle SILENCE?!
FINE!

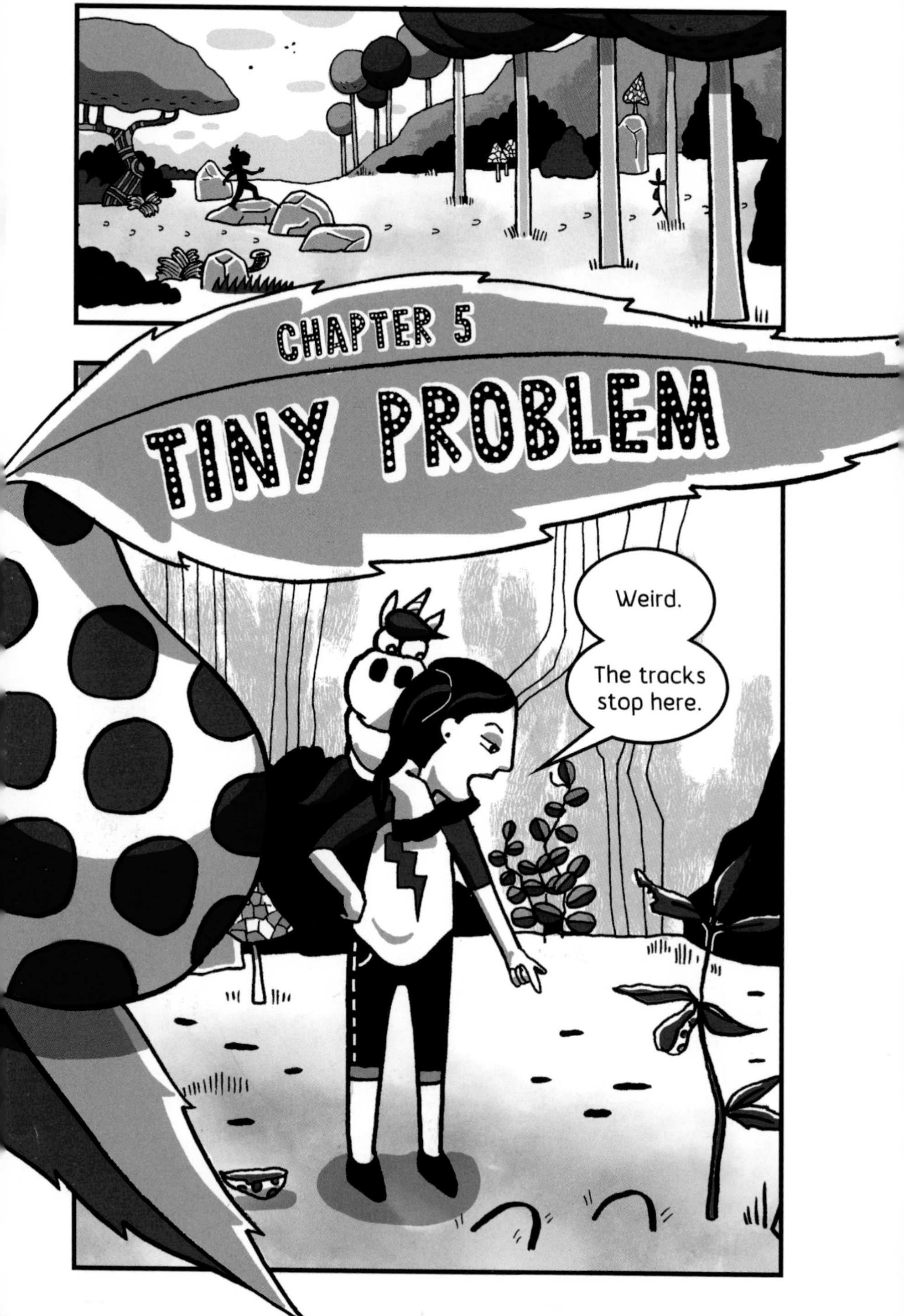
CHAPTER 5
TINY PROBLEM
Weird.
The tracks stop here.

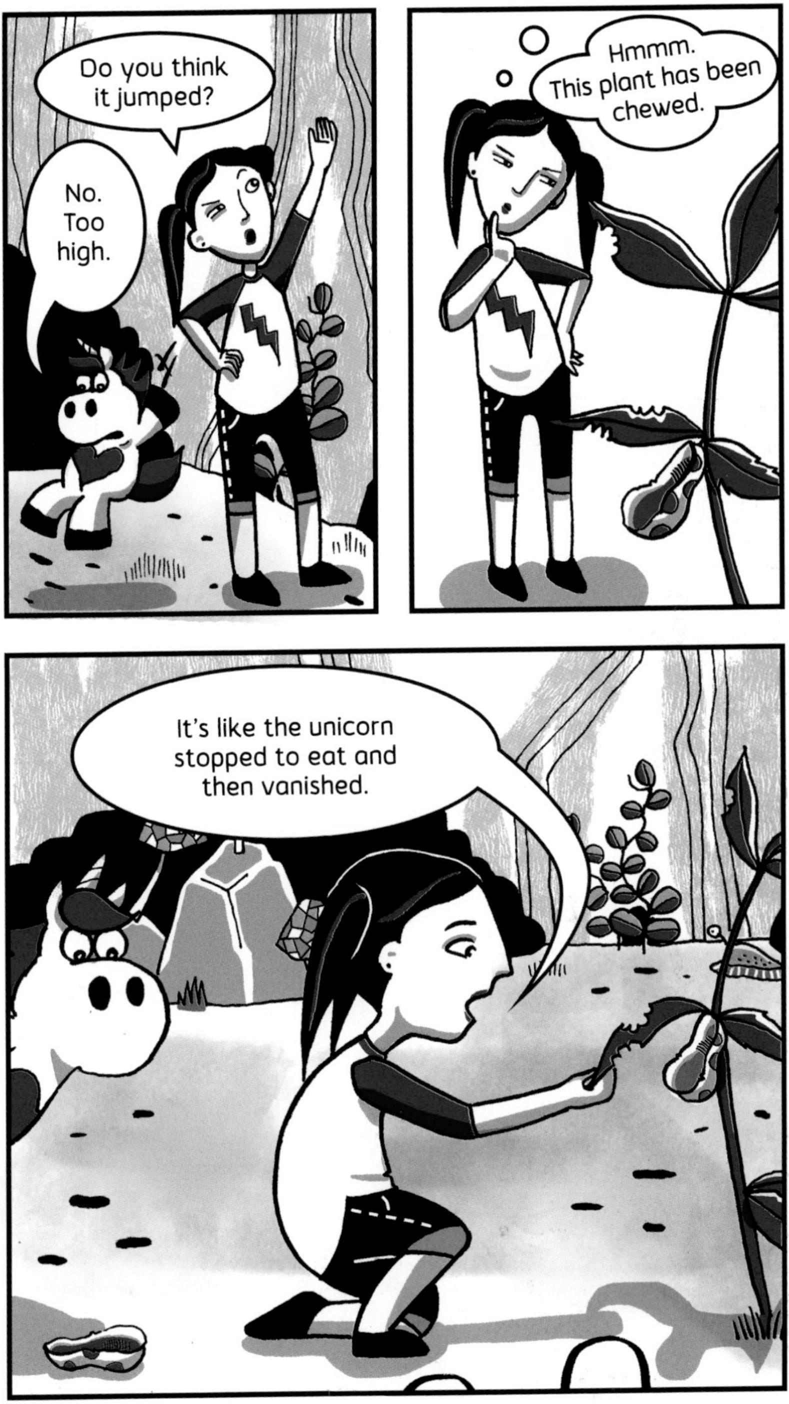
Do you think it jumped?
No. Too high.
Hmmm. This plant has been chewed.
It's like the unicorn stopped to eat and then vanished.

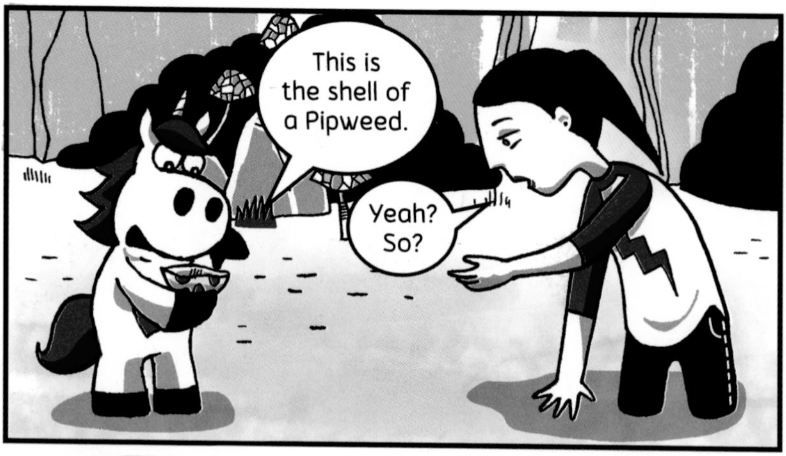
This is the shell of a Pipweed.
Yeah? So?

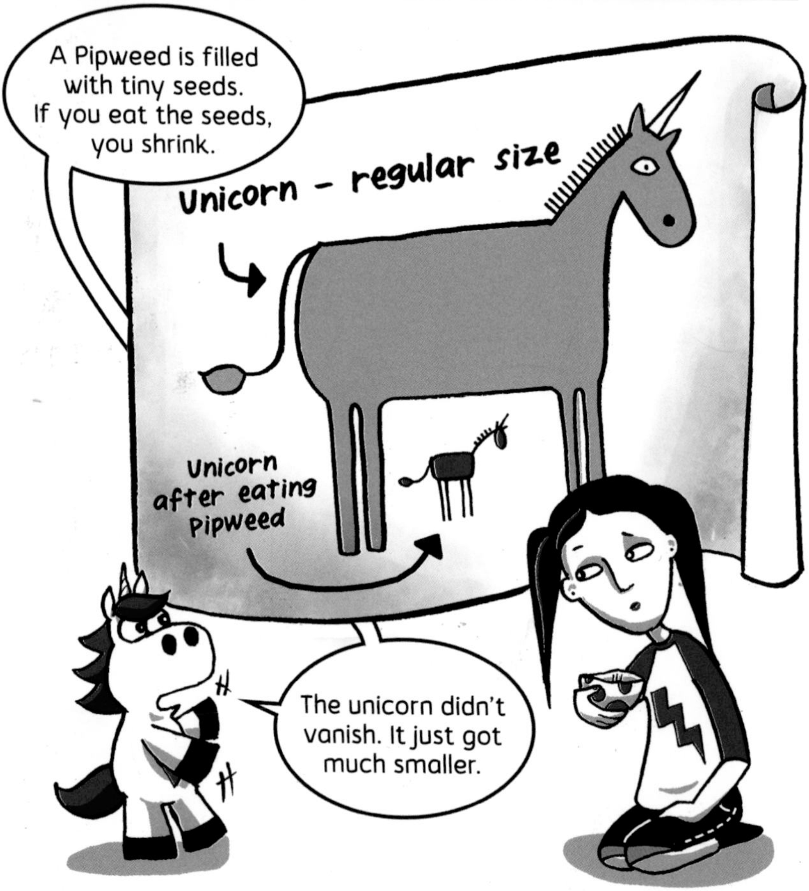
A Pipweed is filled with tiny seeds. If you eat the seeds, you shrink.
Unicorn - regular size
Unicorn after eating Pipweed
The unicorn didn't vanish. It just got much smaller.

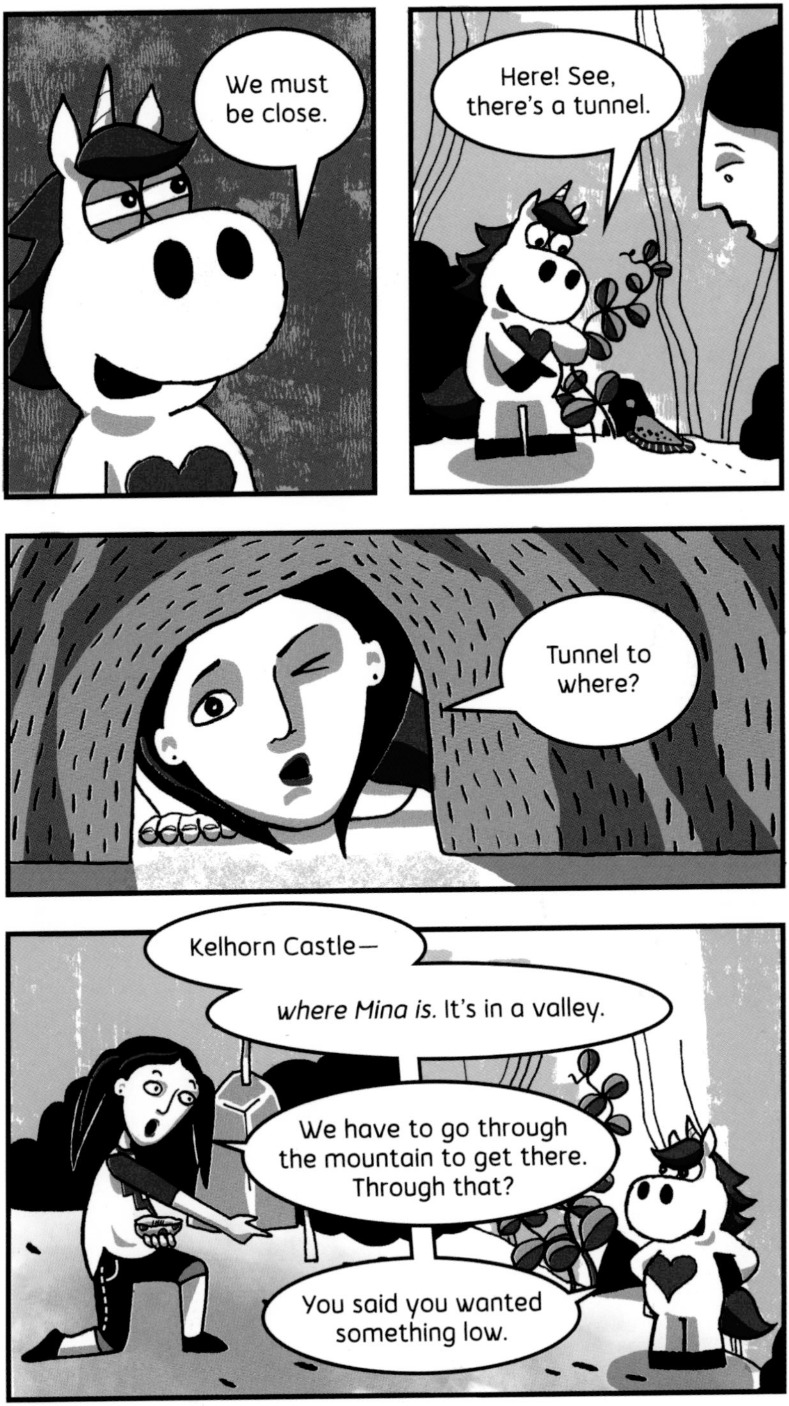
We must be close.
Here! See, there's a tunnel.
Tunnel to where?
Kelhorn Castle—
where Mina is. It's in a valley.
We have to go through the mountain to get there. Through that?
You said you wanted something low.

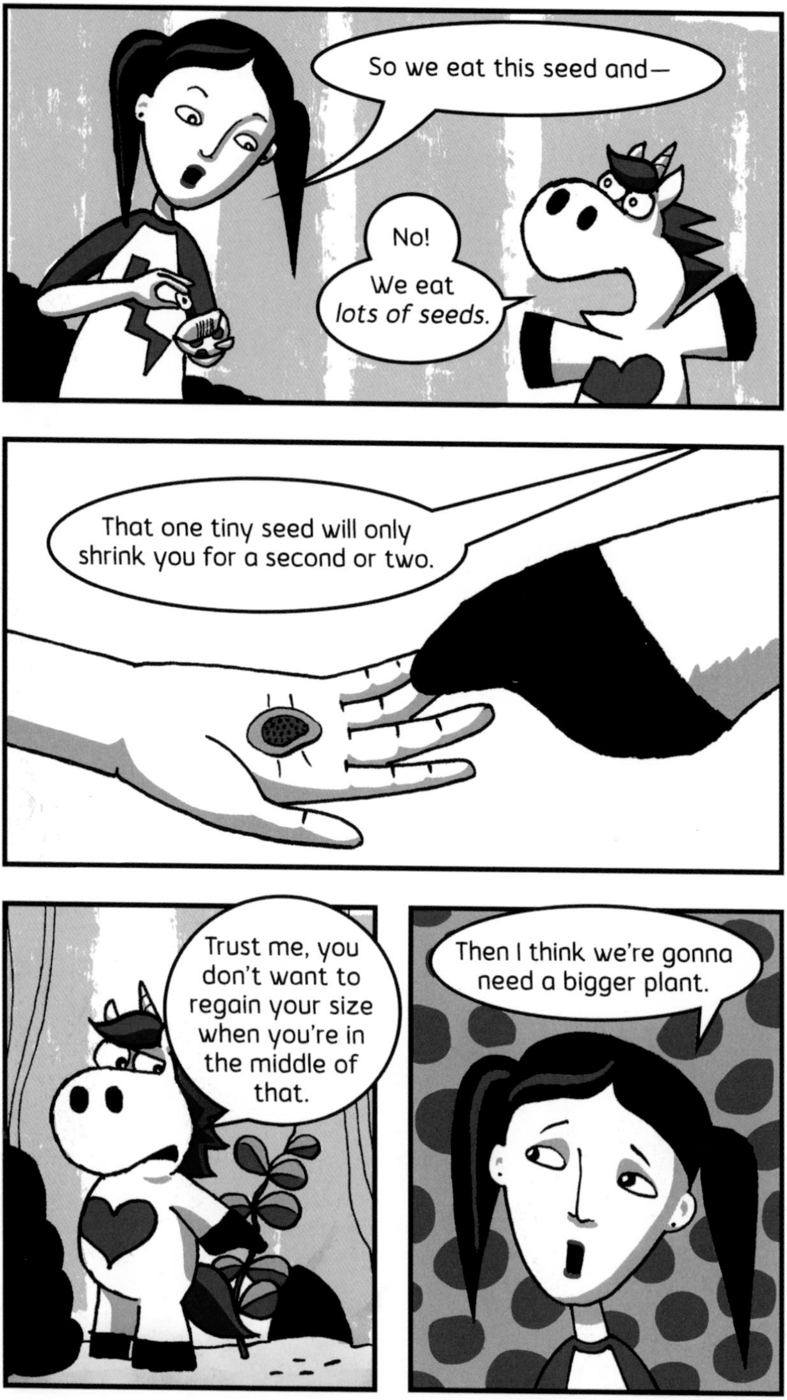

So we eat this seed and—
No! We eat *lots of seeds.*
That one tiny seed will only shrink you for a second or two.
Trust me, you don't want to regain your size when you're in the middle of that.
Then I think we're gonna need a bigger plant.

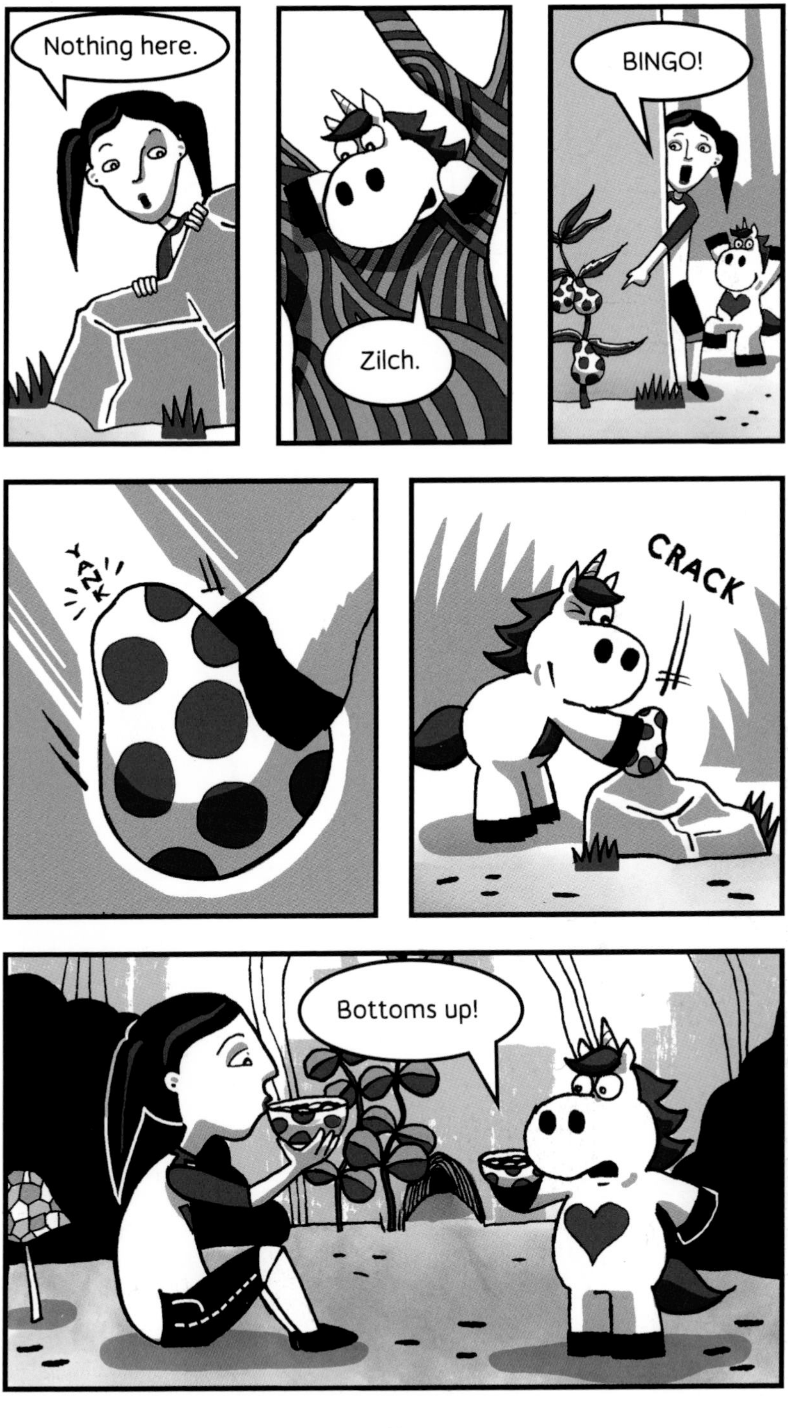
Nothing here.
Zilch.
BINGO!
YANK
CRACK
Bottoms up!

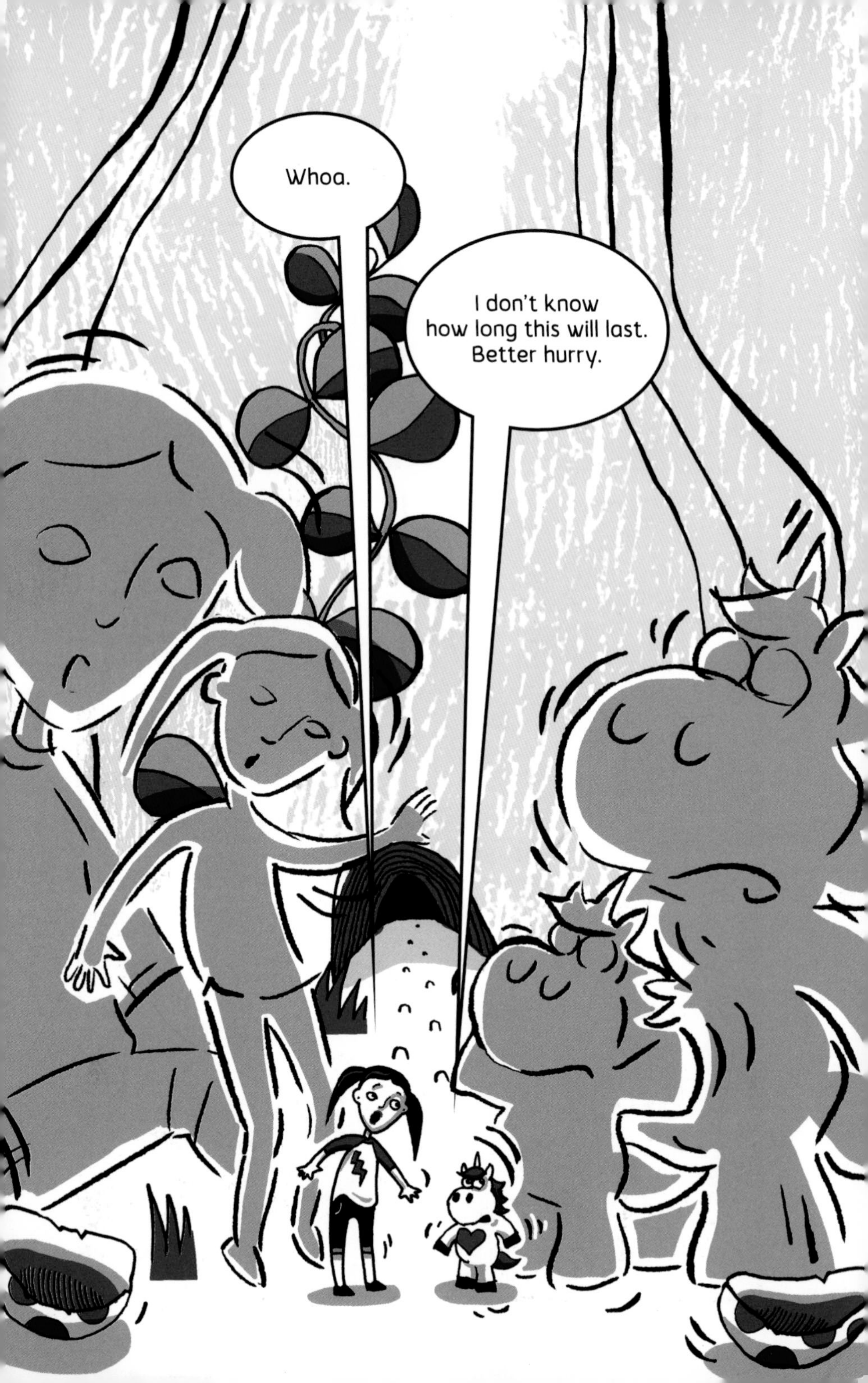
Whoa.
I don't know how long this will last. Better hurry.

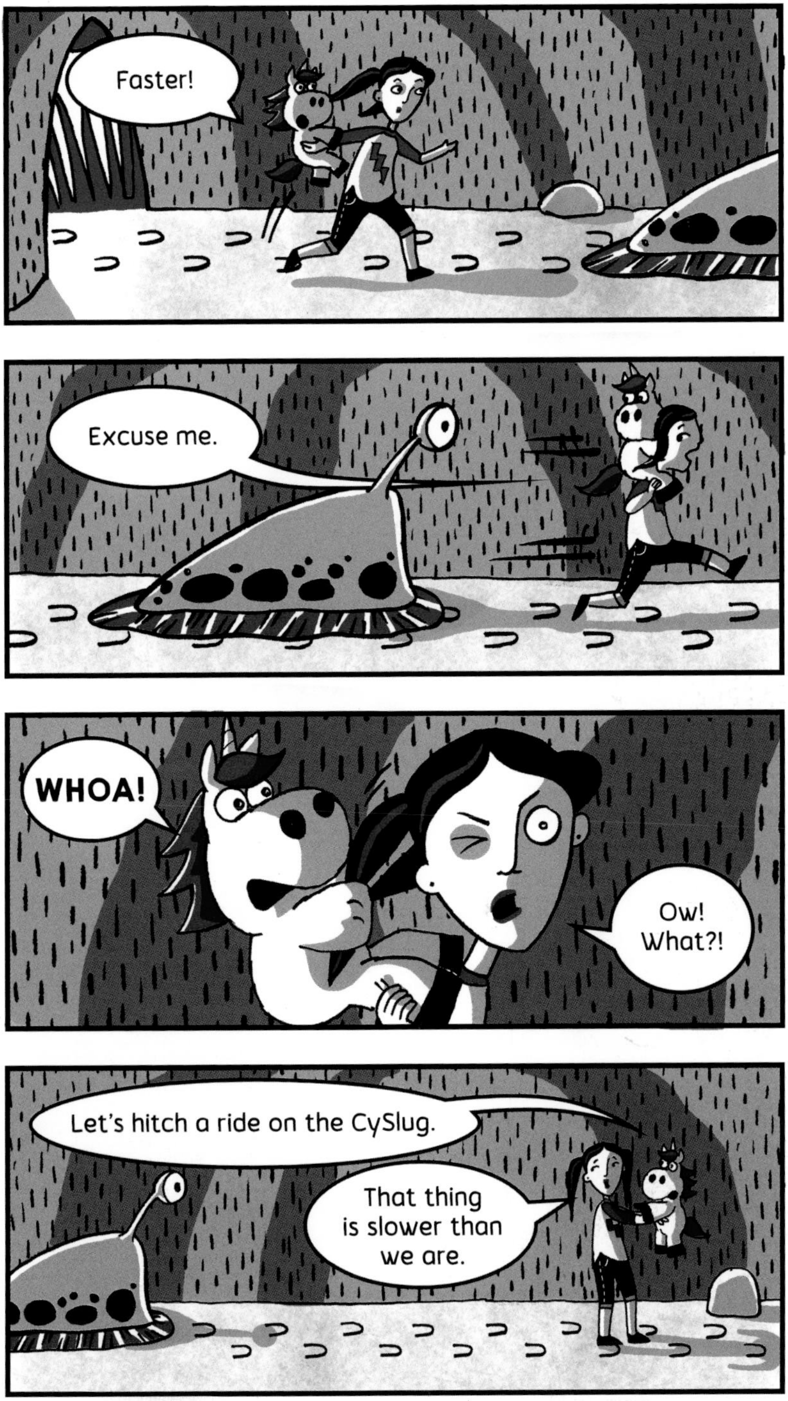
Faster!
Excuse me.
WHOA!
Ow! What?!
Let's hitch a ride on the CySlug.
That thing is slower than we are.

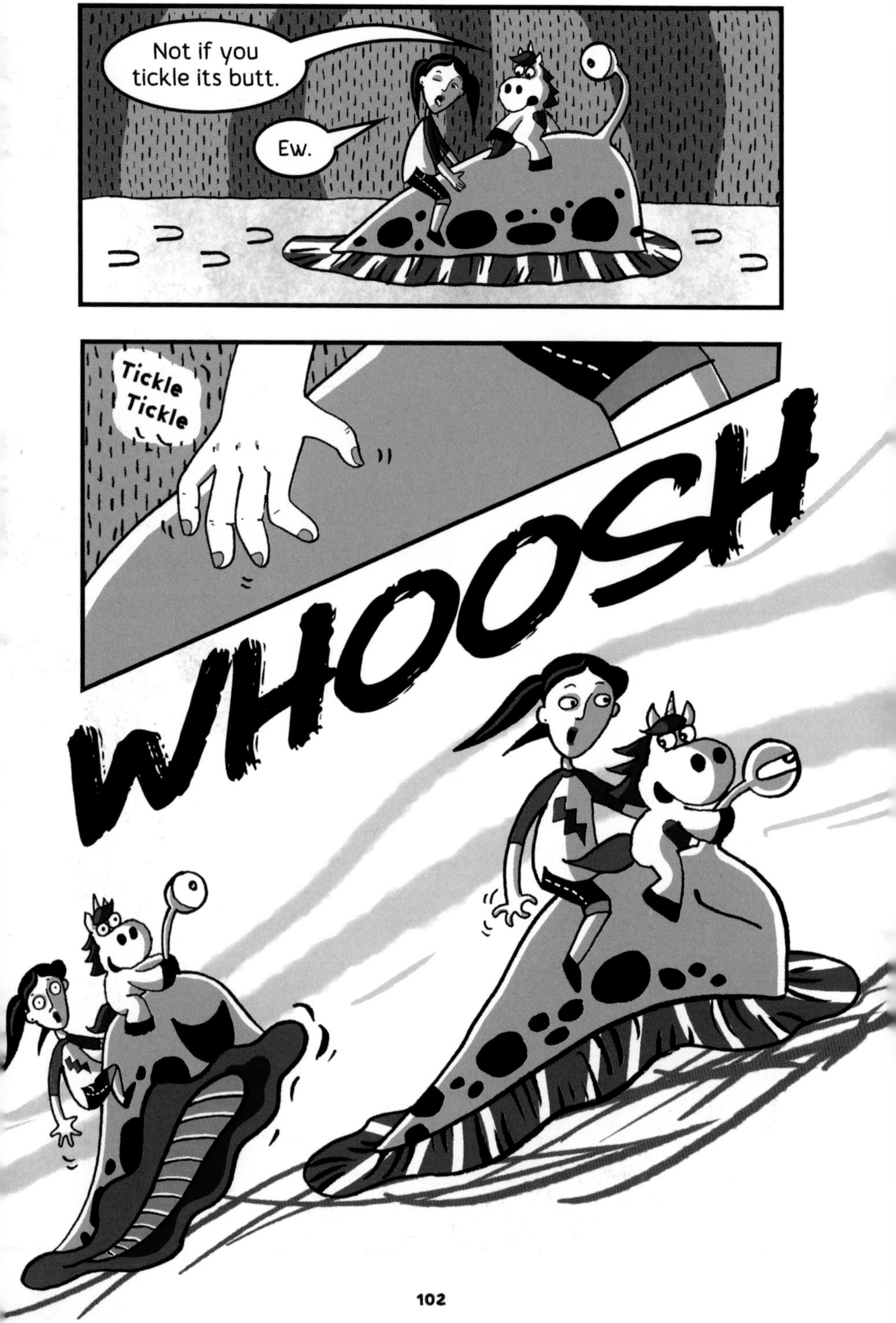

Not if you tickle its butt.
Ew.
Tickle Tickle
WHOOOSH

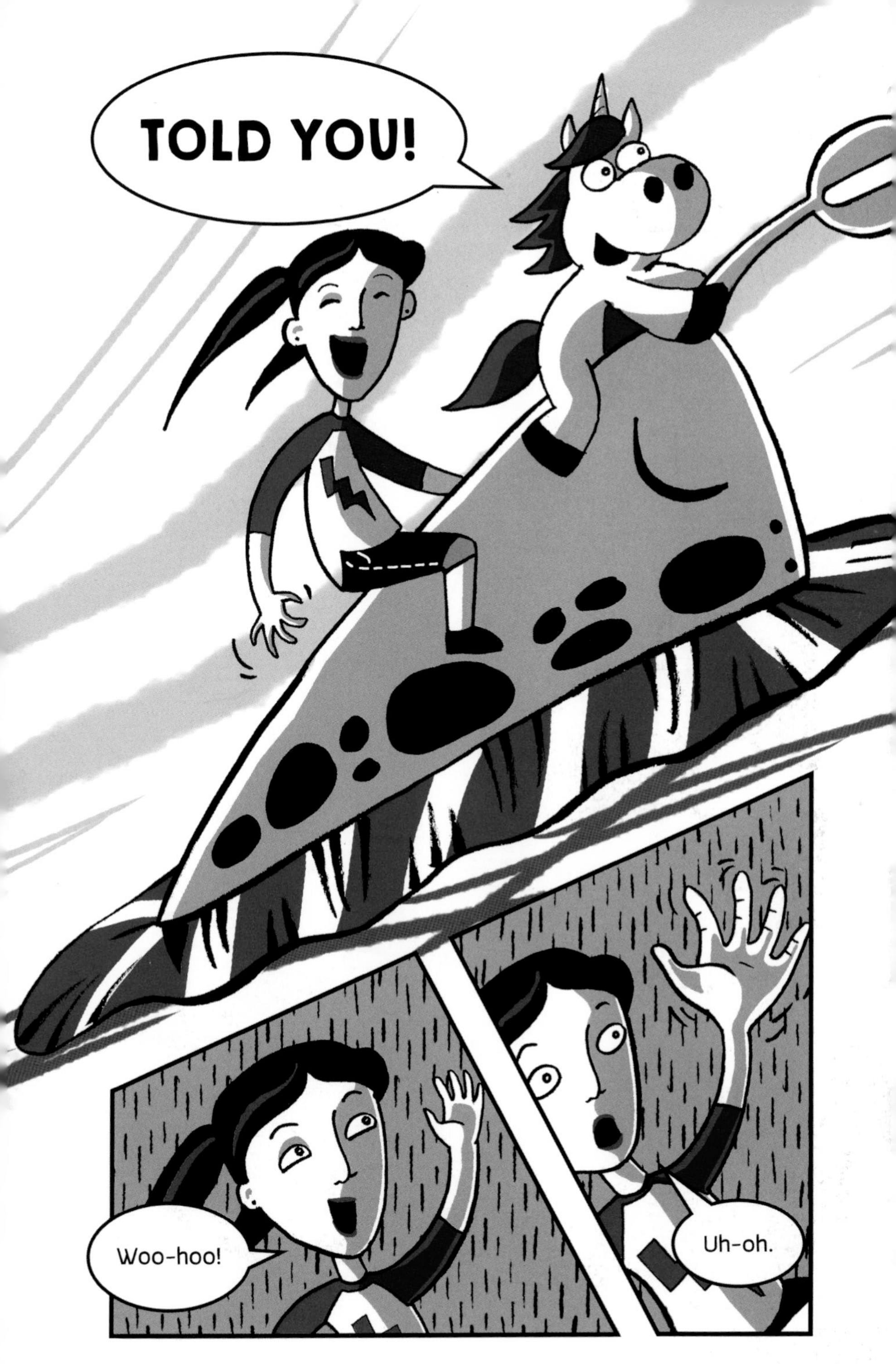
TOLD YOU!
Woo-hoo!
Uh-oh.

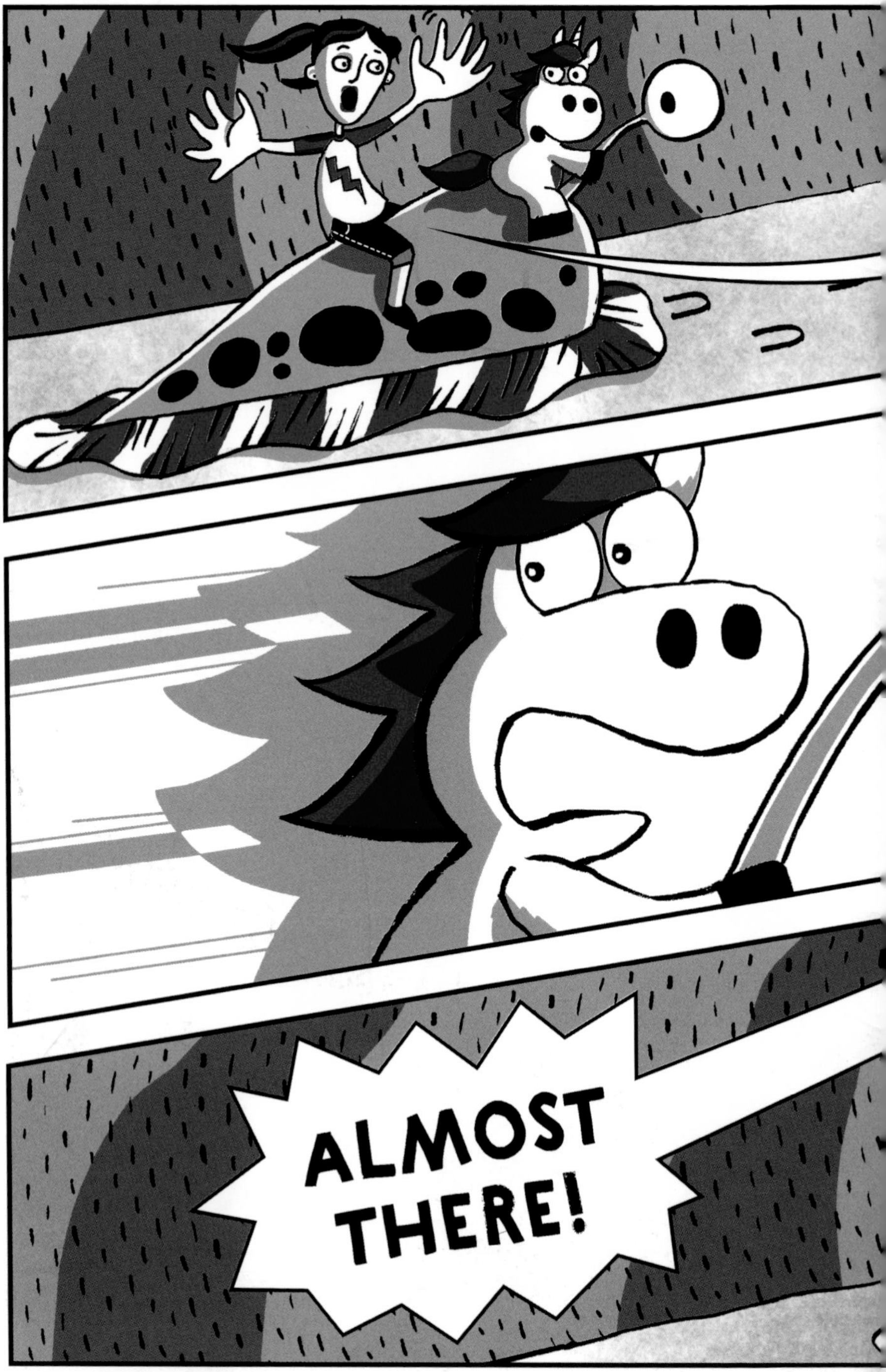
ALMOST THERE!

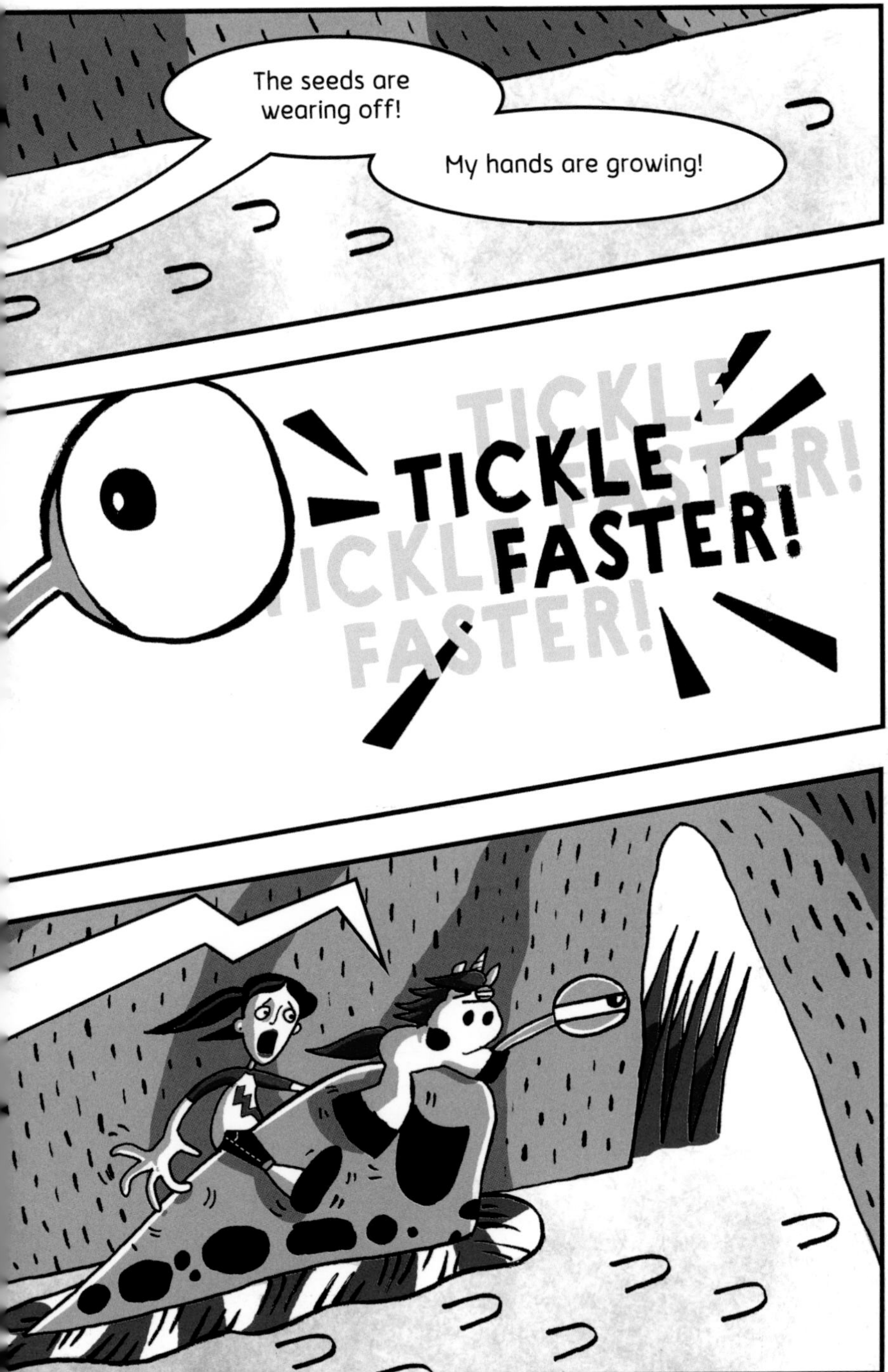
The seeds are wearing off!
My hands are growing!
TICKLE FASTER!
TICKLE FASTER!
TICKLE FASTER!

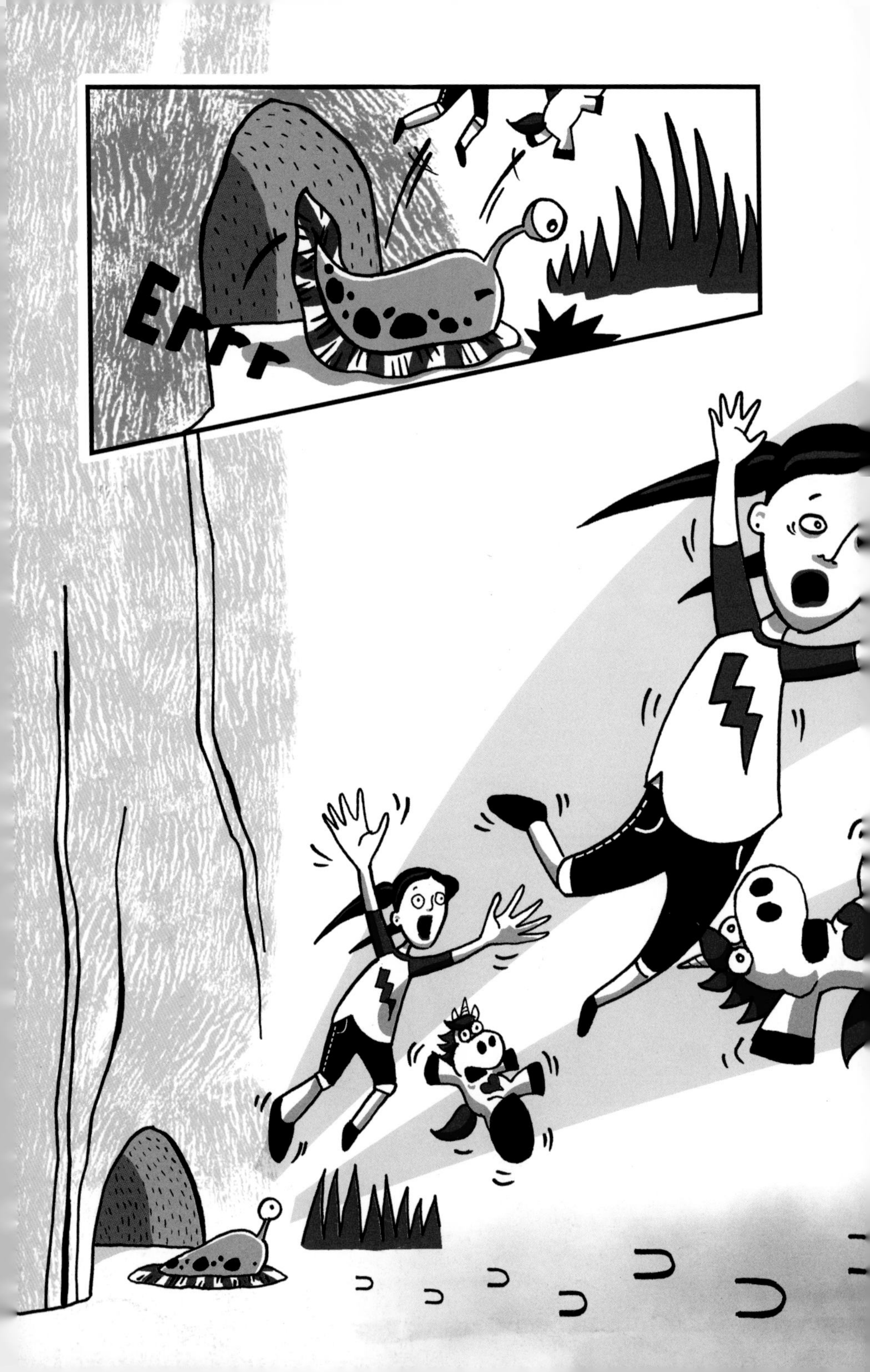
Errr

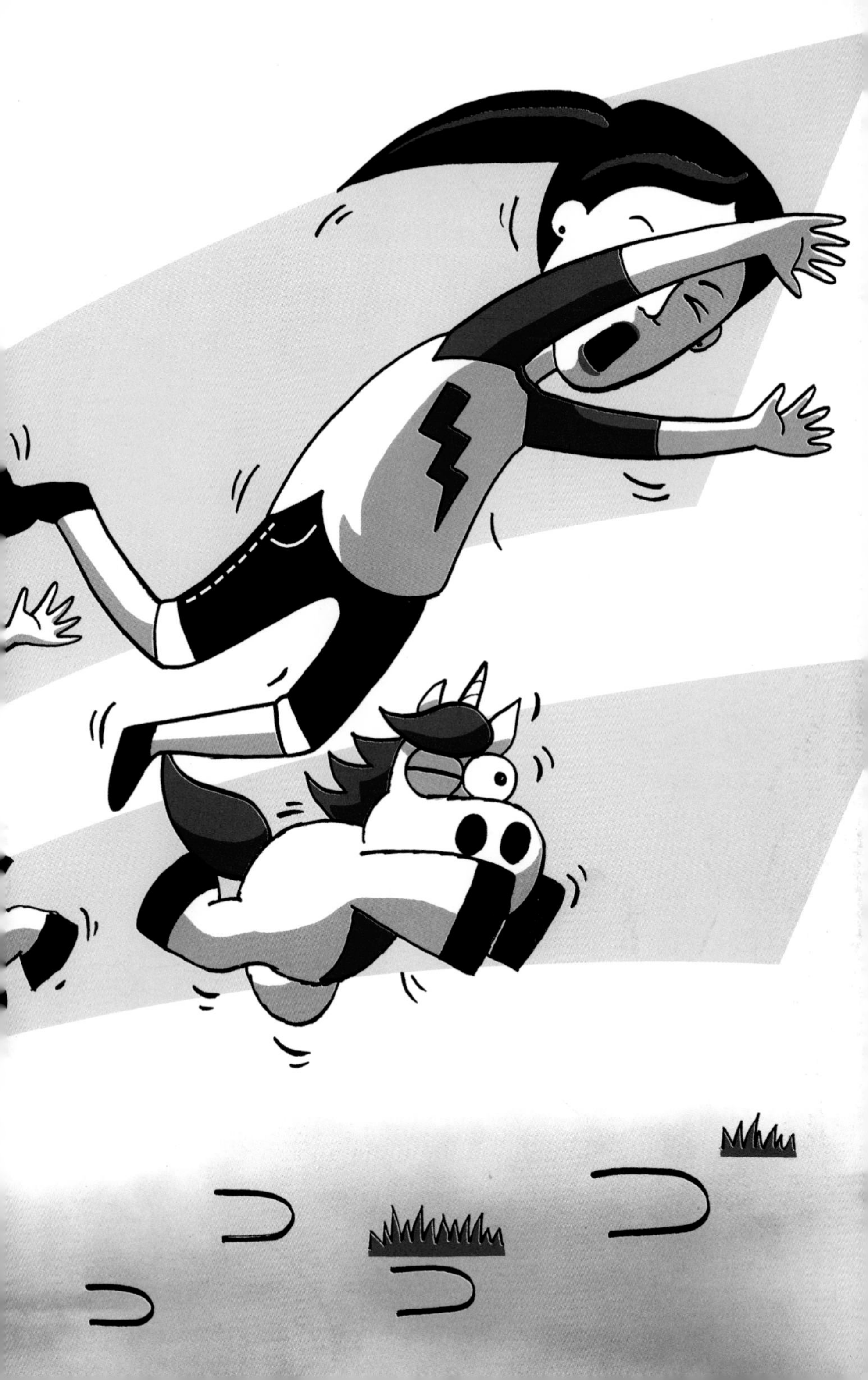

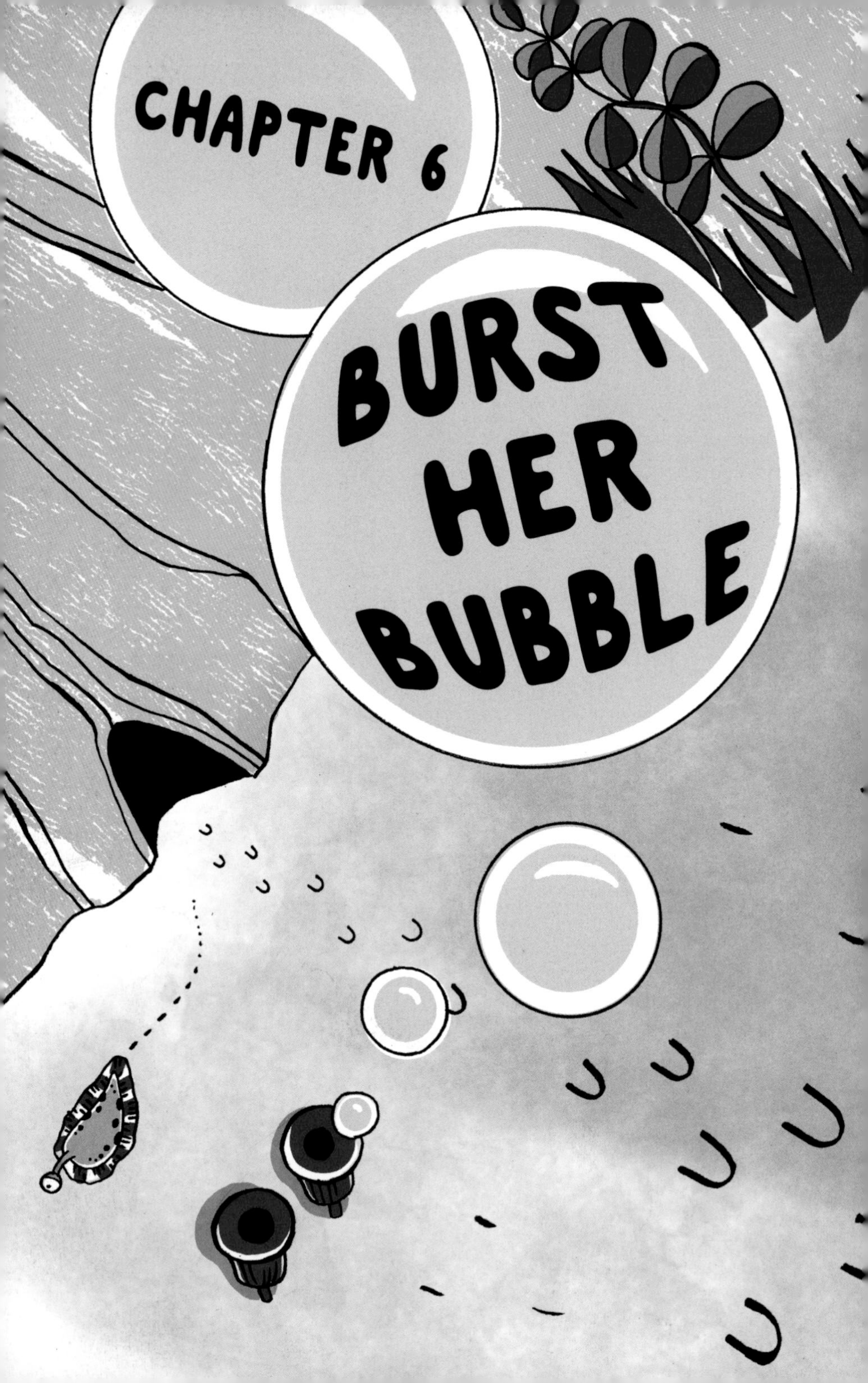
CHAPTER 6
BURST HER BUBBLE

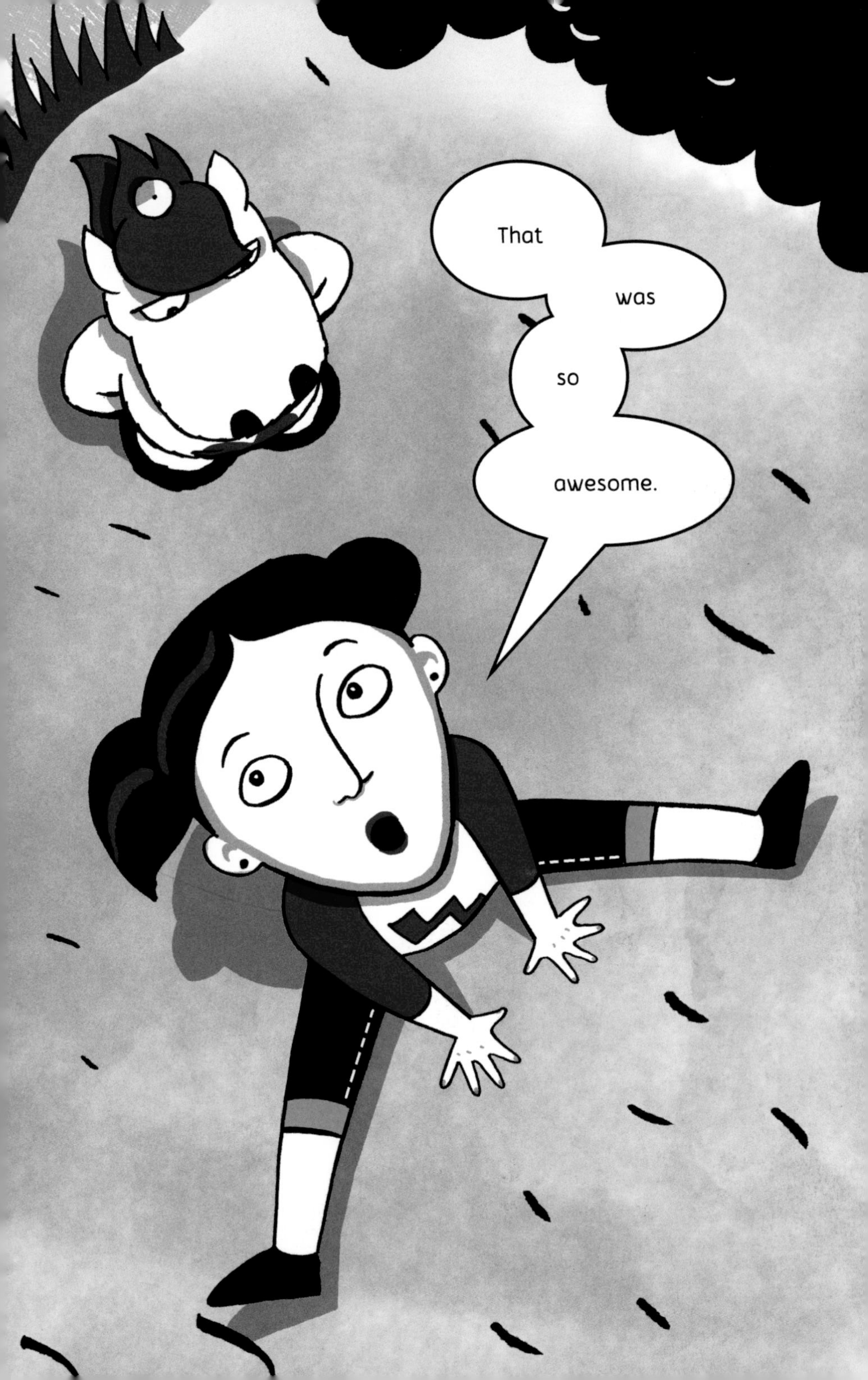
That was so awesome.

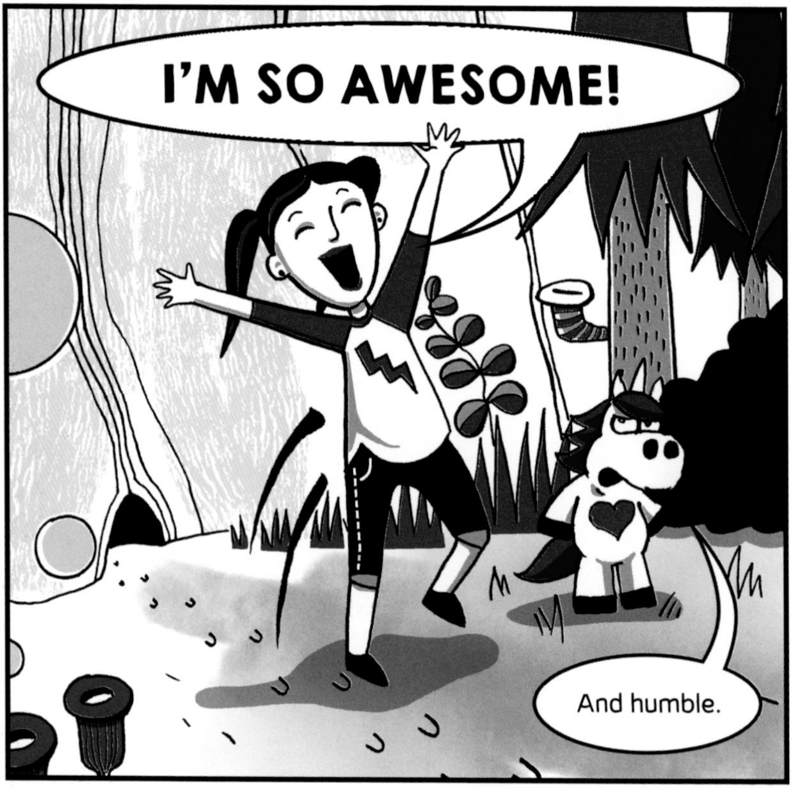
I'M SO AWESOME!
And humble.

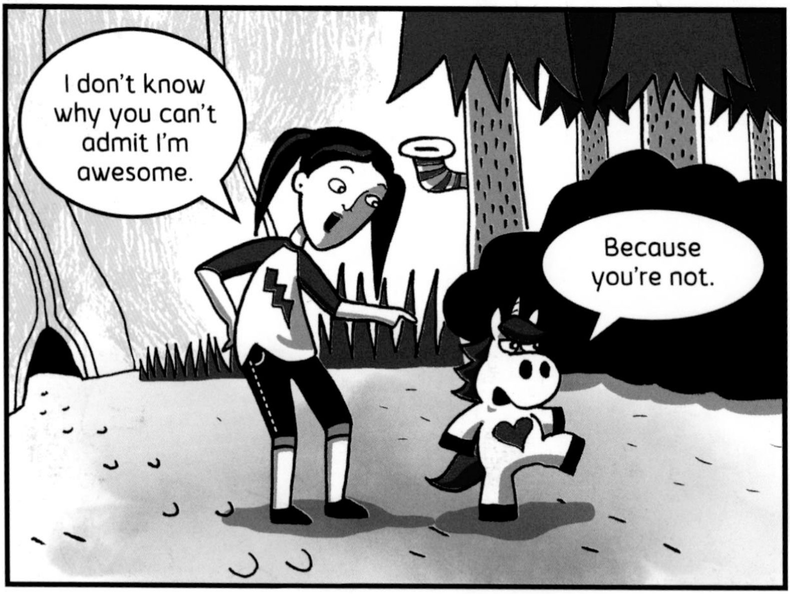
I don't know why you can't admit I'm awesome.
Because you're not.

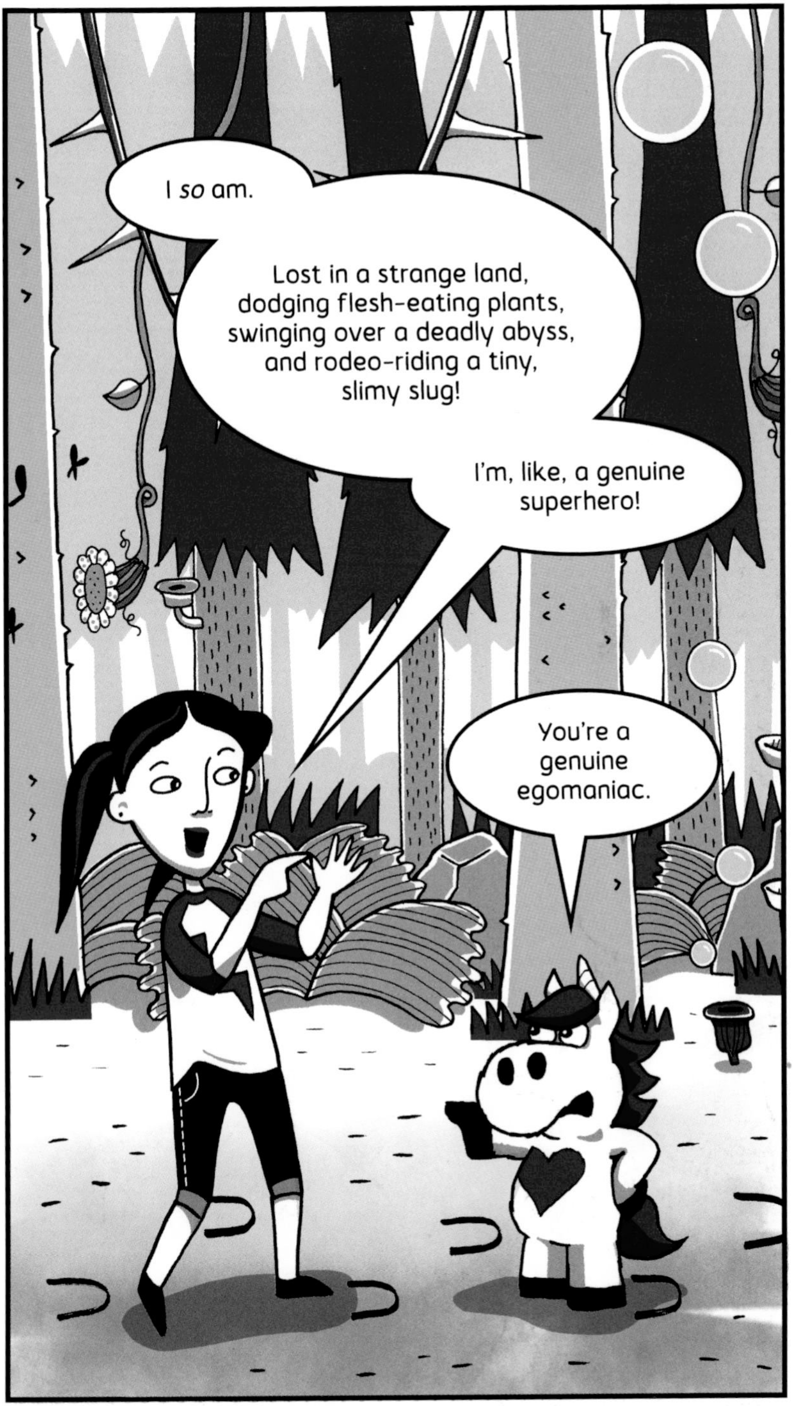
I *so* am.
Lost in a strange land, dodging flesh-eating plants, swinging over a deadly abyss, and rodeo-riding a tiny, slimy slug!
I'm, like, a genuine superhero!
You're a genuine egomaniac.

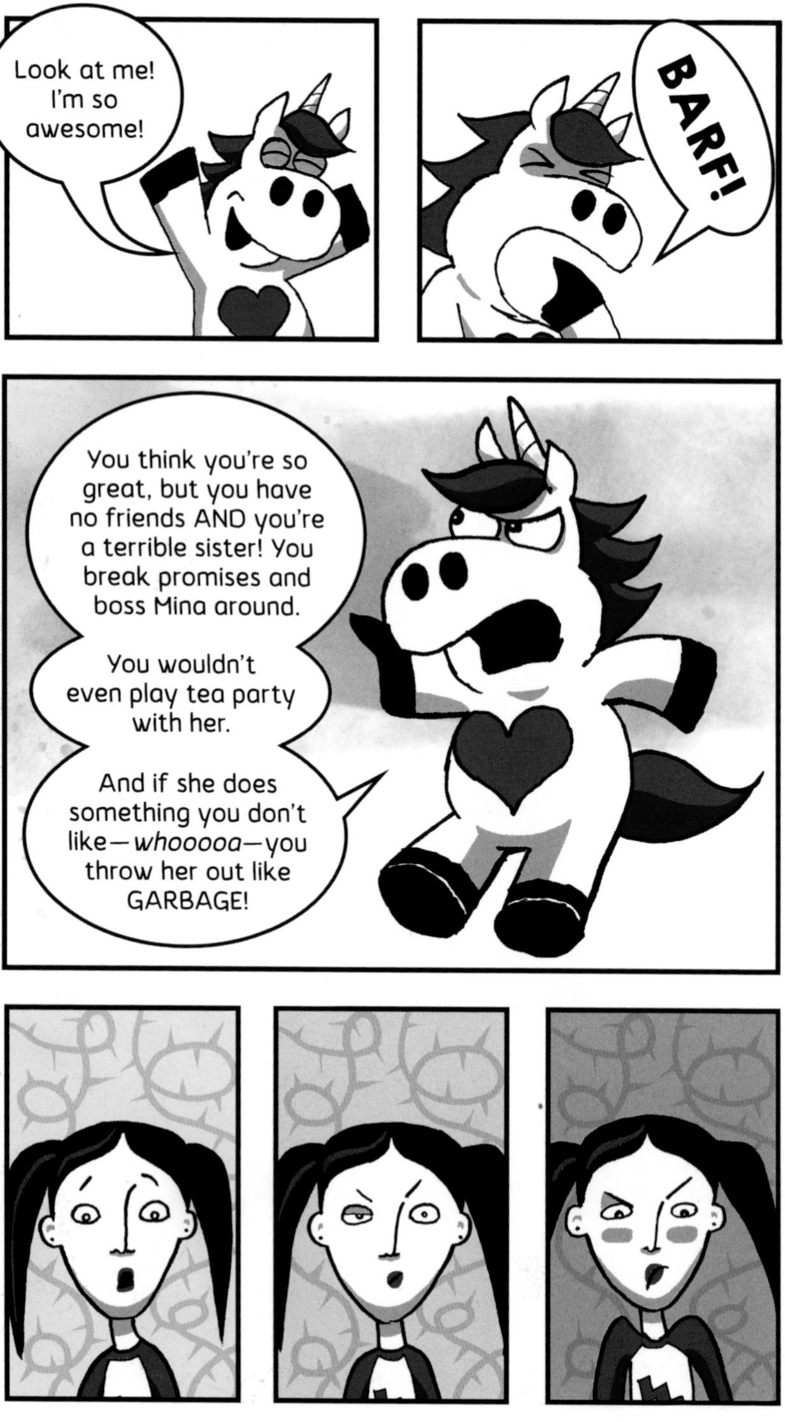

Look at me! I'm so awesome!
BARF!
You think you're so great, but you have no friends AND you're a terrible sister! You break promises and boss Mina around.
You wouldn't even play tea party with her.
And if she does something you don't like—*whooooa*—you throw her out like GARBAGE!

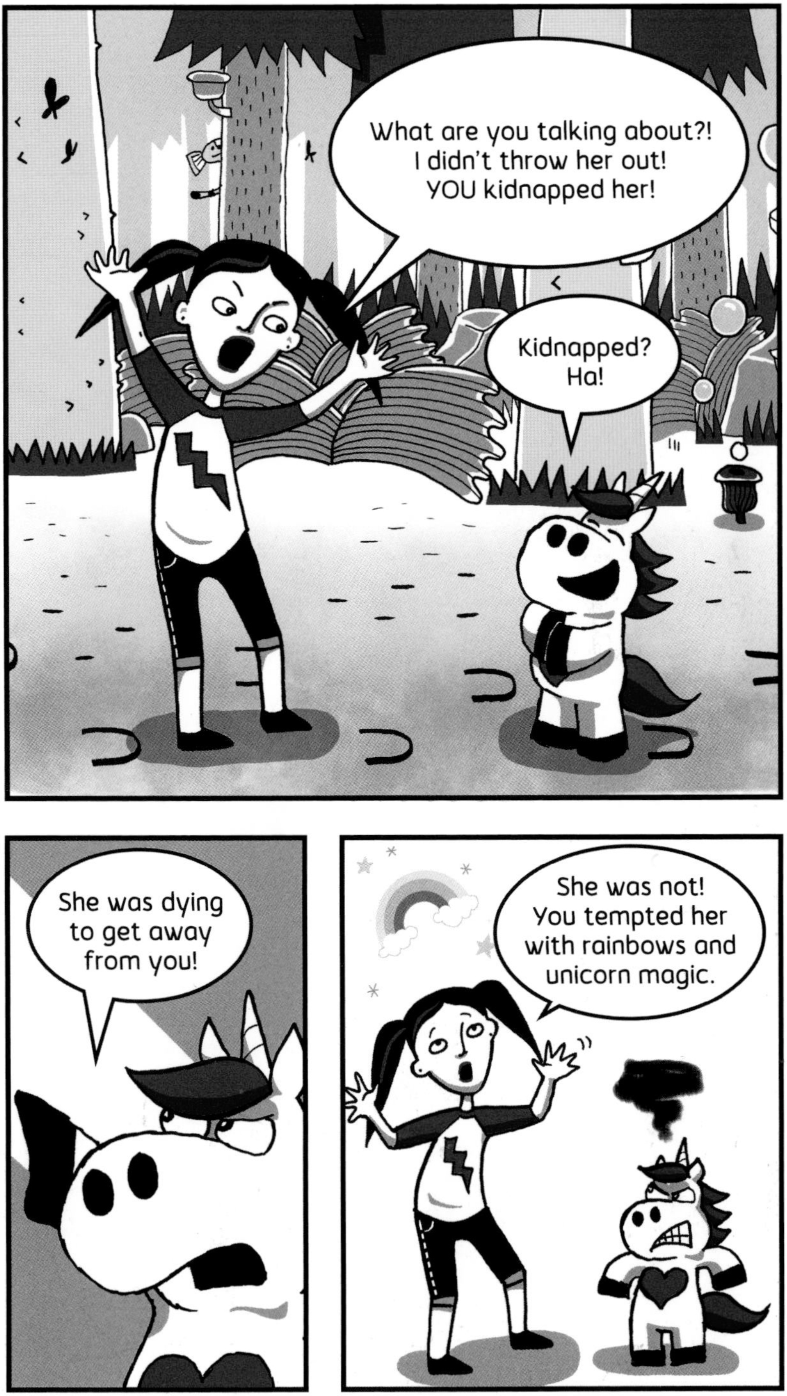
What are you talking about?!
I didn't throw her out!
YOU kidnapped her!
Kidnapped?
Ha!
She was dying
to get away
from you!
She was not!
You tempted her
with rainbows and
unicorn magic.

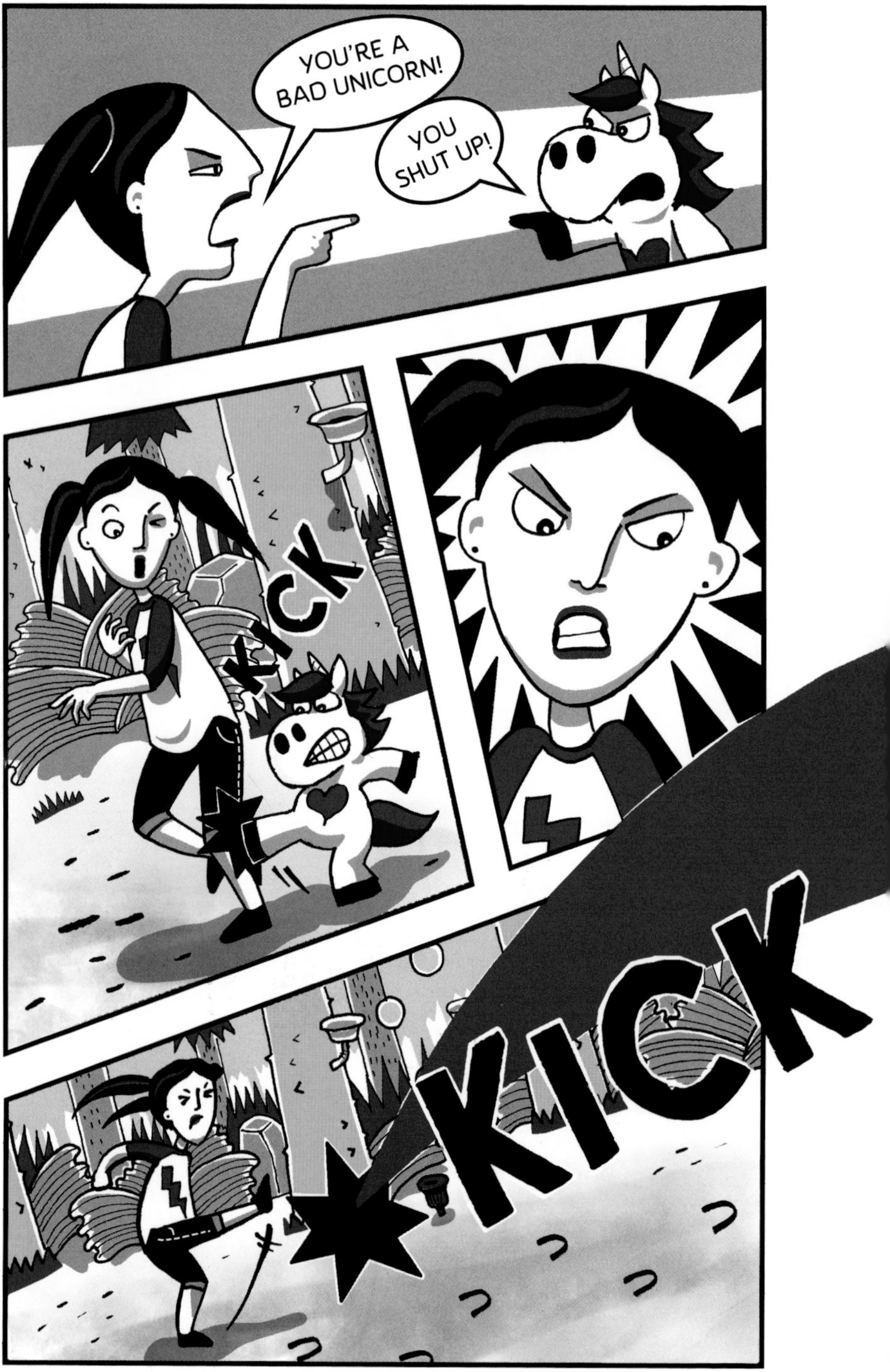
YOU'RE A BAD UNICORN!
YOU SHUT UP!
KICK
KICK

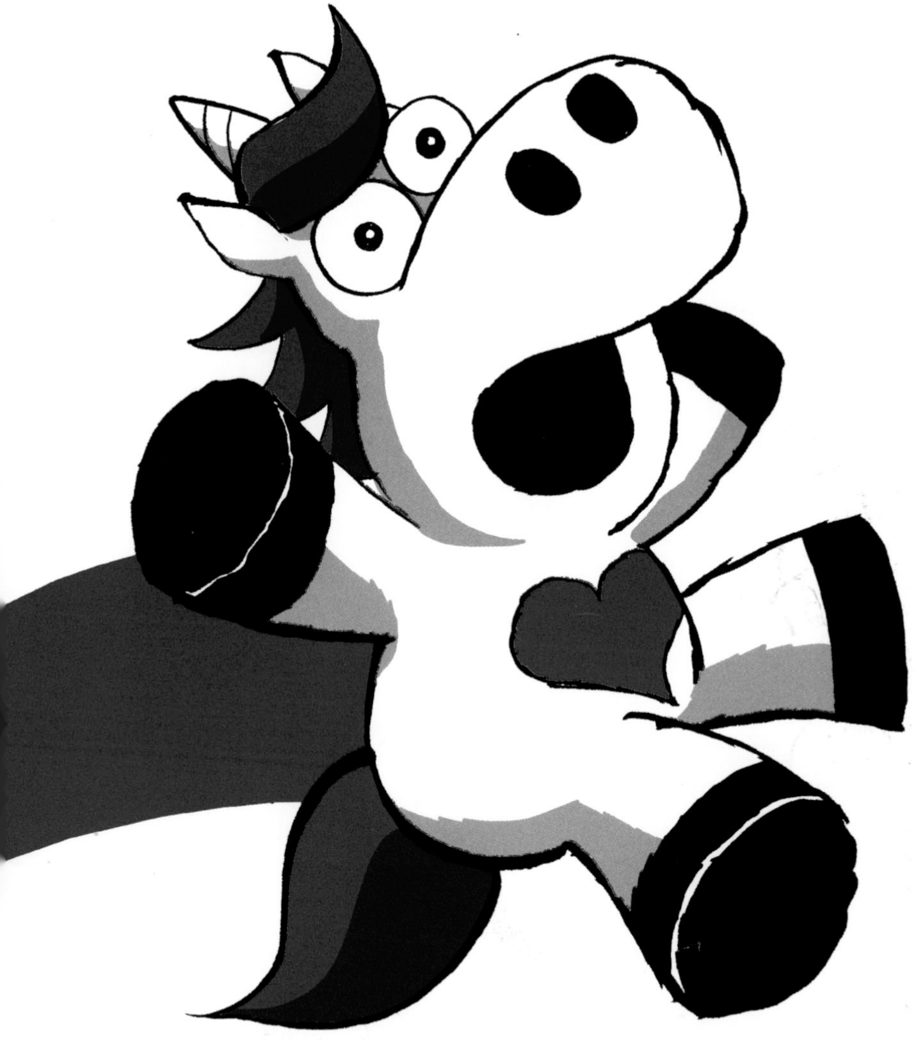

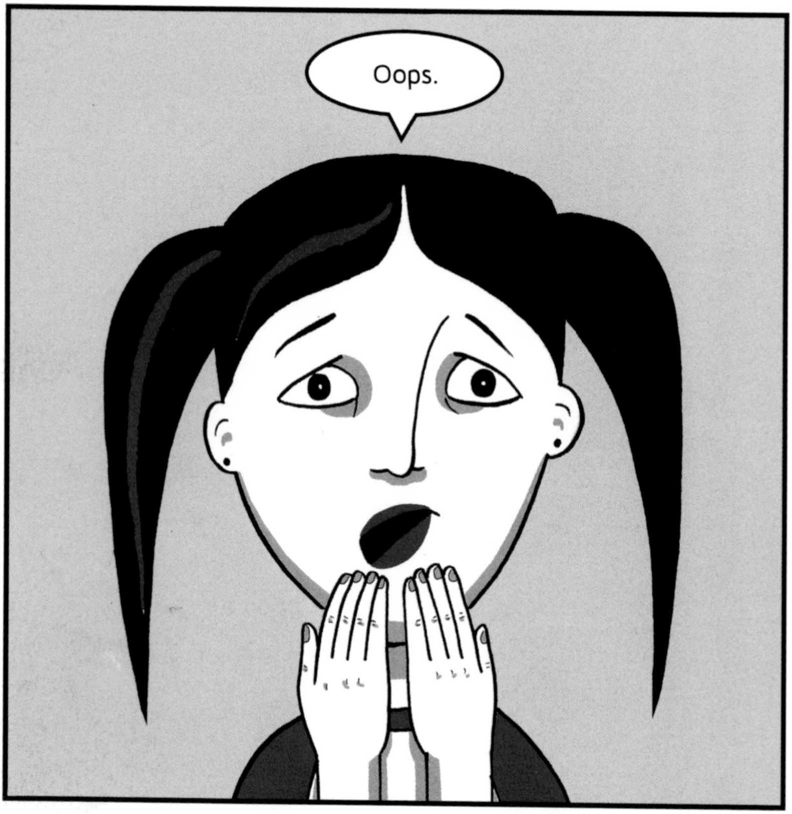
Oops.

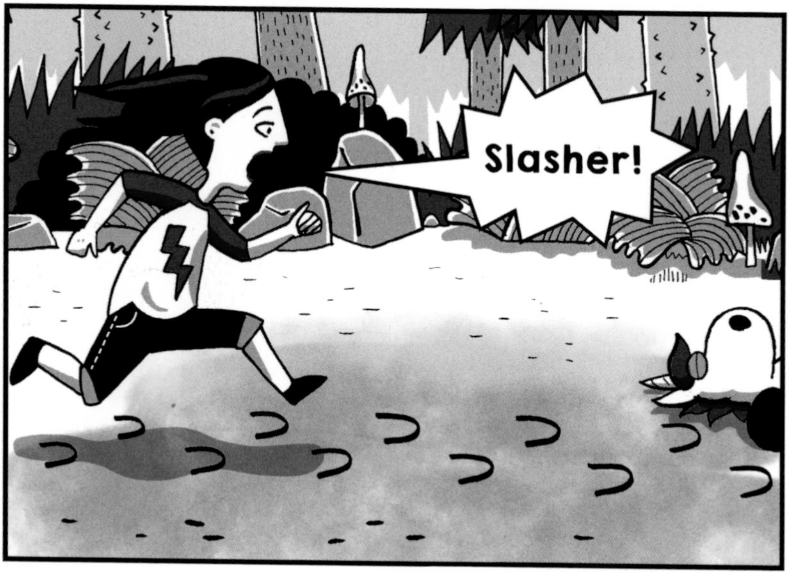
Slasher!

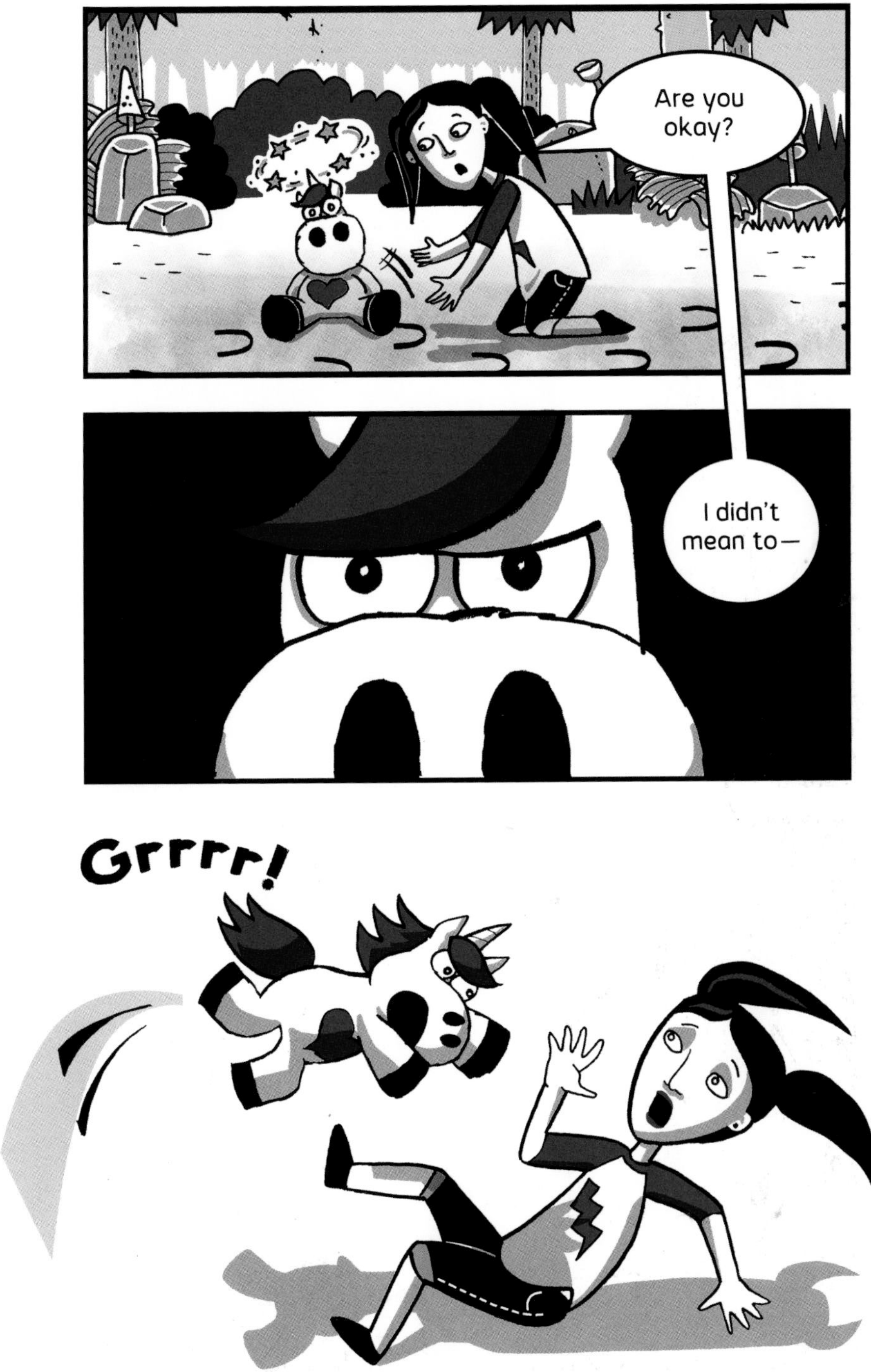
Are you okay?
I didn't mean to—
Grrrr!

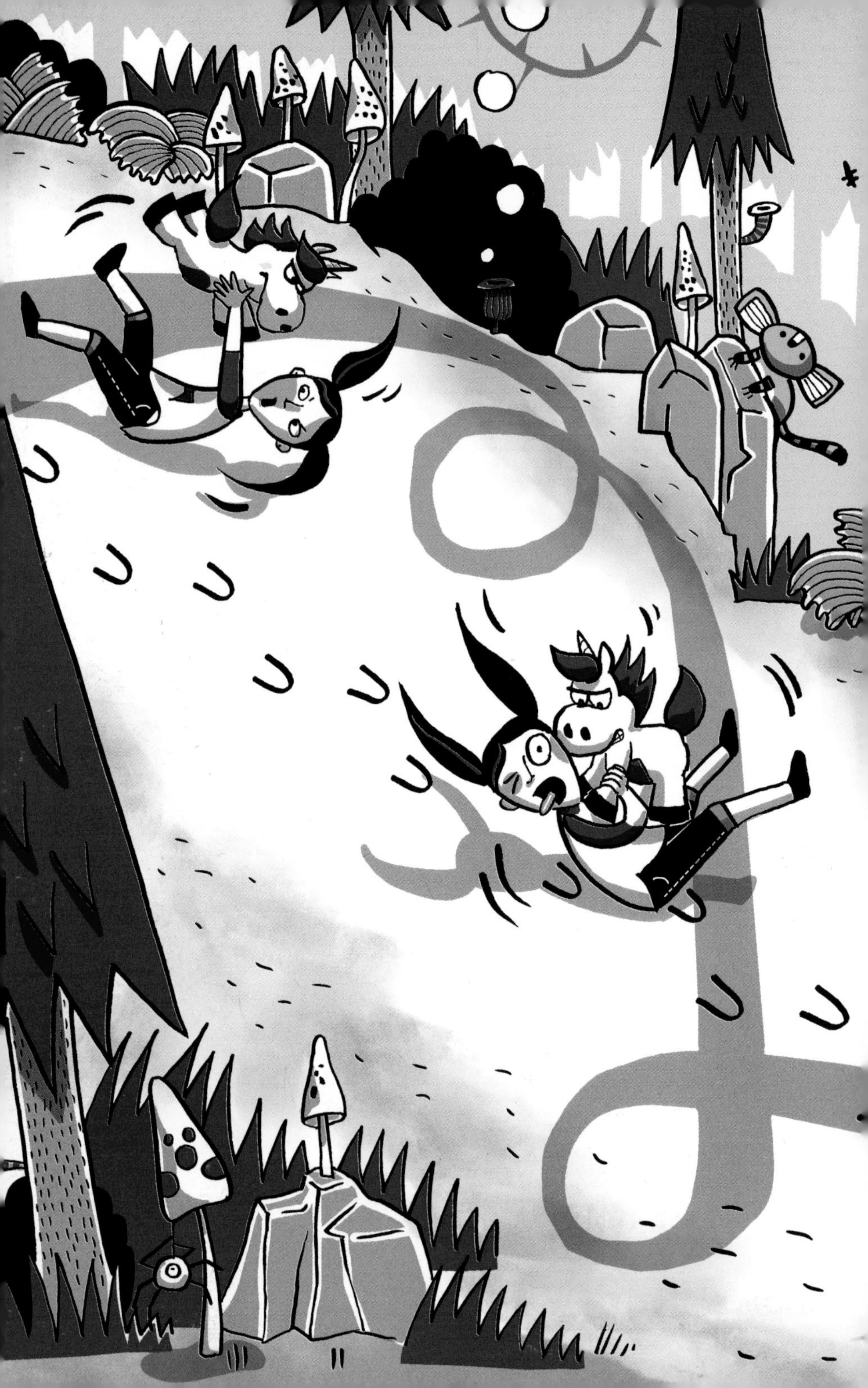

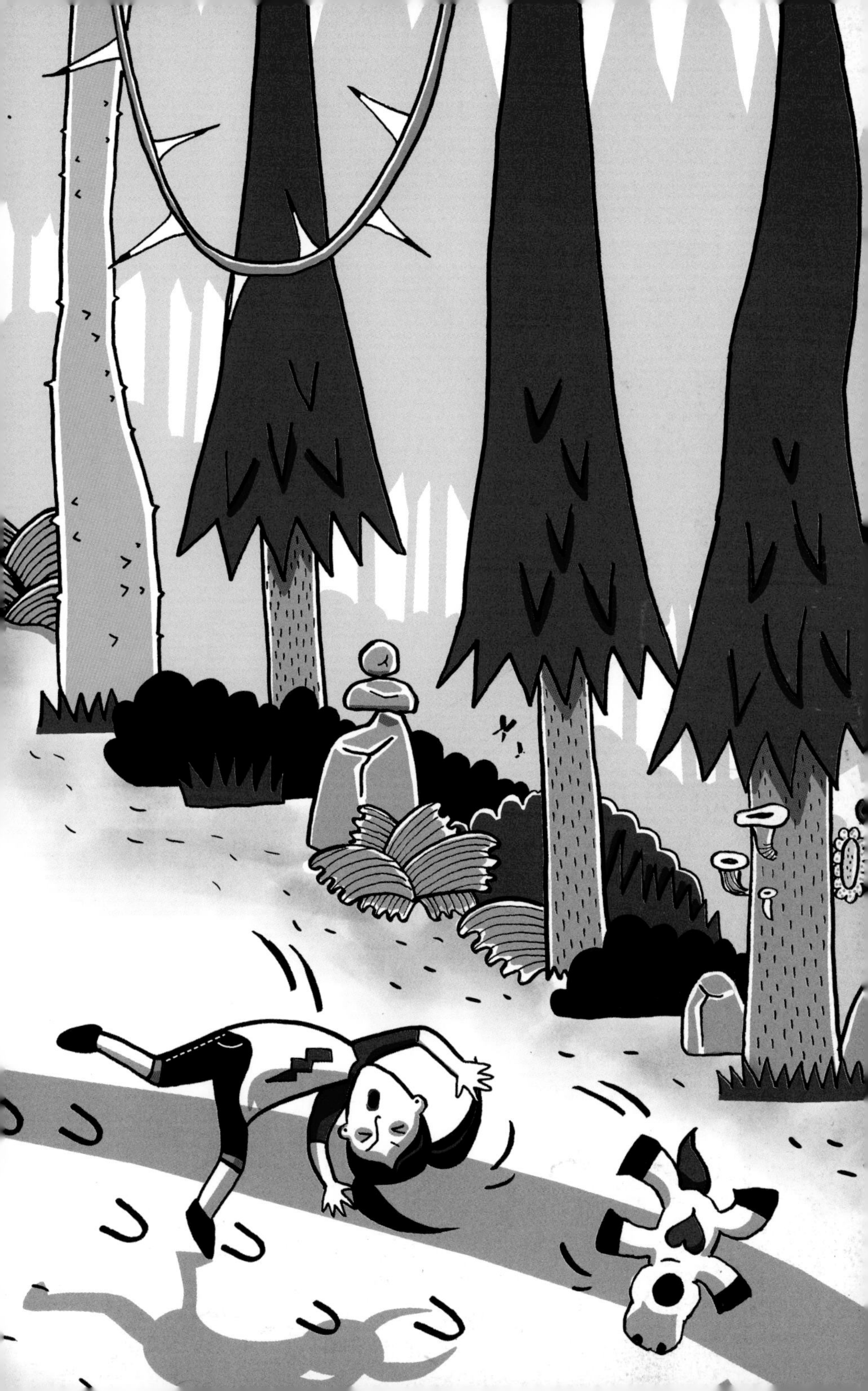

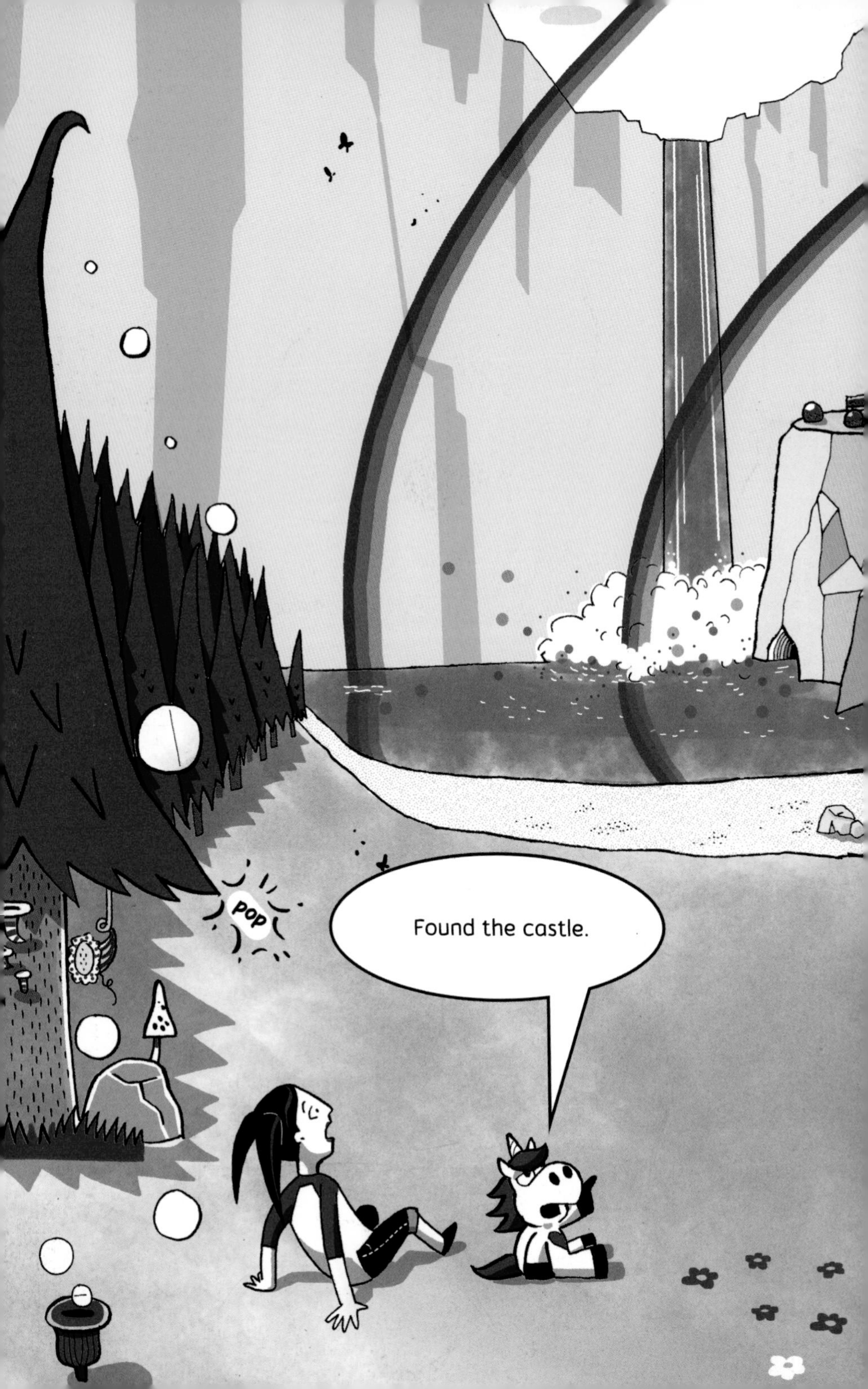
pop
Found the castle.

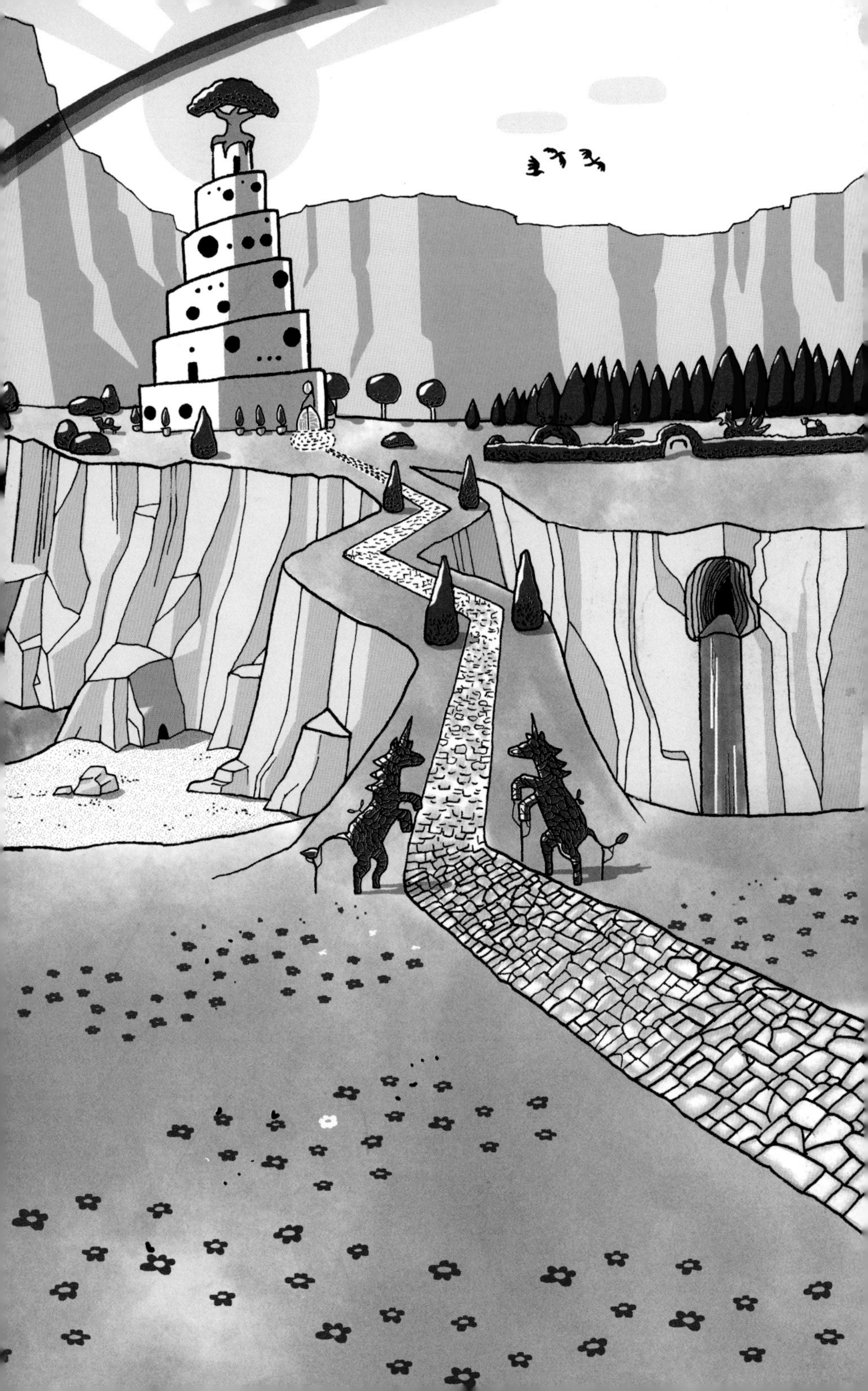

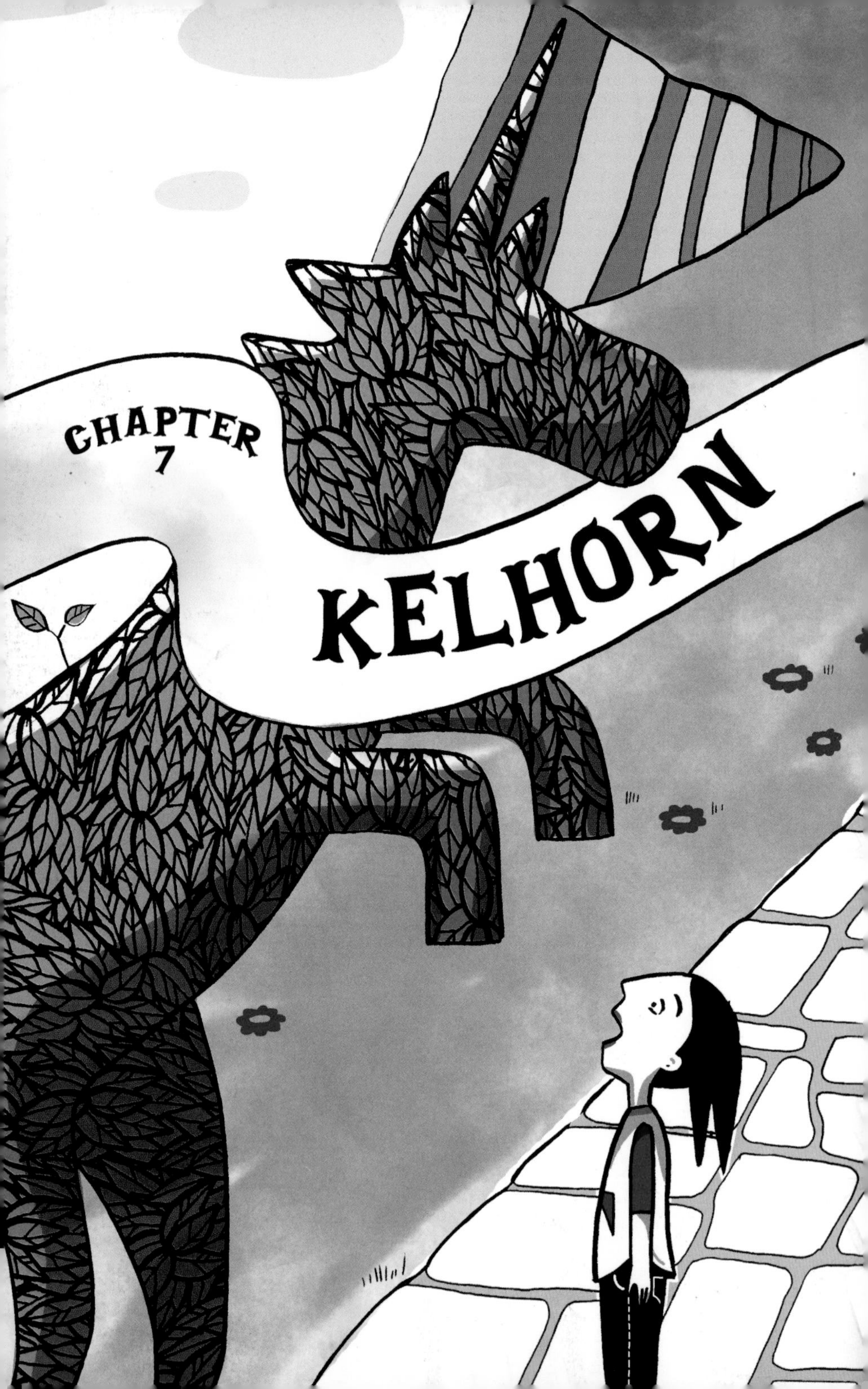
CHAPTER 7
KELHORN

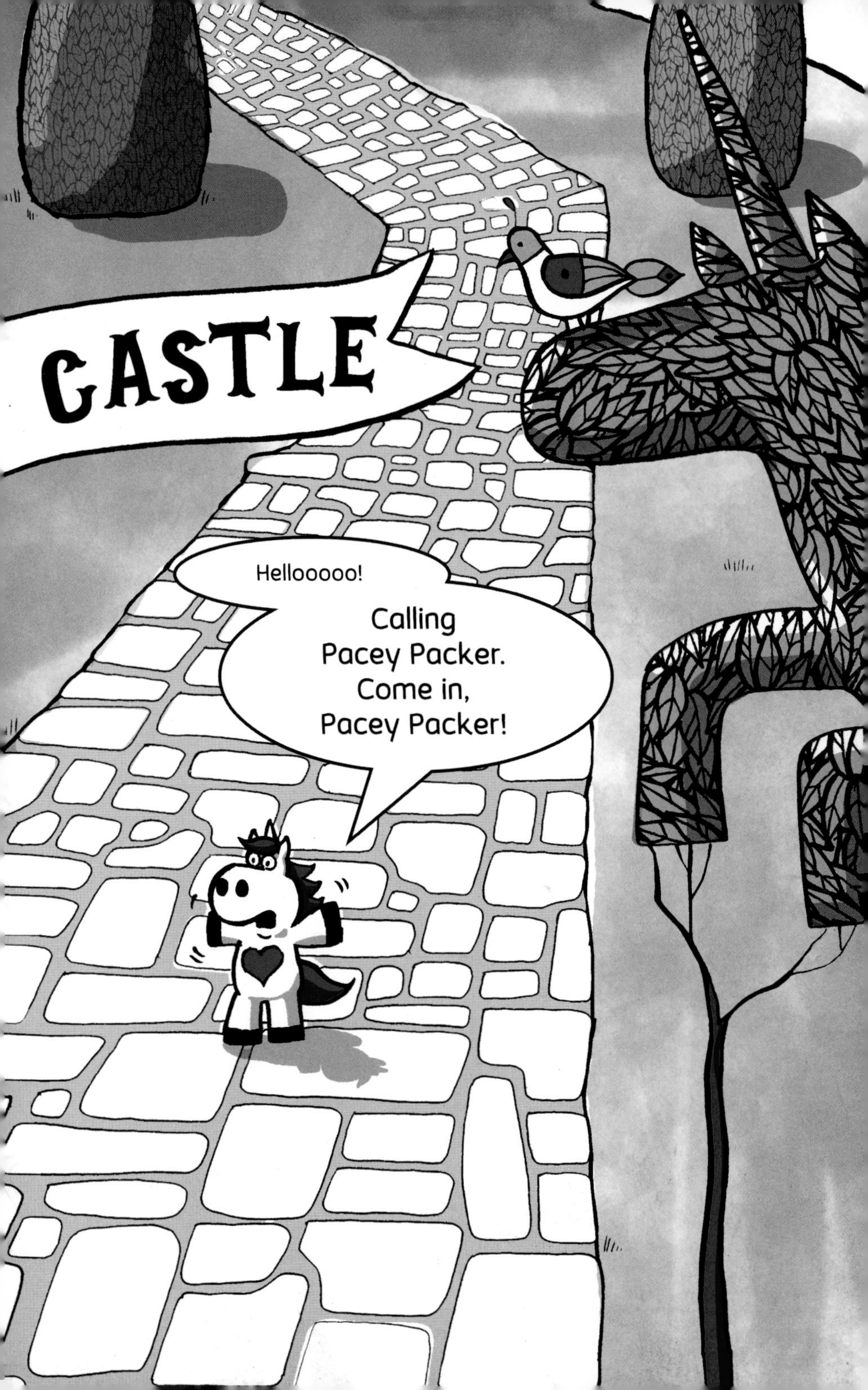
CASTLE
Hellooooo!
Calling Pacey Packer. Come in, Pacey Packer!

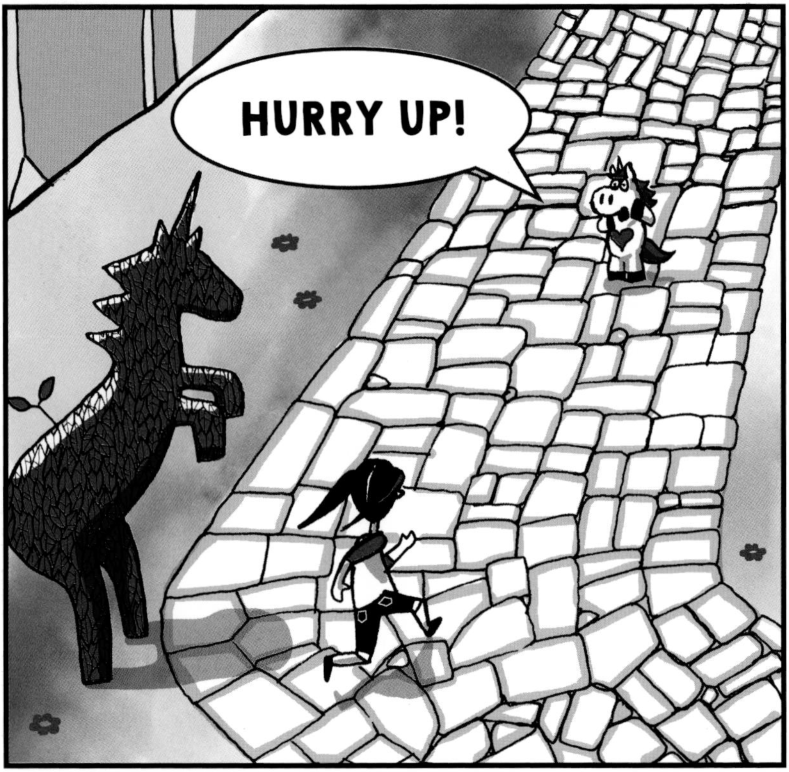
HURRY UP!

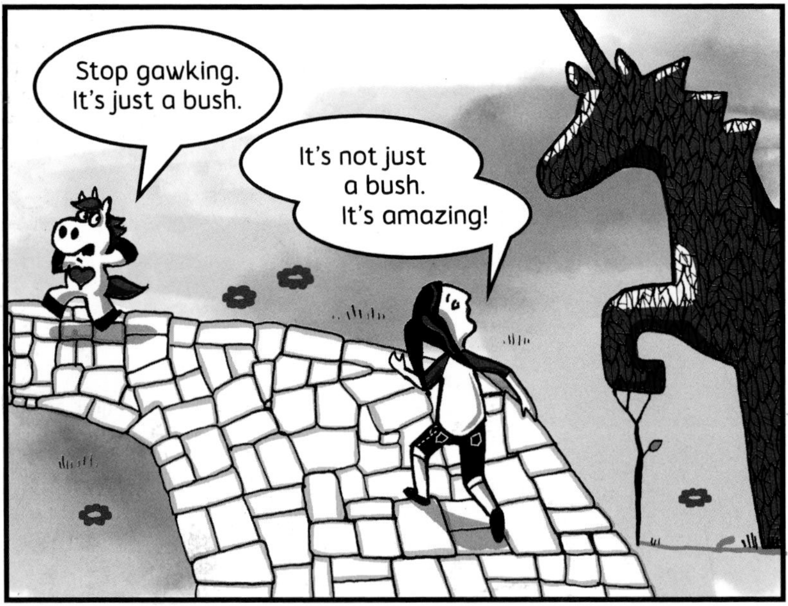
Stop gawking. It's just a bush.
It's not just a bush. It's amazing!

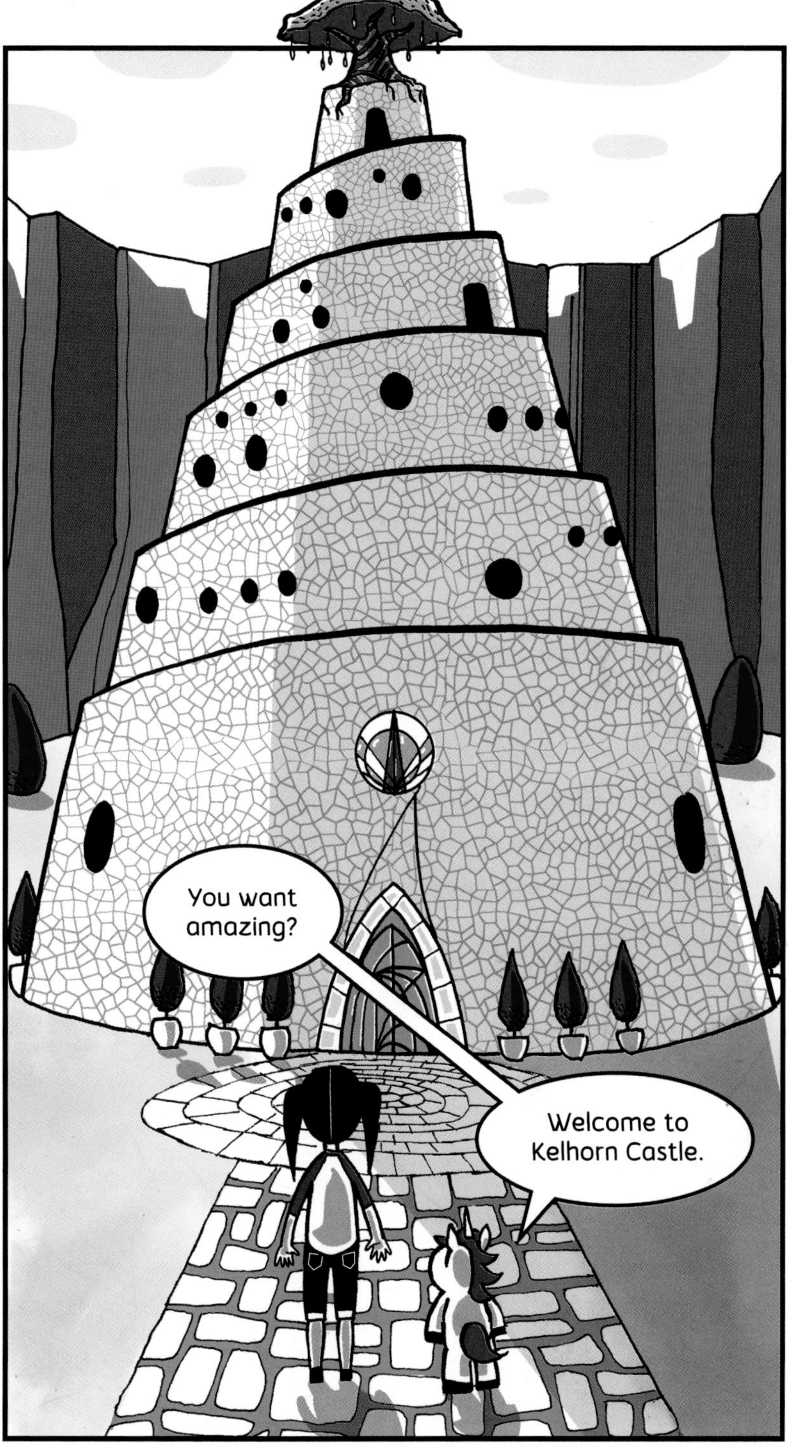
You want amazing?
Welcome to Kelhorn Castle.

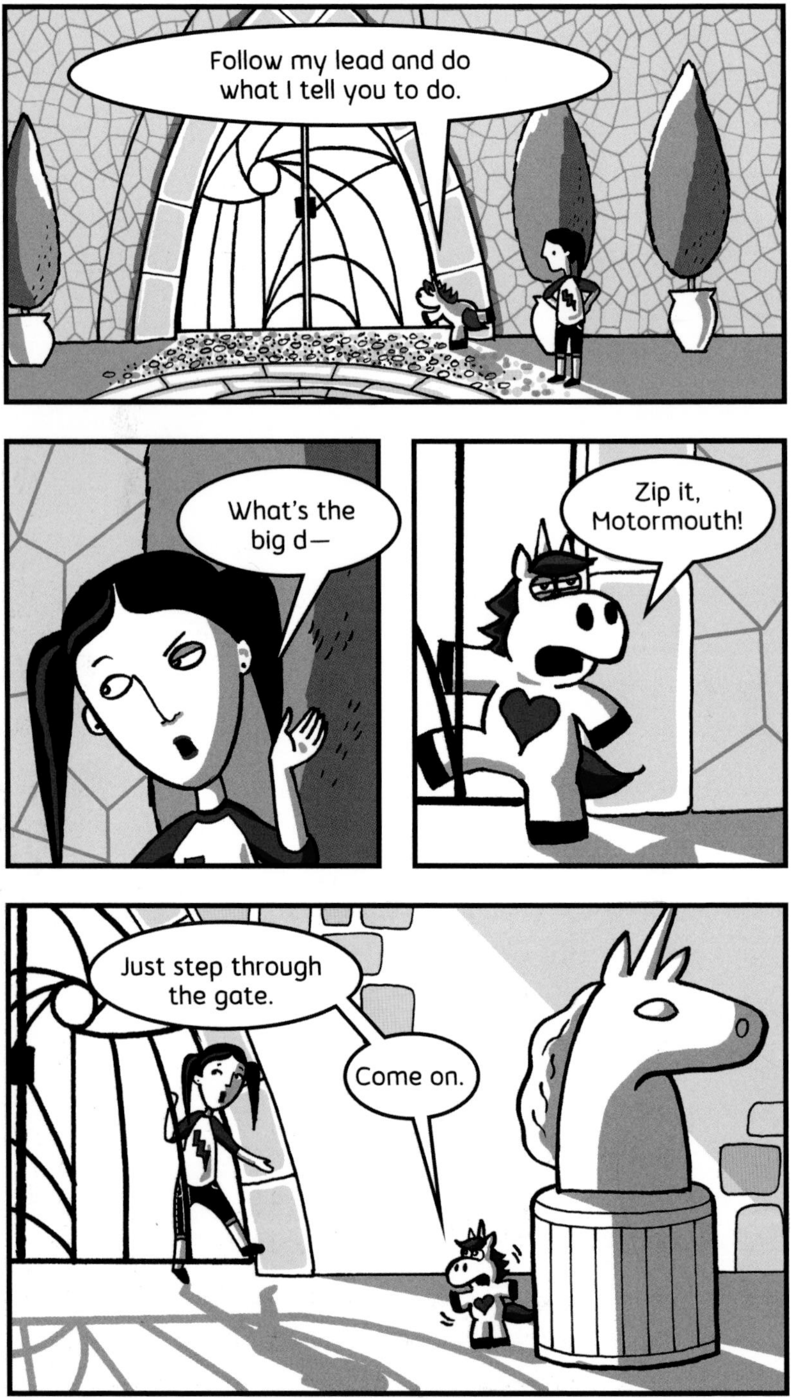
Follow my lead and do what I tell you to do.
What's the big d—
Zip it, Motormouth!
Just step through the gate.
Come on.

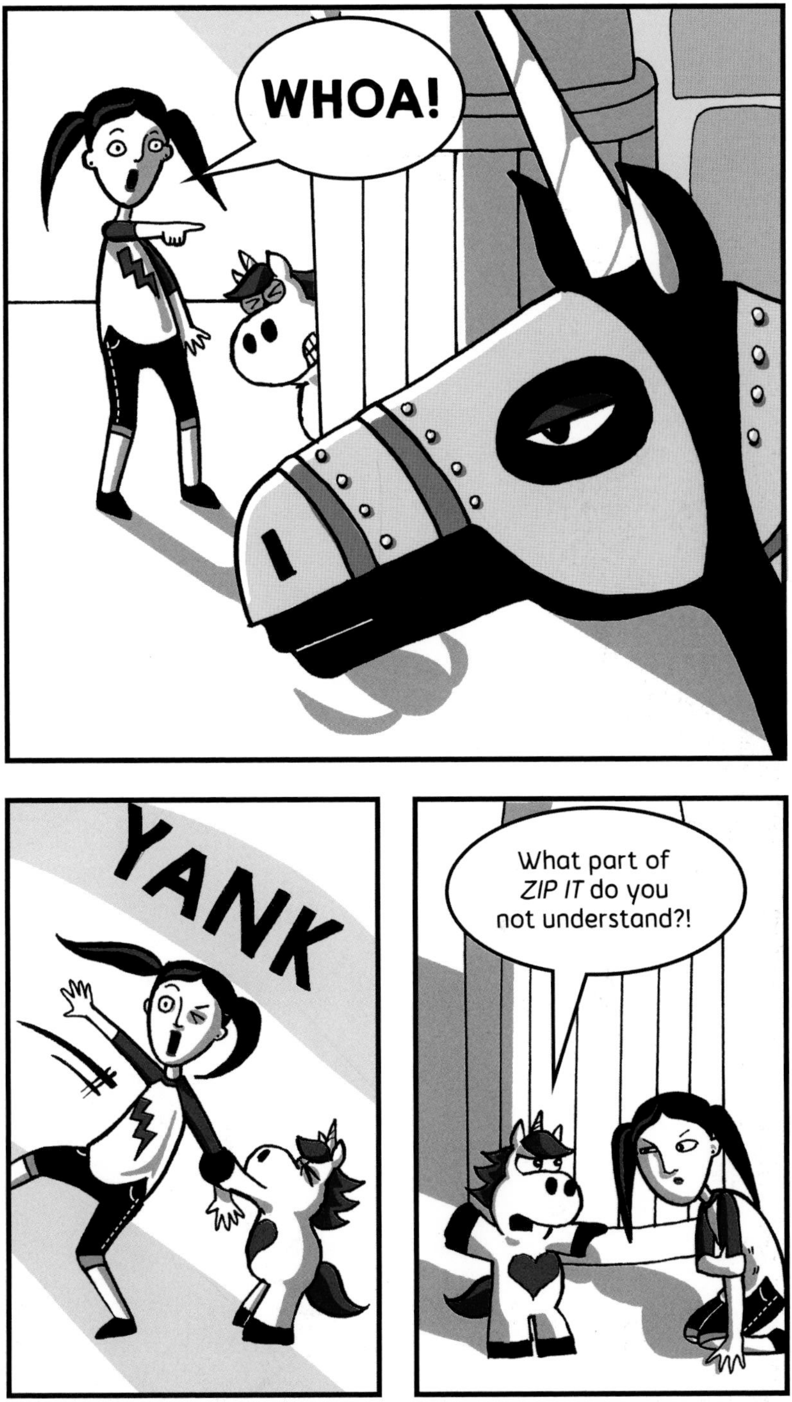
WHOA!
YANK
What part of *ZIP IT* do you not understand?!

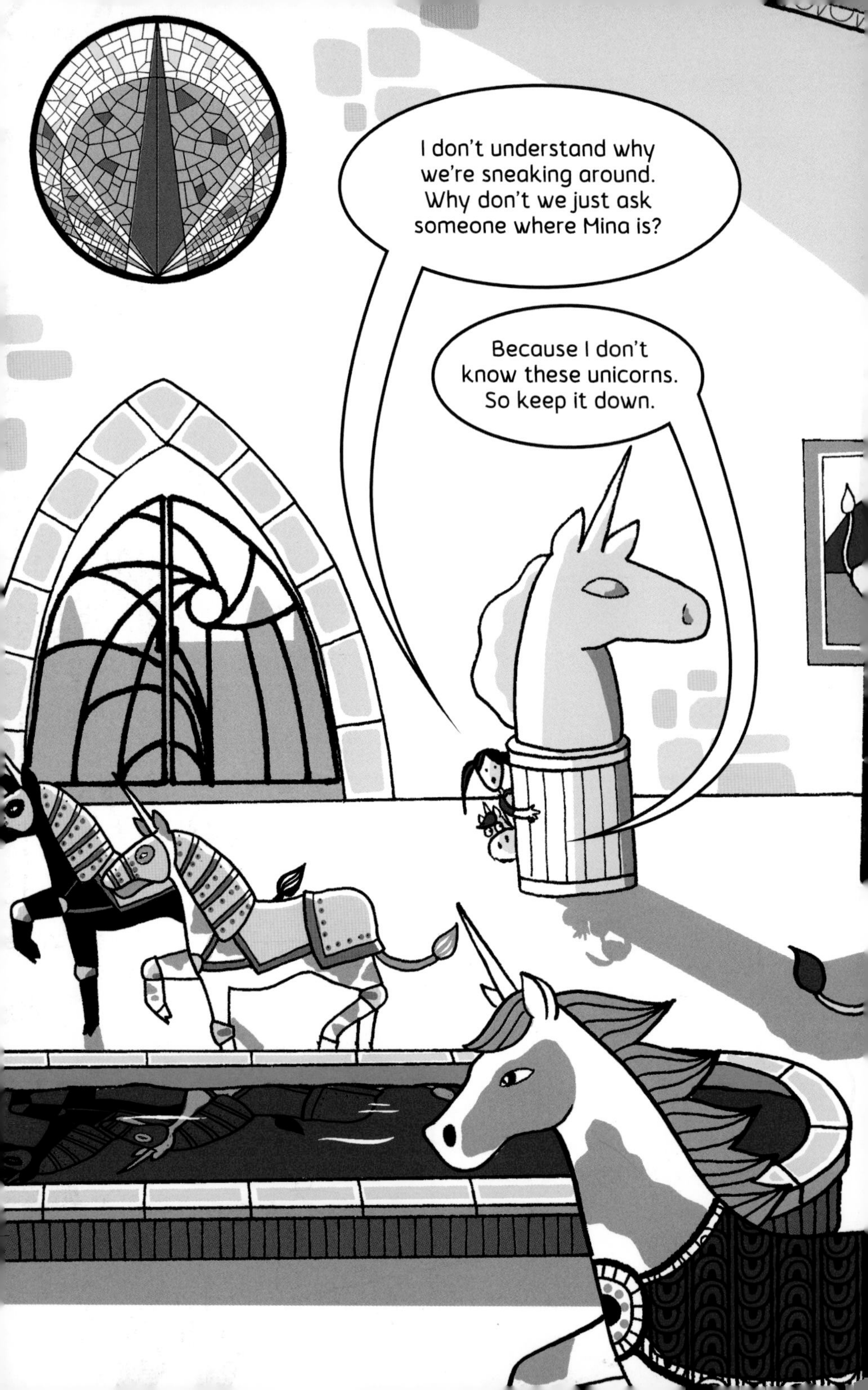
I don't understand why we're sneaking around. Why don't we just ask someone where Mina is?
Because I don't know these unicorns. So keep it down.

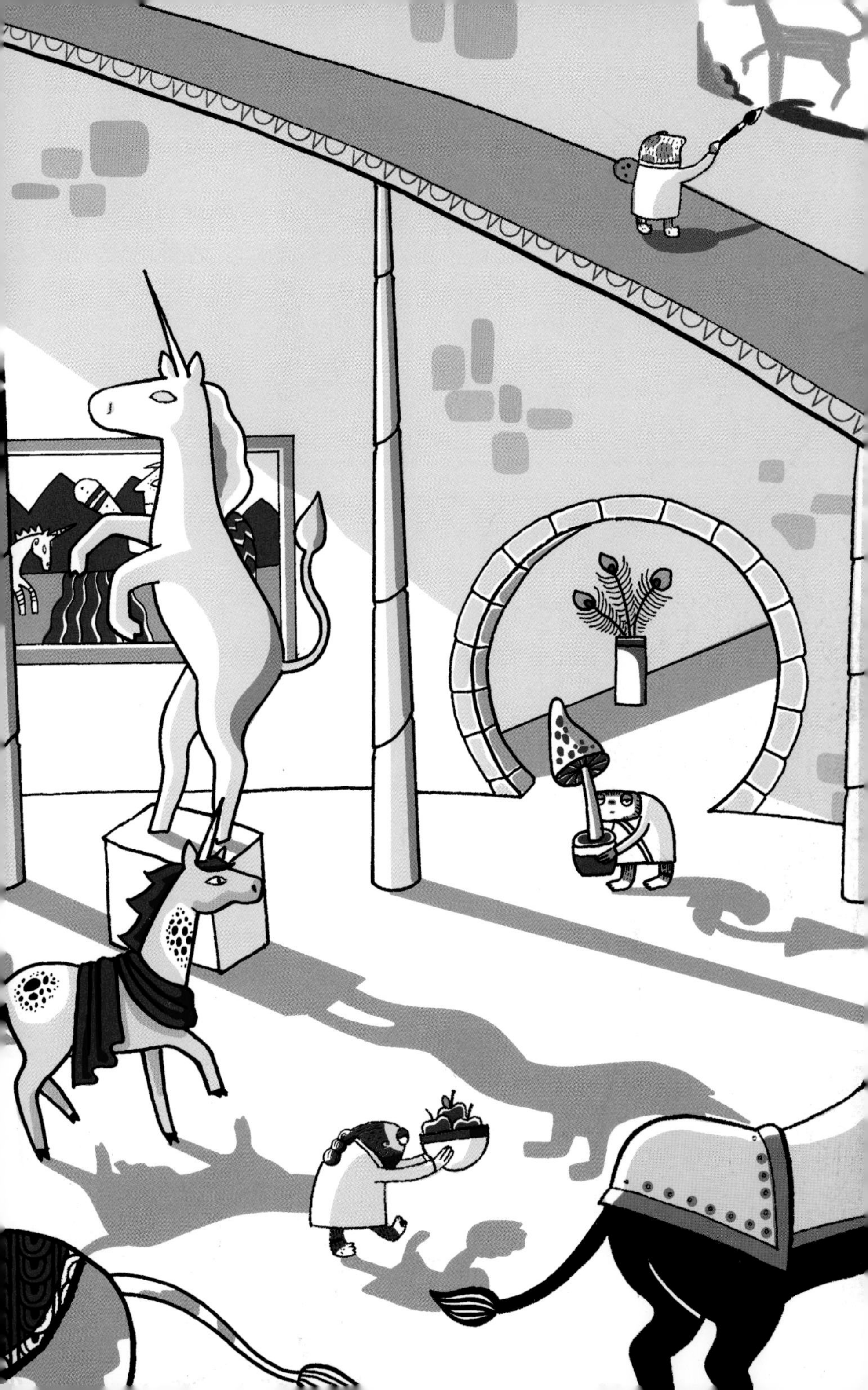

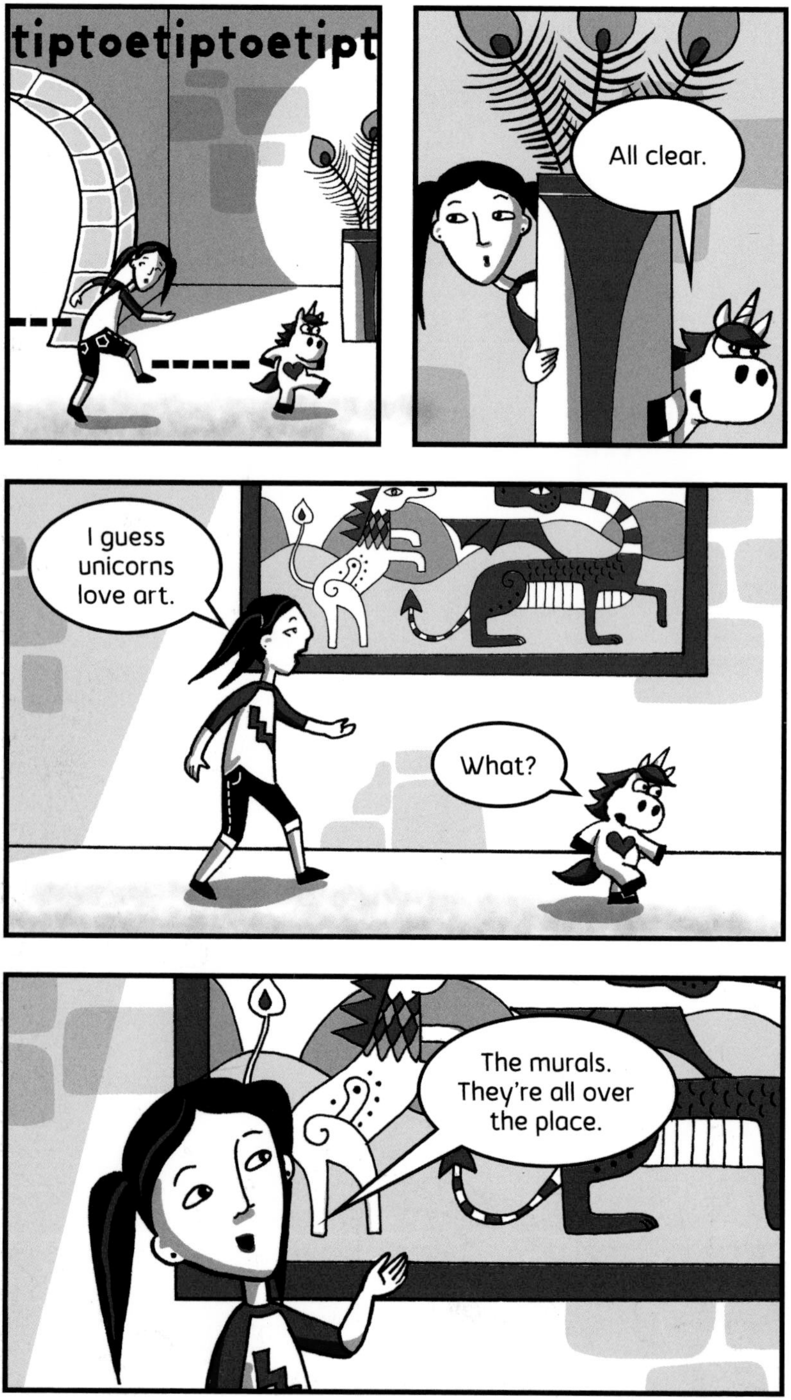
tiptoetiptoetipt
All clear.
I guess unicorns love art.
What?
The murals. They're all over the place.

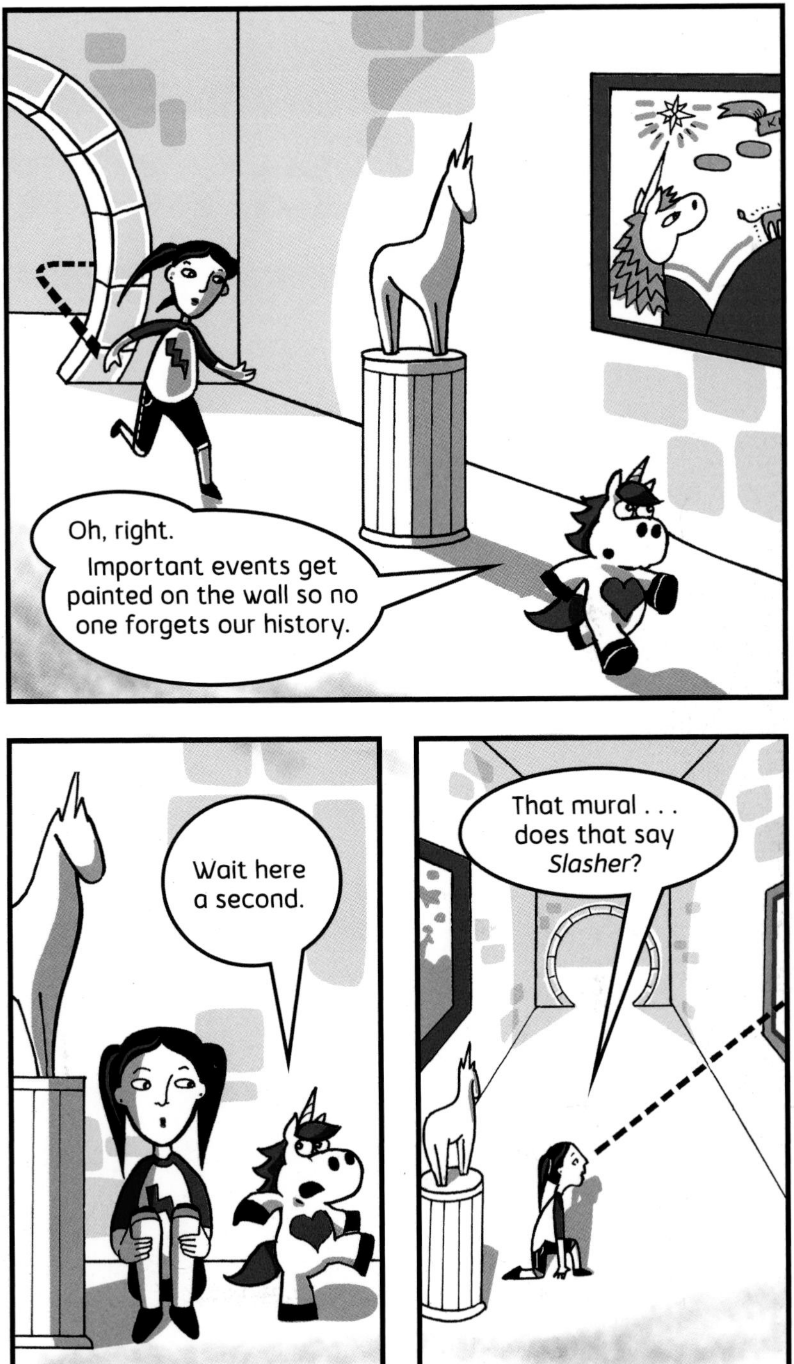
Oh, right.
Important events get painted on the wall so no one forgets our history.
Wait here a second.
That mural . . . does that say *Slasher*?

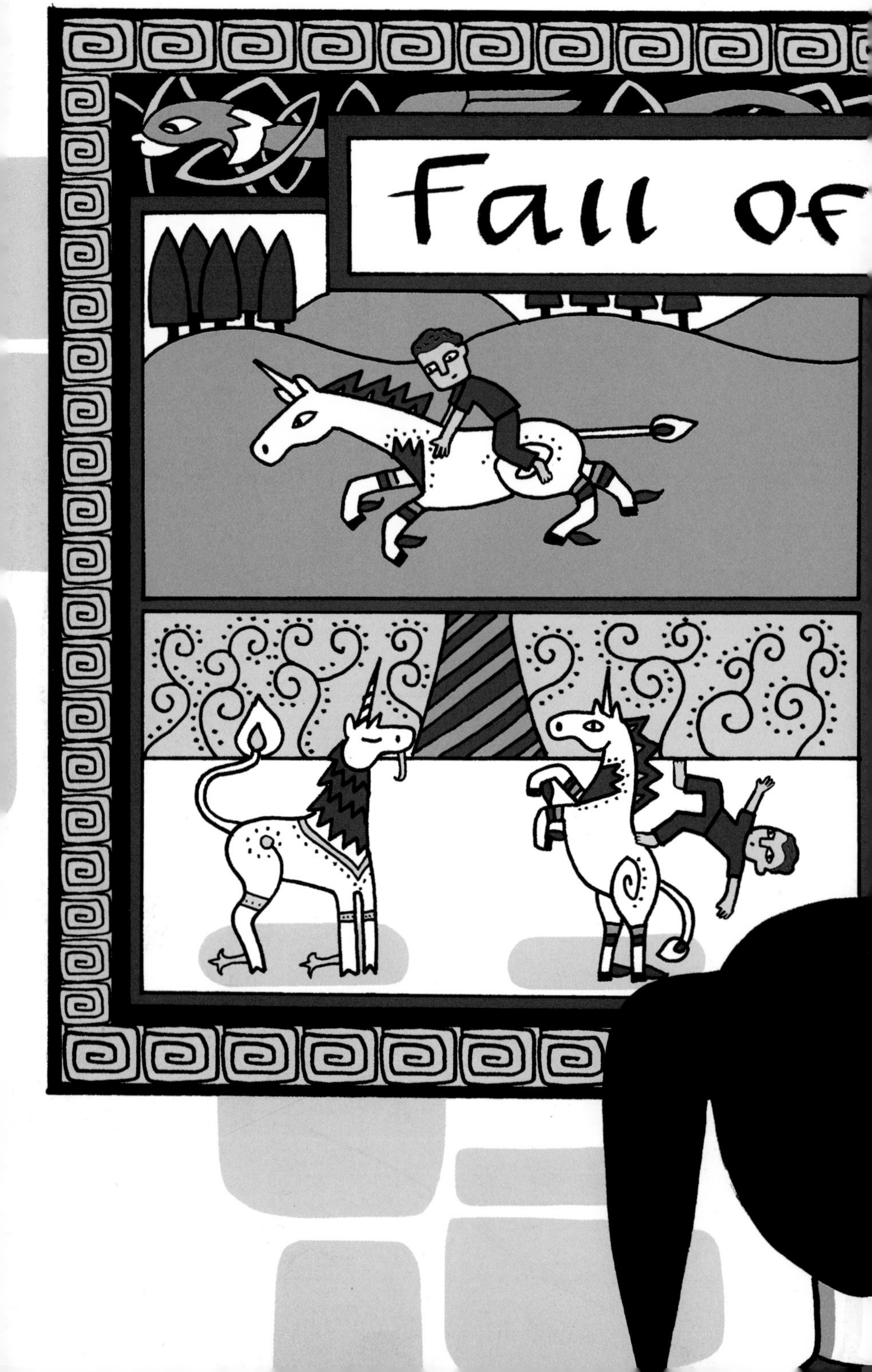
Fall of

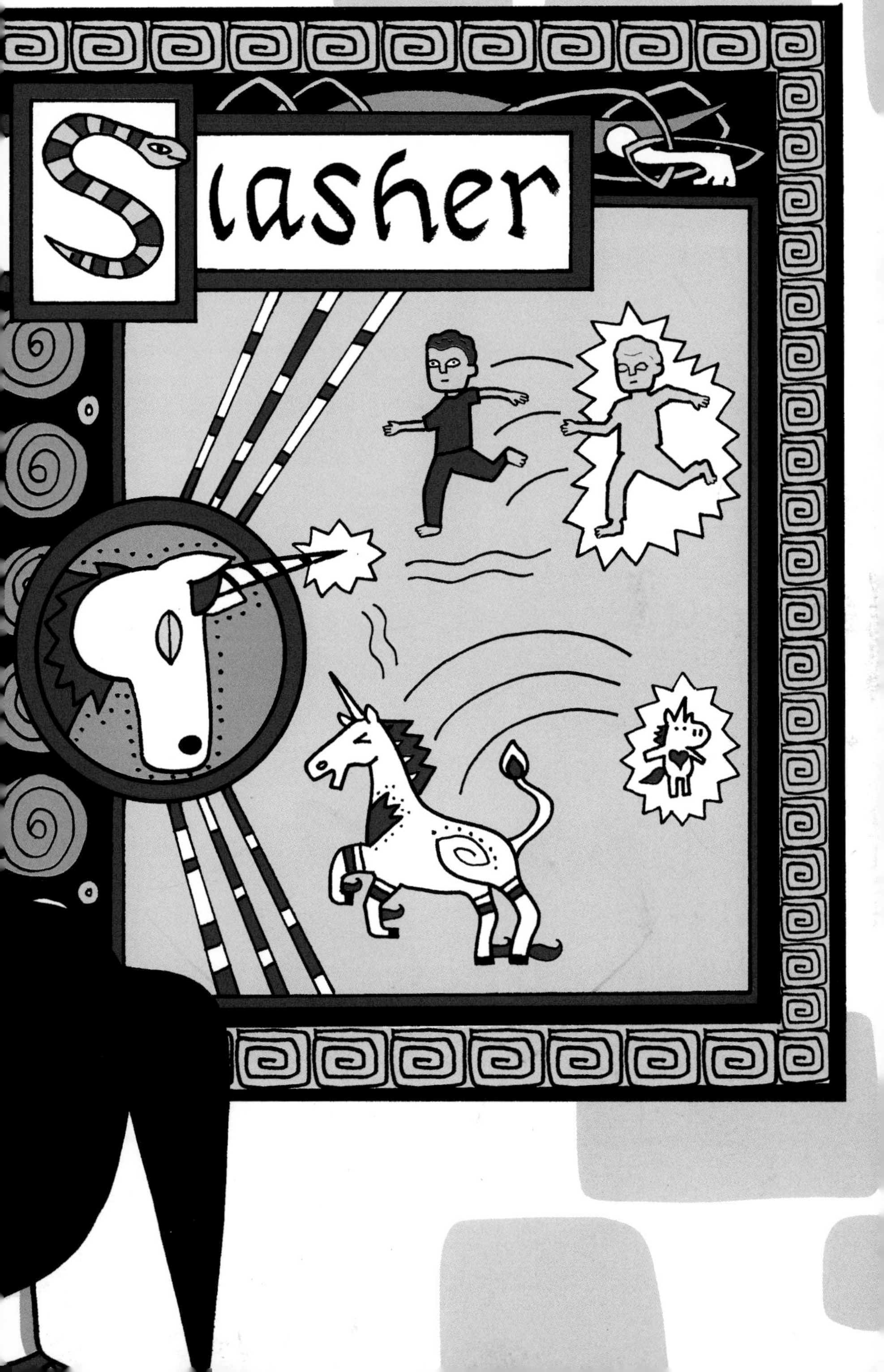
Slasher

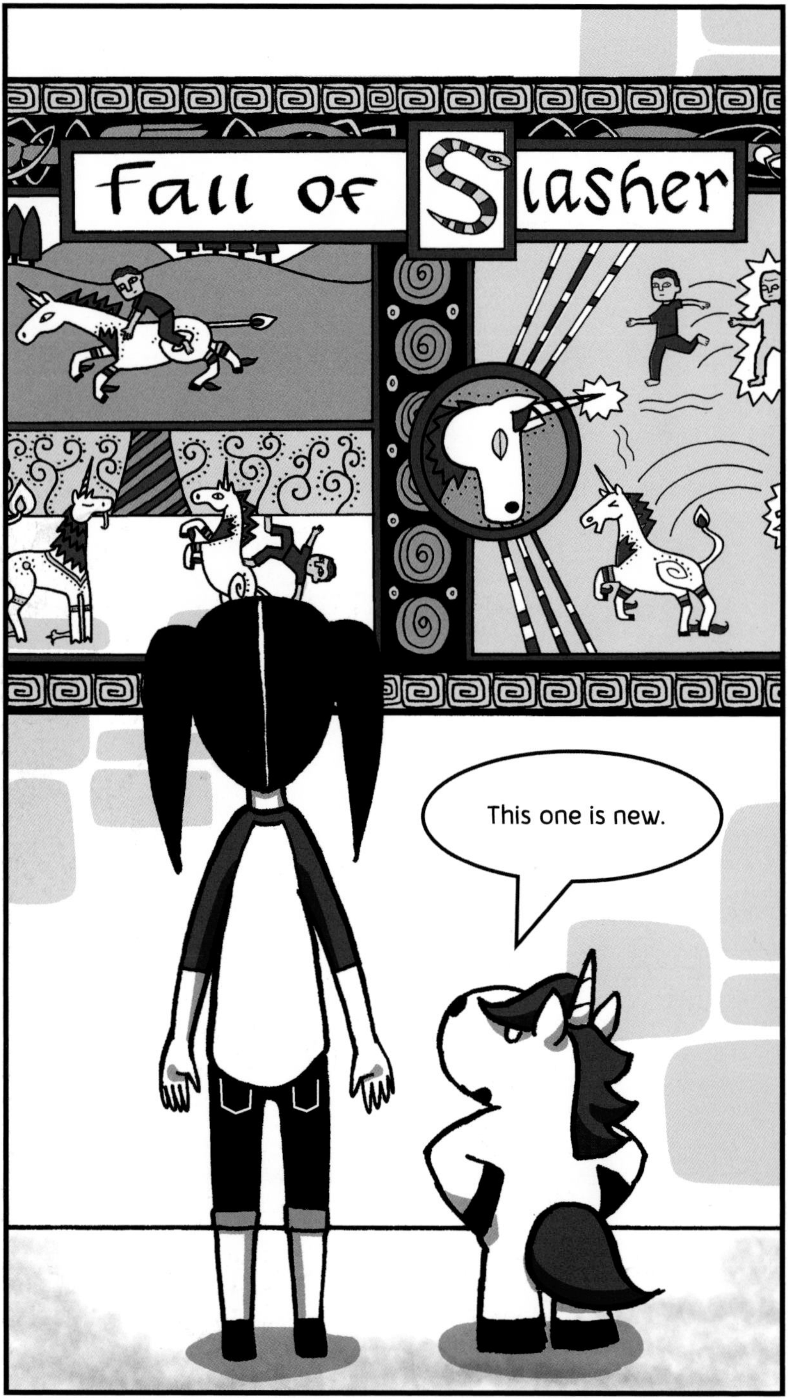
Fall of Slasher
This one is new.

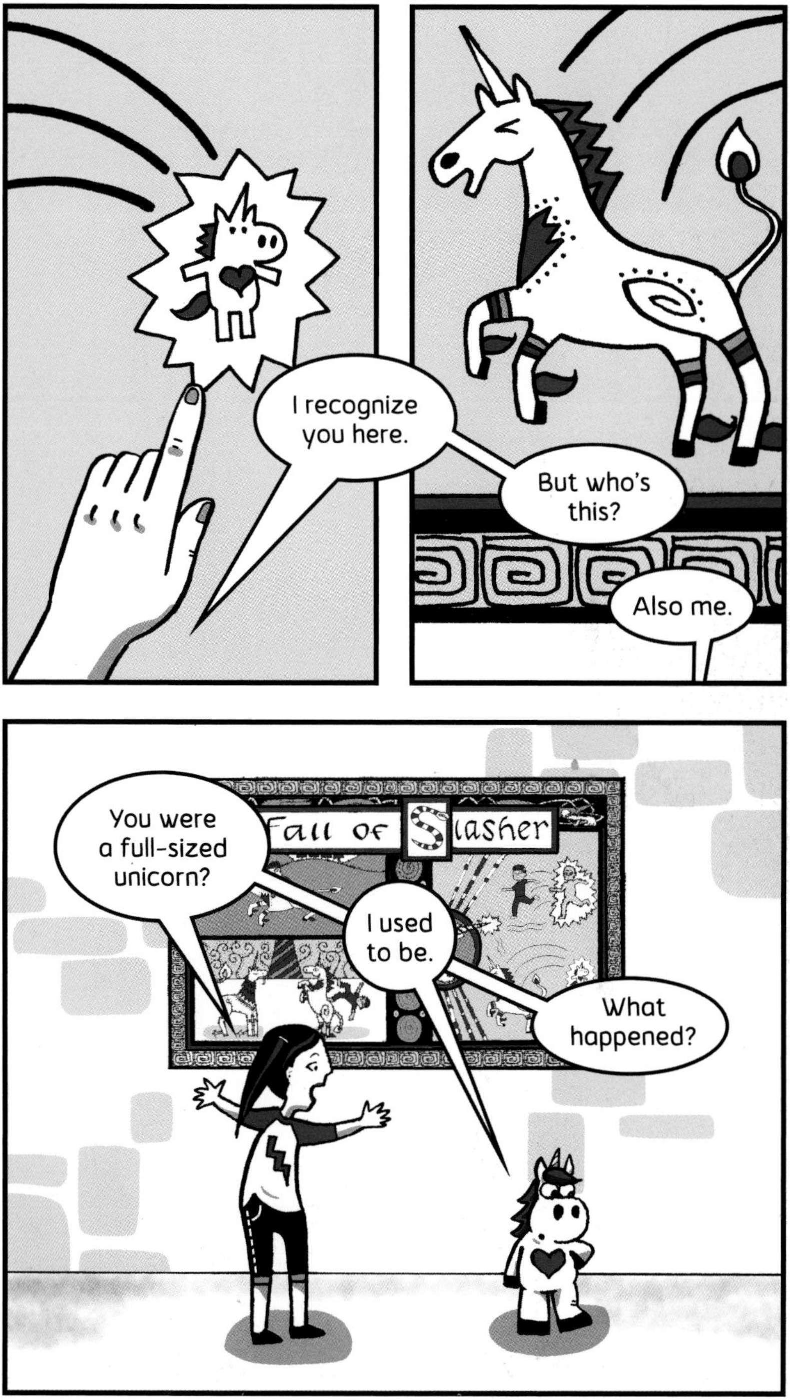
I recognize you here.
But who's this?
Also me.
Fall of Slasher
You were a full-sized unicorn?
I used to be.
What happened?

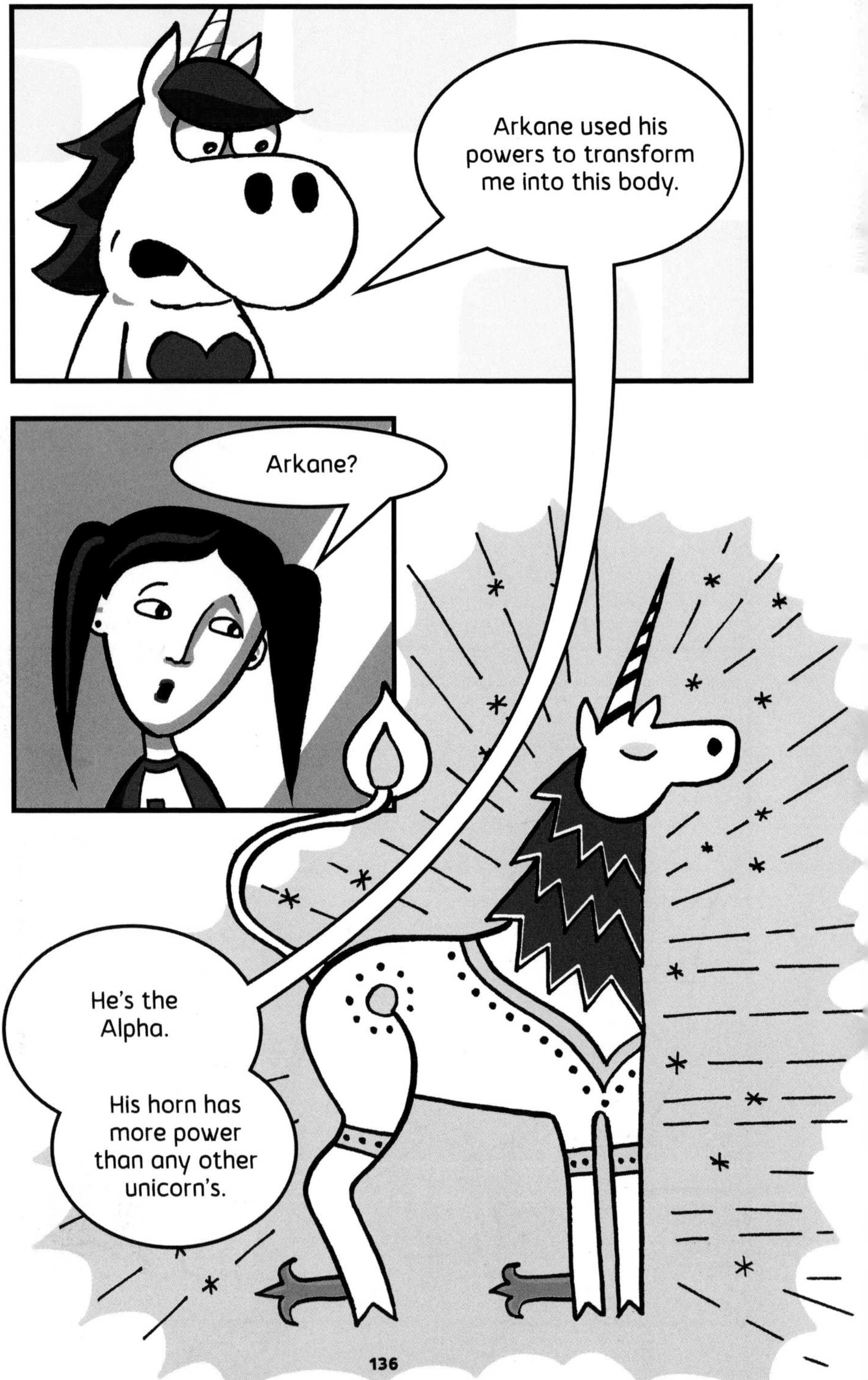
Arkane used his powers to transform me into this body.
Arkane?
He's the Alpha.
His horn has more power than any other unicorn's.

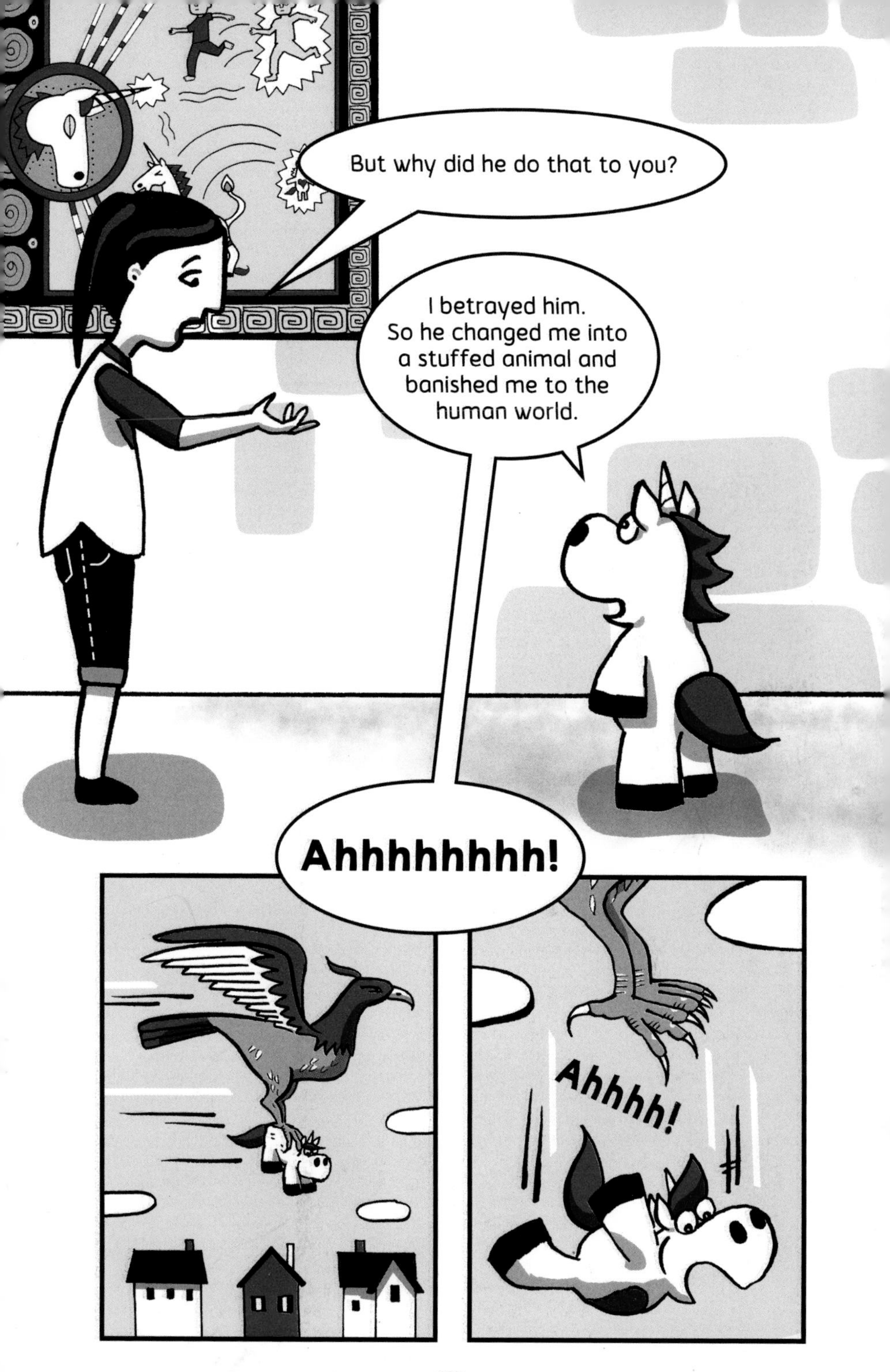

But why did he do that to you?
I betrayed him. So he changed me into a stuffed animal and banished me to the human world.
Ahhhhhhhh!
Ahhhh!

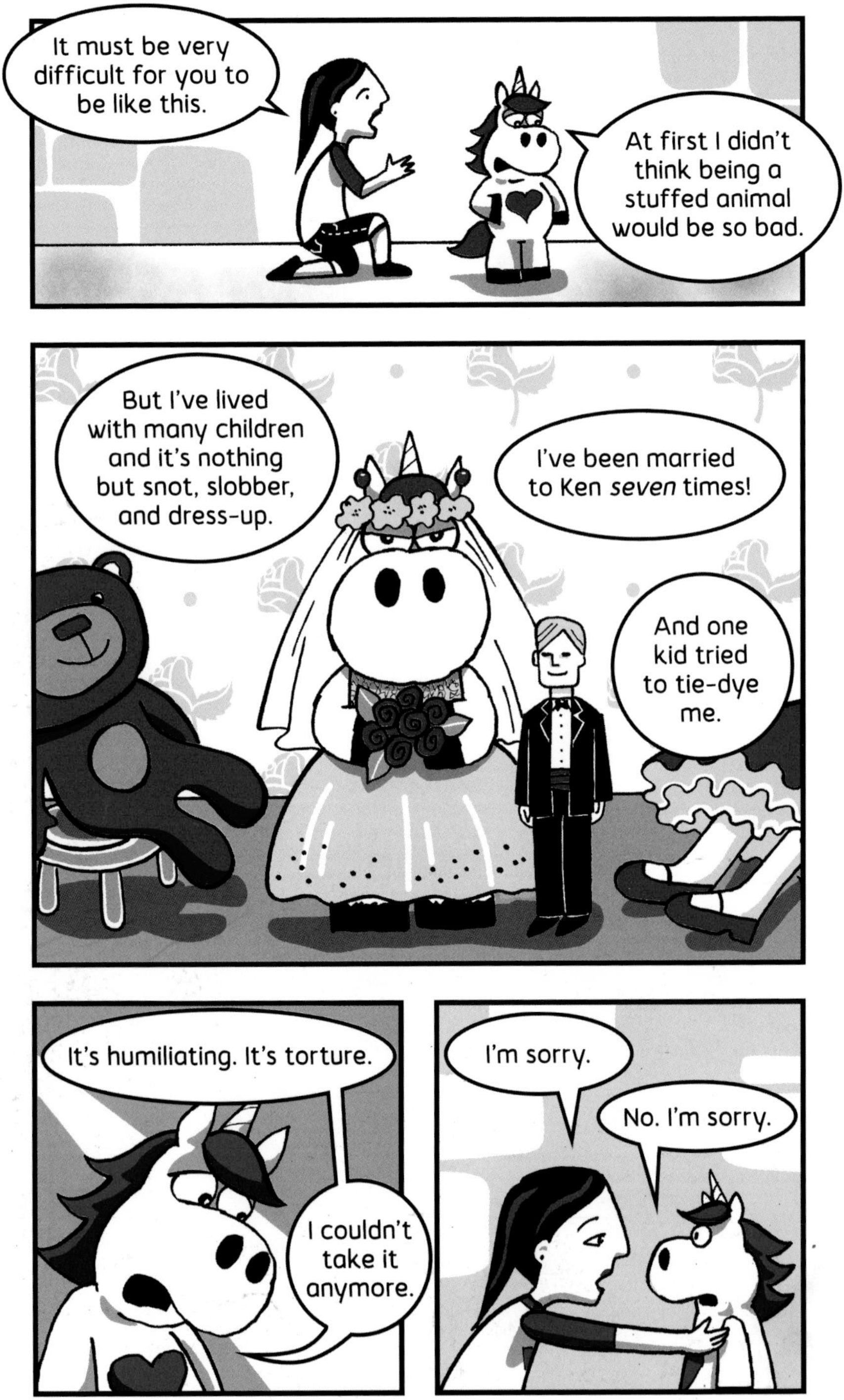

It must be very difficult for you to be like this.
At first I didn't think being a stuffed animal would be so bad.
But I've lived with many children and it's nothing but snot, slobber, and dress-up.
I've been married to Ken *seven* times!
And one kid tried to tie-dye me.
It's humiliating. It's torture.
I couldn't take it anymore.
I'm sorry.
No. I'm sorry.

For what?

FWUMF

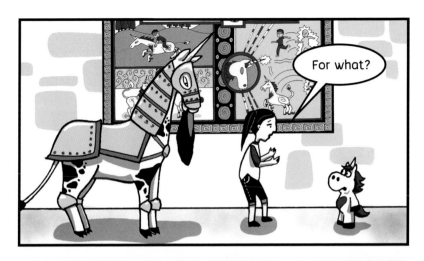

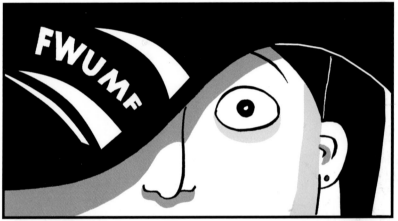

CHAPTER 8

THE GREAT ARKANE

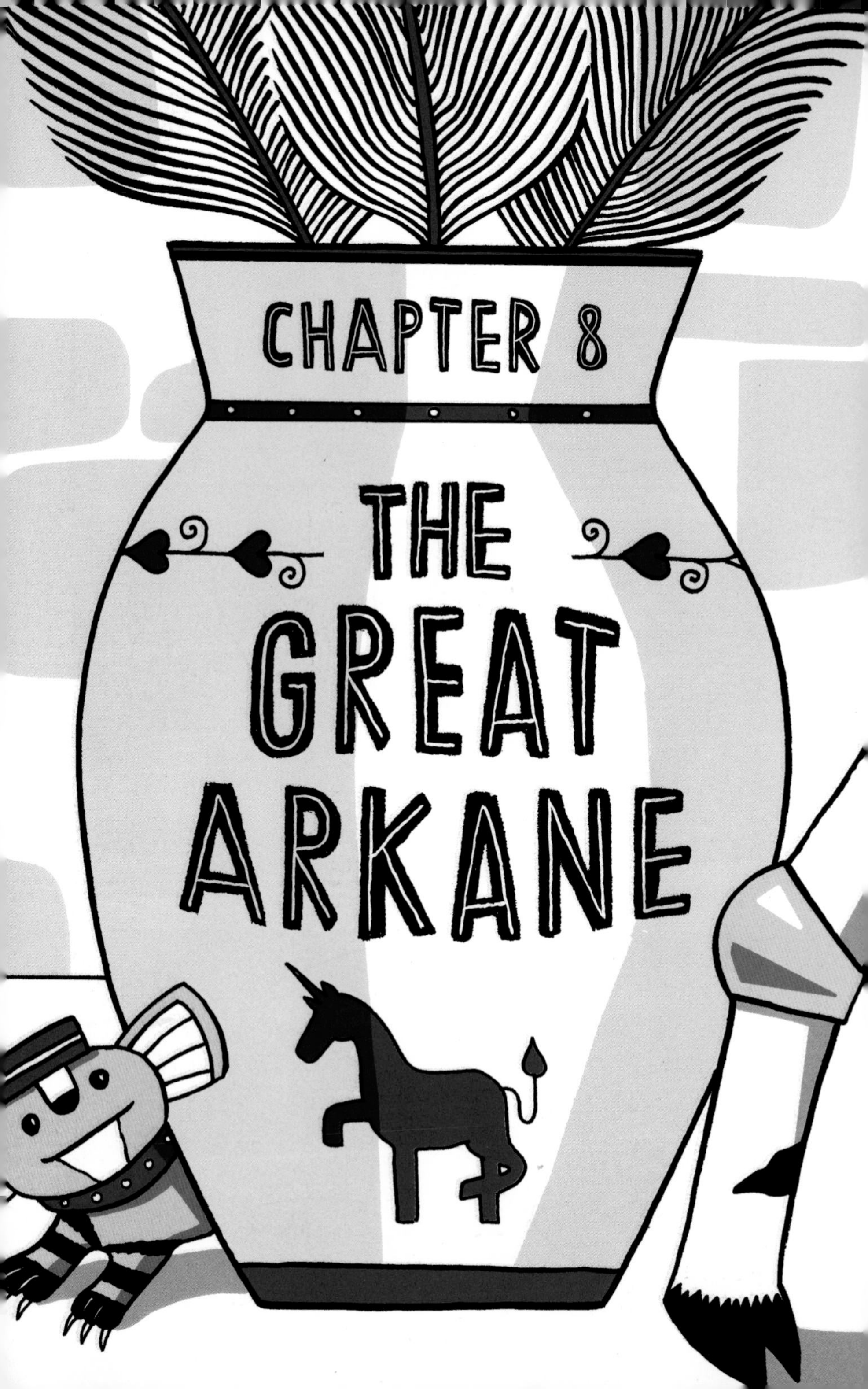

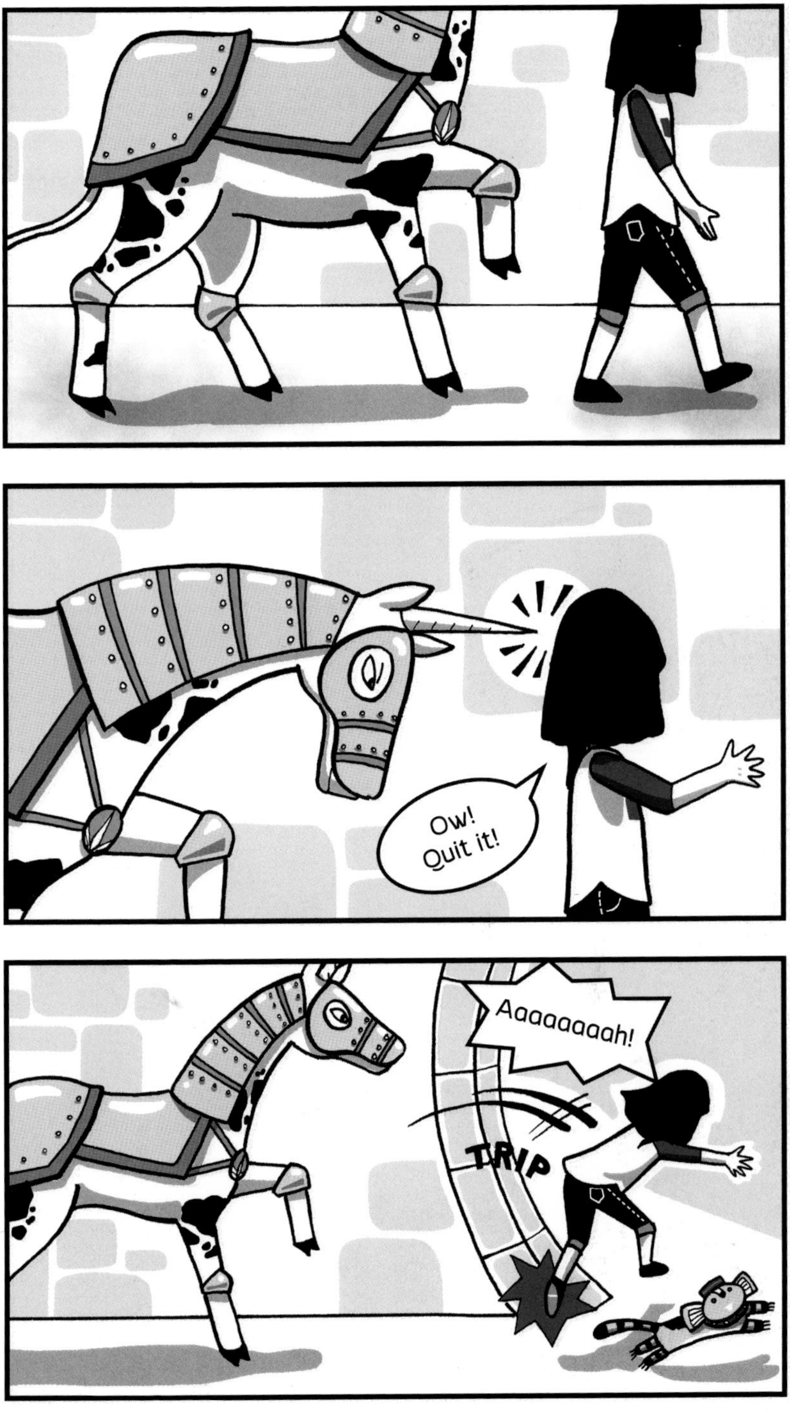
Ow!
Quit it!
Aaaaaaaah!
TRIP

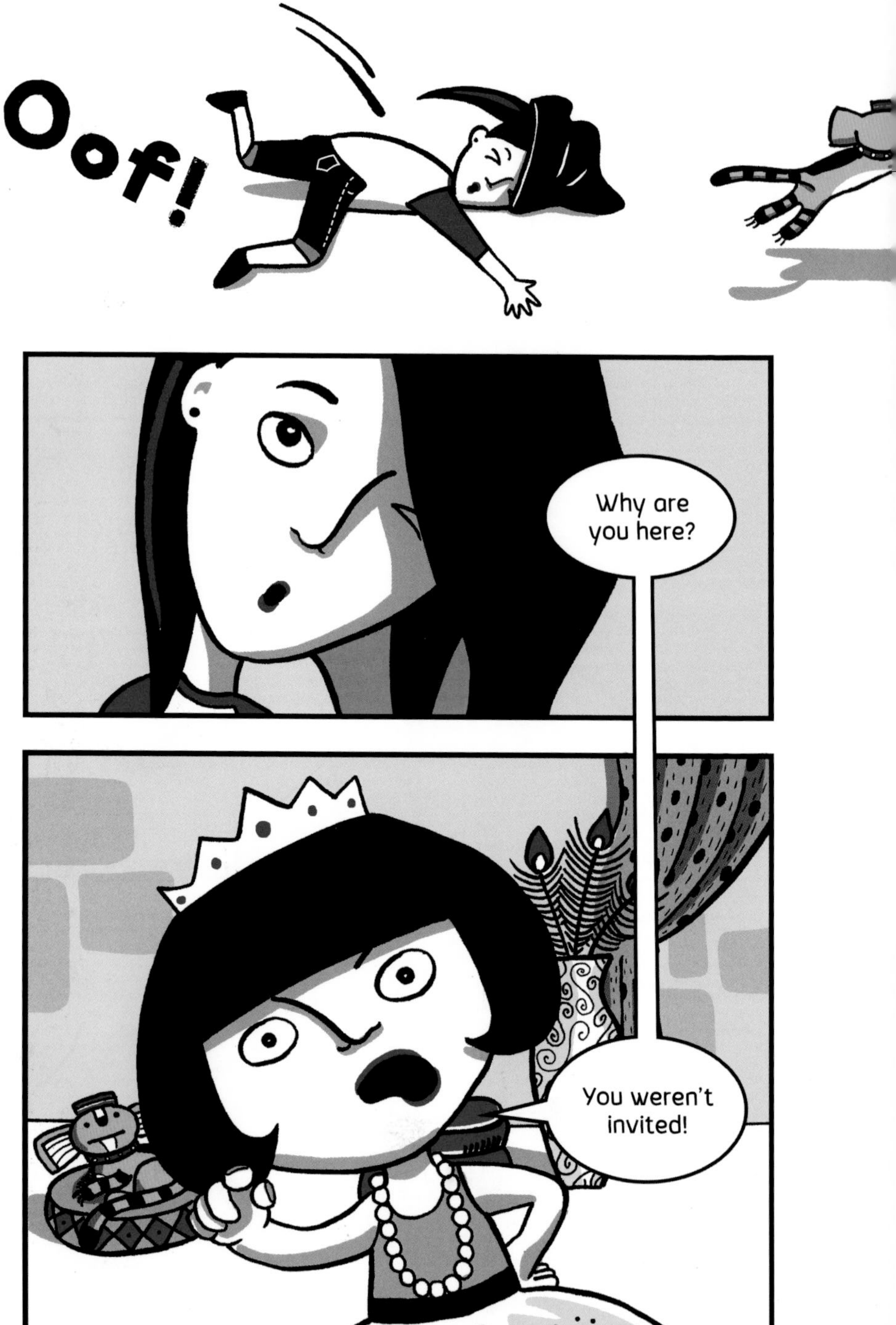
Oof!
Why are you here?
You weren't invited!

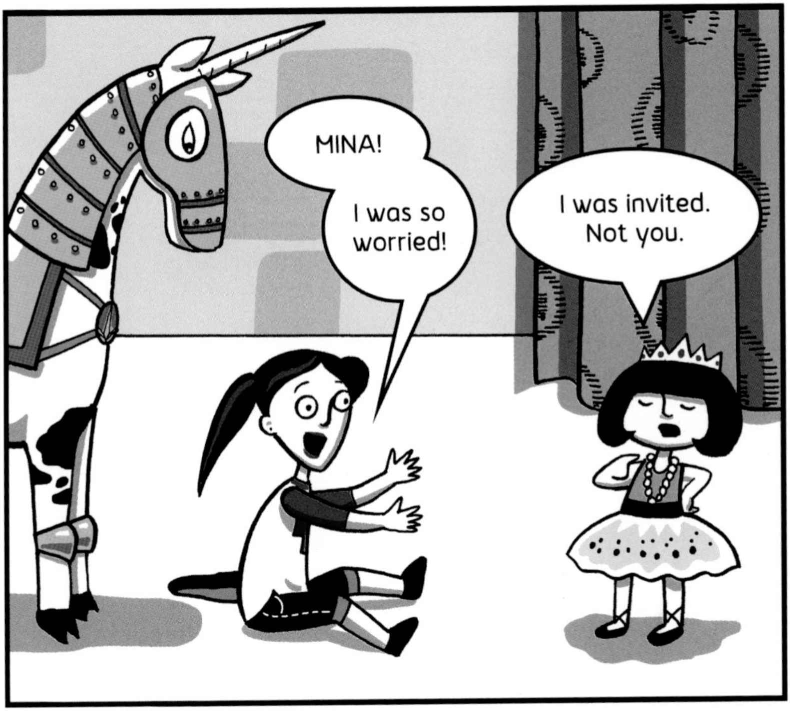
MINA!
I was so worried!
I was invited. Not you.

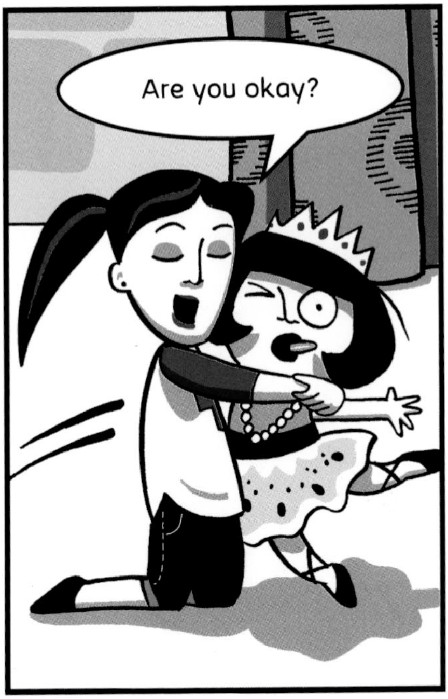
Are you okay?

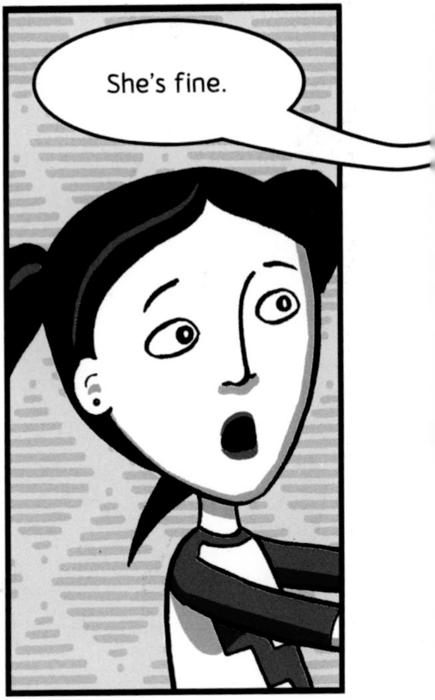
She's fine.

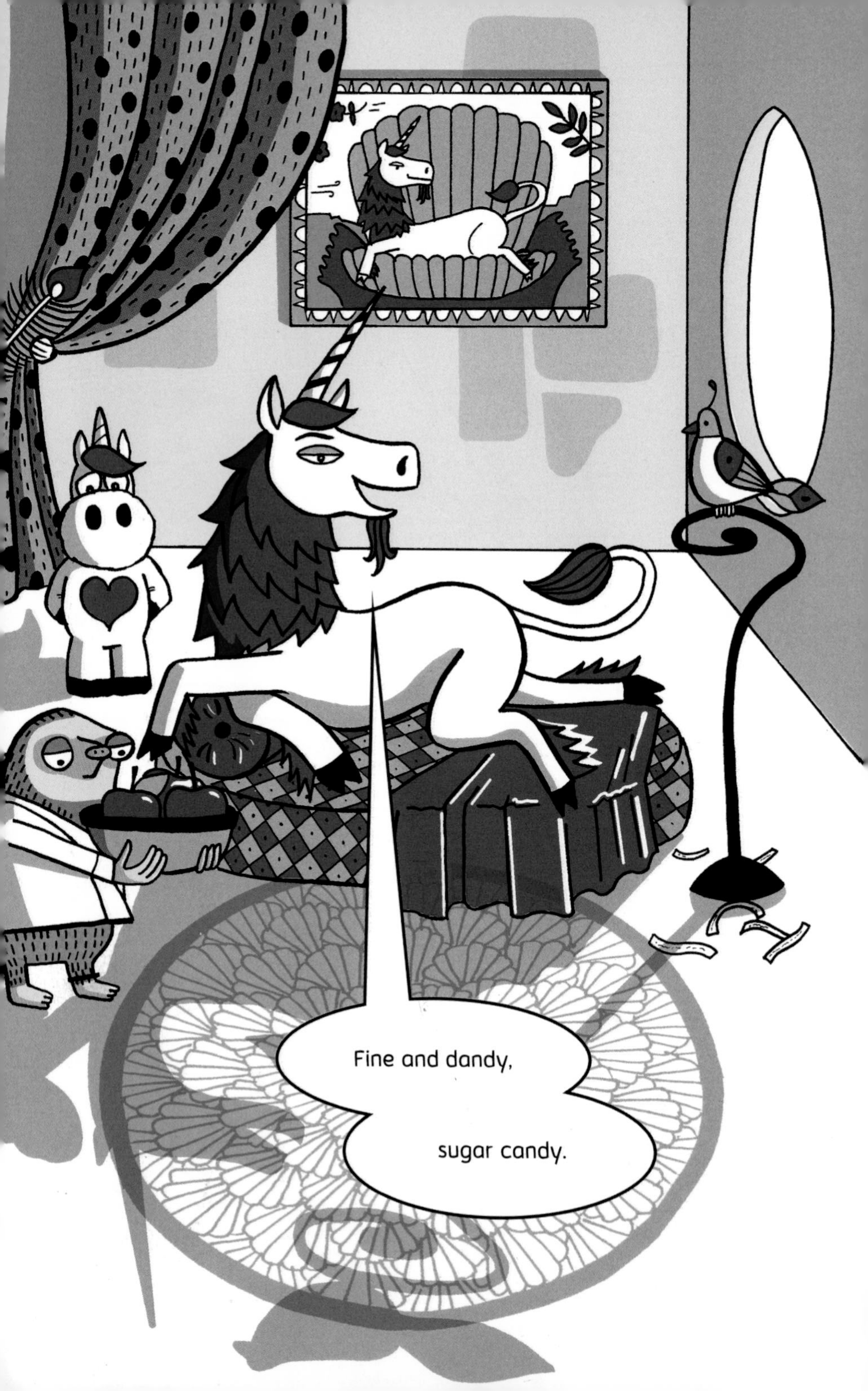
Fine and dandy,
sugar candy.

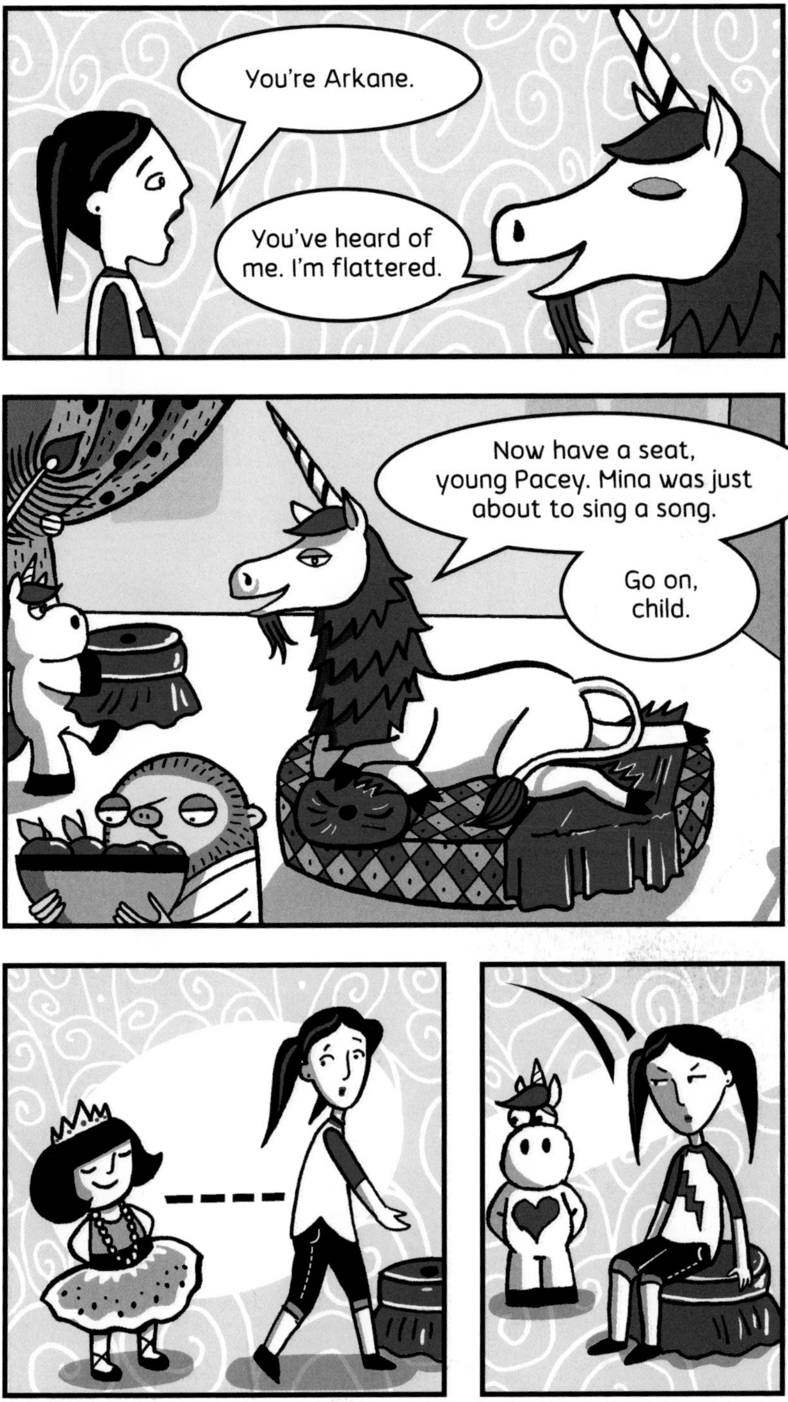

You're Arkane.
You've heard of me. I'm flattered.
Now have a seat, young Pacey. Mina was just about to sing a song.
Go on, child.

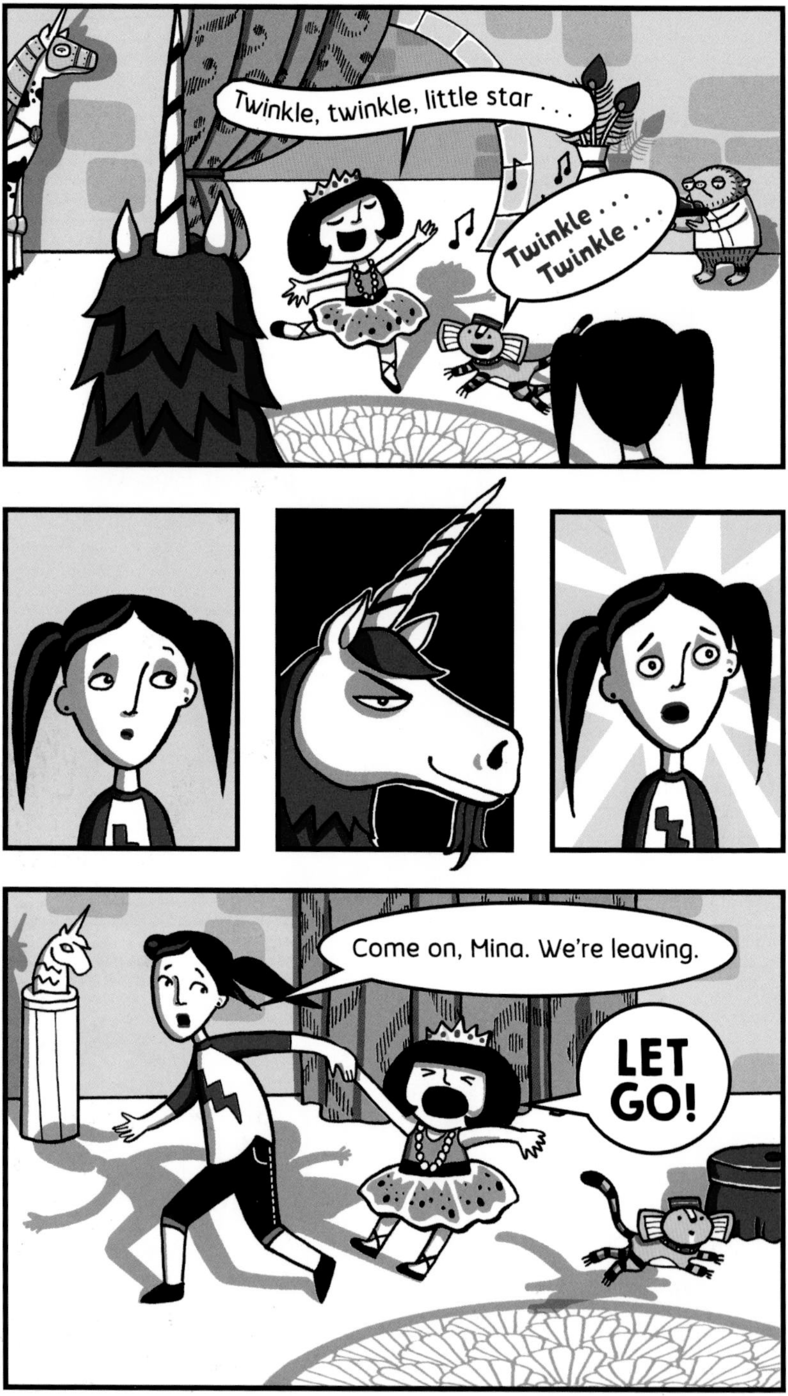
Twinkle, twinkle, little star . . .
Twinkle . . .
Twinkle . . .
Come on, Mina. We're leaving.
LET GO!

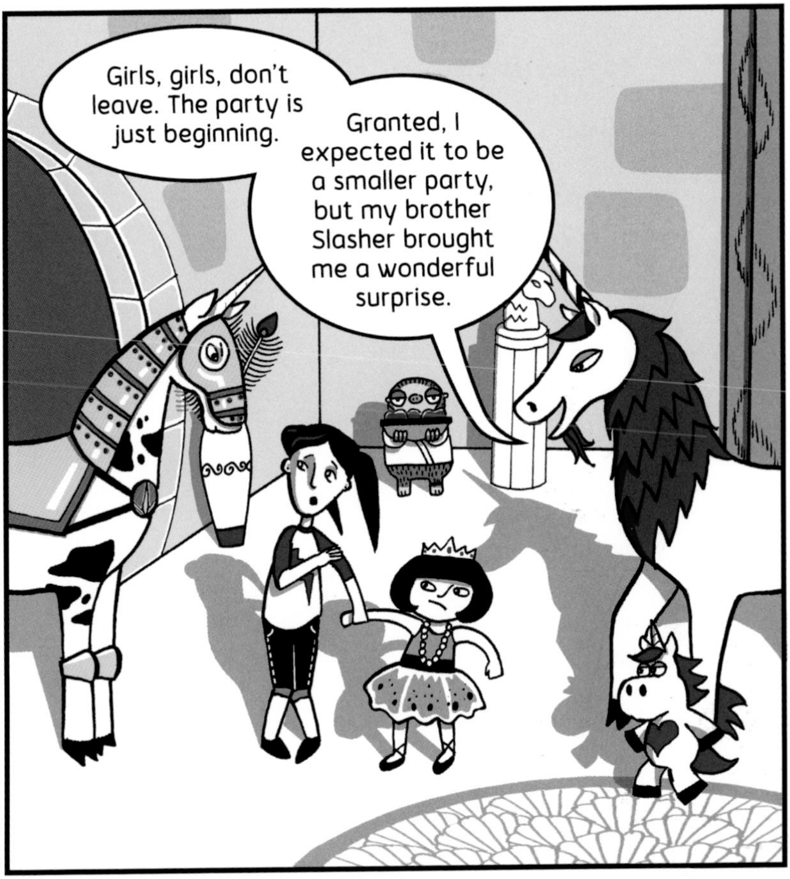
Girls, girls, don't leave. The party is just beginning.
Granted, I expected it to be a smaller party, but my brother Slasher brought me a wonderful surprise.

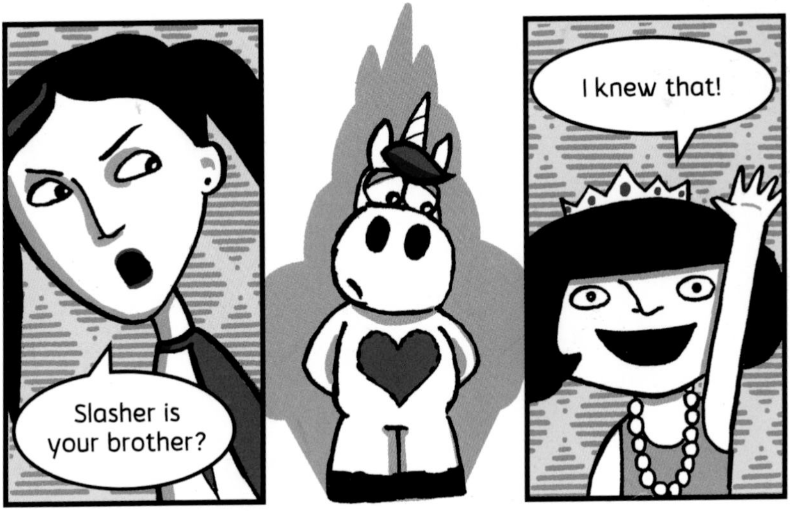
Slasher is your brother?
I knew that!

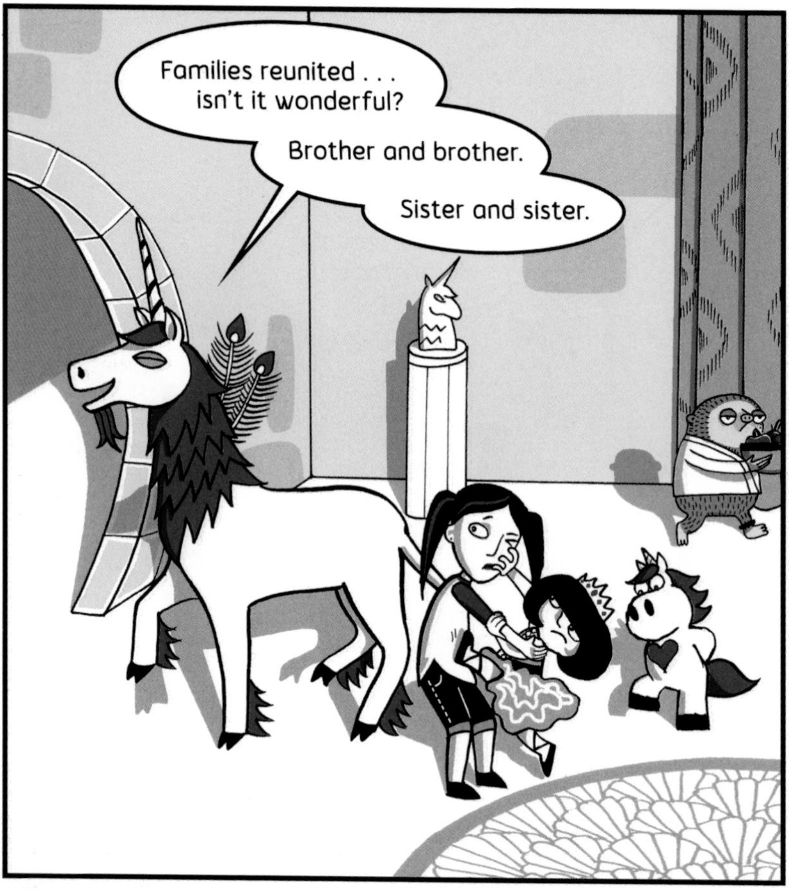
Families reunited . . . isn't it wonderful?
Brother and brother.
Sister and sister.

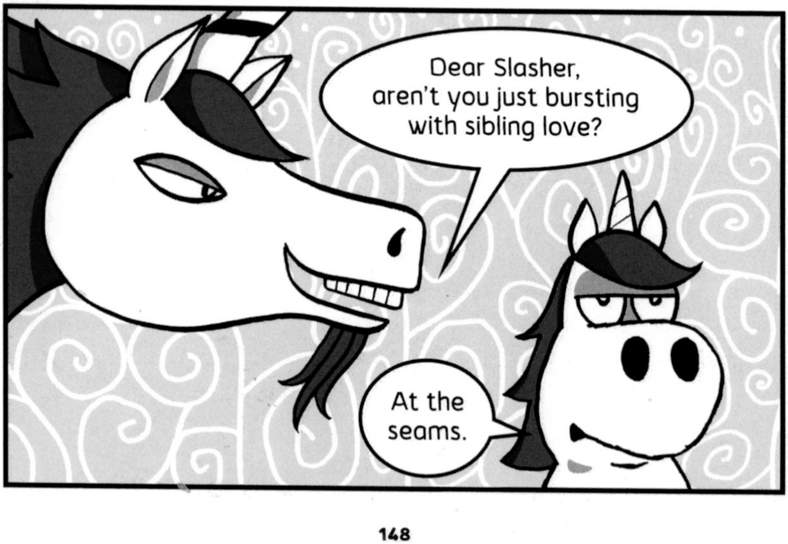
Dear Slasher, aren't you just bursting with sibling love?
At the seams.

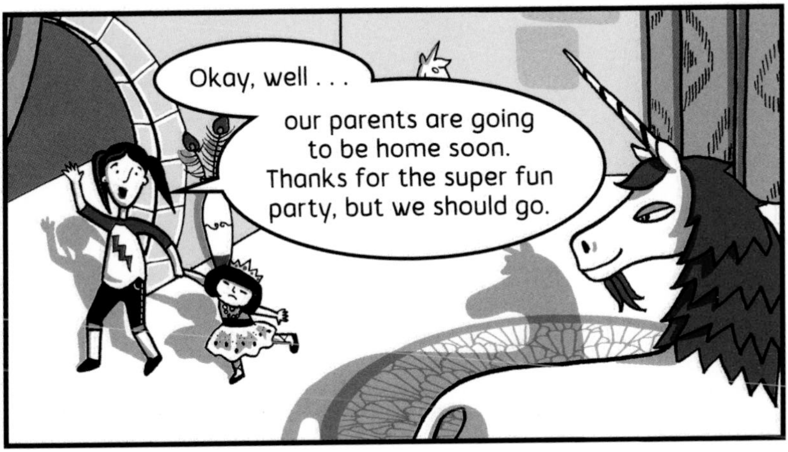
Okay, well . . .
our parents are going to be home soon. Thanks for the super fun party, but we should go.

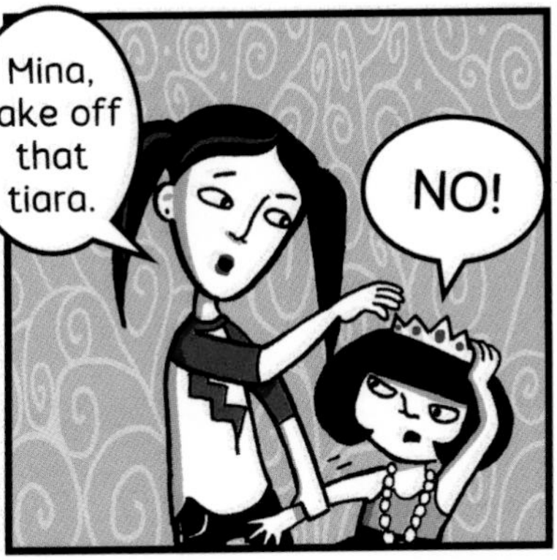
Mina, take off that tiara.
NO!

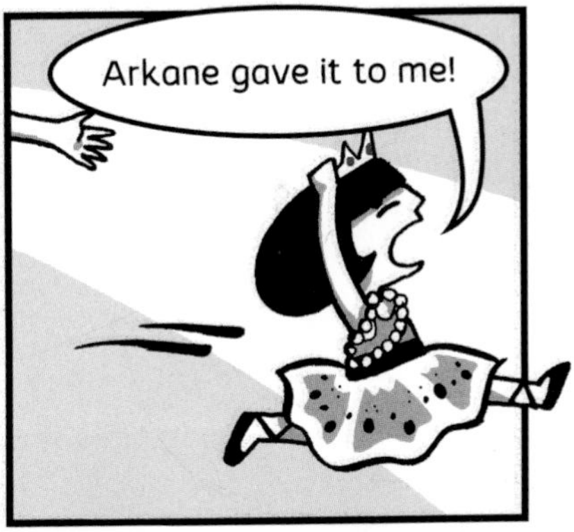
Arkane gave it to me!

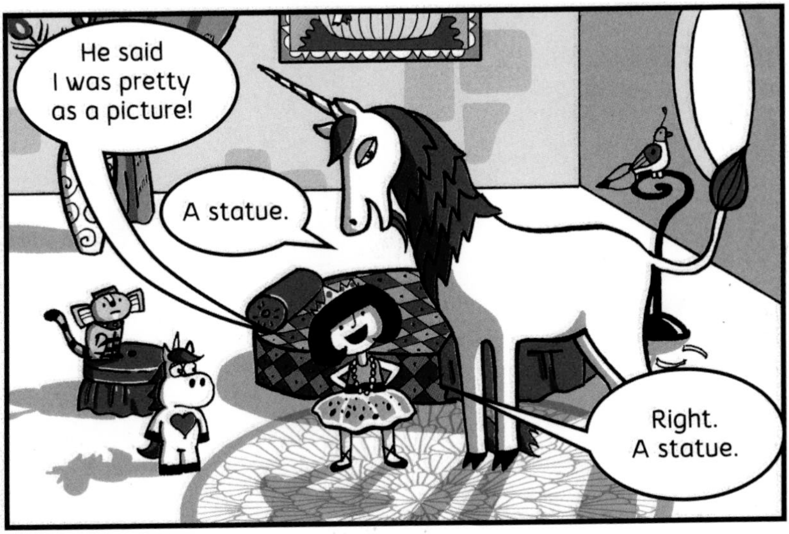
He said I was pretty as a picture!
A statue.
Right. A statue.

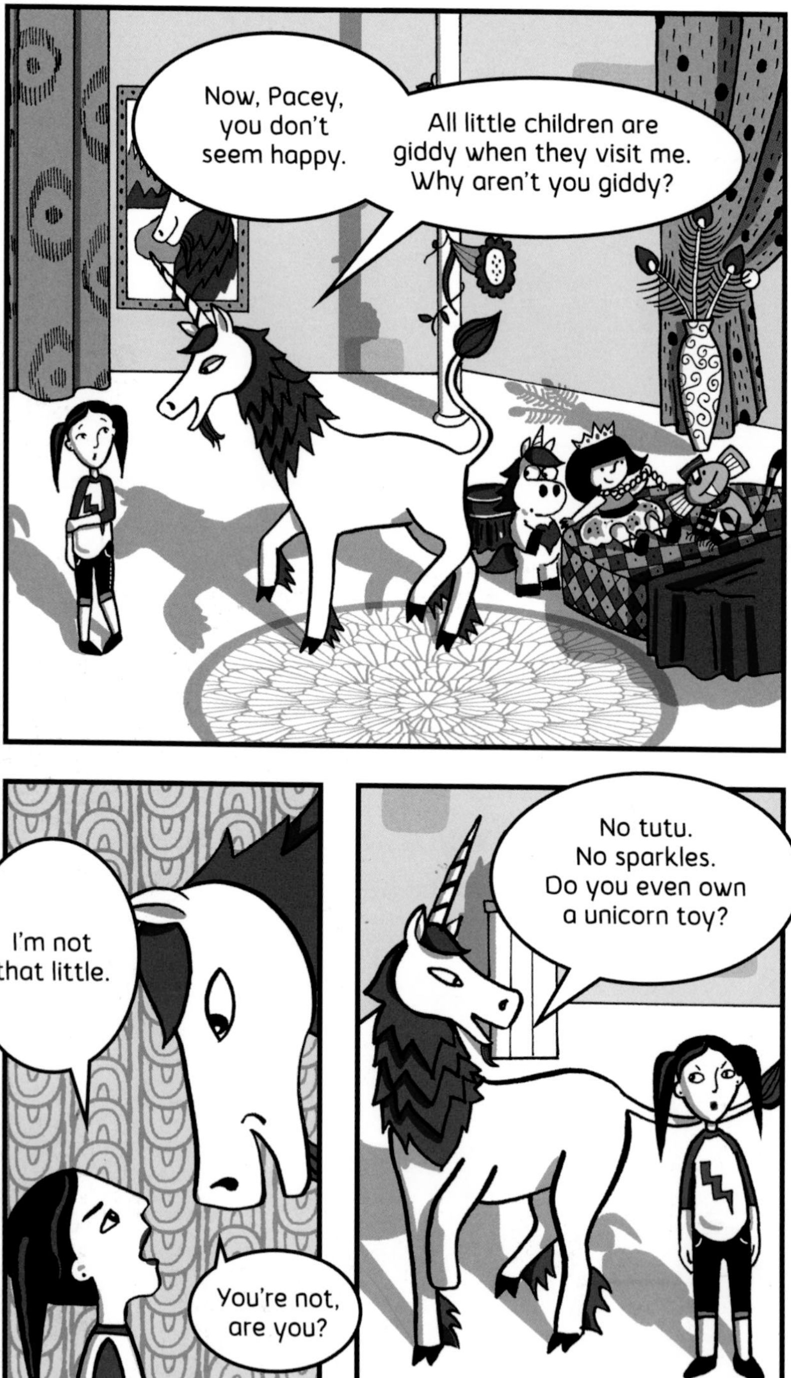
Now, Pacey, you don't seem happy.
All little children are giddy when they visit me. Why aren't you giddy?
I'm not that little.
You're not, are you?
No tutu. No sparkles. Do you even own a unicorn toy?

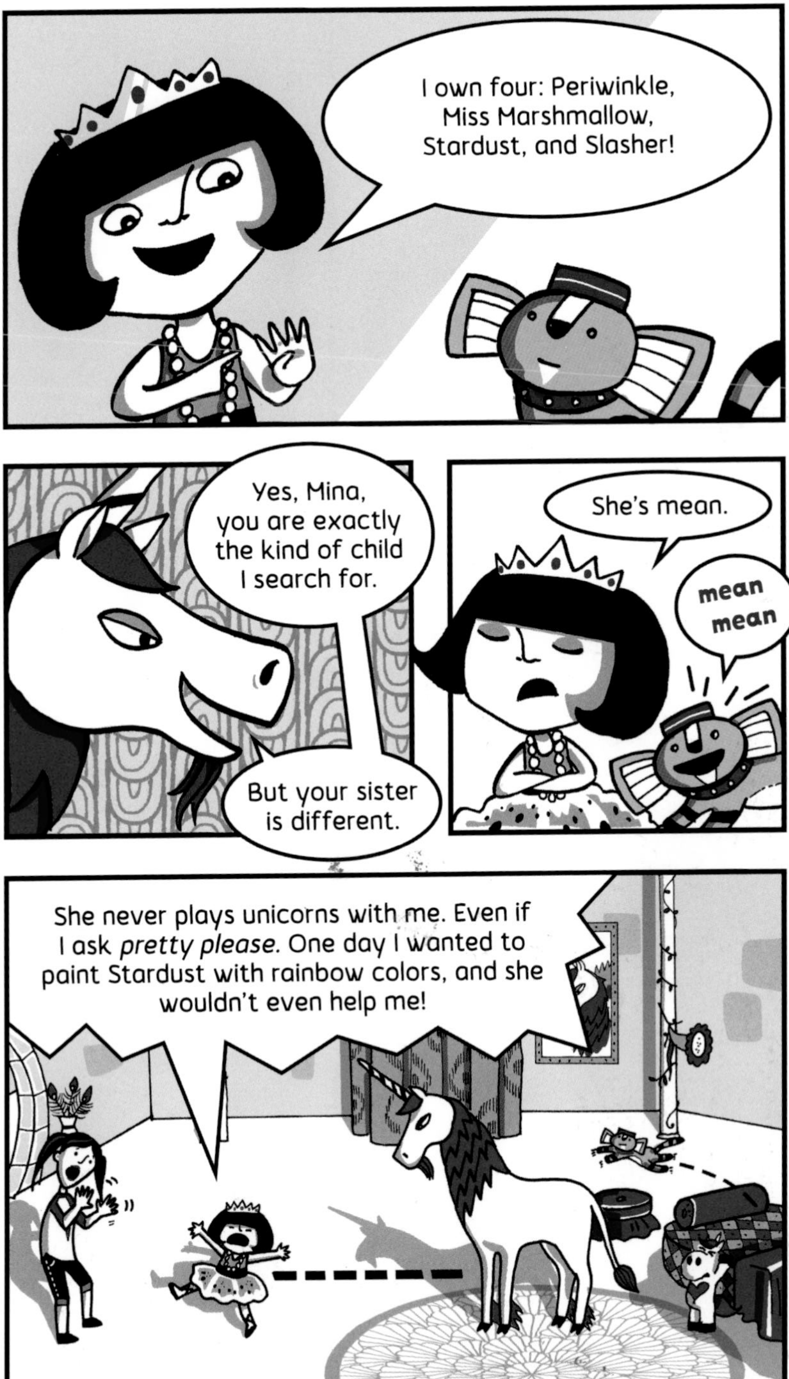
I own four: Periwinkle, Miss Marshmallow, Stardust, and Slasher!
Yes, Mina, you are exactly the kind of child I search for.
But your sister is different.
She's mean.
mean mean
She never plays unicorns with me. Even if I ask *pretty please.* One day I wanted to paint Stardust with rainbow colors, and she wouldn't even help me!

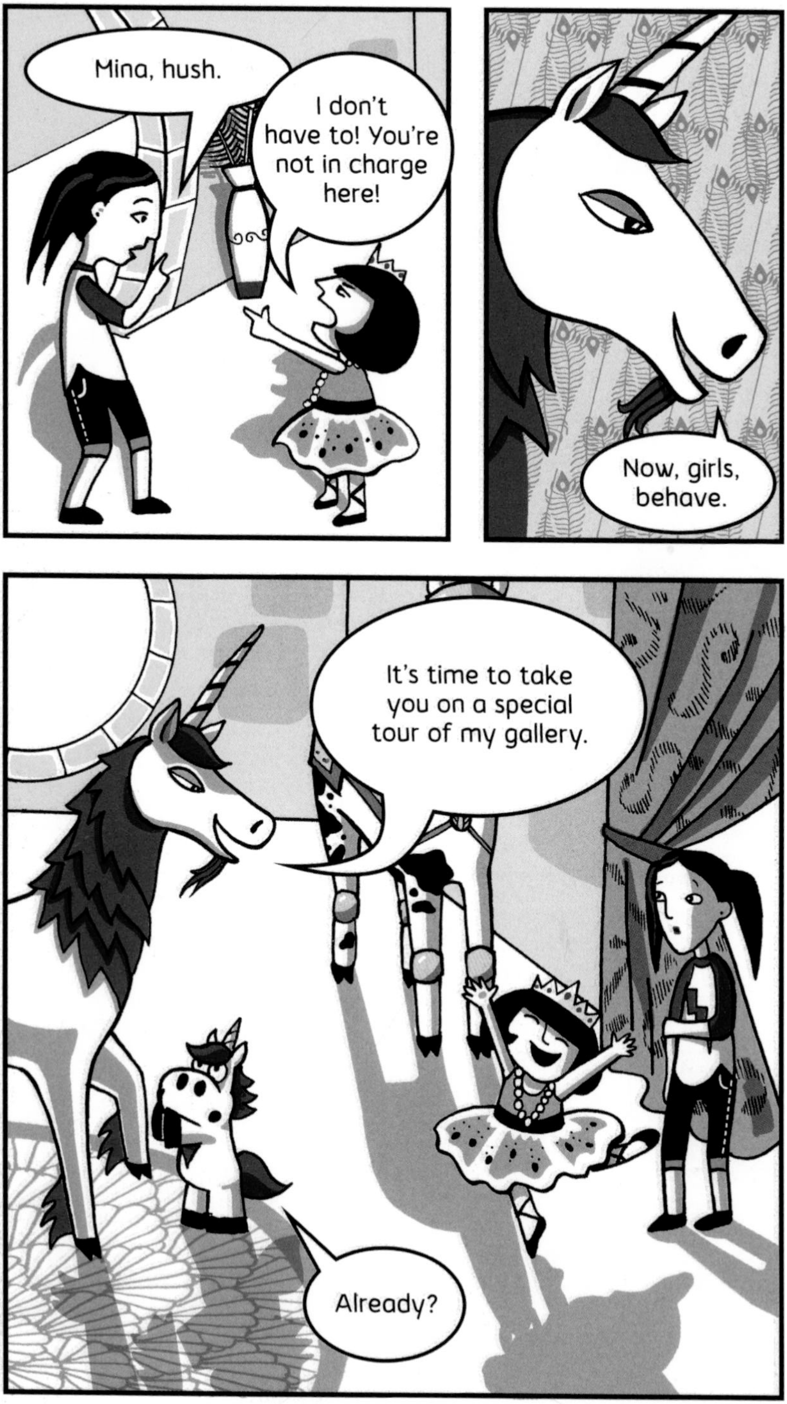
Mina, hush.
I don't have to! You're not in charge here!
Now, girls, behave.
It's time to take you on a special tour of my gallery.
Already?

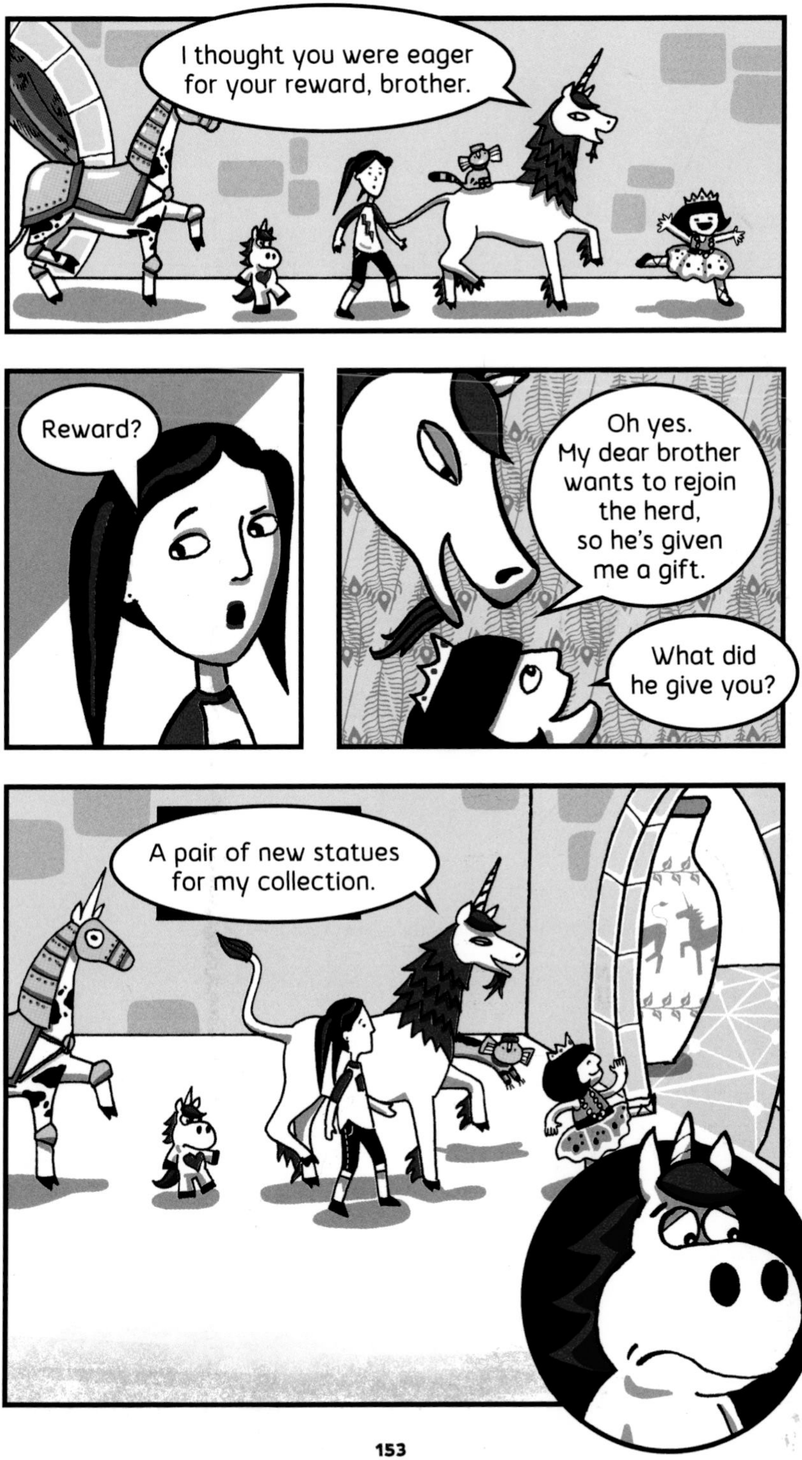

I thought you were eager for your reward, brother.
Reward?
Oh yes. My dear brother wants to rejoin the herd, so he's given me a gift.
What did he give you?
A pair of new statues for my collection.

CHAPTER 9
STONE COLD

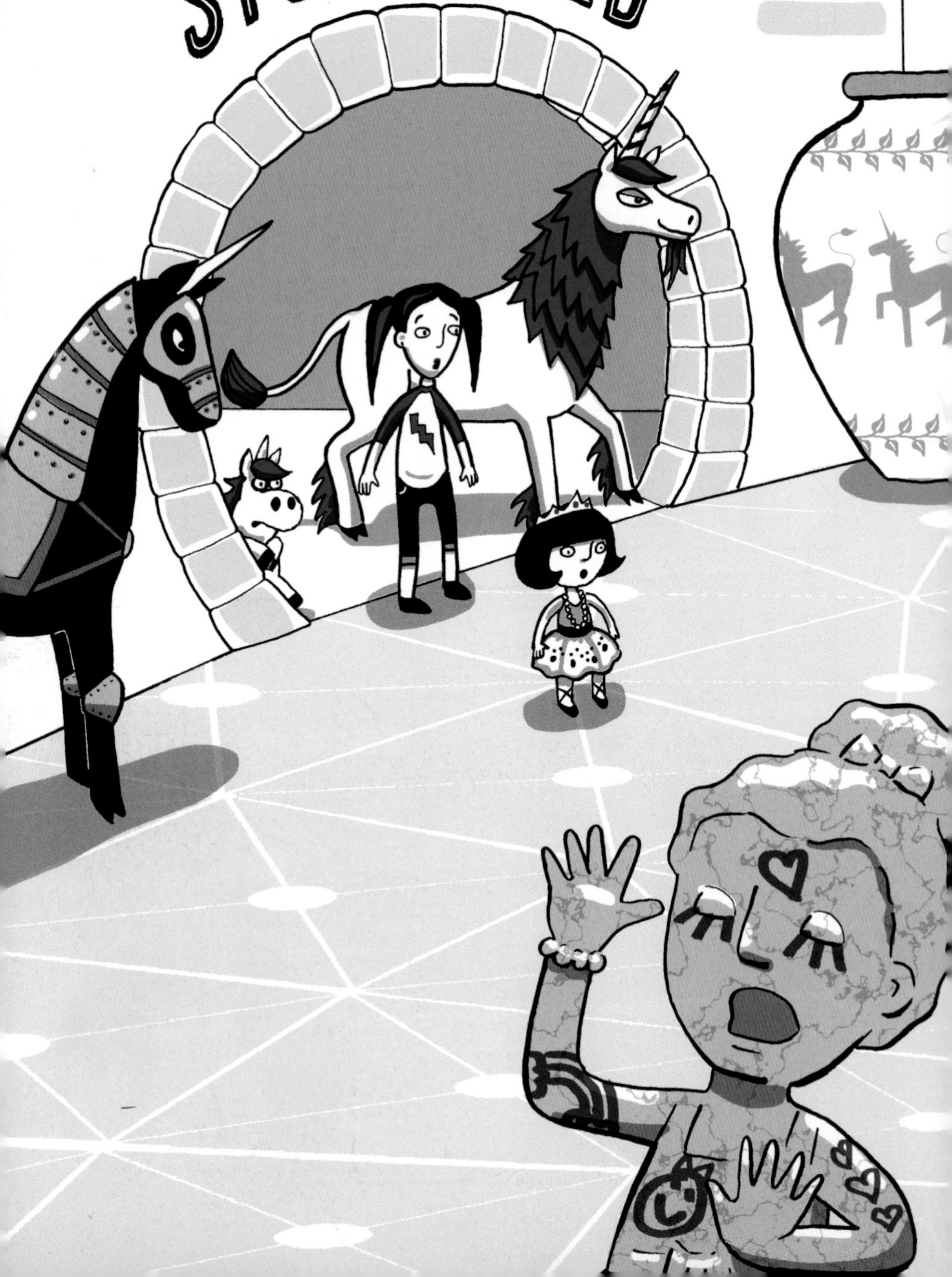

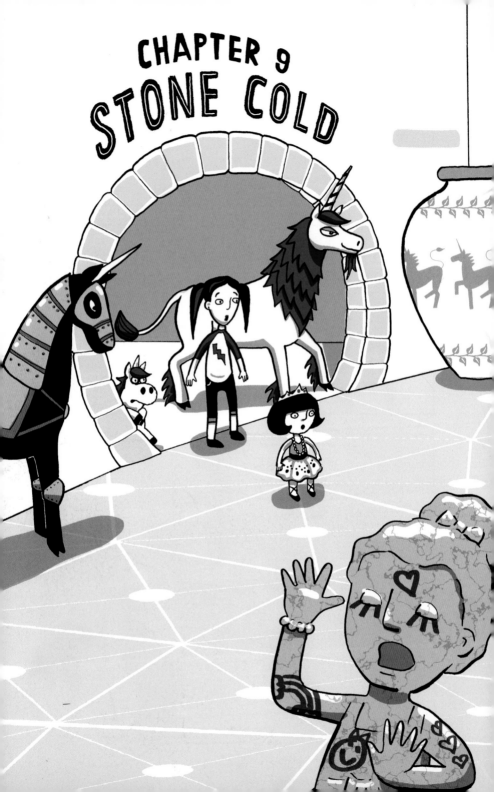

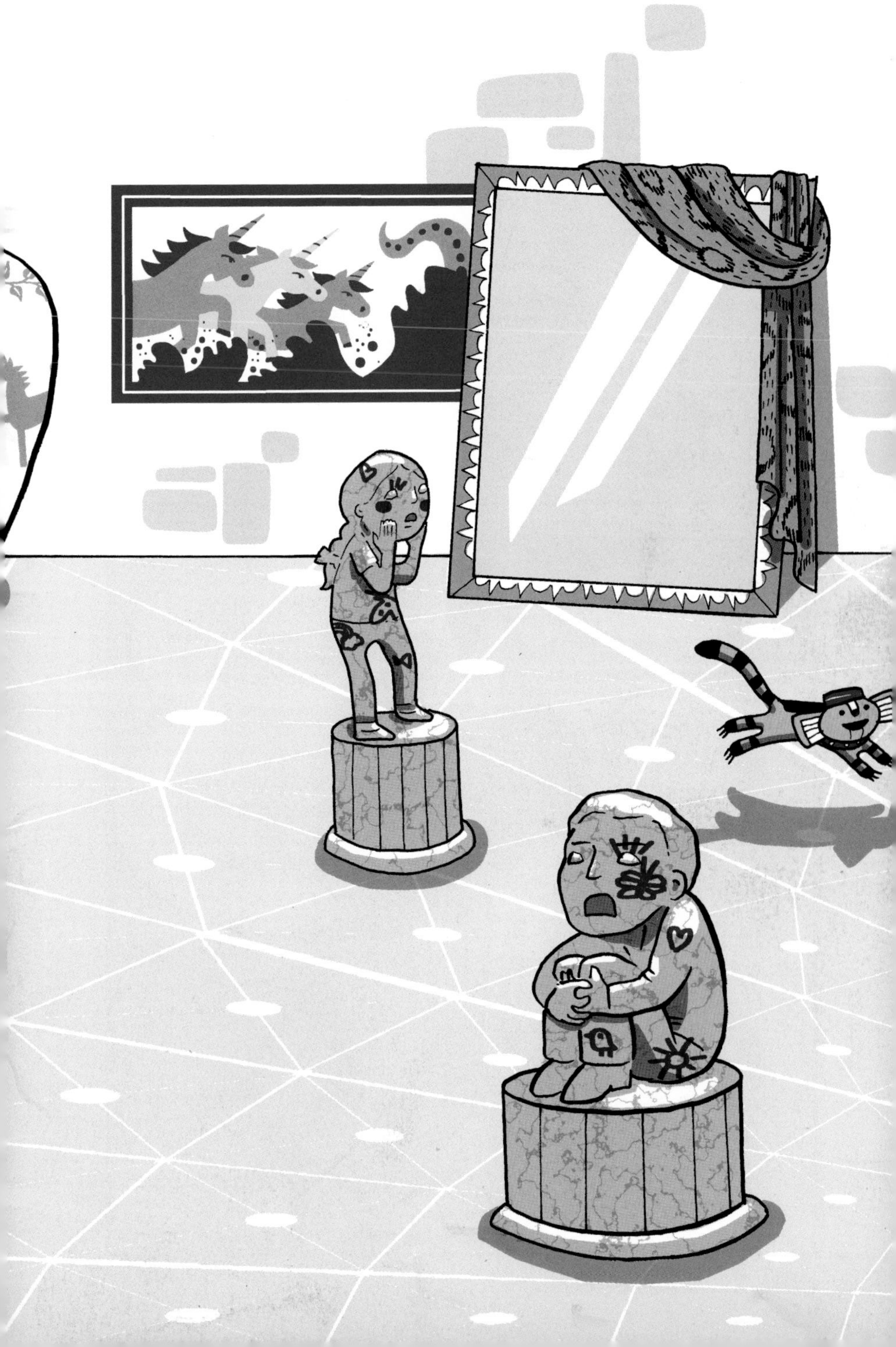

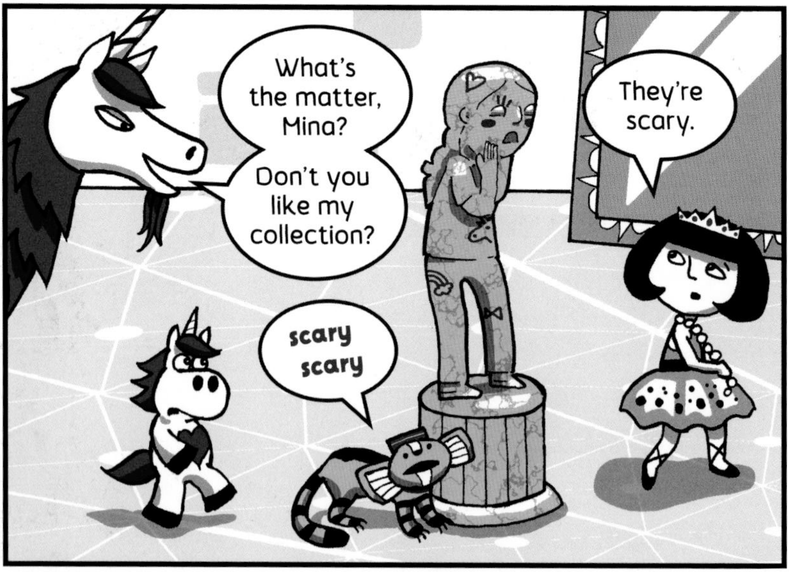
What's the matter, Mina?
Don't you like my collection?
They're scary.
scary scary

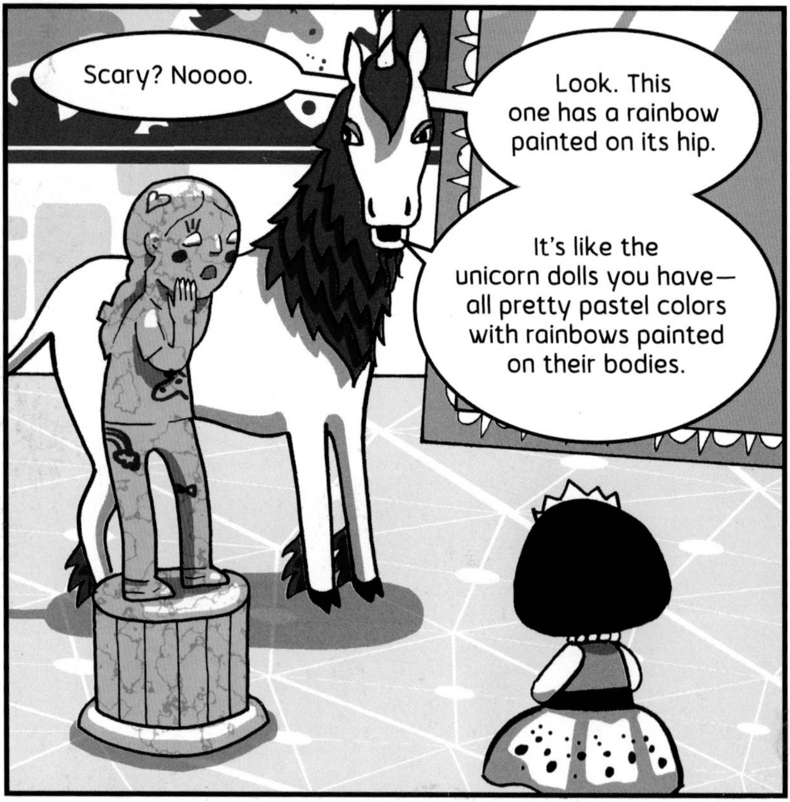
Scary? Noooo.
Look. This one has a rainbow painted on its hip.
It's like the unicorn dolls you have—all pretty pastel colors with rainbows painted on their bodies.

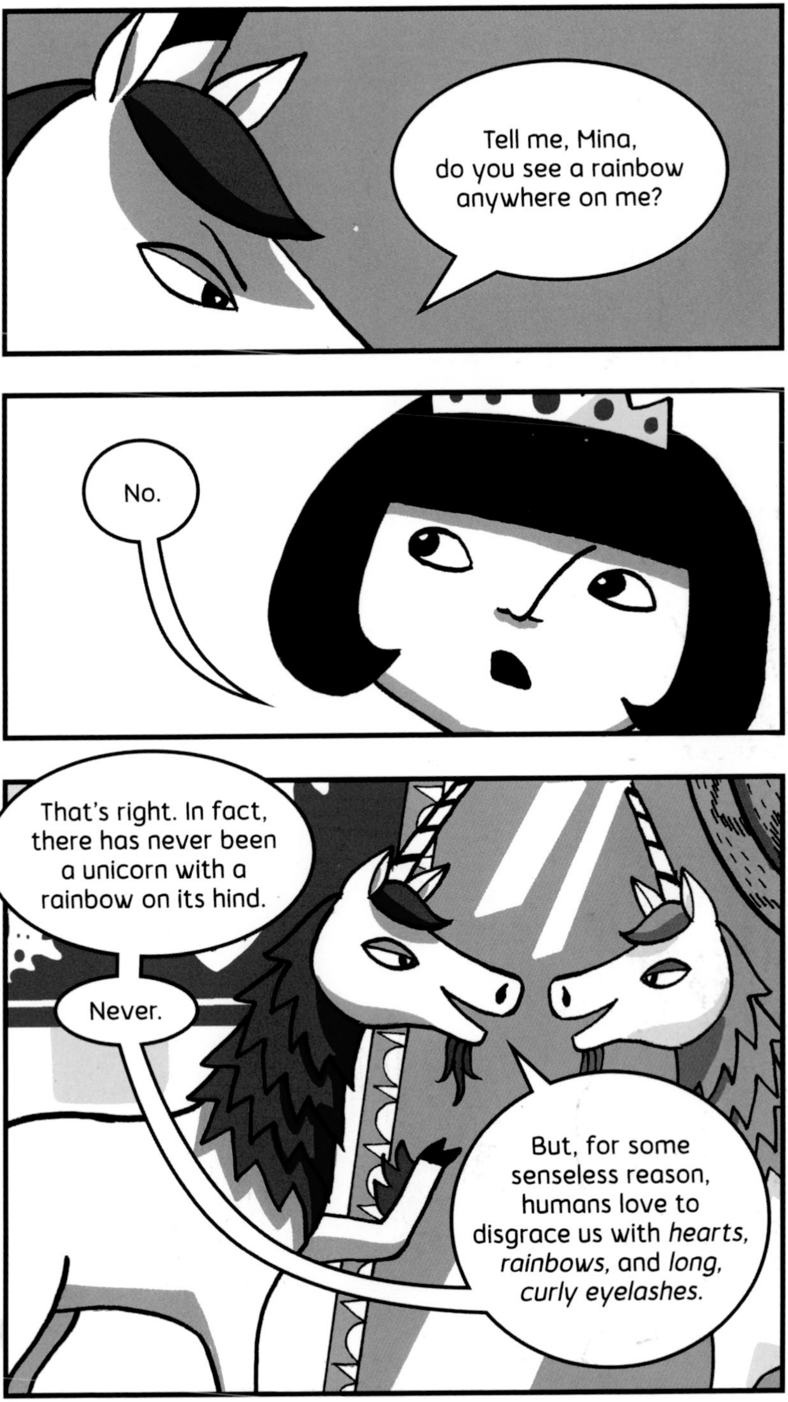
Tell me, Mina, do you see a rainbow anywhere on me?
No.
That's right. In fact, there has never been a unicorn with a rainbow on its hind.
Never.
But, for some senseless reason, humans love to disgrace us with *hearts*, *rainbows*, and *long, curly eyelashes*.

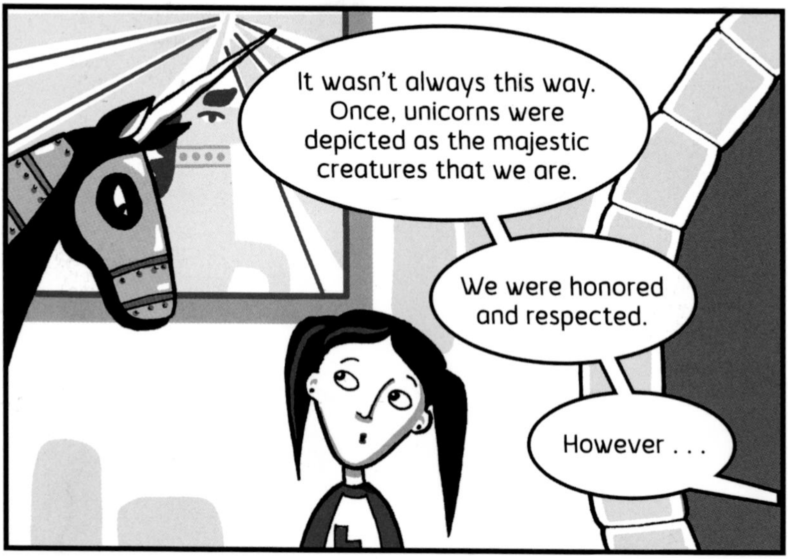
It wasn't always this way. Once, unicorns were depicted as the majestic creatures that we are.
We were honored and respected.
However . . .

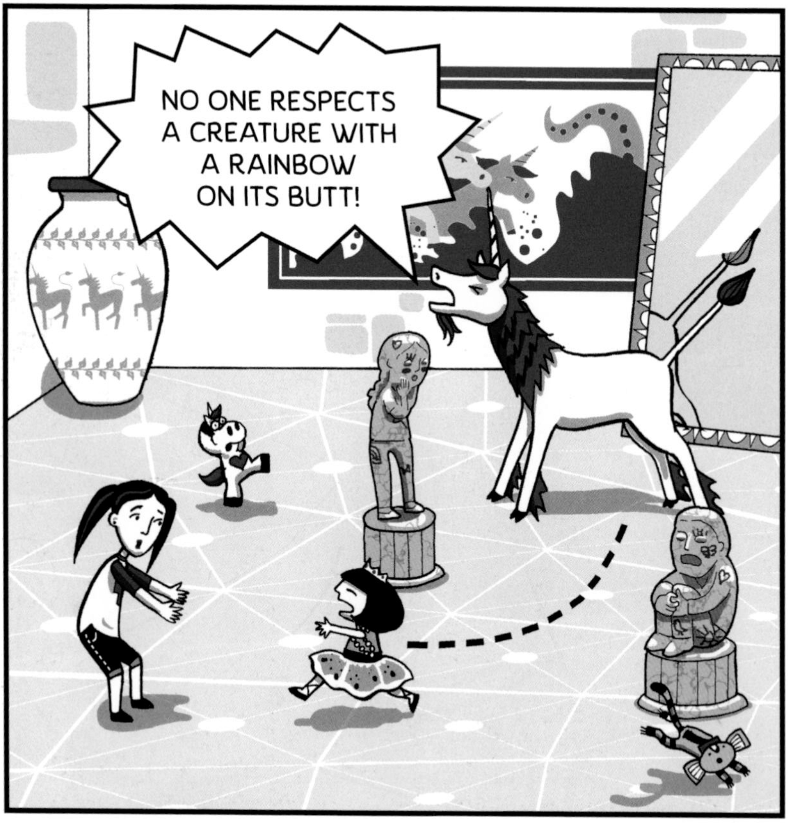
NO ONE RESPECTS A CREATURE WITH A RAINBOW ON ITS BUTT!

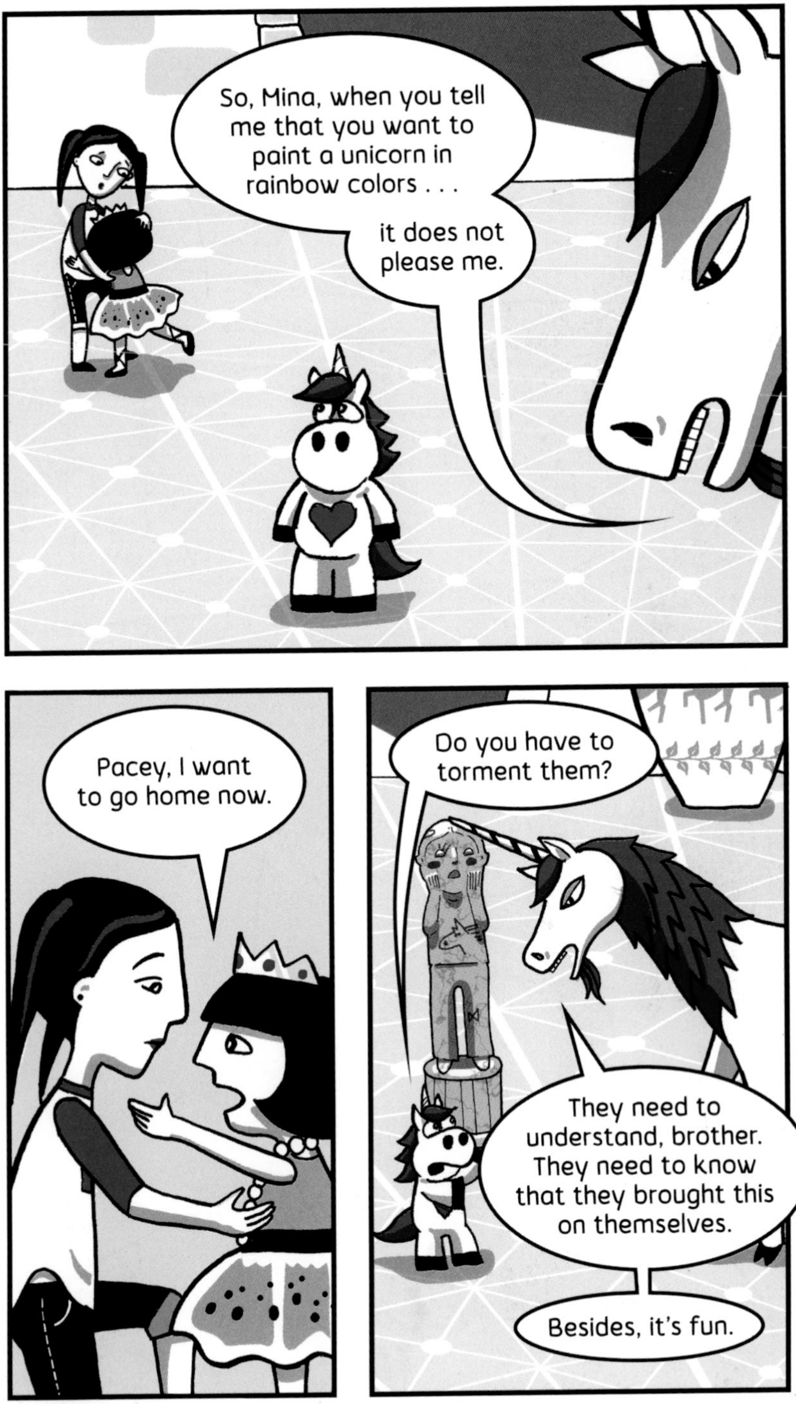
So, Mina, when you tell me that you want to paint a unicorn in rainbow colors . . .
it does not please me.
Pacey, I want to go home now.
Do you have to torment them?
They need to understand, brother. They need to know that they brought this on themselves.
Besides, it's fun.

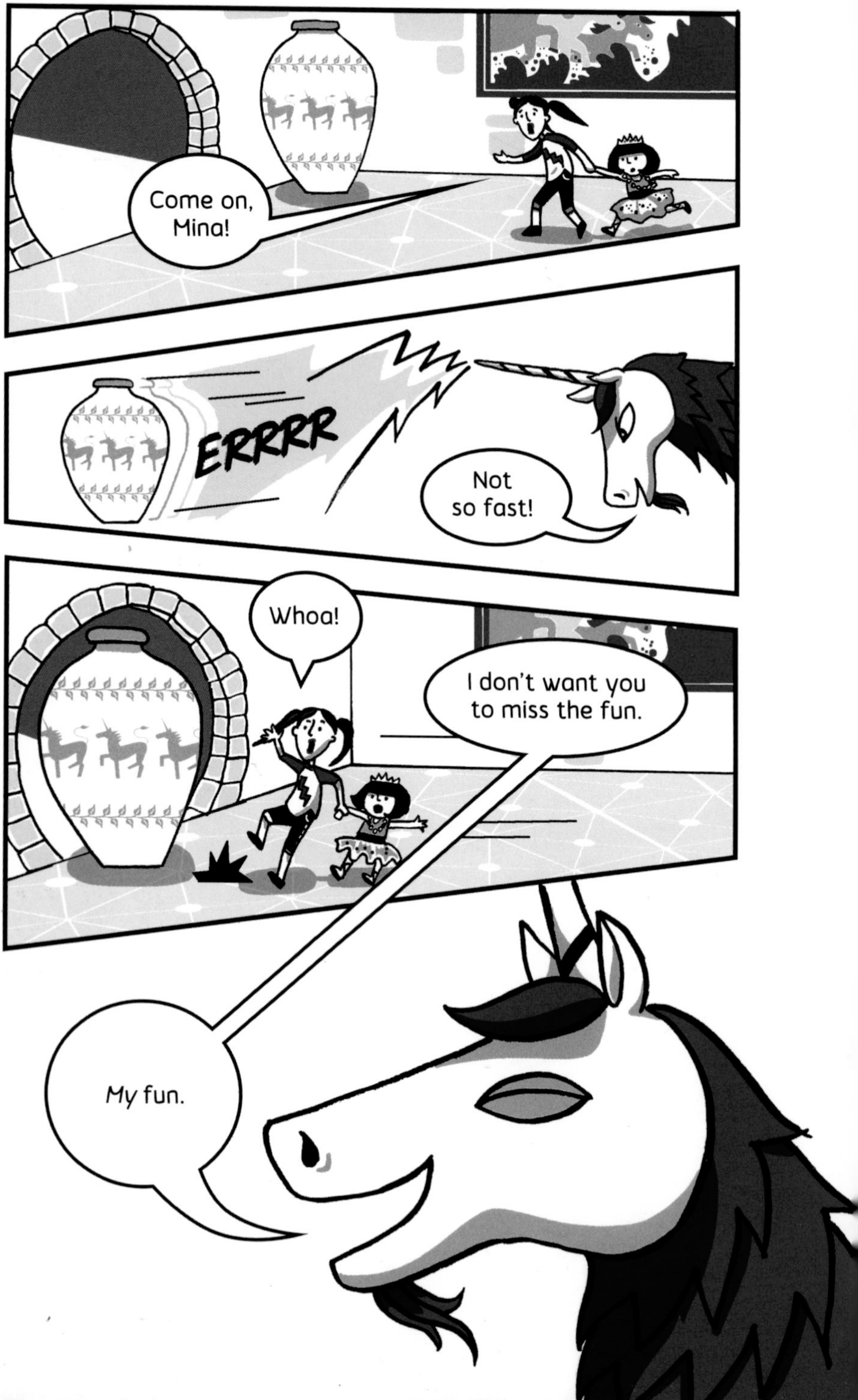
Come on, Mina!
ERRRR
Not so fast!
Whoa!
I don't want you to miss the fun.
My fun.

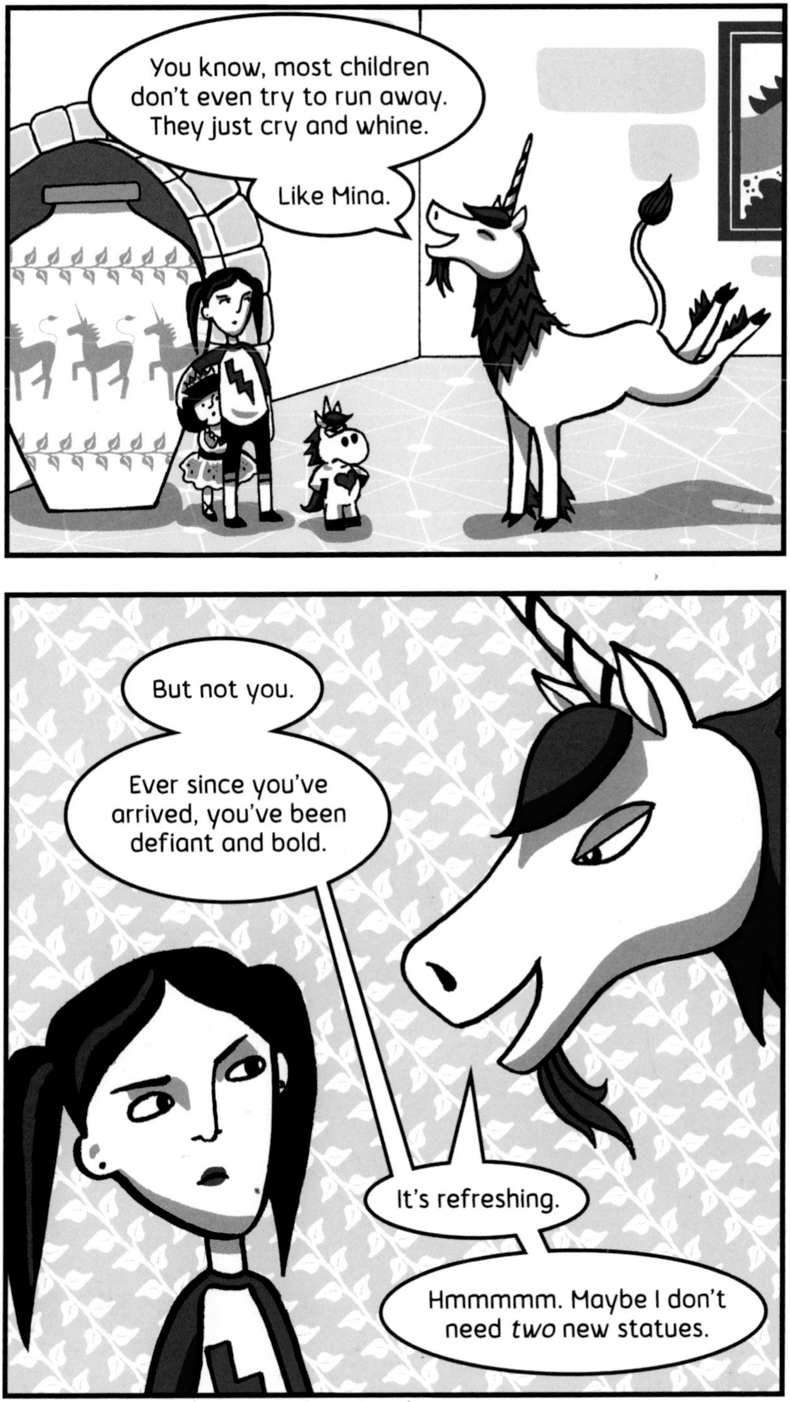
You know, most children don't even try to run away. They just cry and whine.
Like Mina.
But not you.
Ever since you've arrived, you've been defiant and bold.
It's refreshing.
Hmmmmm. Maybe I don't need *two* new statues.

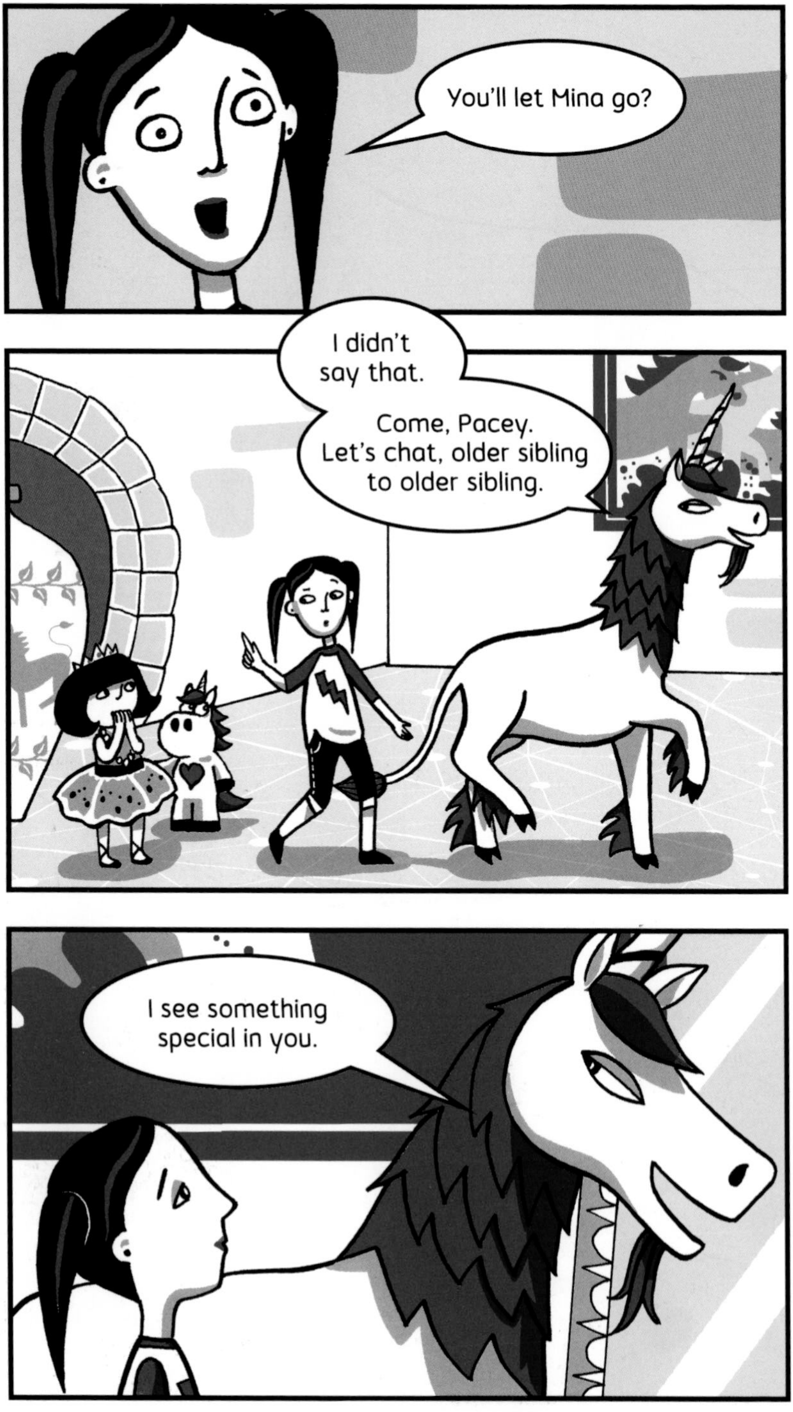
You'll let Mina go?
I didn't say that.
Come, Pacey. Let's chat, older sibling to older sibling.
I see something special in you.

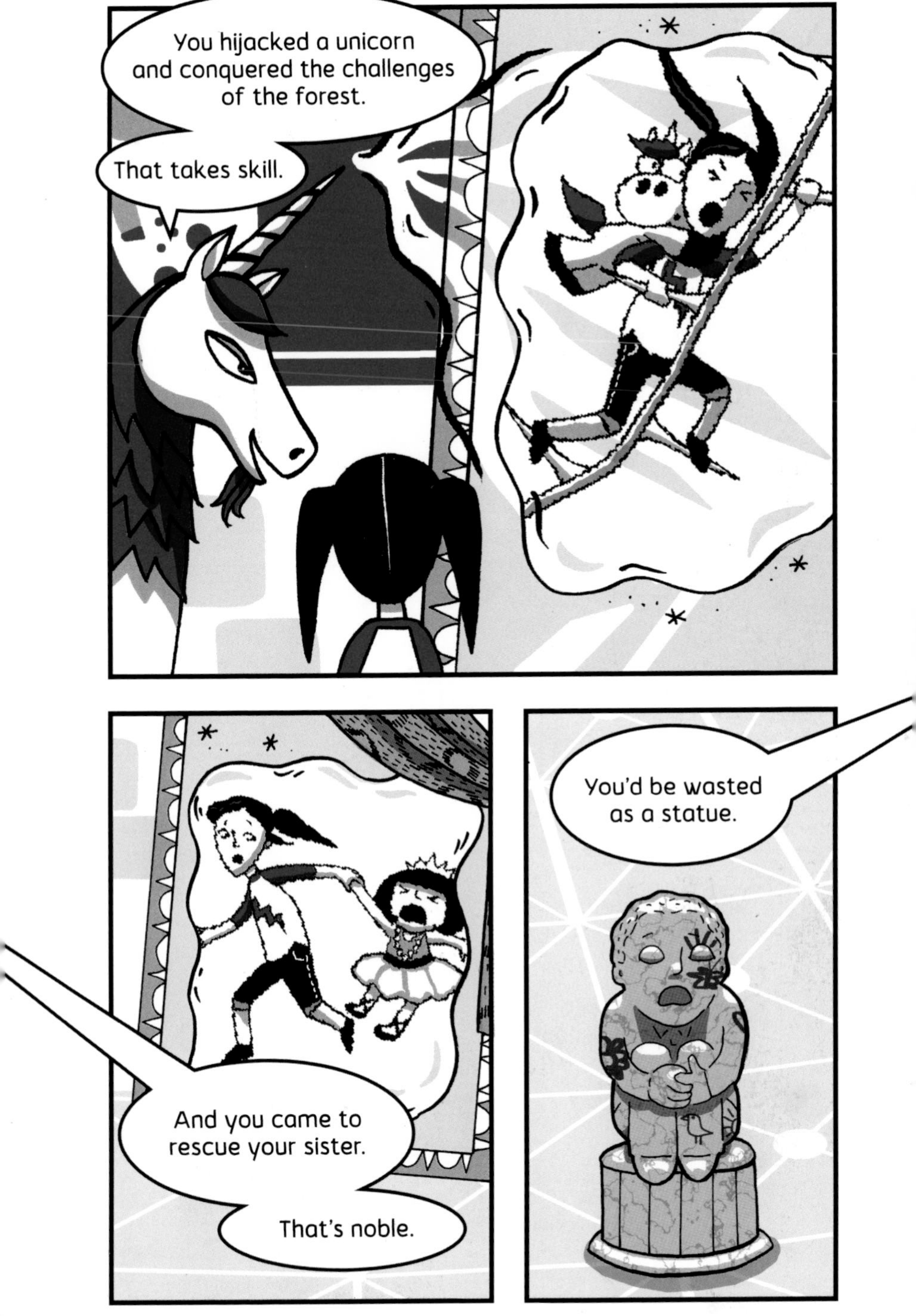
You hijacked a unicorn and conquered the challenges of the forest.
That takes skill.
And you came to rescue your sister.
That's noble.
You'd be wasted as a statue.

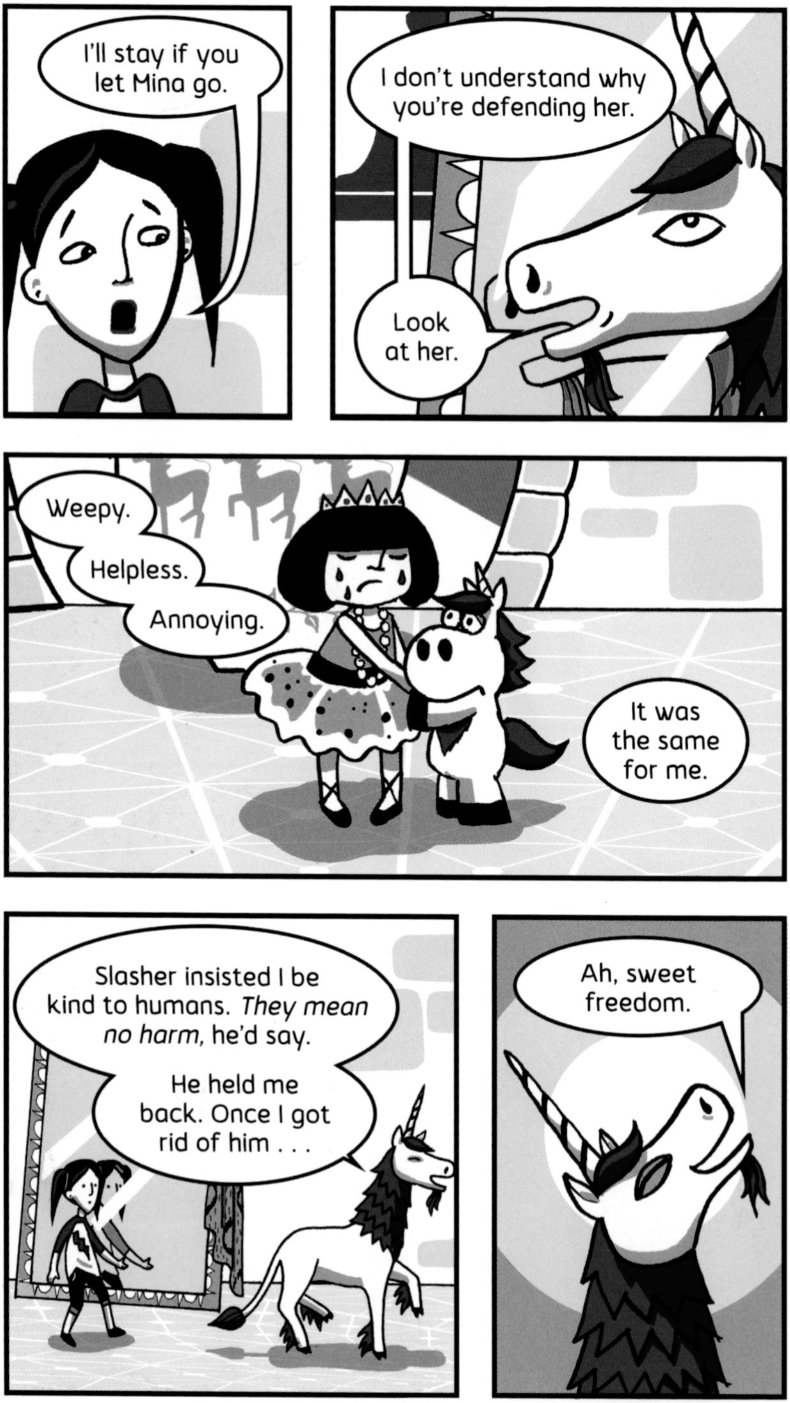
I'll stay if you let Mina go.
I don't understand why you're defending her.
Look at her.
Weepy.
Helpless.
Annoying.
It was the same for me.
Slasher insisted I be kind to humans. *They mean no harm,* he'd say.
He held me back. Once I got rid of him . . .
Ah, sweet freedom.

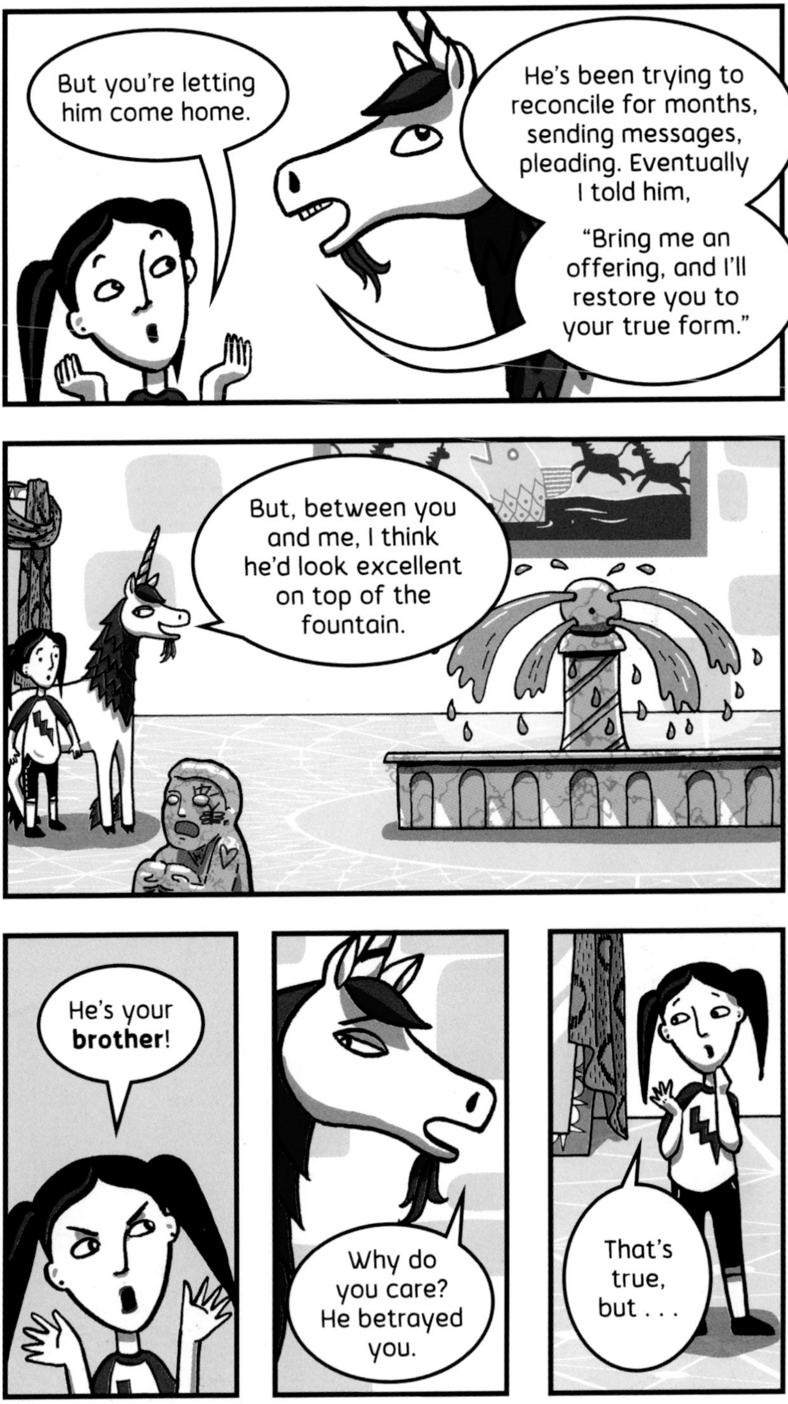
But you're letting him come home.
He's been trying to reconcile for months, sending messages, pleading. Eventually I told him,
"Bring me an offering, and I'll restore you to your true form."
But, between you and me, I think he'd look excellent on top of the fountain.
He's your **brother**!
Why do you care? He betrayed you.
That's true, but . . .

Shhhh. It's going to be okay.
I understand you, Pacey. You are valiant, like me.
You need the freedom to—
I'm not like you! I love my sister!
You can't stand her.
That's not true! I—
Bored now.
Mina, strike a pose.

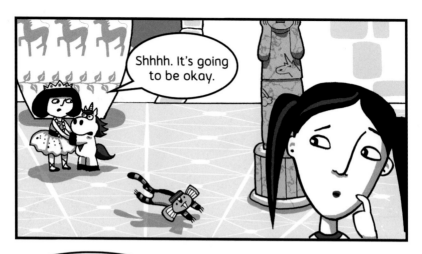

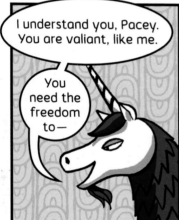

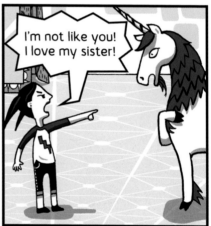

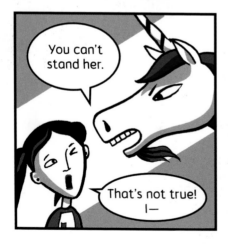

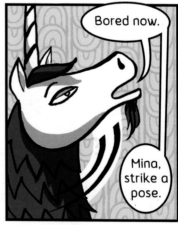

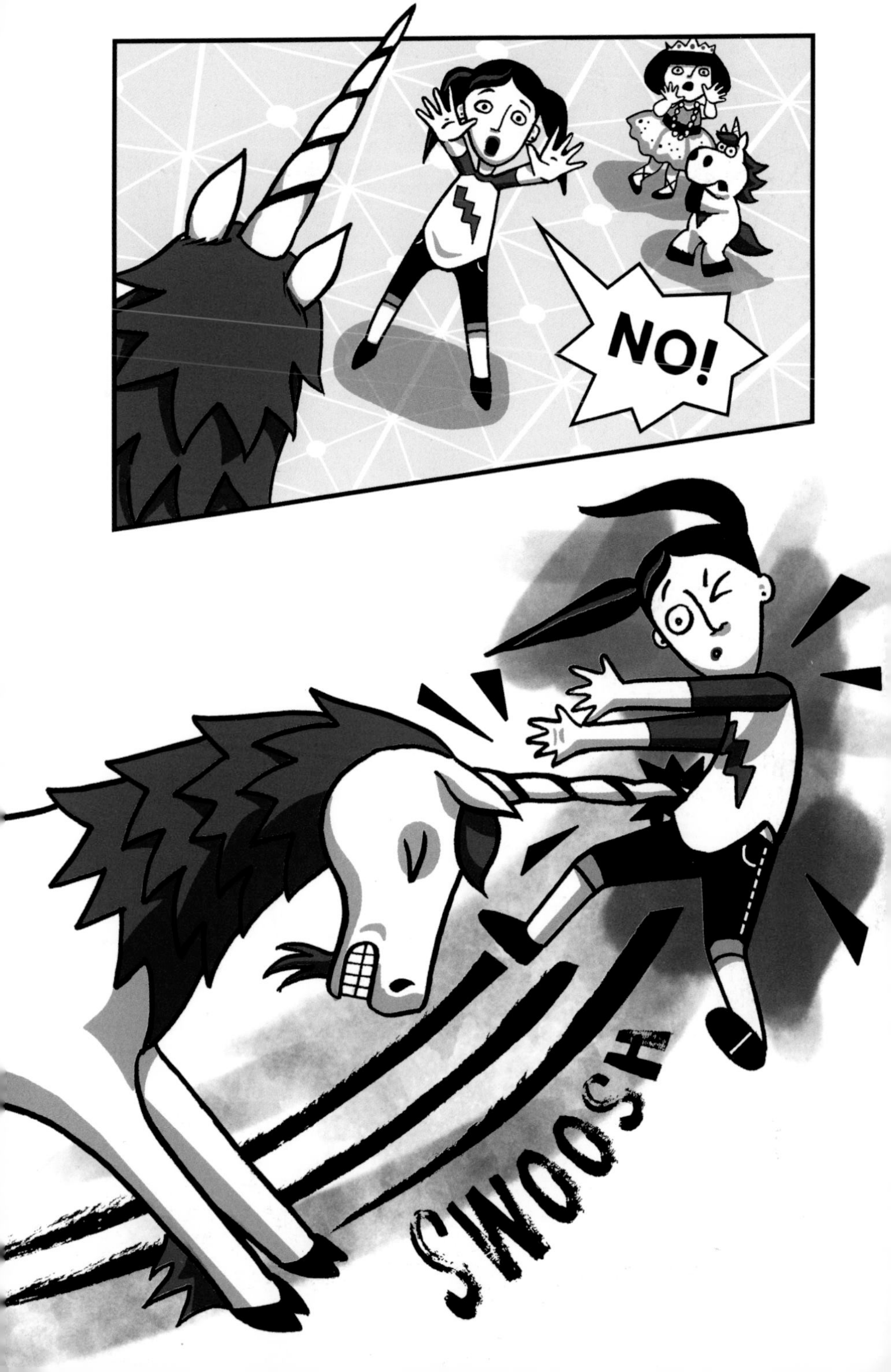
NO!
SWOOSH

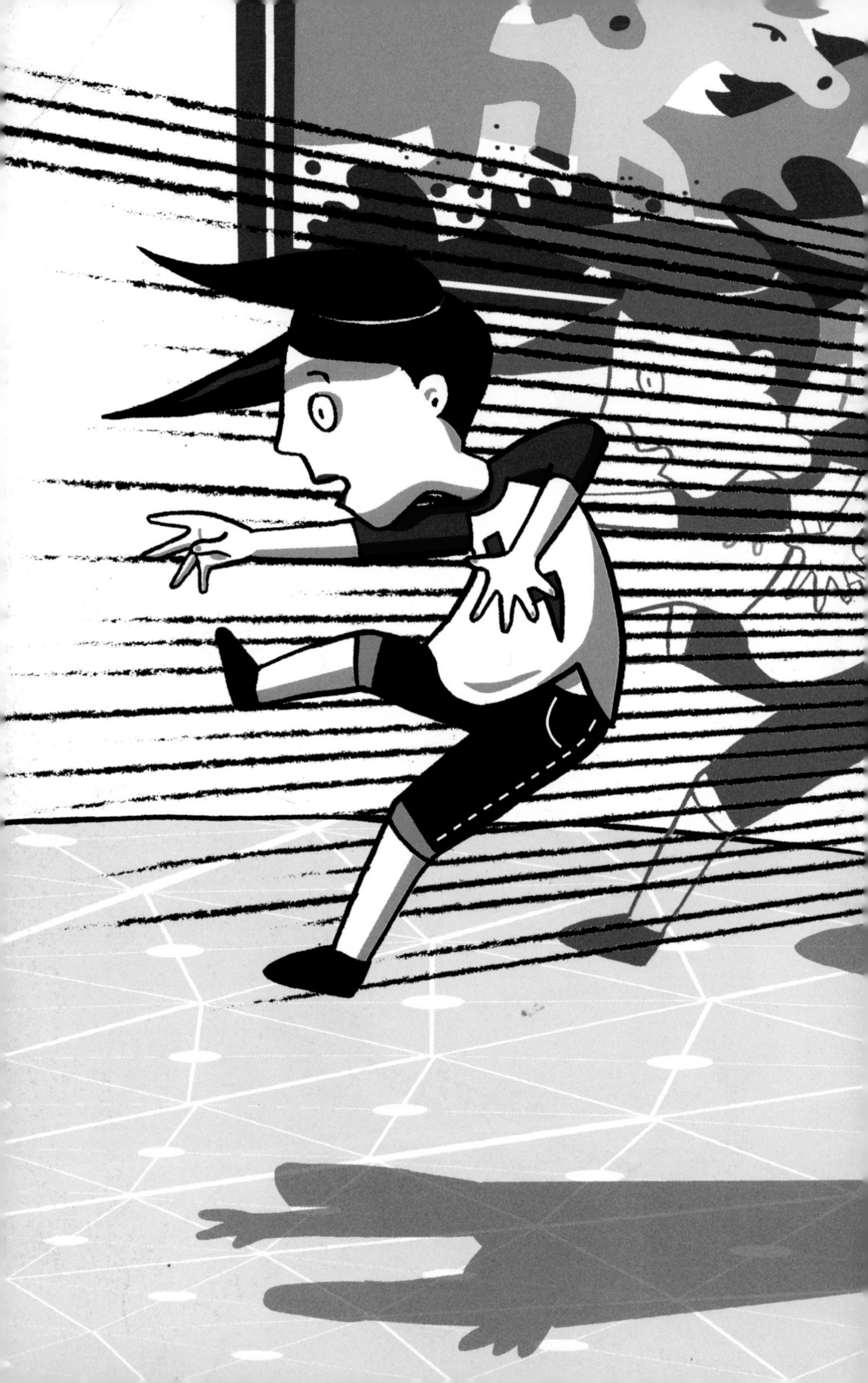

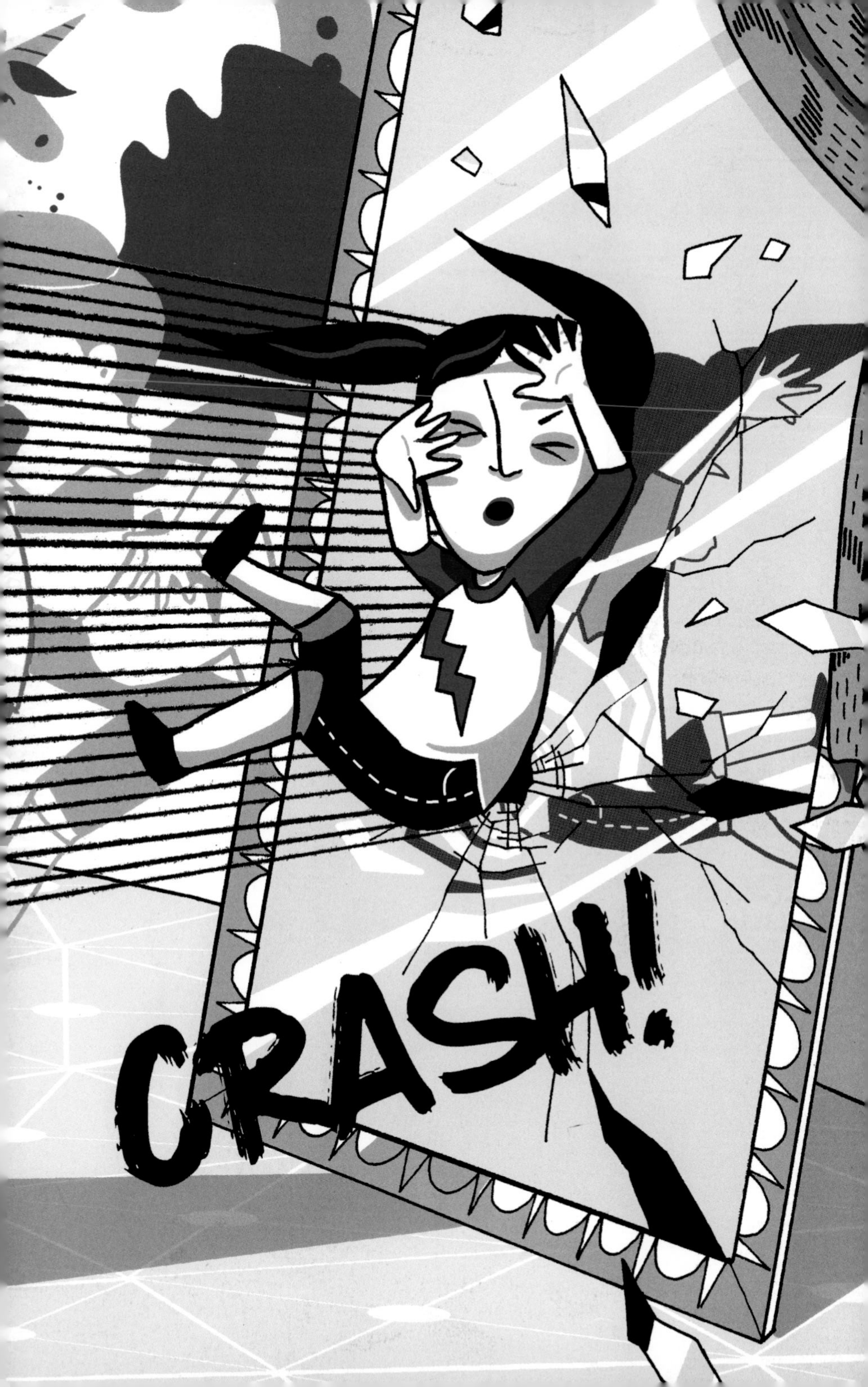
CRASH!

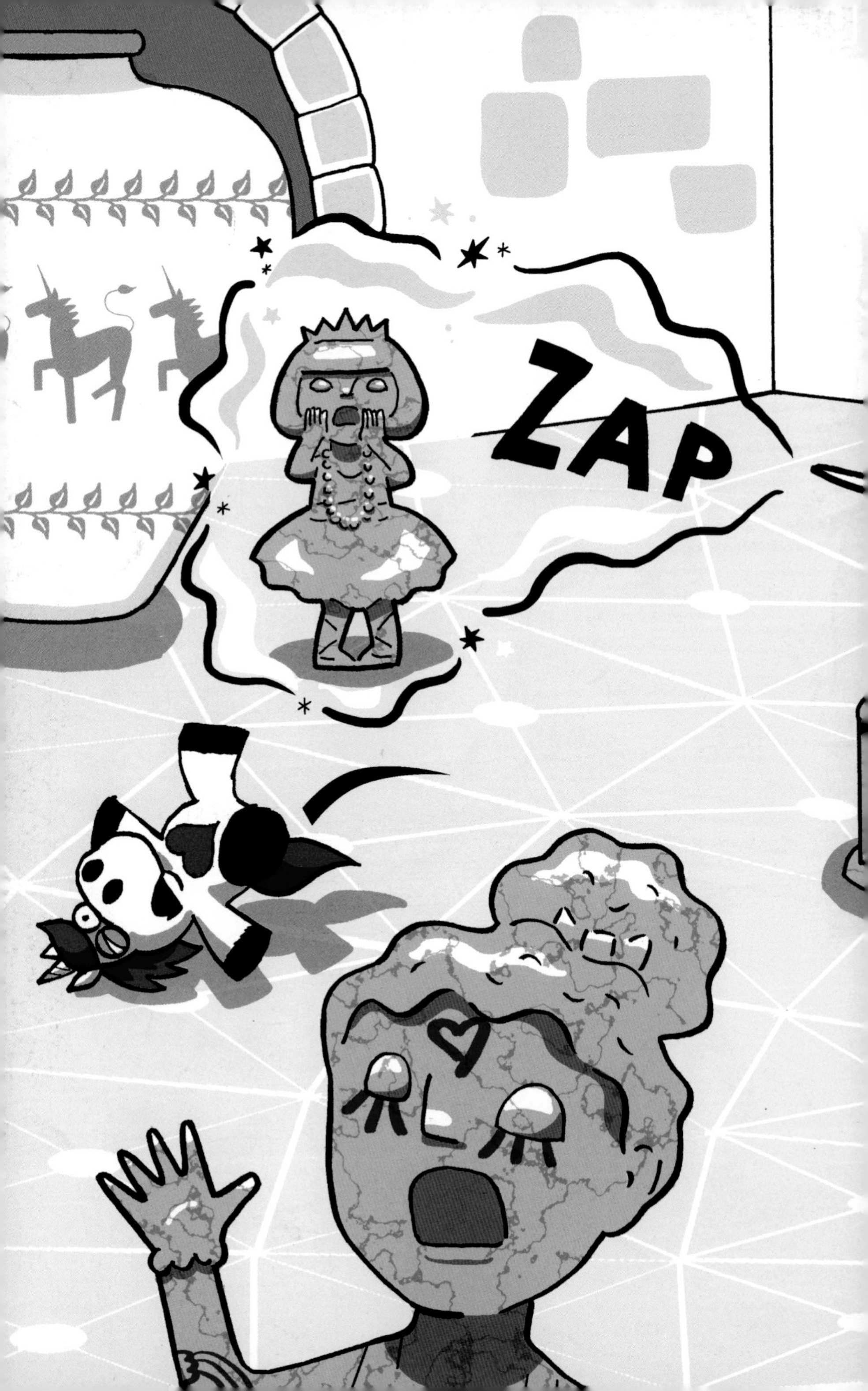
ZAP

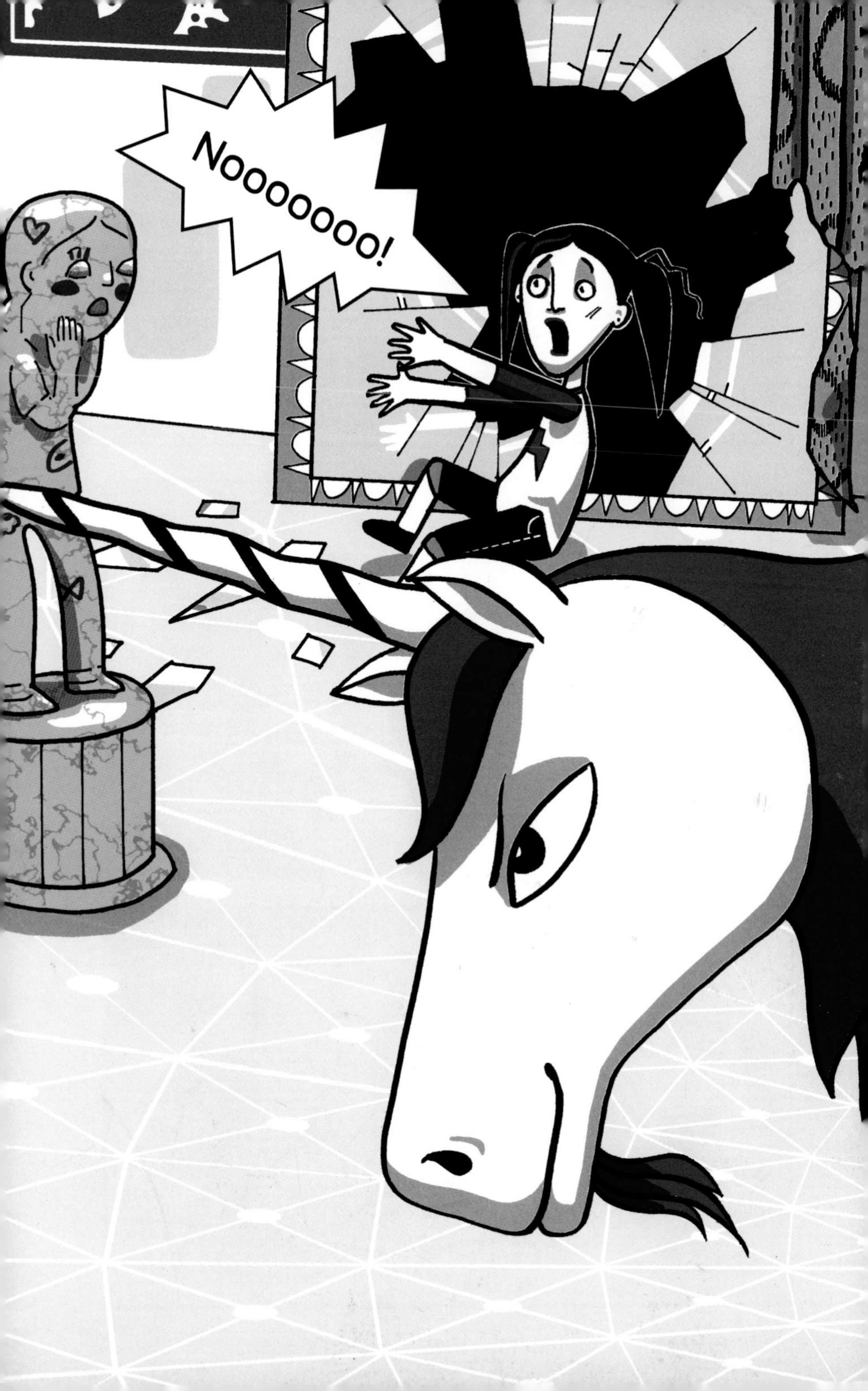
Nooooooo!

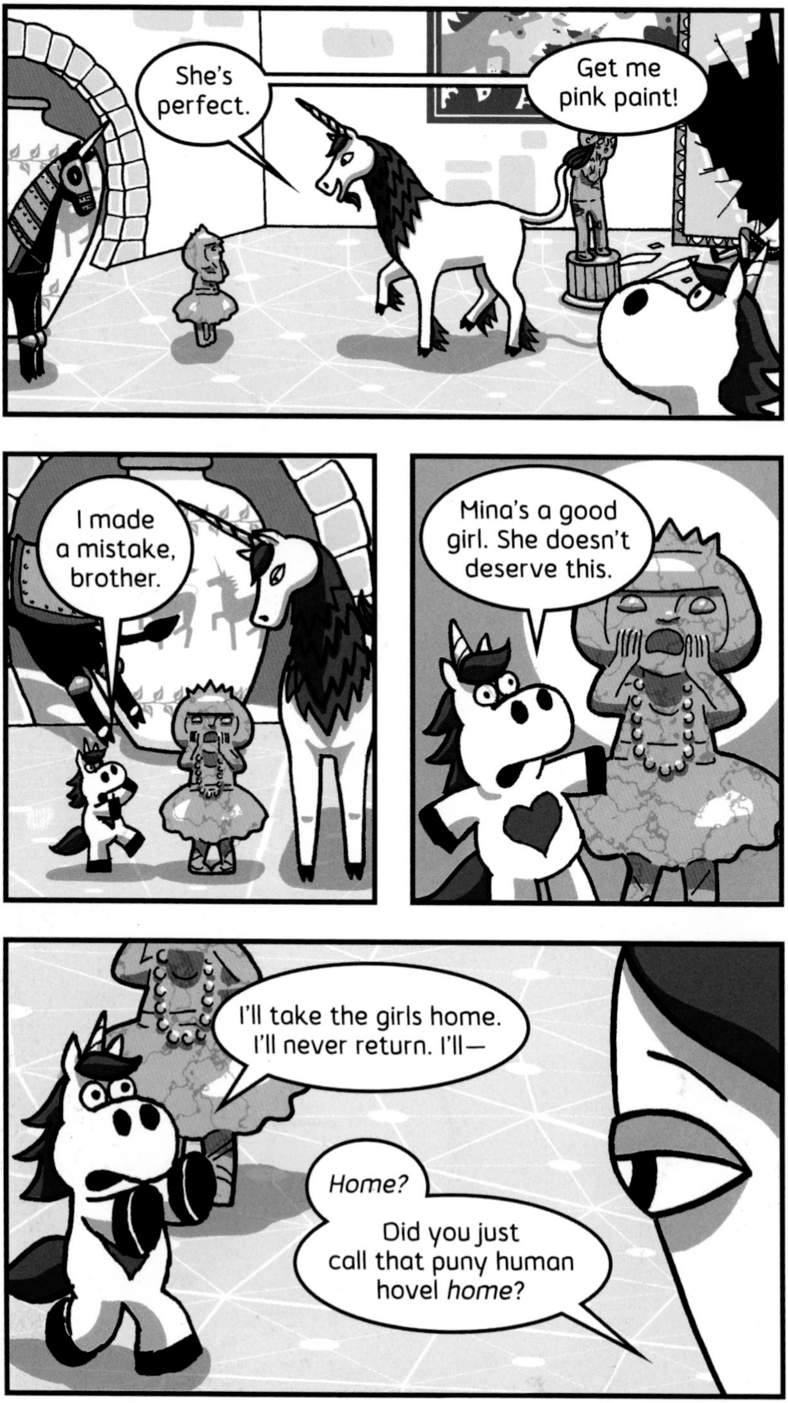
She's perfect.
Get me pink paint!
I made a mistake, brother.
Mina's a good girl. She doesn't deserve this.
I'll take the girls home. I'll never return. I'll—
Home?
Did you just call that puny human hovel *home*?

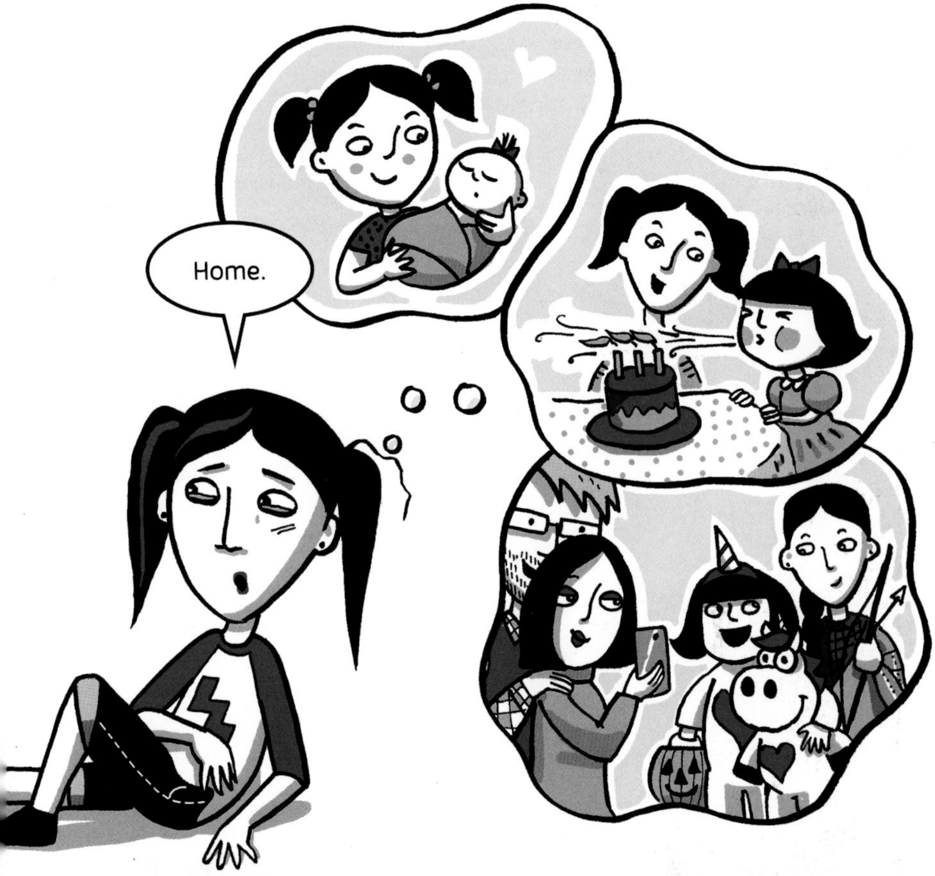
Home.

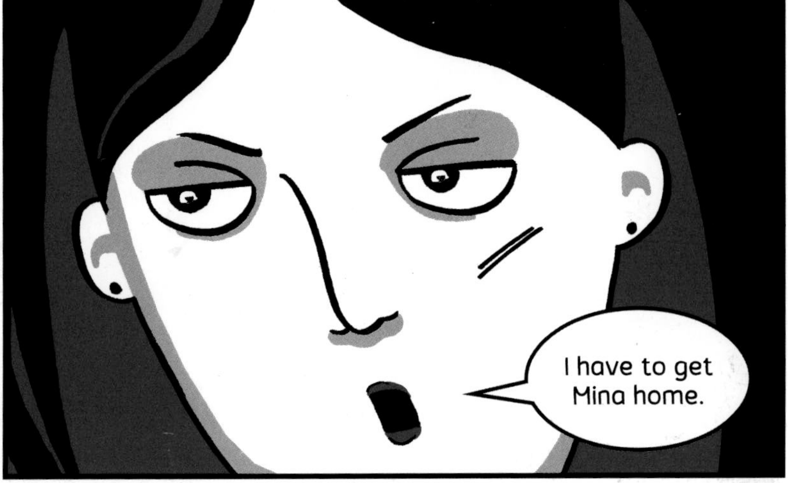
I have to get
Mina home.

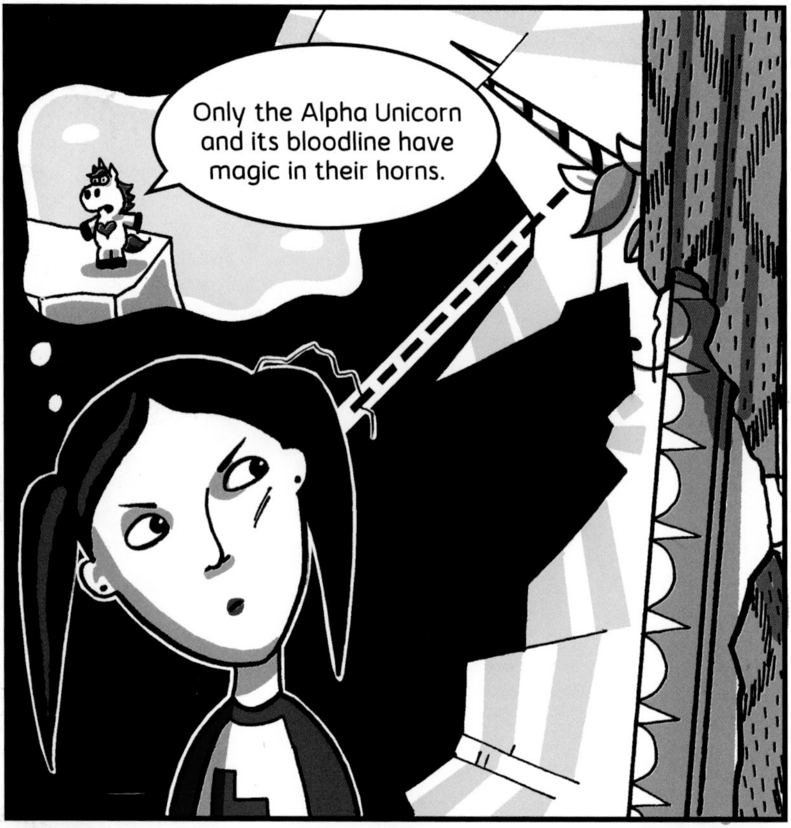
Only the Alpha Unicorn and its bloodline have magic in their horns.

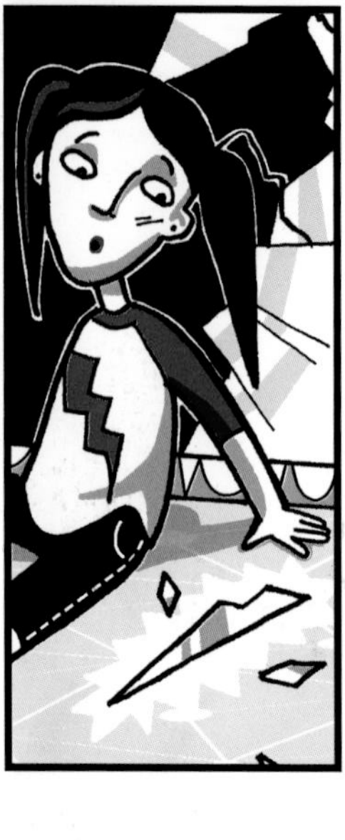

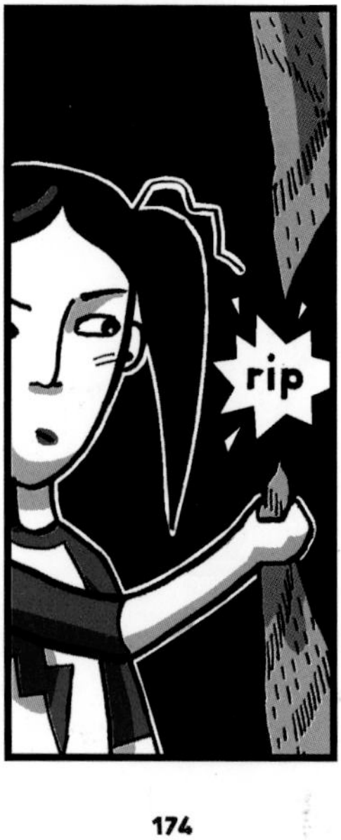
rip

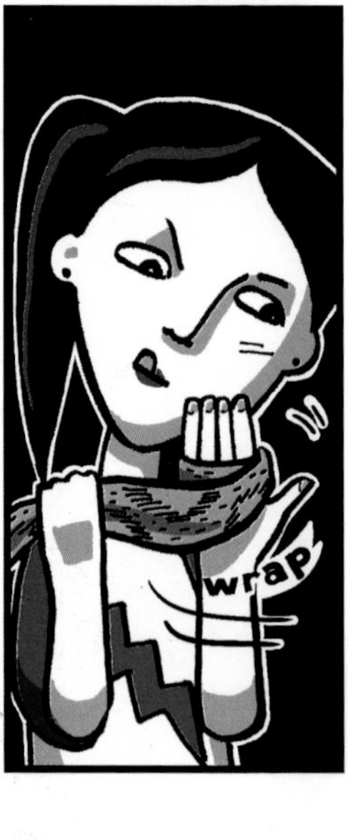
wrap

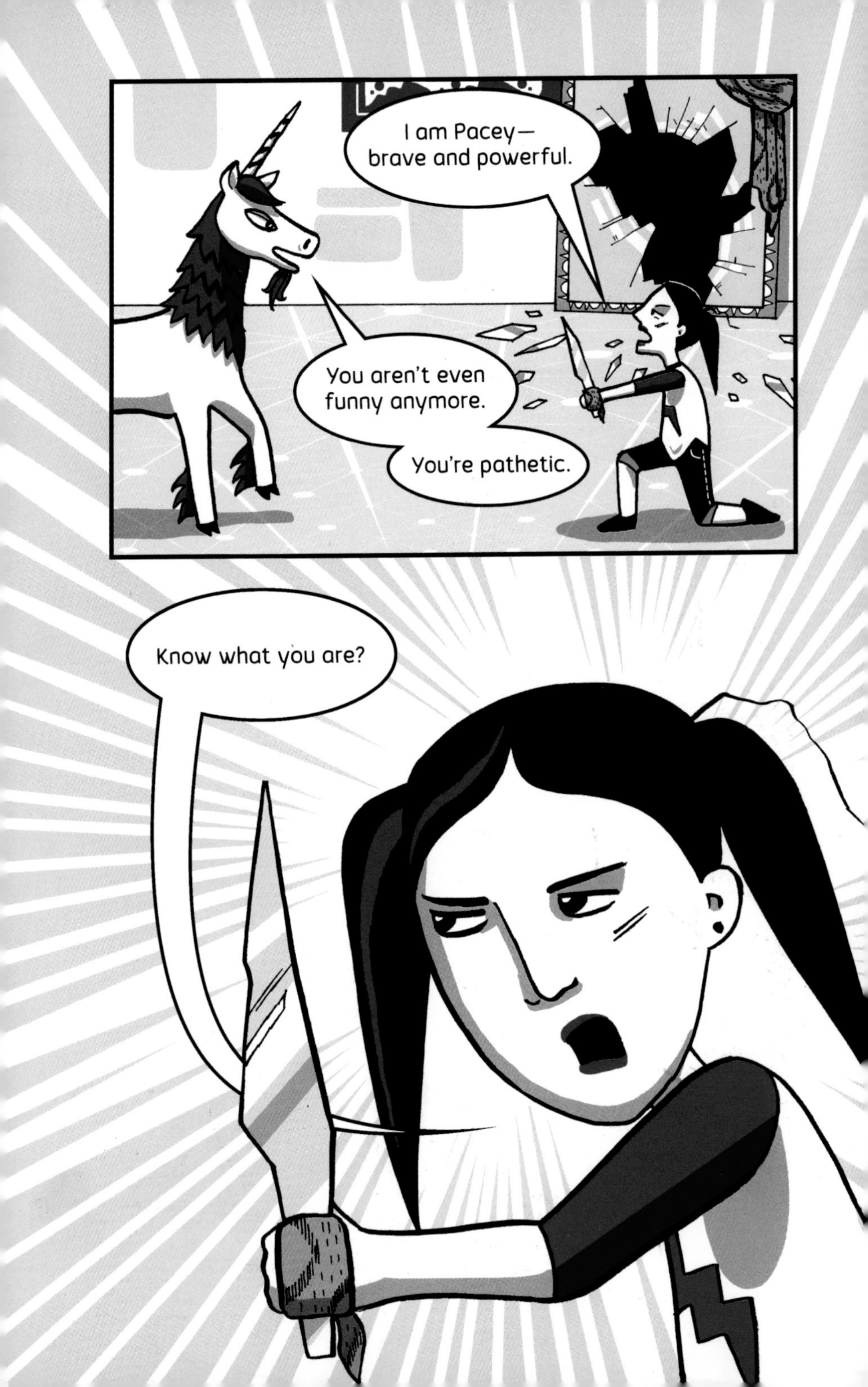
I am Pacey—
brave and powerful.
You aren't even funny anymore.
You're pathetic.
Know what you are?

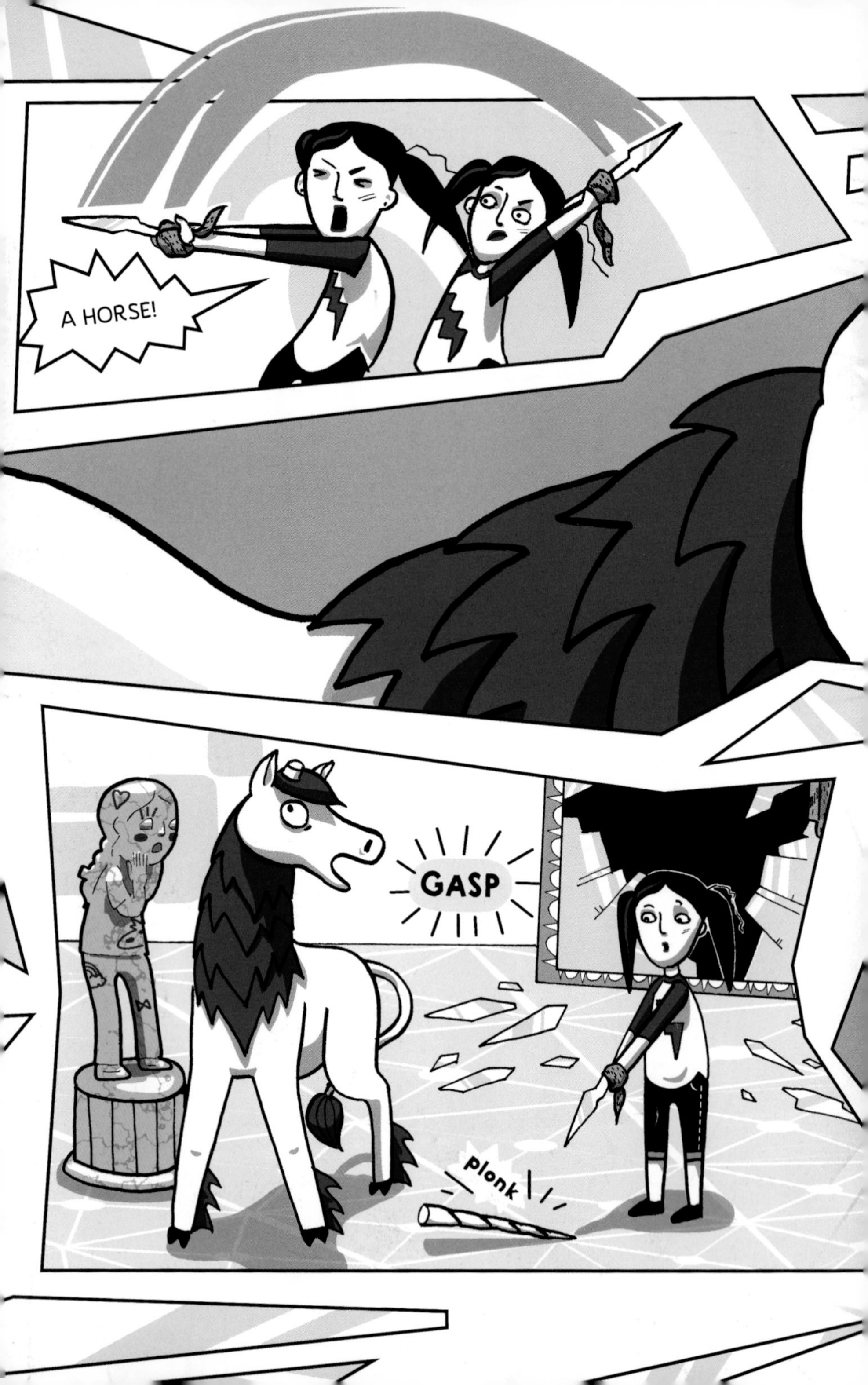
A HORSE!
GASP
plonk

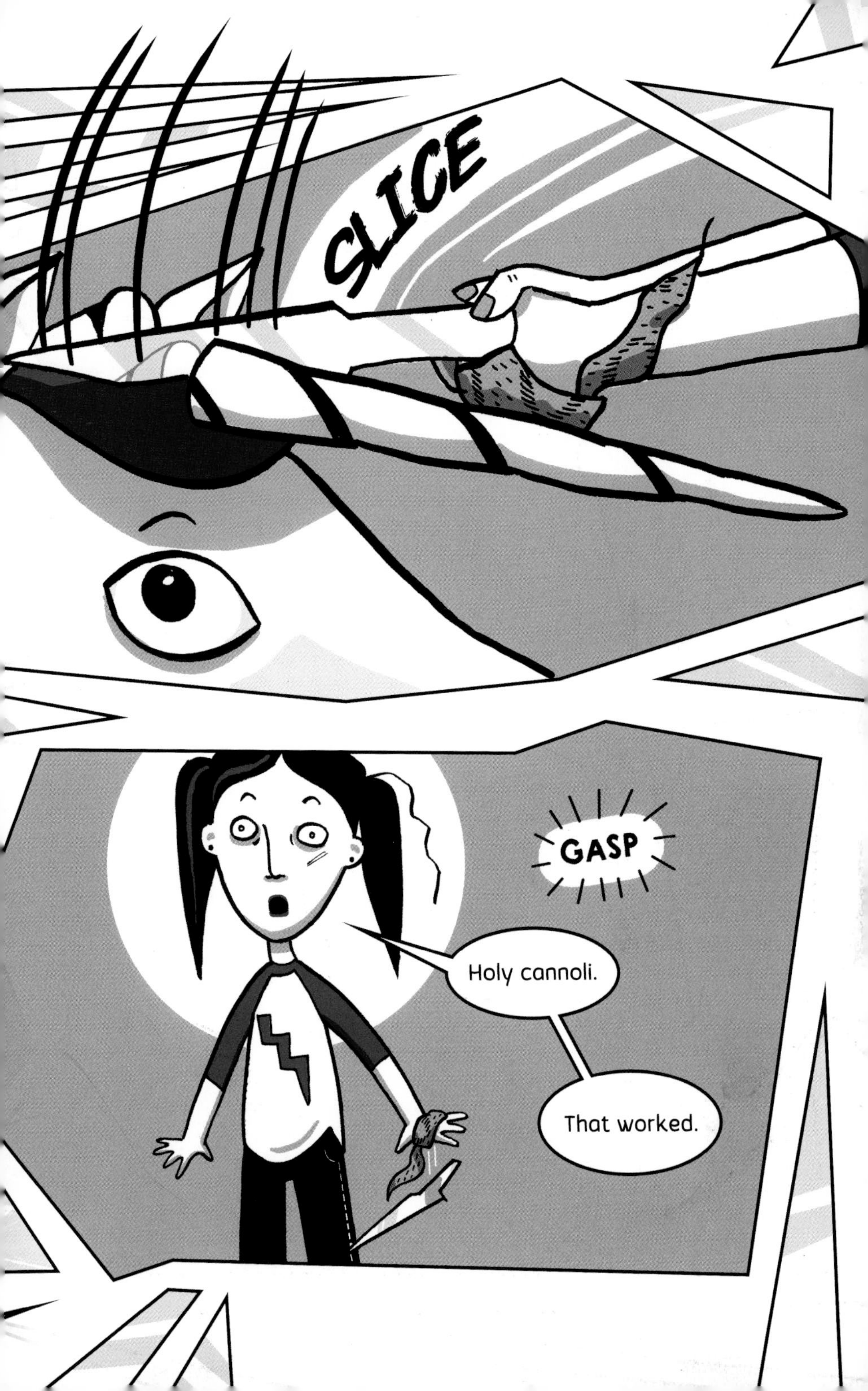
SLICE
GASP
Holy cannoli.
That worked.

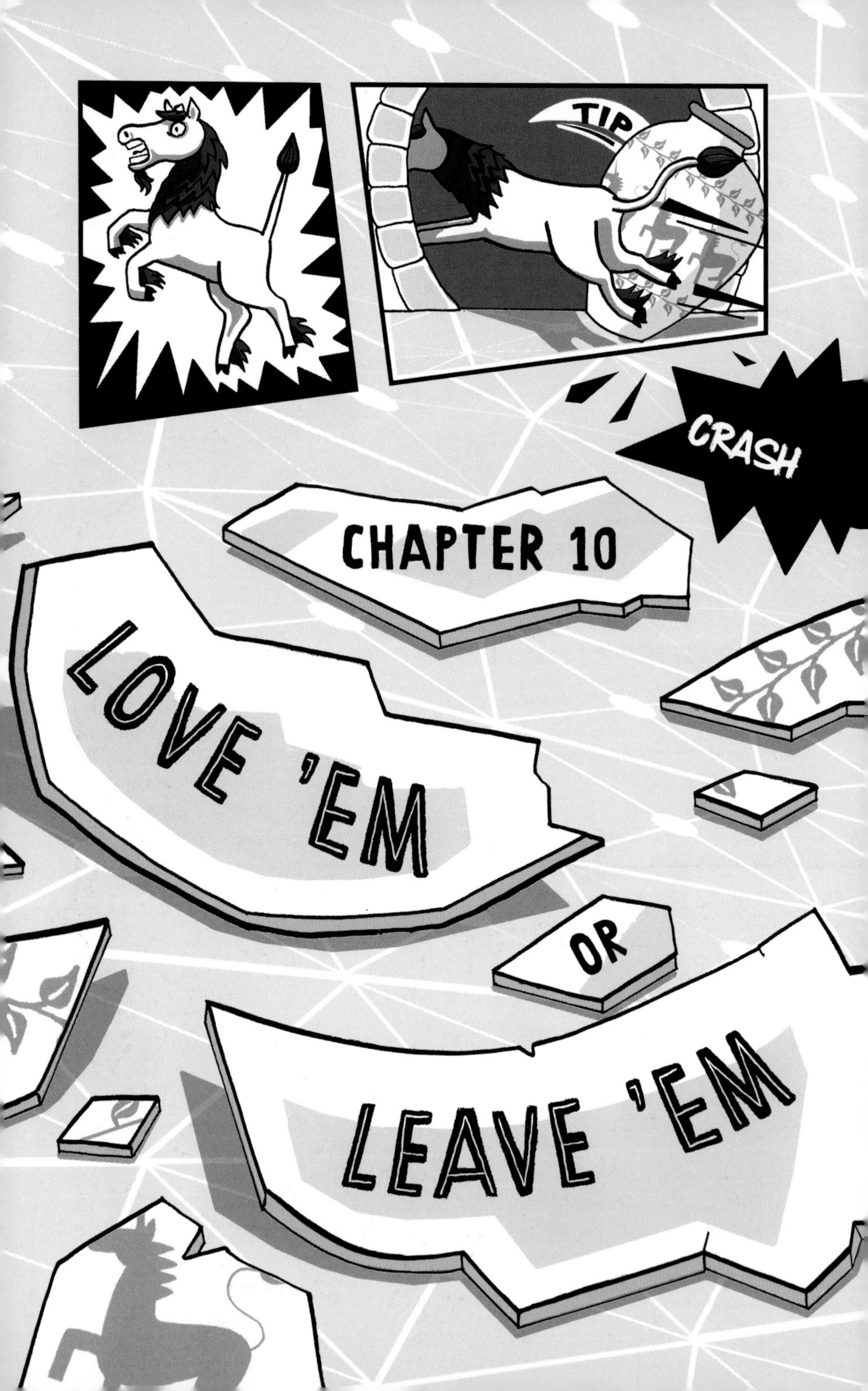
TIP
CRASH
CHAPTER 10
LOVE 'EM
OR
LEAVE 'EM

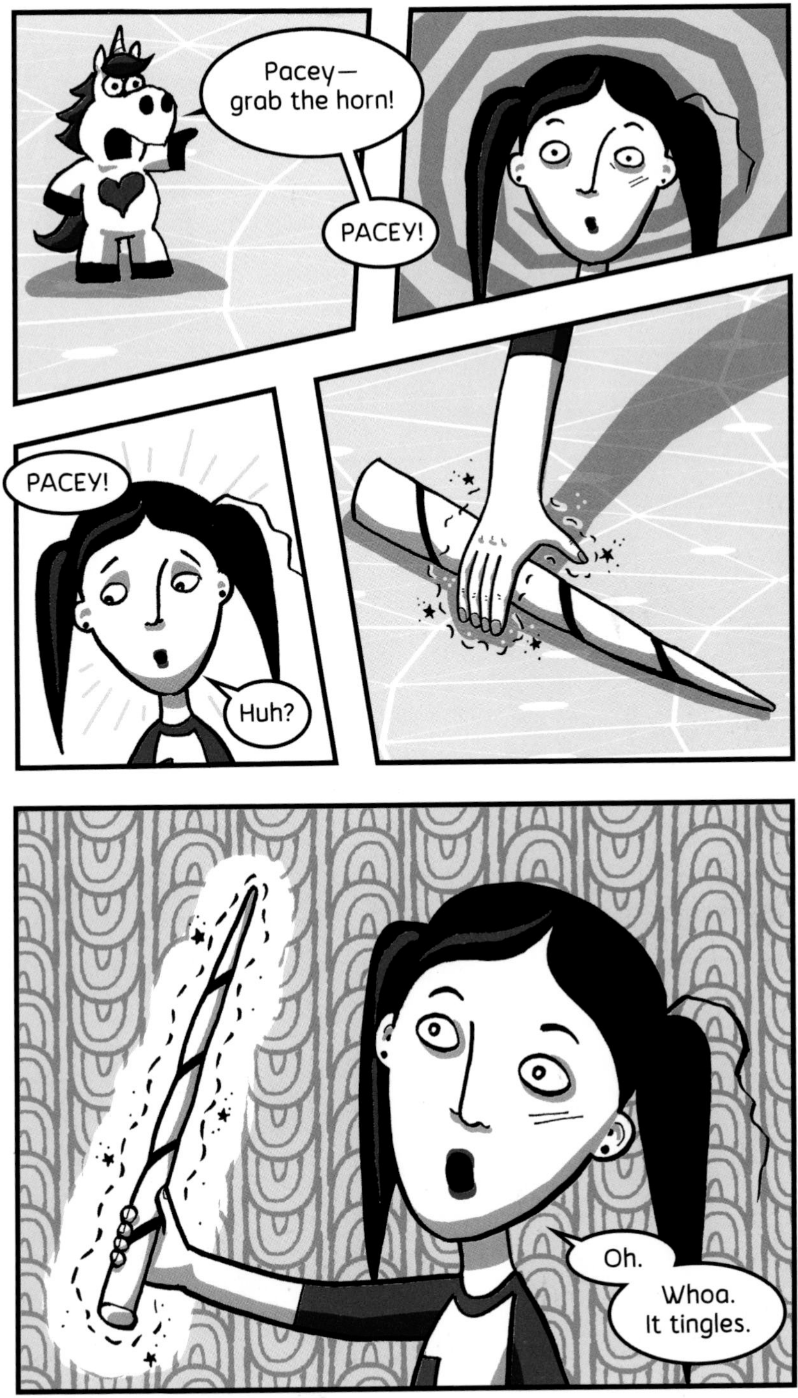
Pacey—
grab the horn!
PACEY!
PACEY!
Huh?
Oh.
Whoa.
It tingles.

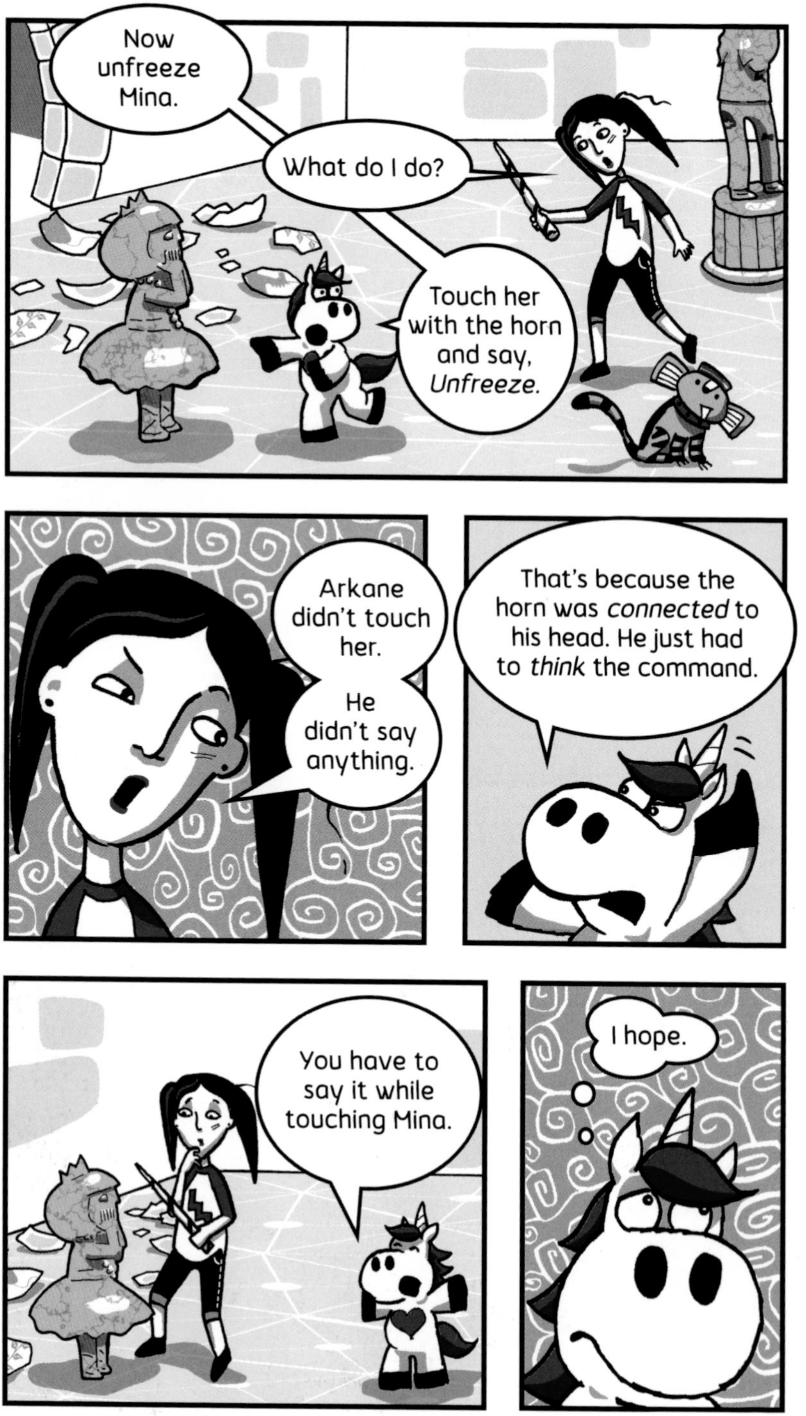

Now unfreeze Mina.
What do I do?
Touch her with the horn and say, *Unfreeze.*
Arkane didn't touch her.
He didn't say anything.
That's because the horn was *connected* to his head. He just had to *think* the command.
You have to say it while touching Mina.
I hope.

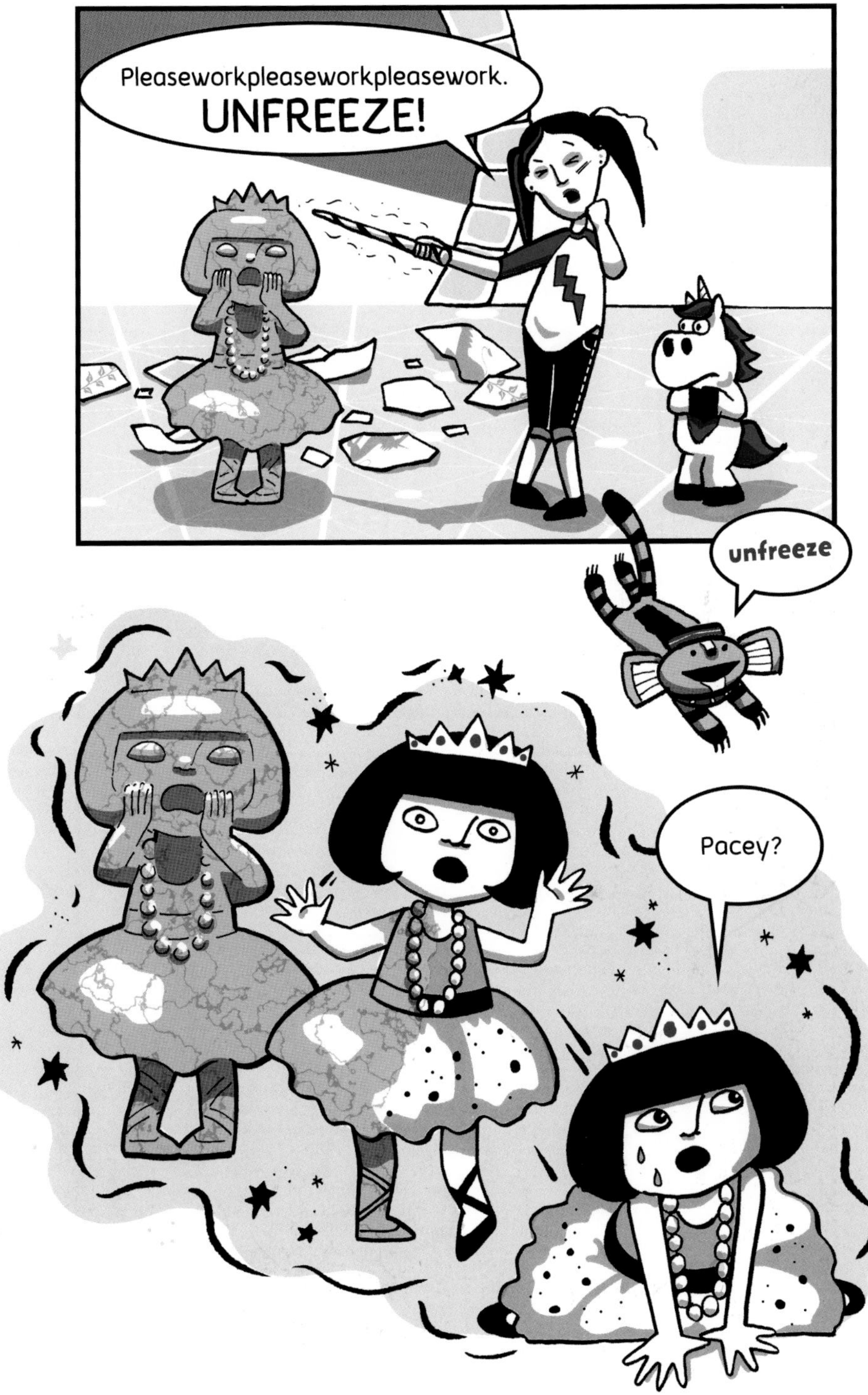
Pleaseworkpleaseworkpleasework.
UNFREEZE!
unfreeze
Pacey?

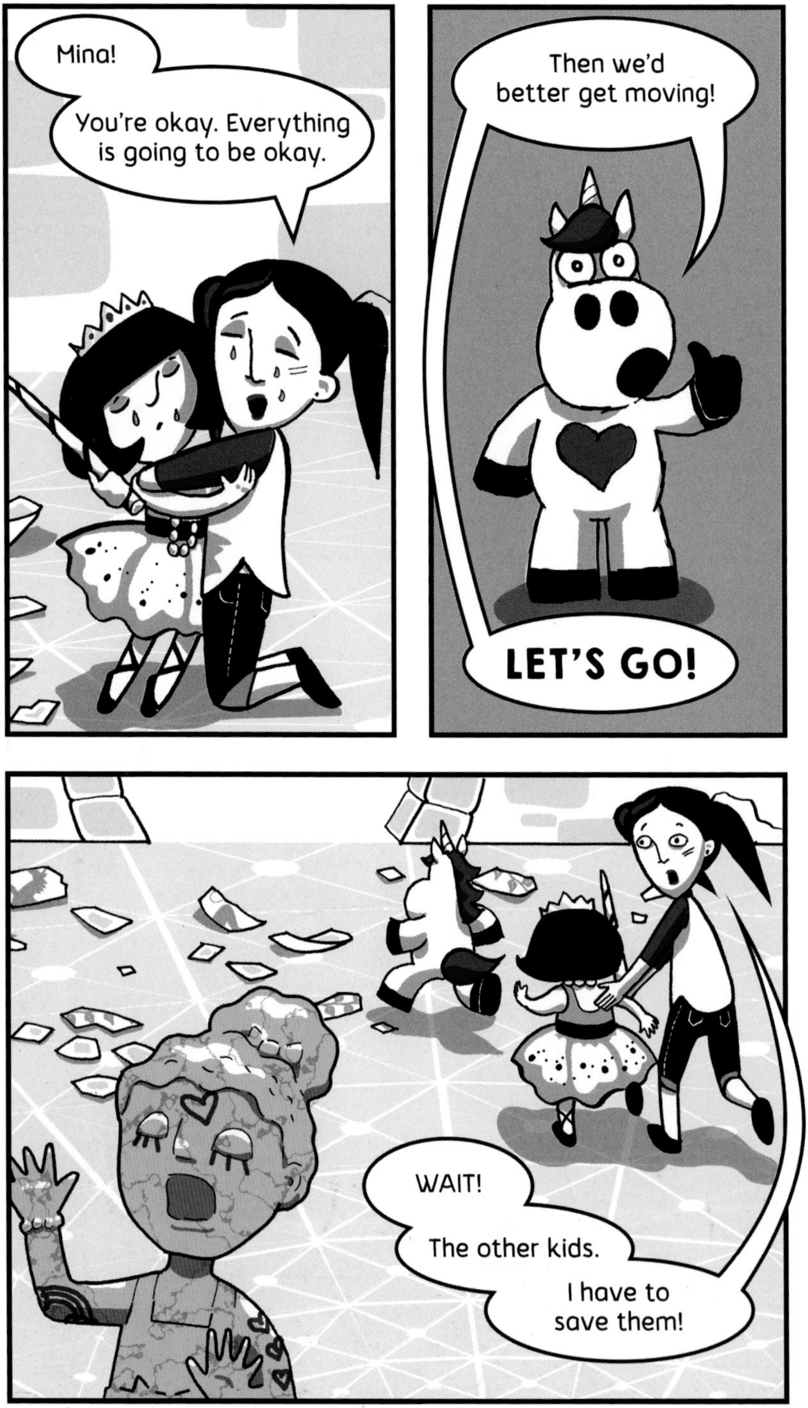
Mina!
You're okay. Everything is going to be okay.
Then we'd better get moving!
LET'S GO!
WAIT!
The other kids.
I have to save them!

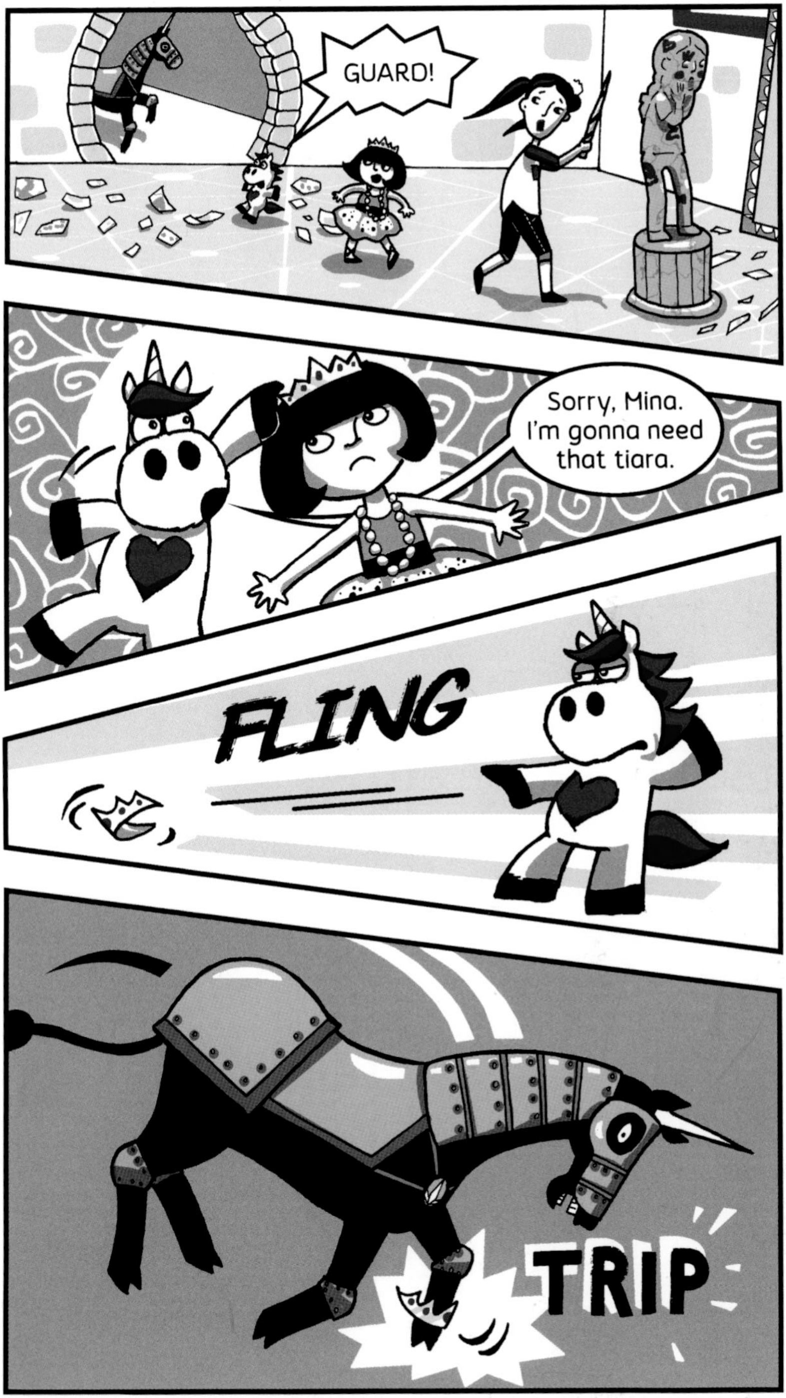
GUARD!
Sorry, Mina. I'm gonna need that tiara.
FLING
TRIP

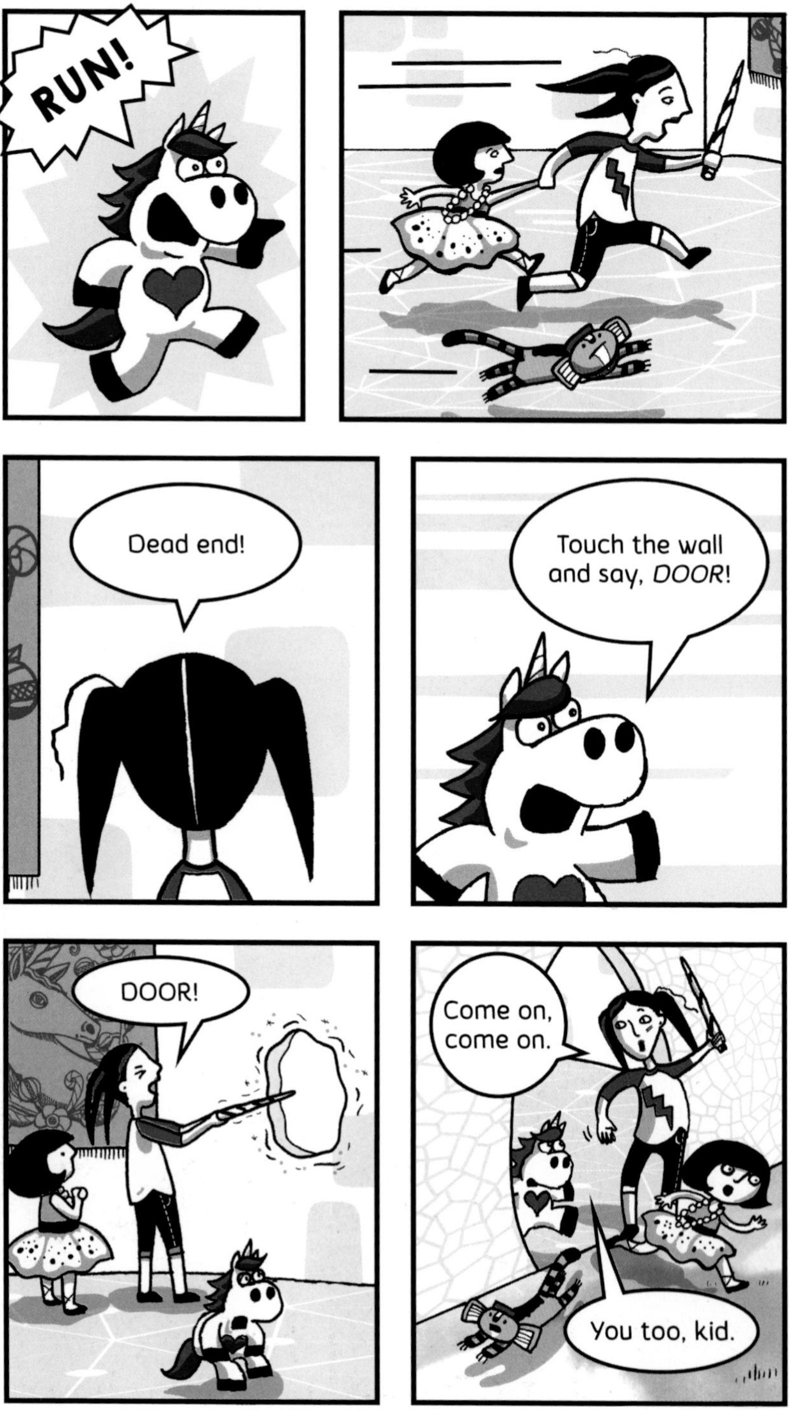
RUN!
Dead end!
Touch the wall and say, *DOOR*!
DOOR!
Come on, come on.
You too, kid.

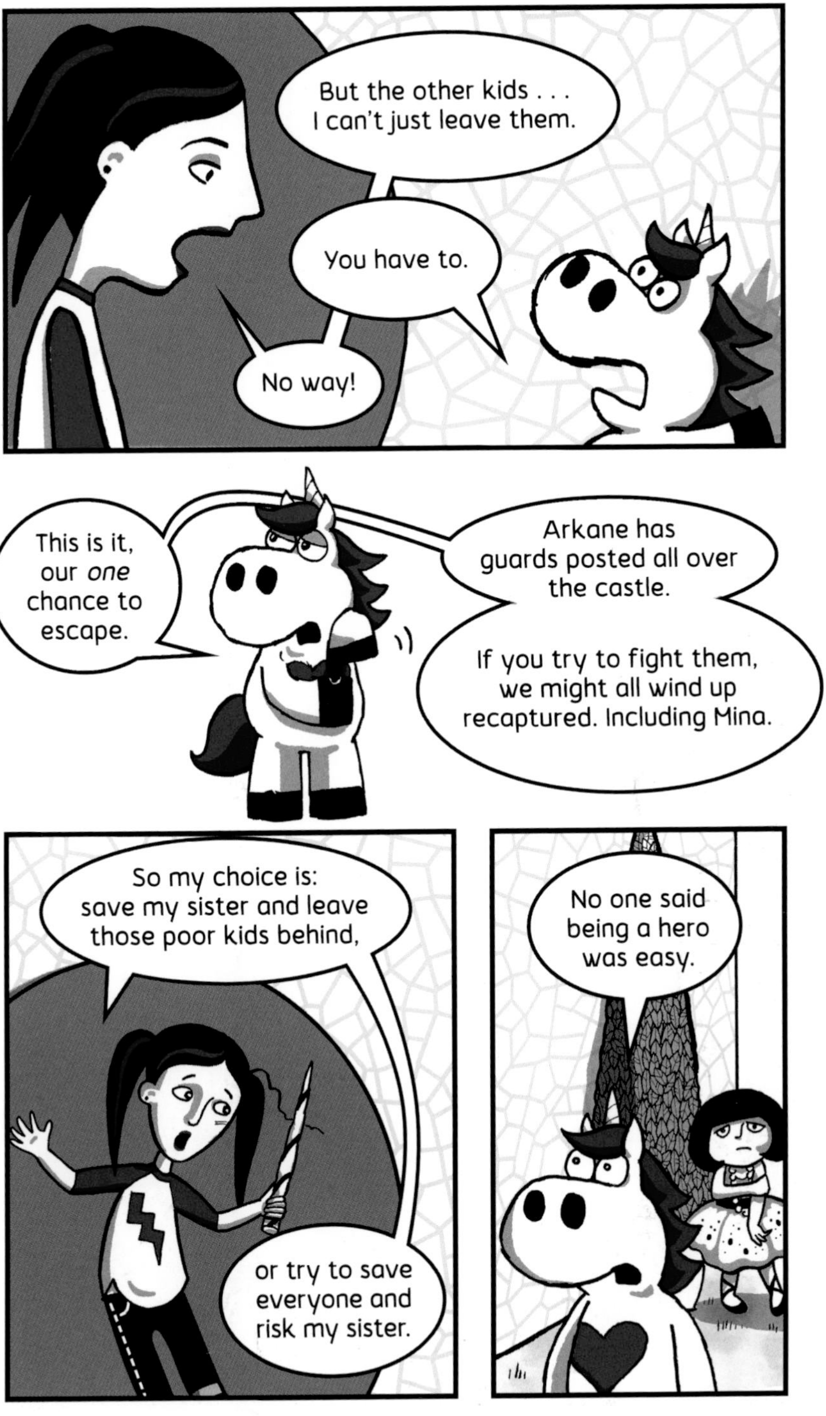
But the other kids . . .
I can't just leave them.
You have to.
No way!
This is it, our *one* chance to escape.
Arkane has guards posted all over the castle.
If you try to fight them, we might all wind up recaptured. Including Mina.
So my choice is: save my sister and leave those poor kids behind,
or try to save everyone and risk my sister.
No one said being a hero was easy.

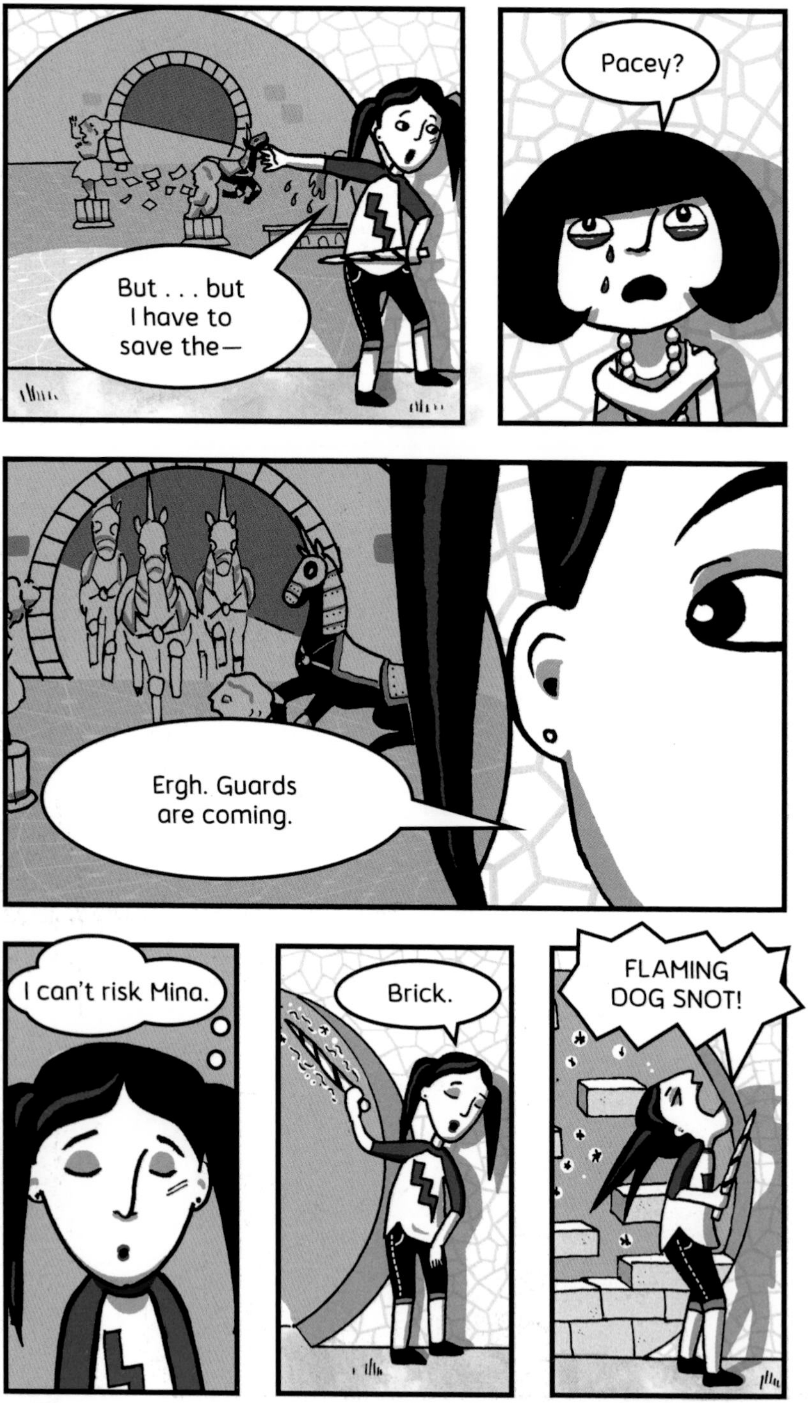
But . . . but I have to save the—
Pacey?
Ergh. Guards are coming.
I can't risk Mina.
Brick.
FLAMING DOG SNOT!

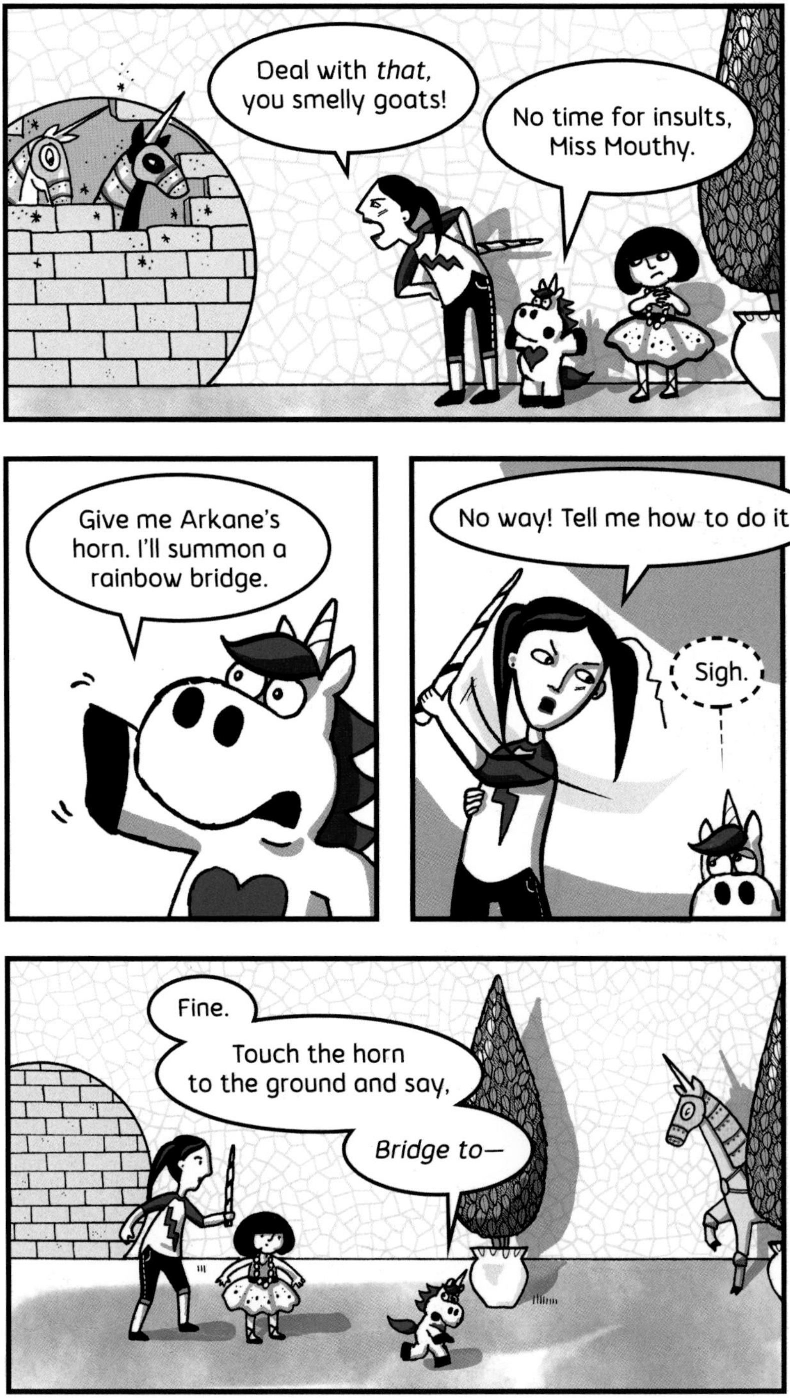
Deal with *that*, you smelly goats!
No time for insults, Miss Mouthy.
Give me Arkane's horn. I'll summon a rainbow bridge.
No way! Tell me how to do it.
Sigh.
Fine.
Touch the horn to the ground and say,
Bridge to—

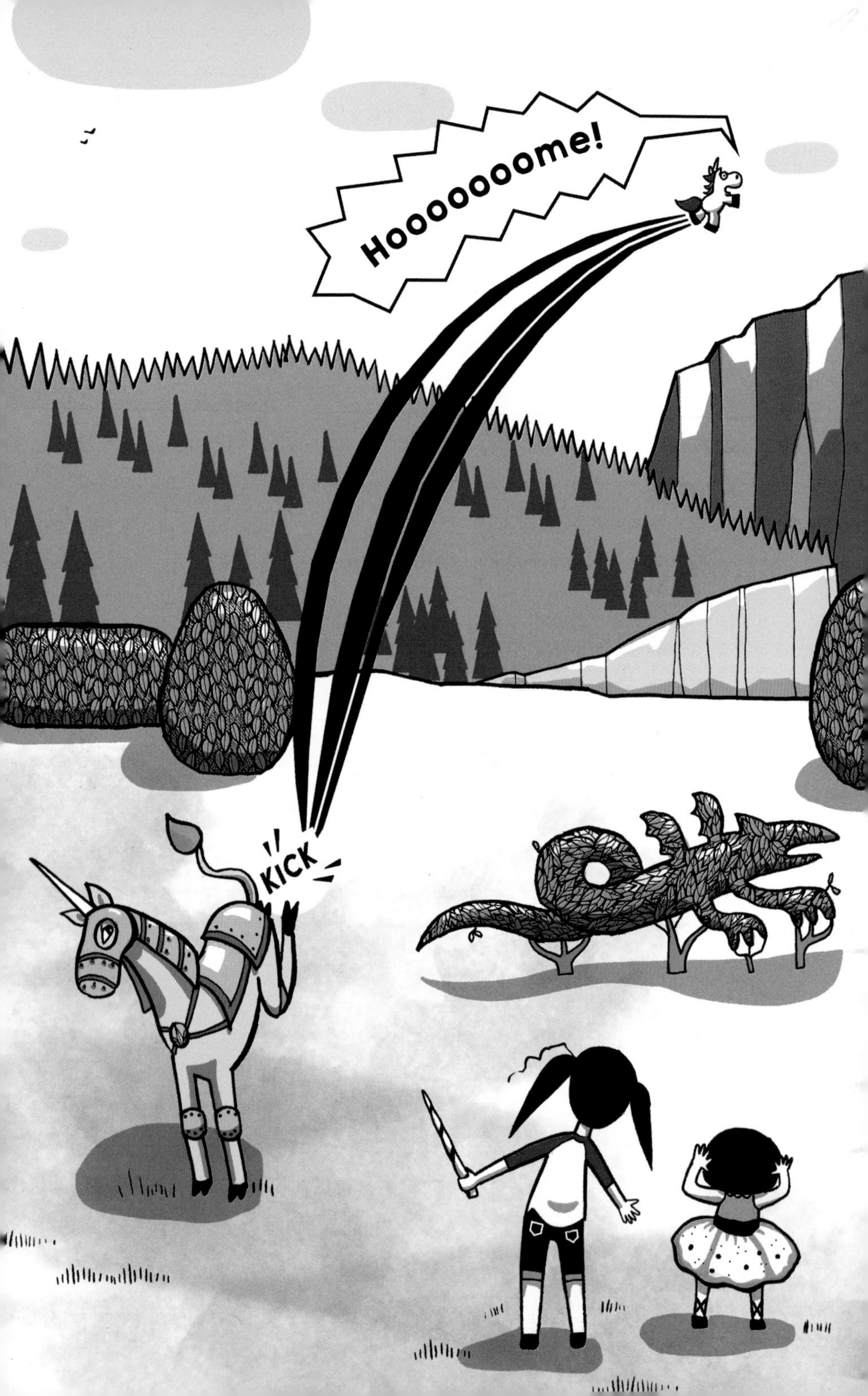
Hoooooooome!
KICK

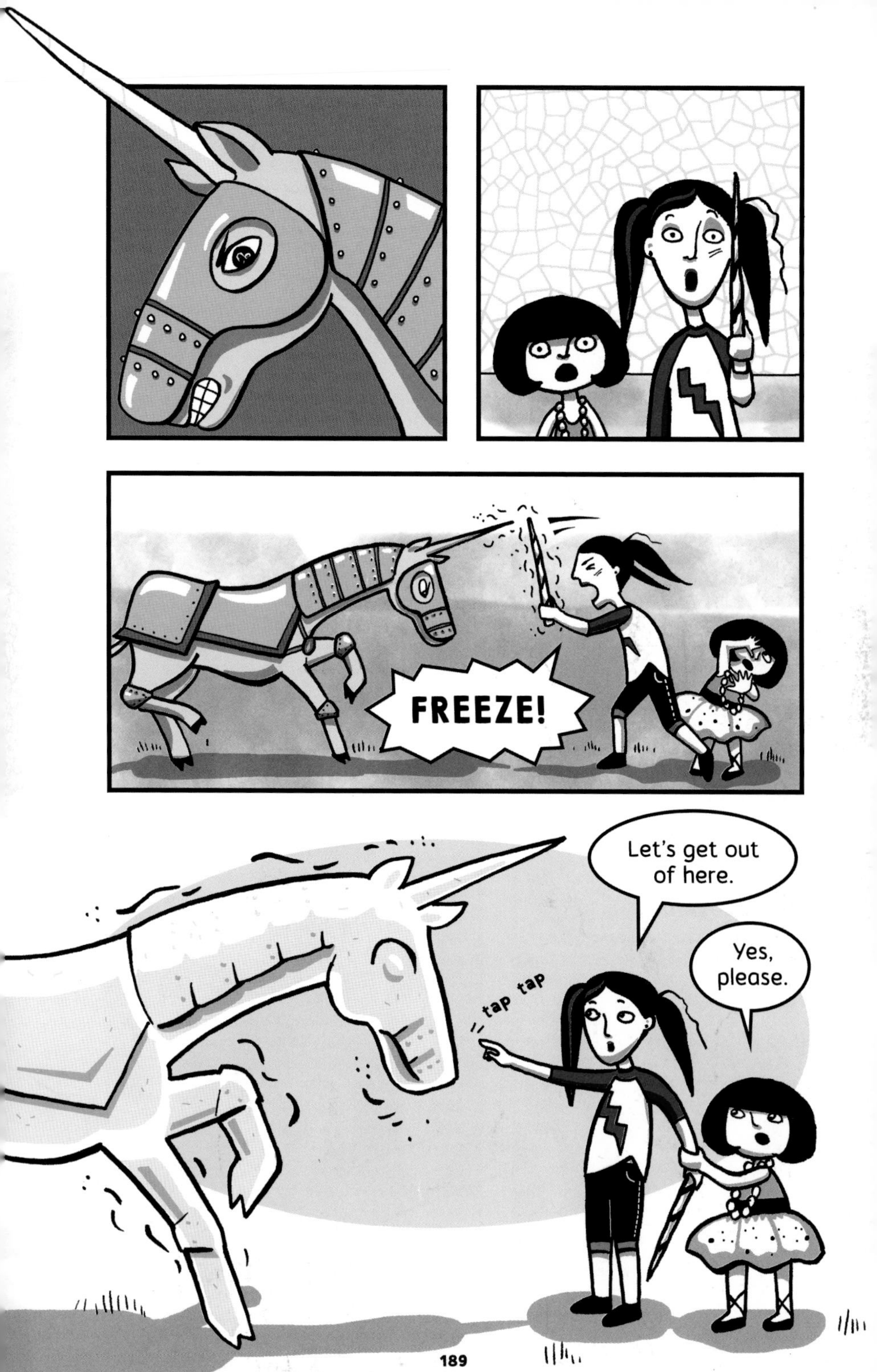
FREEZE!
Let's get out of here.
Yes, please.
tap tap

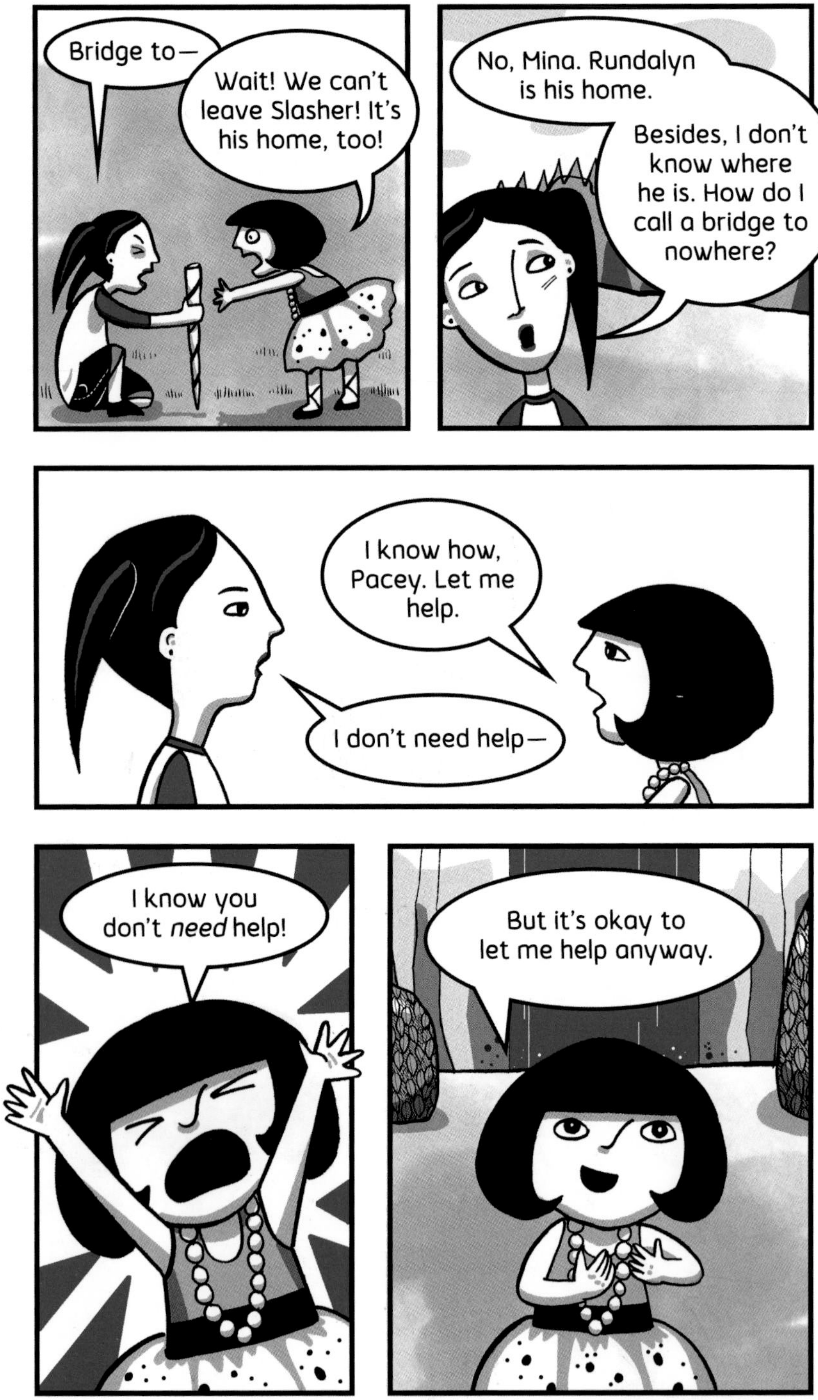
Bridge to—
Wait! We can't leave Slasher! It's his home, too!
No, Mina. Rundalyn is his home.
Besides, I don't know where he is. How do I call a bridge to nowhere?
I know how, Pacey. Let me help.
I don't need help—
I know you don't *need* help!
But it's okay to let me help anyway.

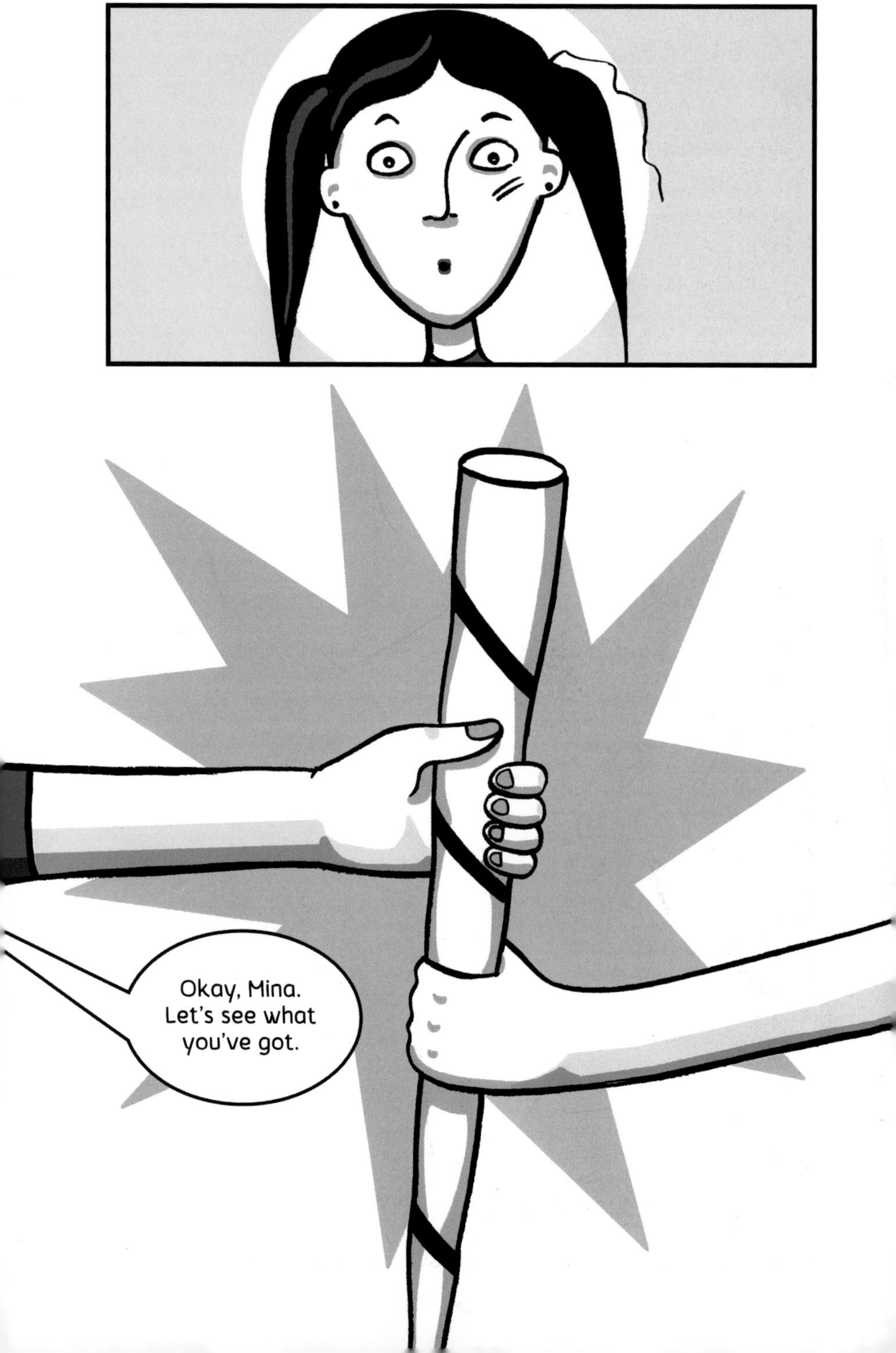
Okay, Mina. Let's see what you've got.

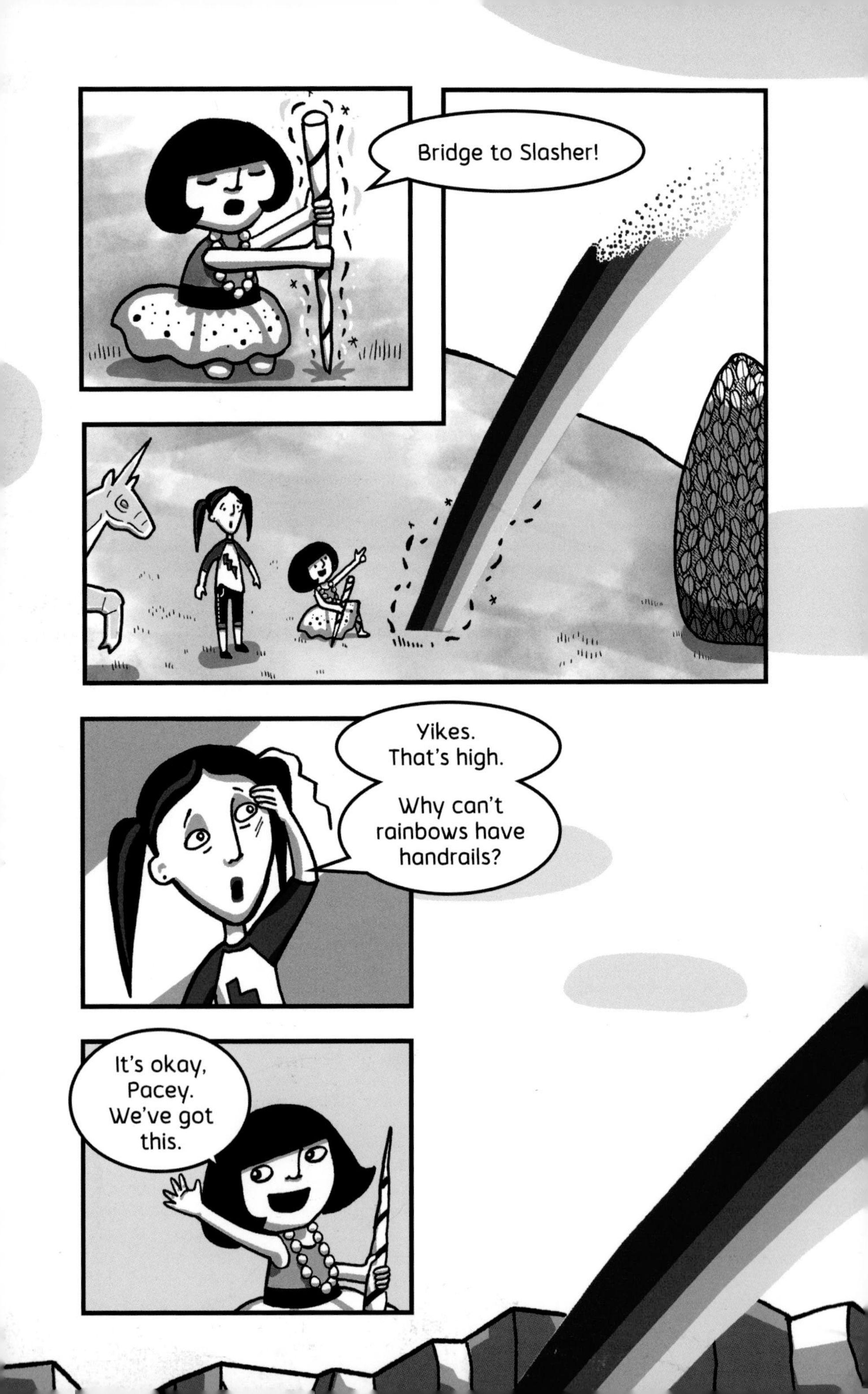
Bridge to Slasher!
Yikes. That's high.
Why can't rainbows have handrails?
It's okay, Pacey. We've got this.

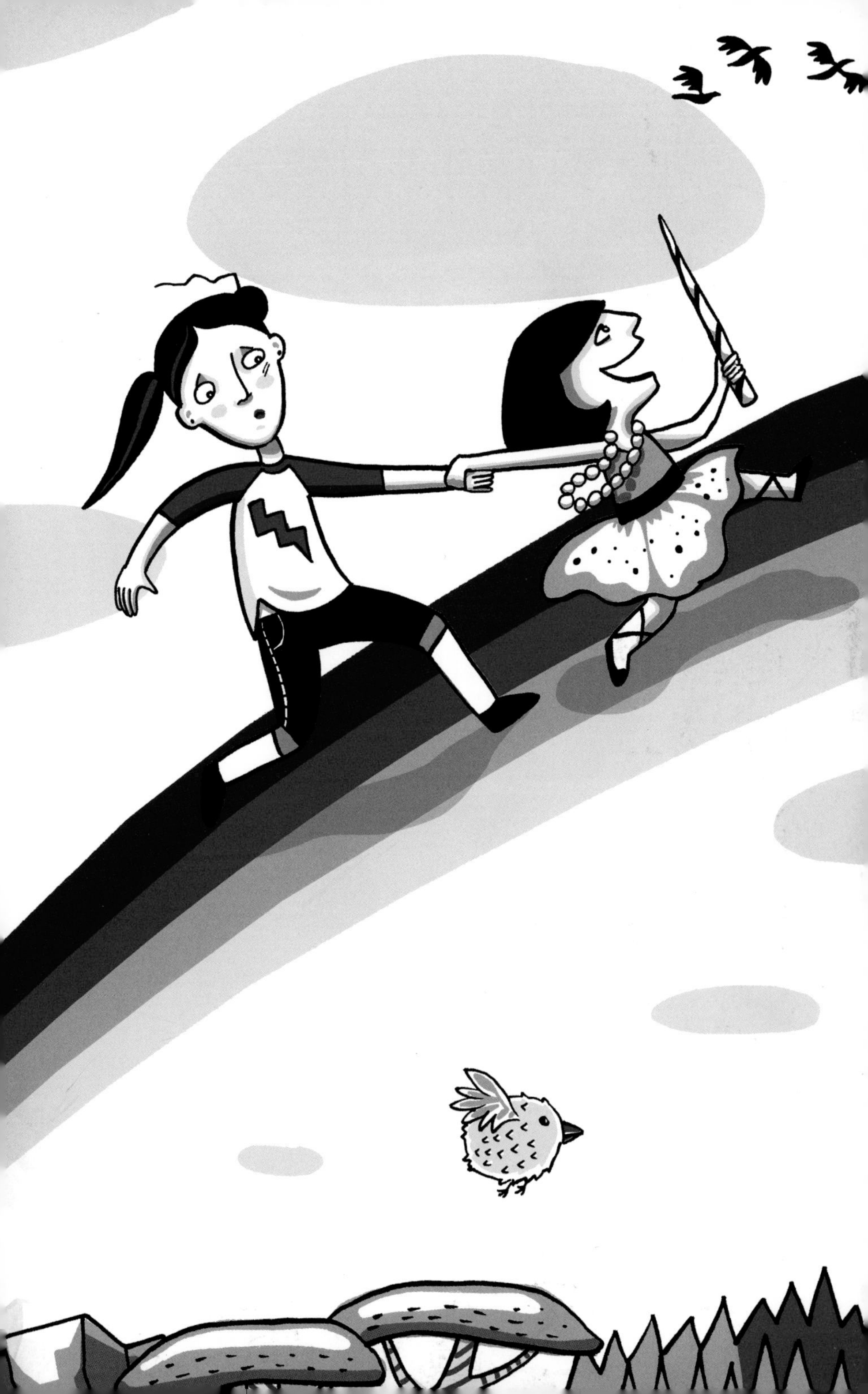

CHAPTER 11
FINAL FRACAS

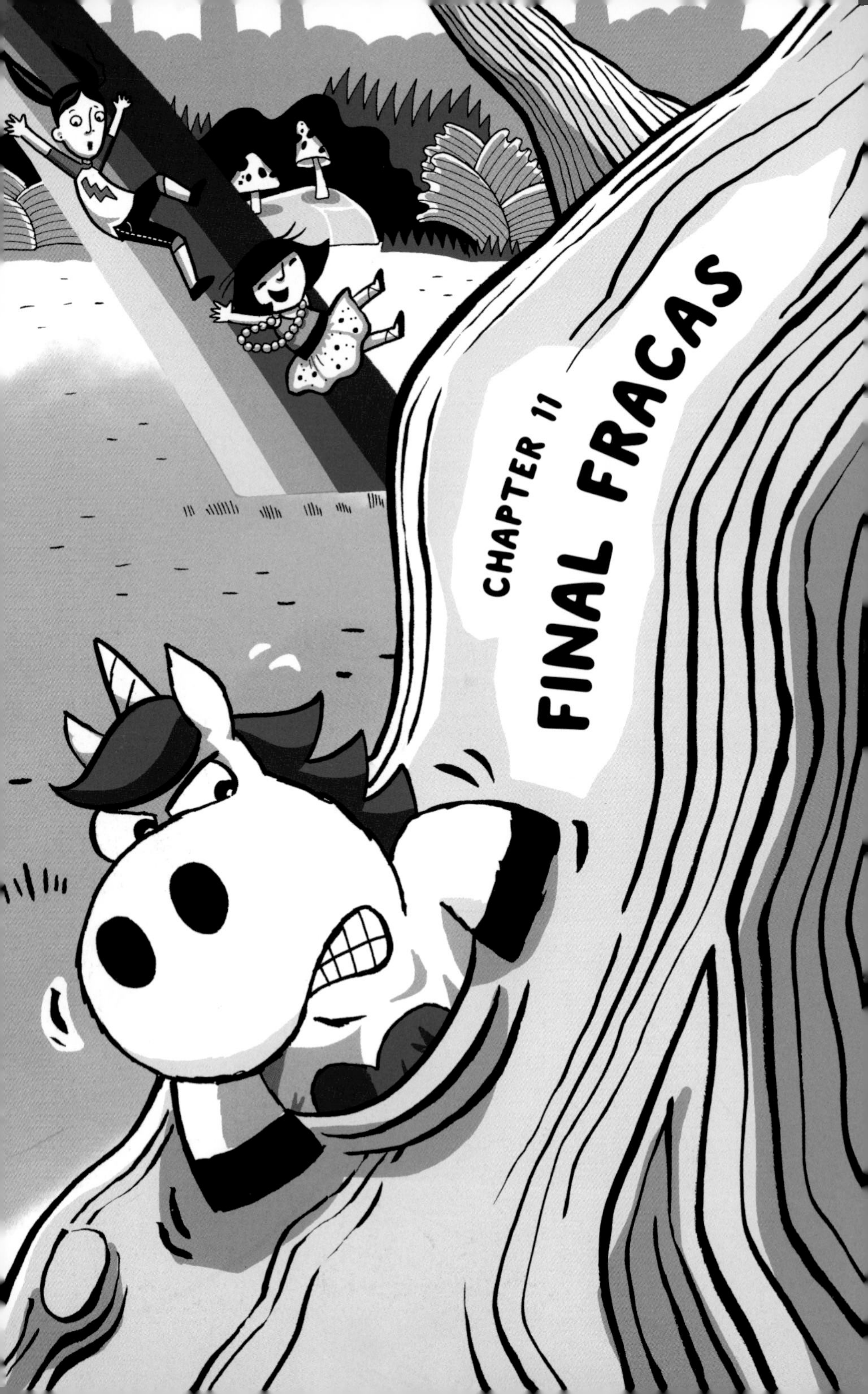

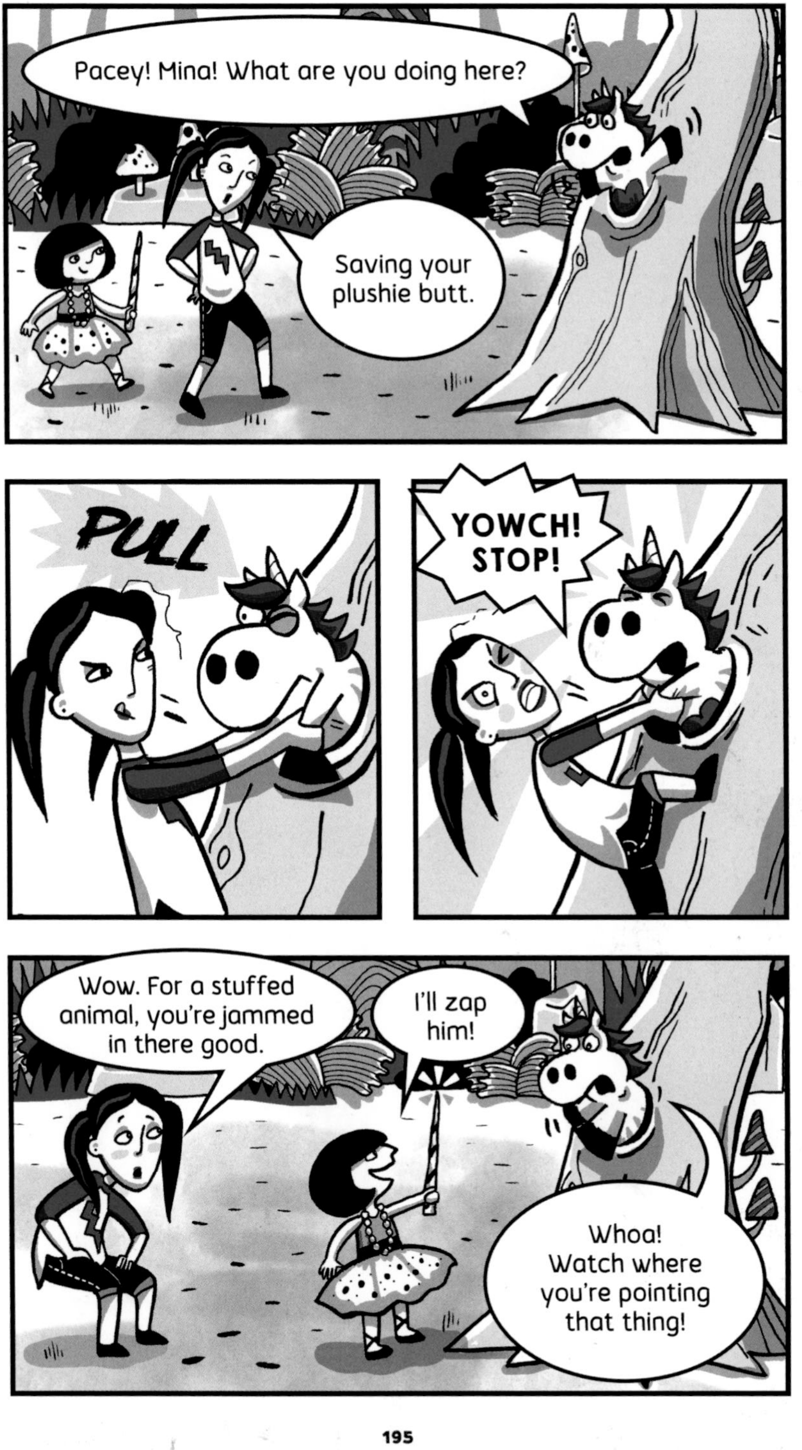
Pacey! Mina! What are you doing here?
Saving your plushie butt.
PULL
YOWCH! STOP!
Wow. For a stuffed animal, you're jammed in there good.
I'll zap him!
Whoa! Watch where you're pointing that thing!

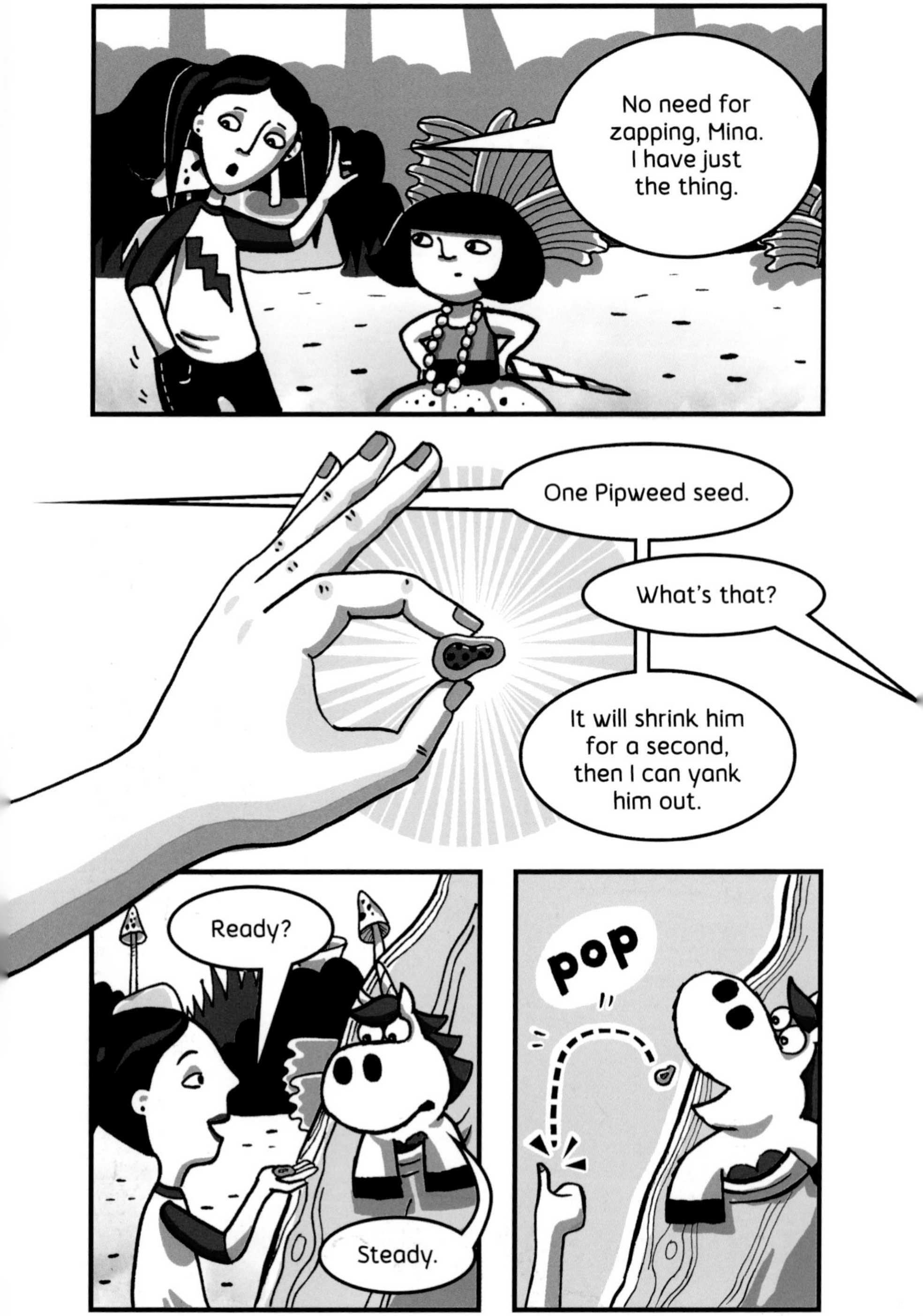
No need for zapping, Mina. I have just the thing.
One Pipweed seed.
What's that?
It will shrink him for a second, then I can yank him out.
Ready?
Steady.
pop

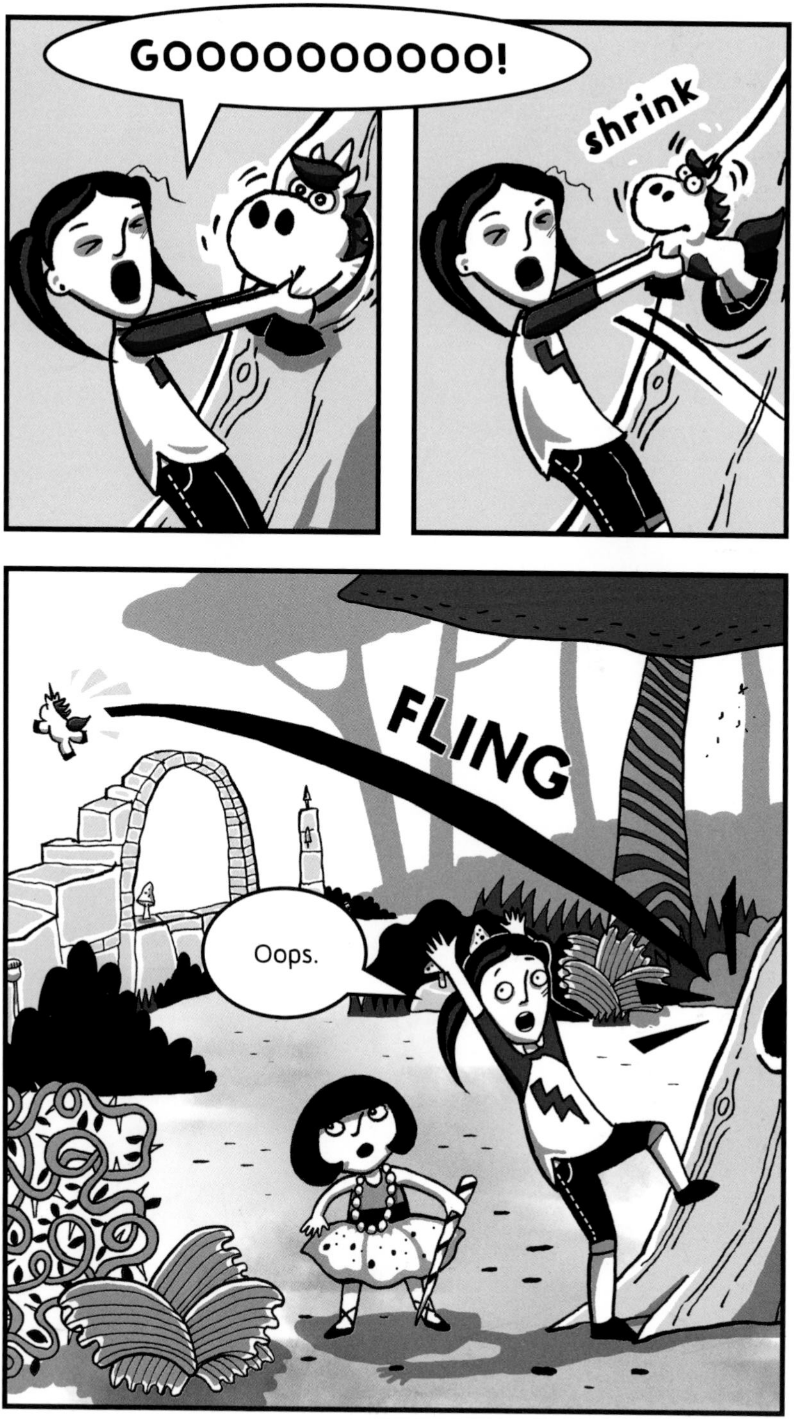
GOOOOOOOOOO!
shrink
FLING
Oops.

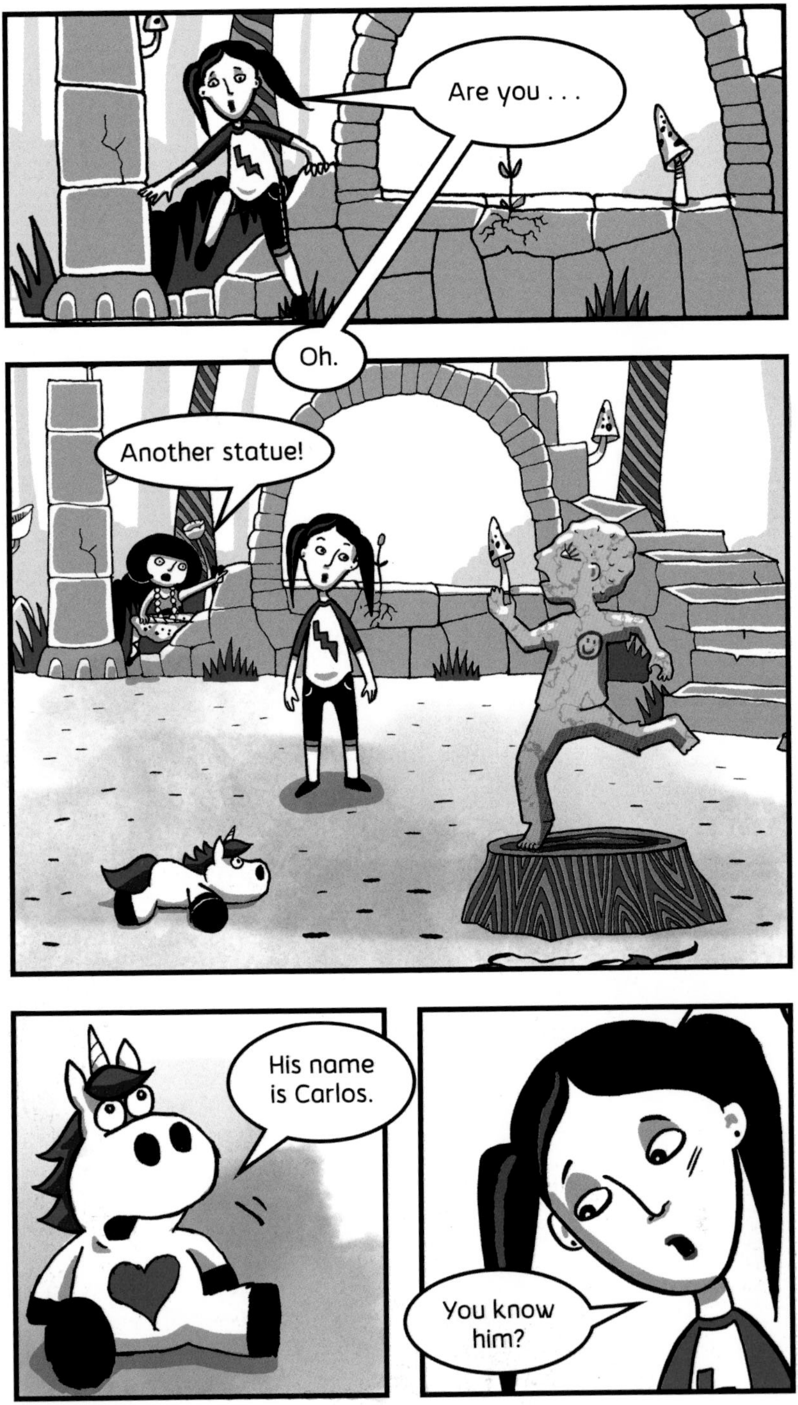
Are you . . .
Oh.
Another statue!
His name is Carlos.
You know him?

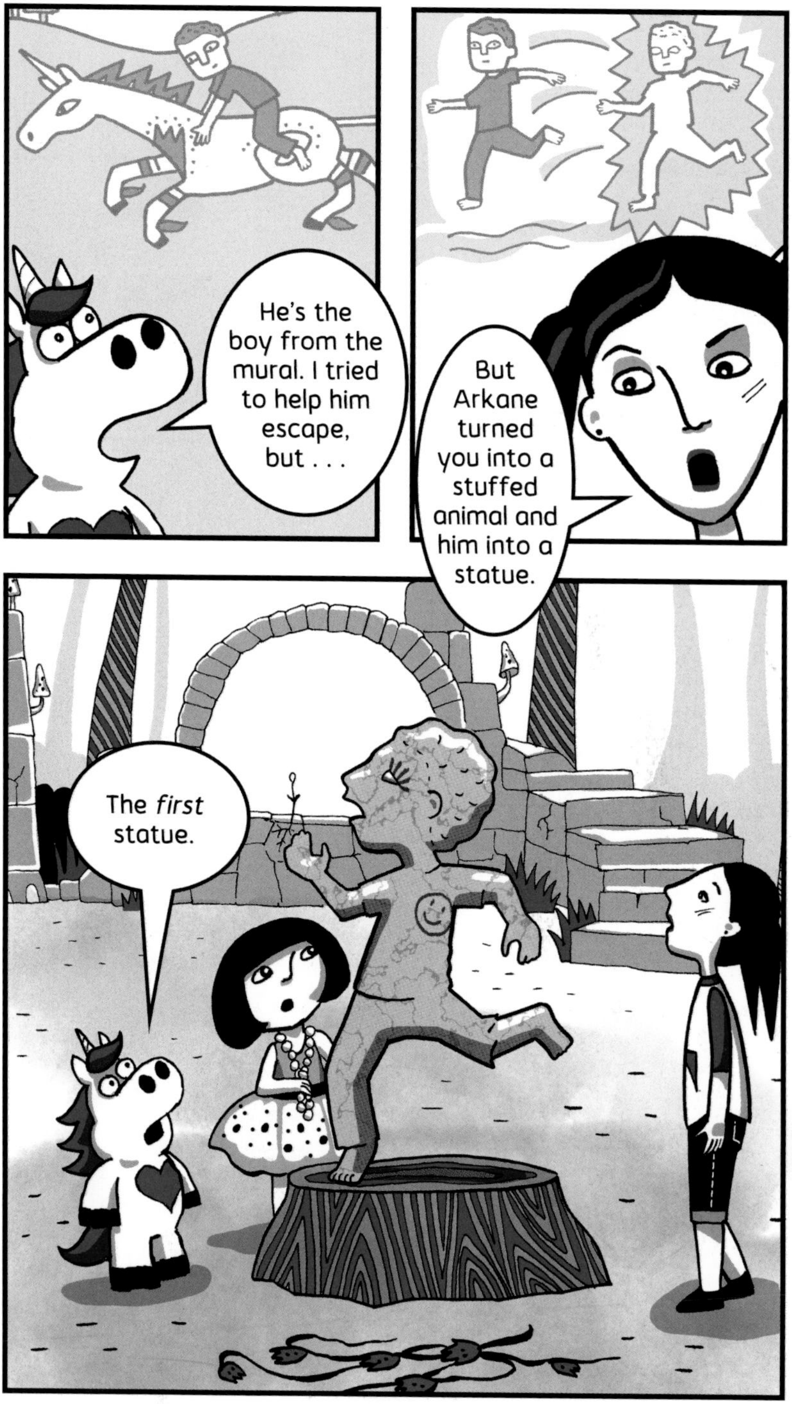
He's the boy from the mural. I tried to help him escape, but . . .
But Arkane turned you into a stuffed animal and him into a statue.
The *first* statue.

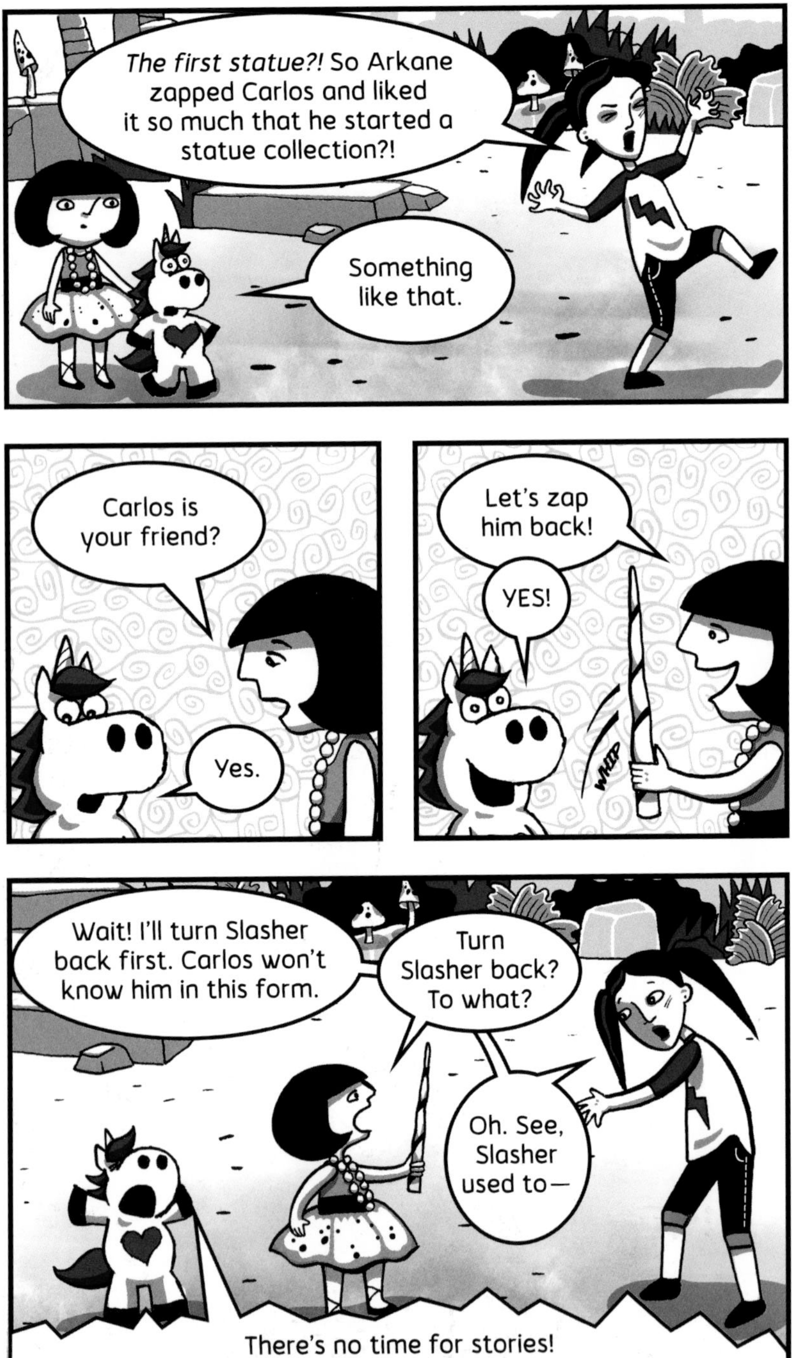
The first statue?! So Arkane zapped Carlos and liked it so much that he started a statue collection?!
Something like that.
Carlos is your friend?
Yes.
Let's zap him back!
YES!
WHIP
Wait! I'll turn Slasher back first. Carlos won't know him in this form.
Turn Slasher back? To what?
Oh. See, Slasher used to—
There's no time for stories! Arkane is probably halfway through the forest!

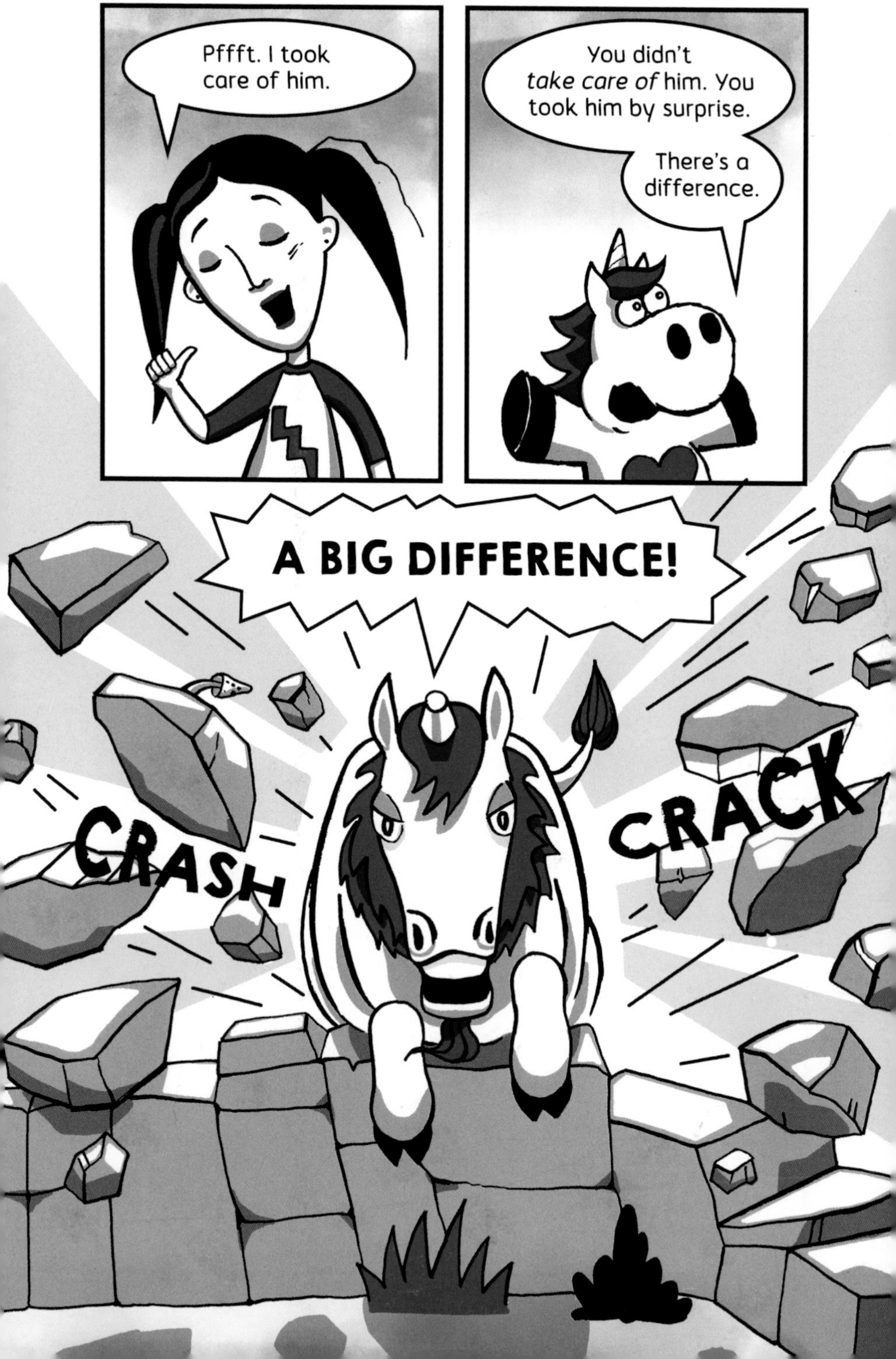
Pffft. I took care of him.
You didn't *take care of* him. You took him by surprise.
There's a difference.
A BIG DIFFERENCE!
CRASH
CRACK

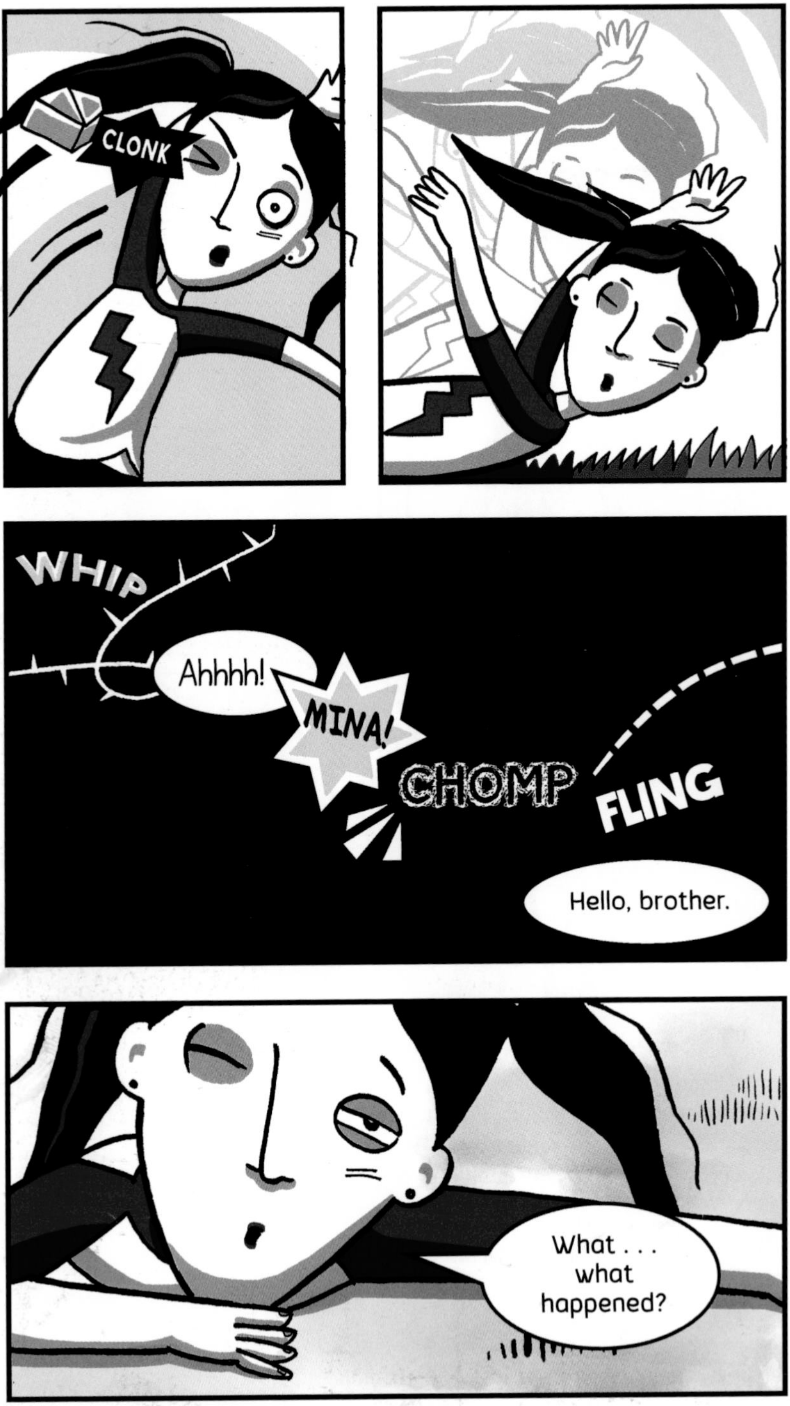
CLONK
WHIP
Ahhhh!
MINA!
CHOMP
FLING
Hello, brother.
What . . . what happened?

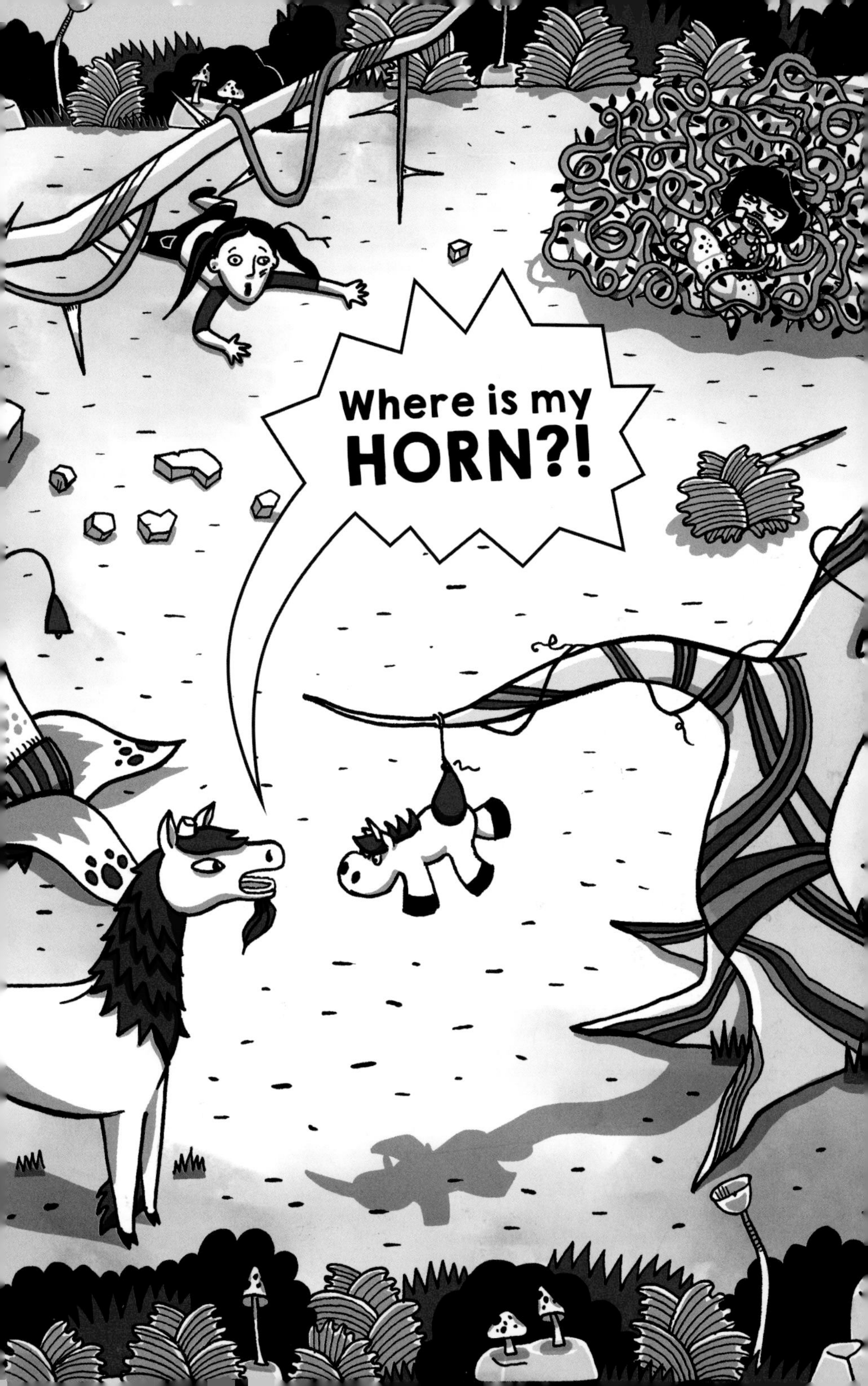
Where is my
HORN?!

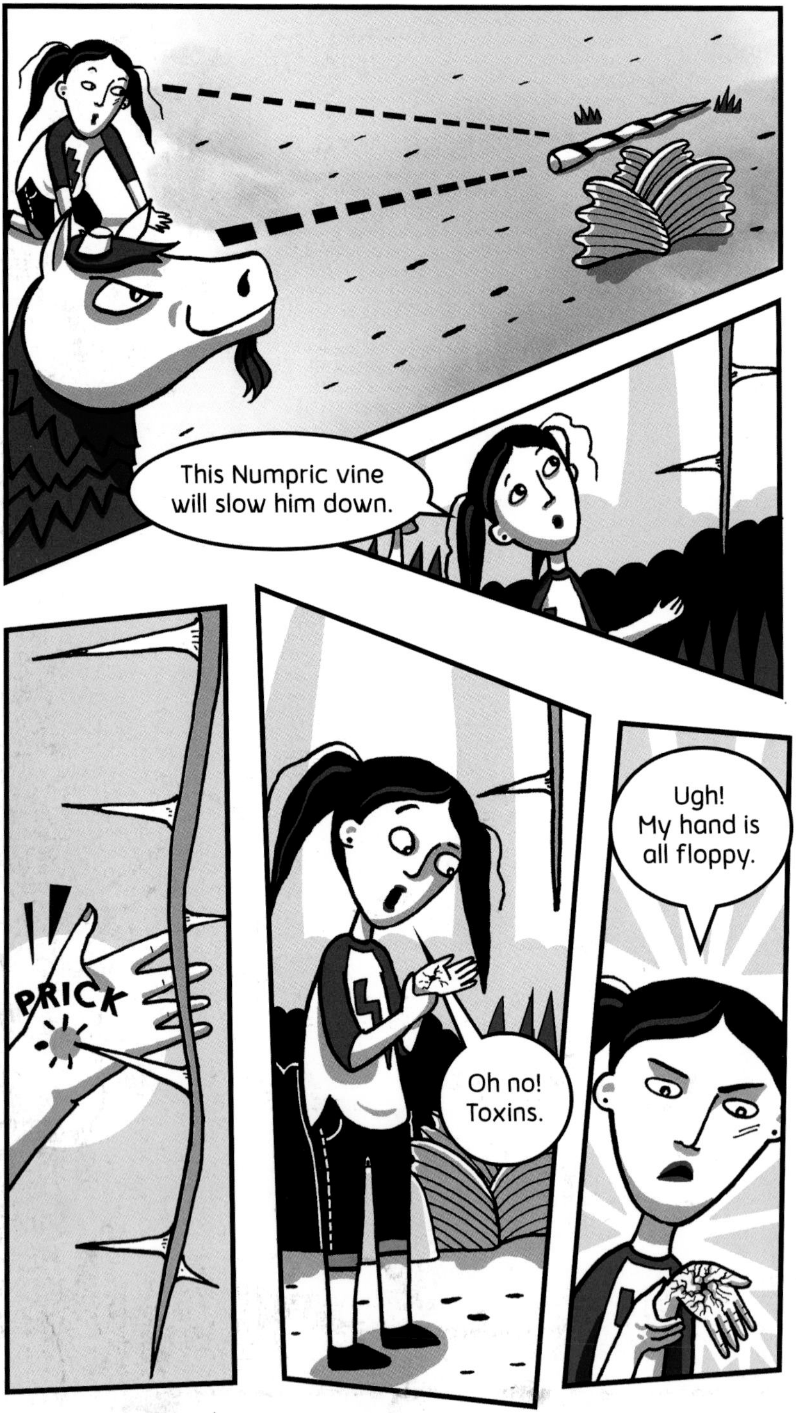
This Numpric vine will slow him down.
PRICK
Oh no! Toxins.
Ugh! My hand is all floppy.

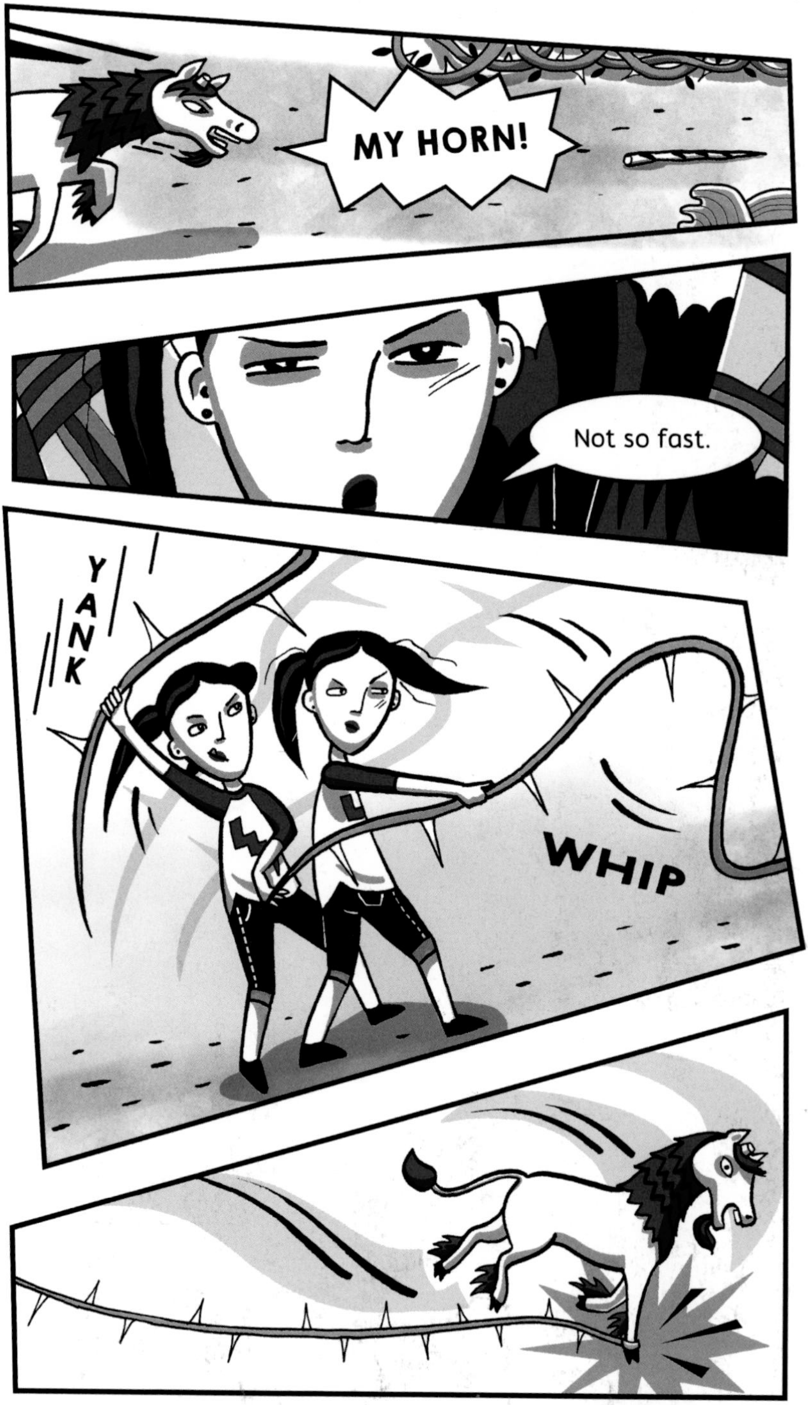
MY HORN!
Not so fast.
YANK
WHIP

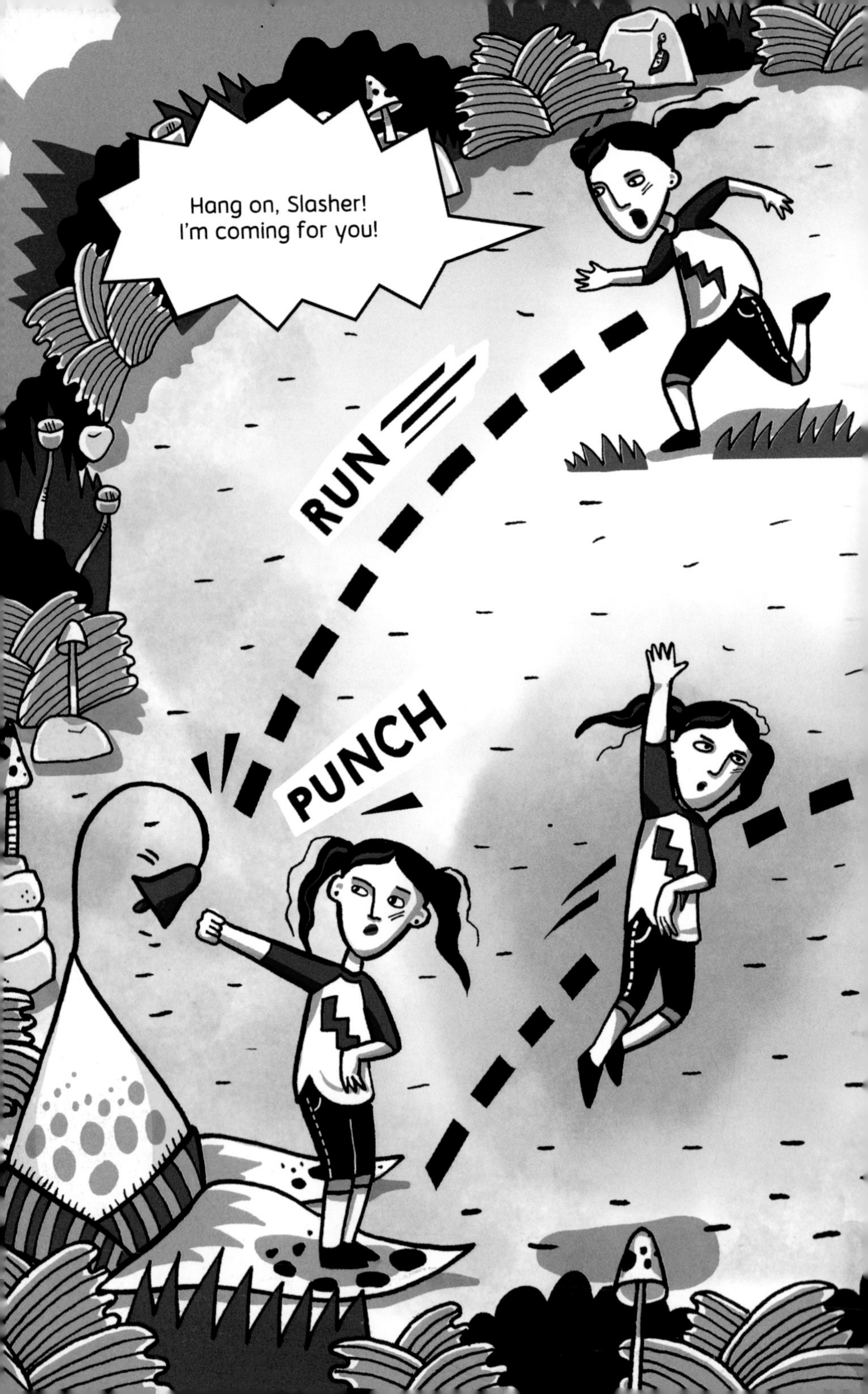
Hang on, Slasher!
I'm coming for you!
RUN
PUNCH

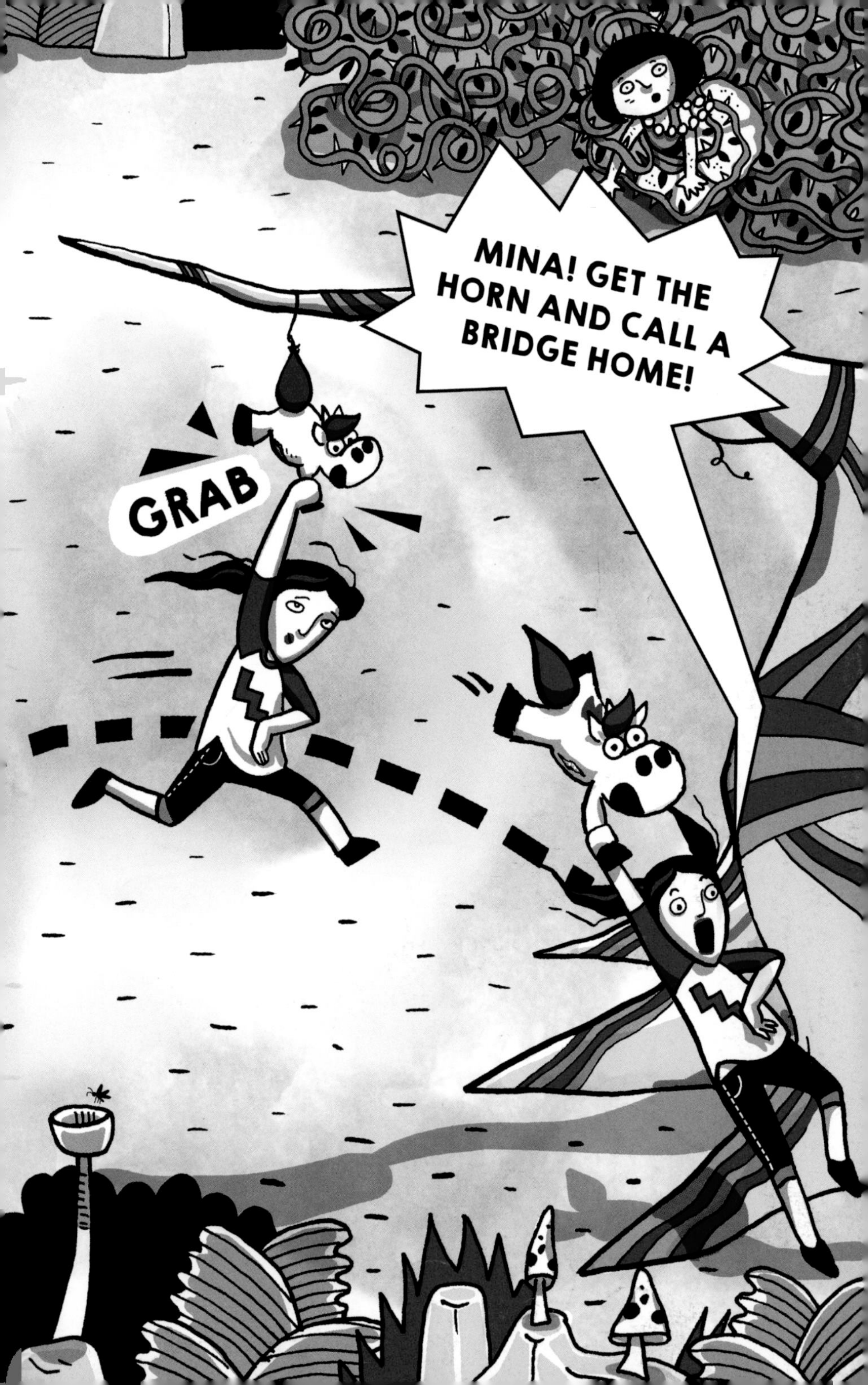
MINA! GET THE HORN AND CALL A BRIDGE HOME!
GRAB

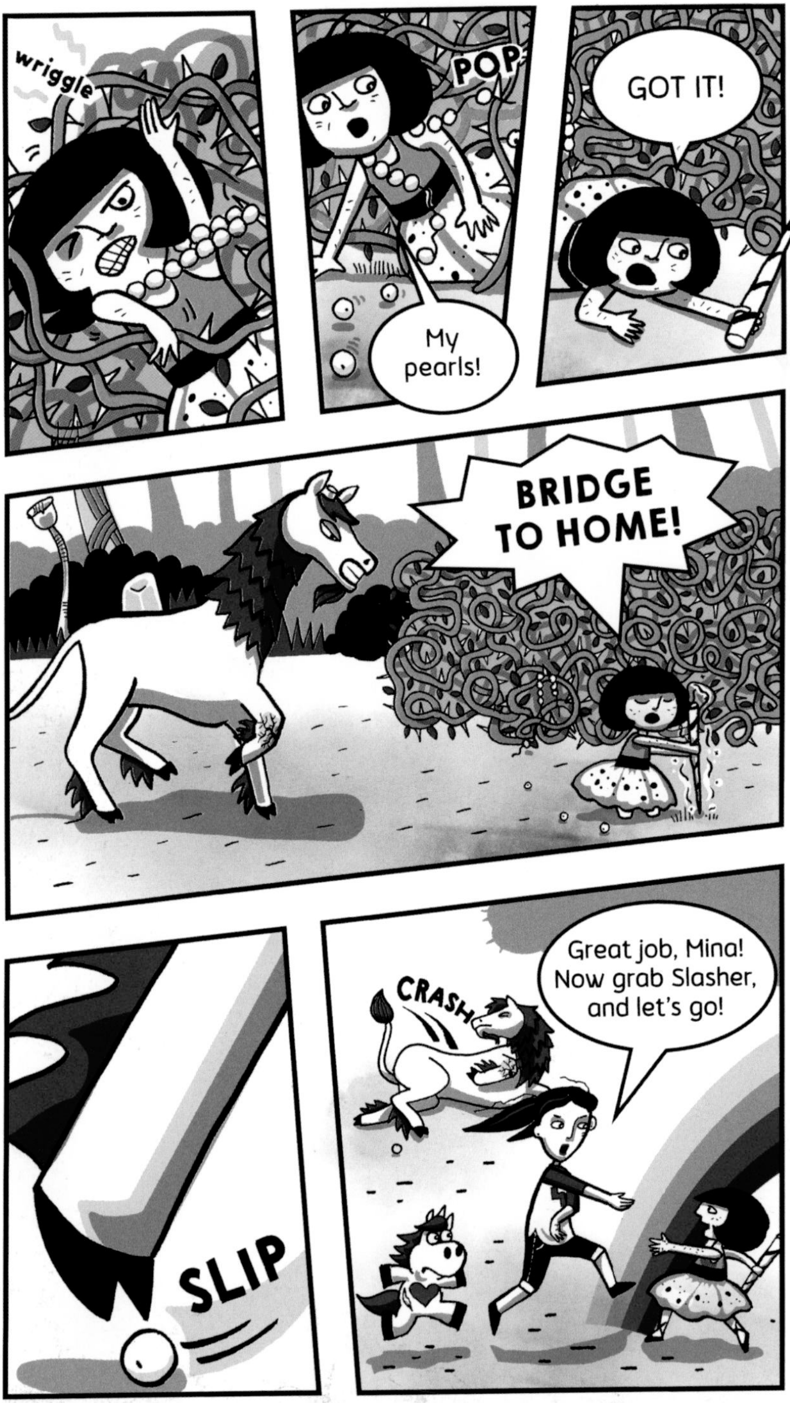
wriggle
POP
My pearls!
GOT IT!
BRIDGE TO HOME!
SLIP
CRASH
Great job, Mina! Now grab Slasher, and let's go!

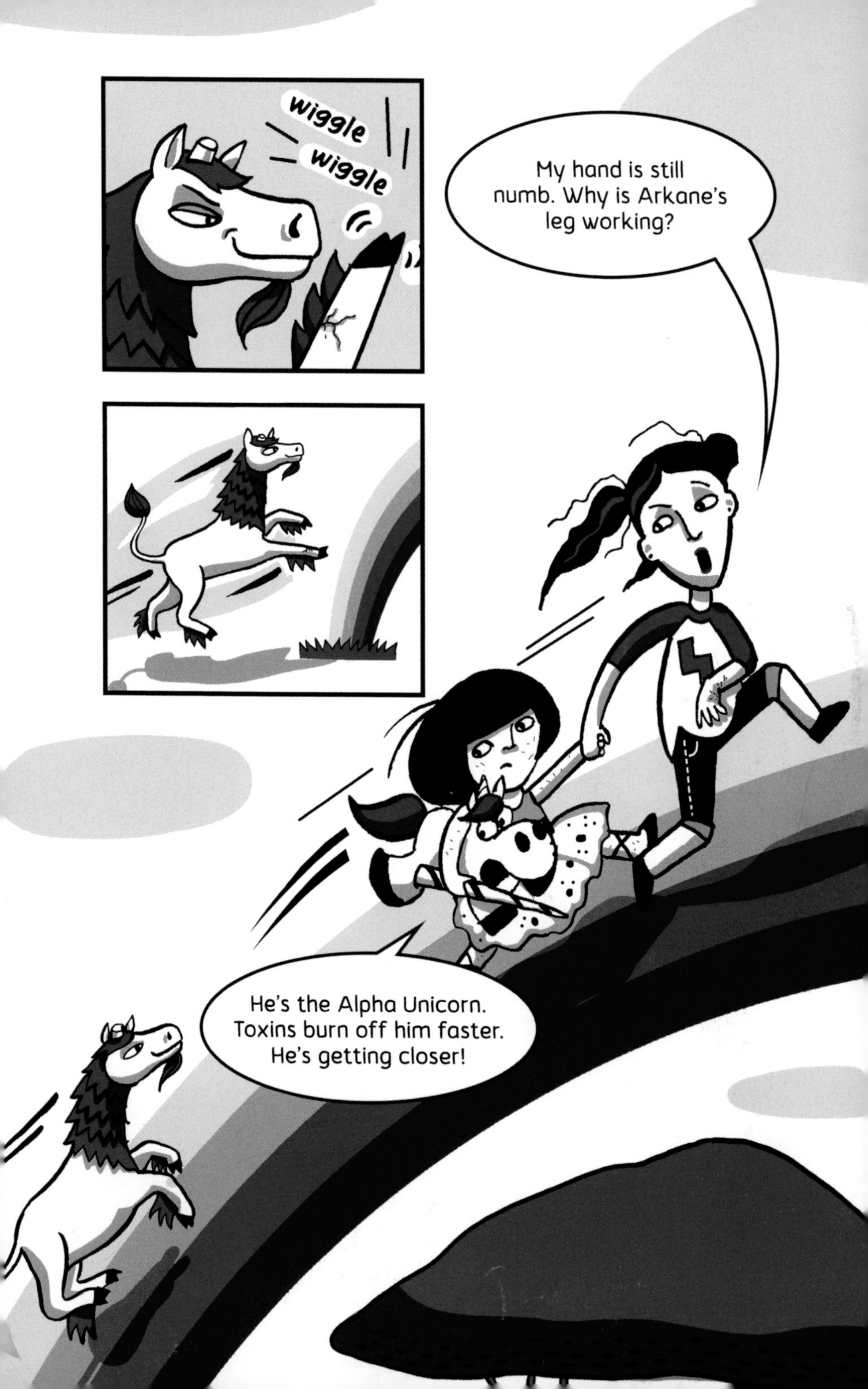
wiggle
wiggle
My hand is still numb. Why is Arkane's leg working?
He's the Alpha Unicorn. Toxins burn off him faster. He's getting closer!

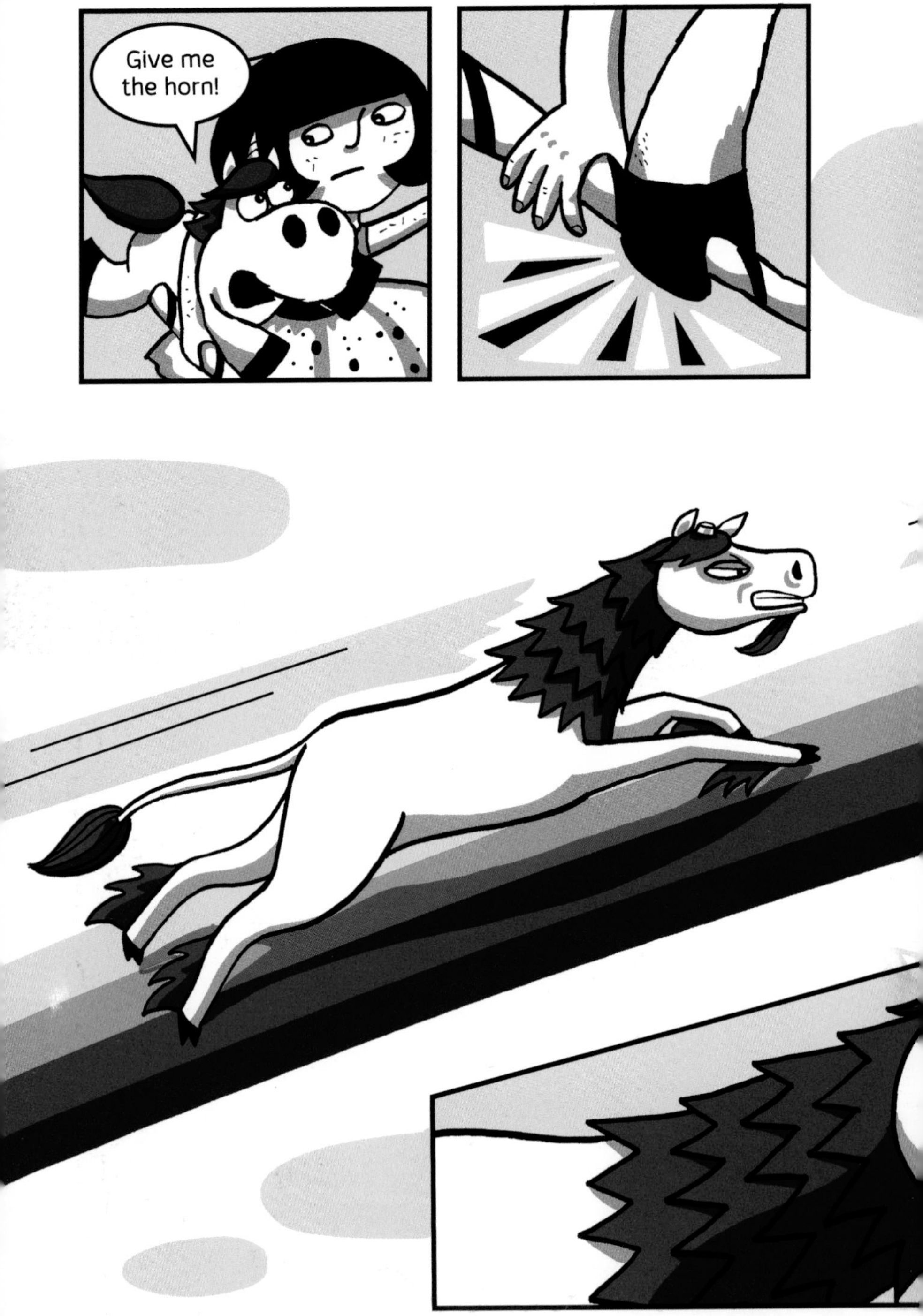
Give me the horn!

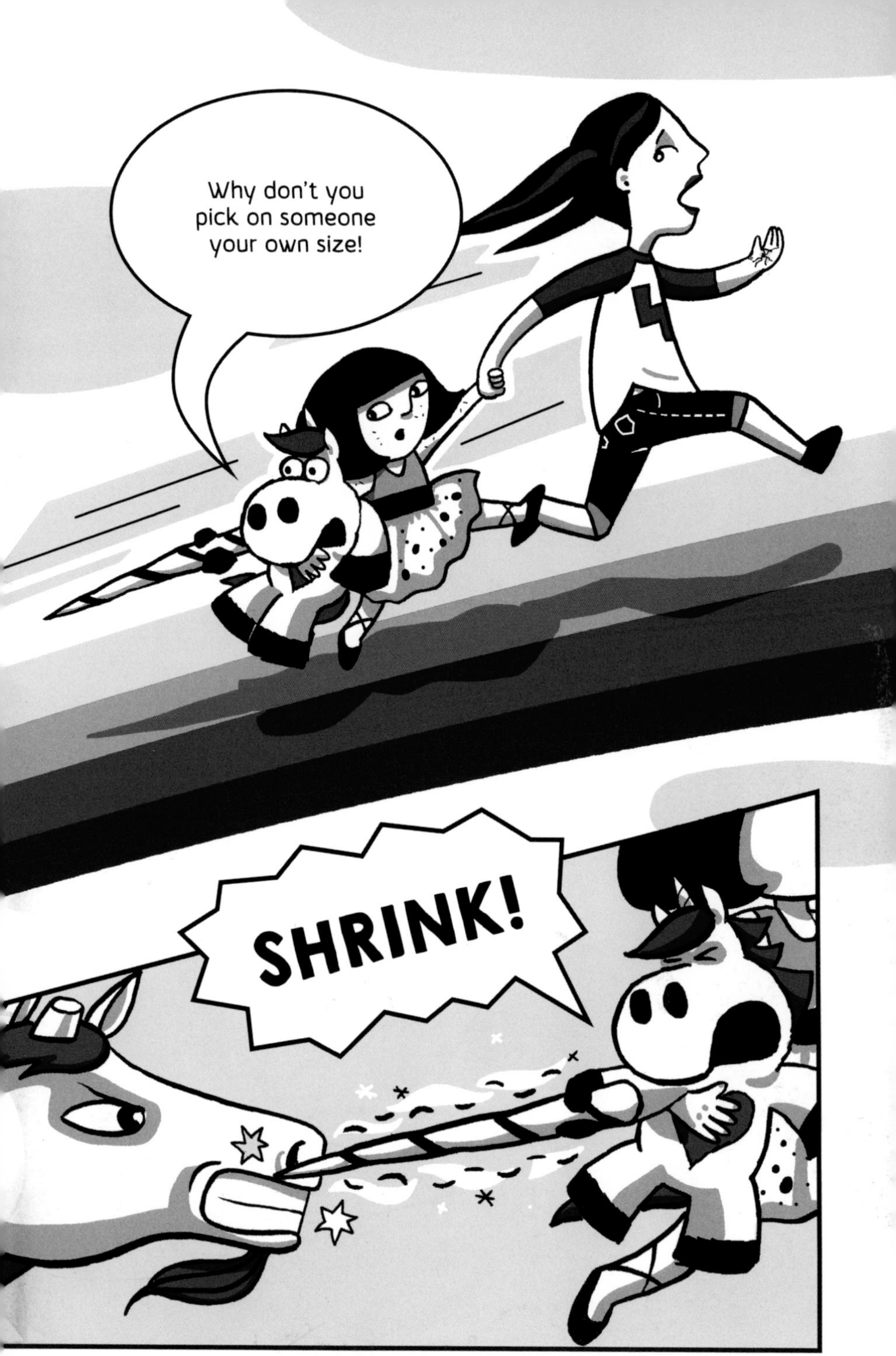
Why don't you pick on someone your own size!
SHRINK!

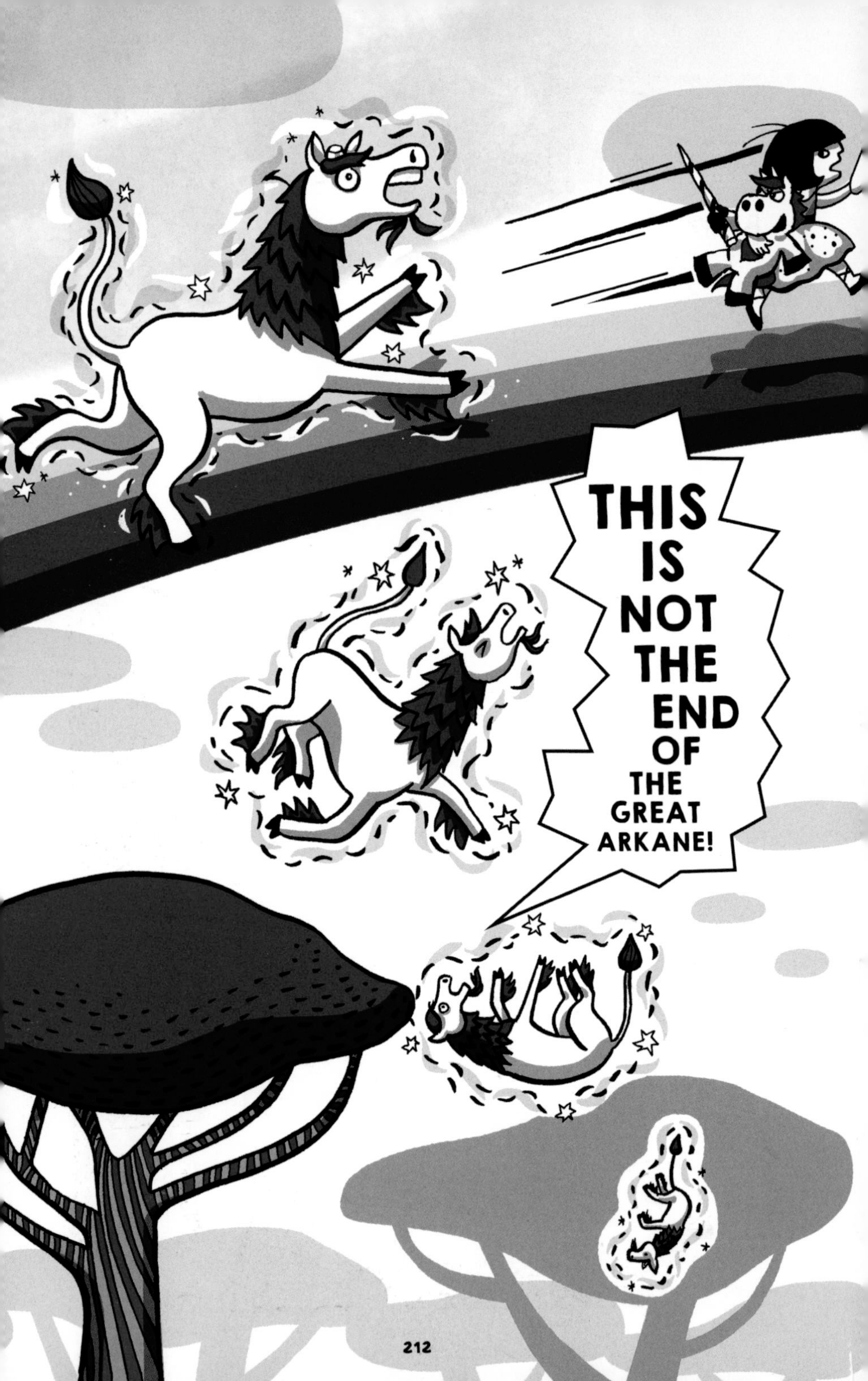
THIS IS NOT THE END OF THE GREAT ARKANE!

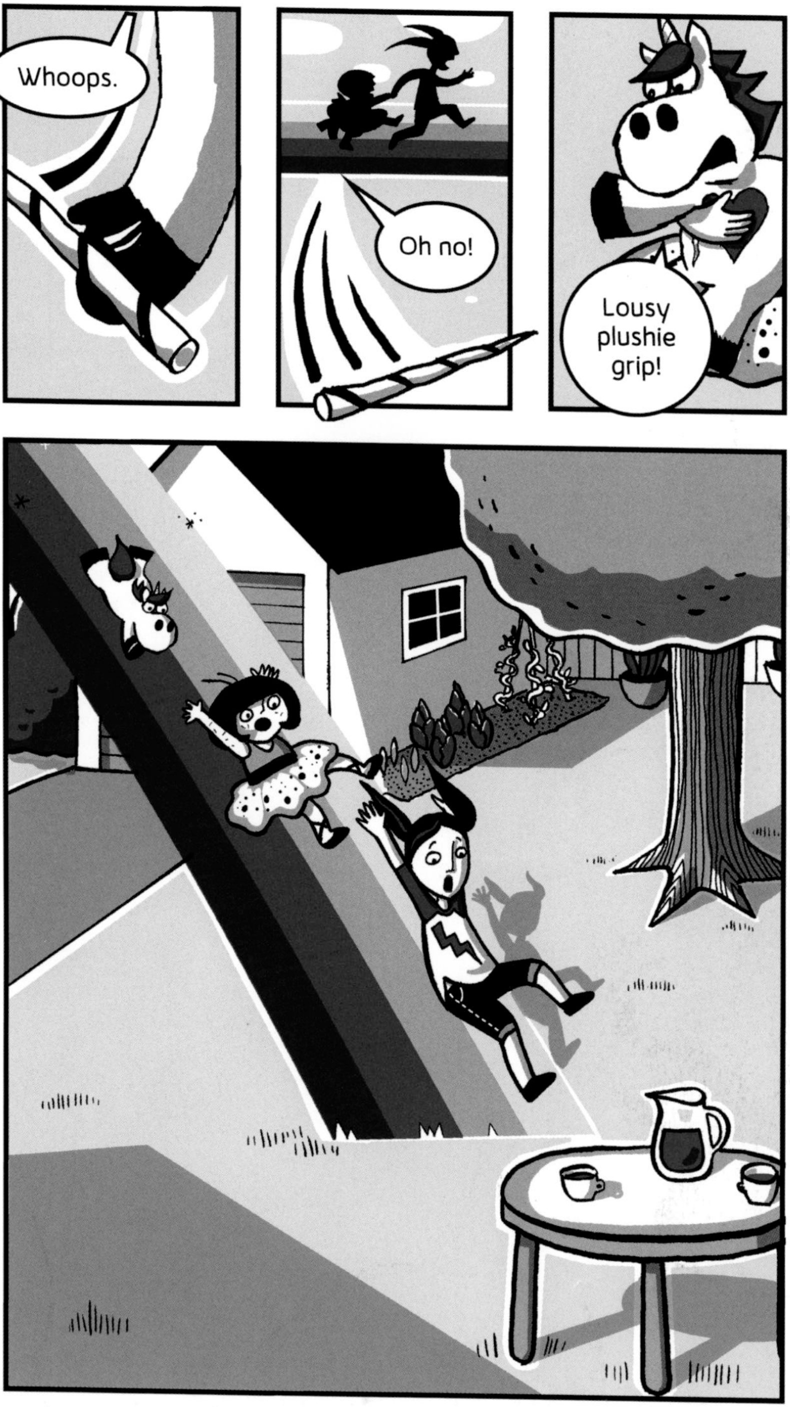
Whoops.
Oh no!
Lousy plushie grip!

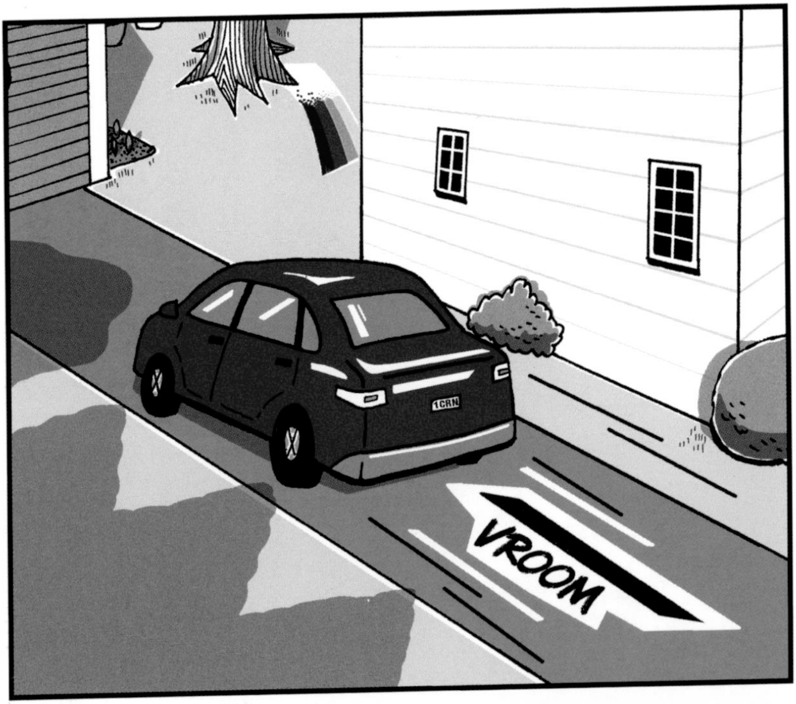
1CRN
VROOM

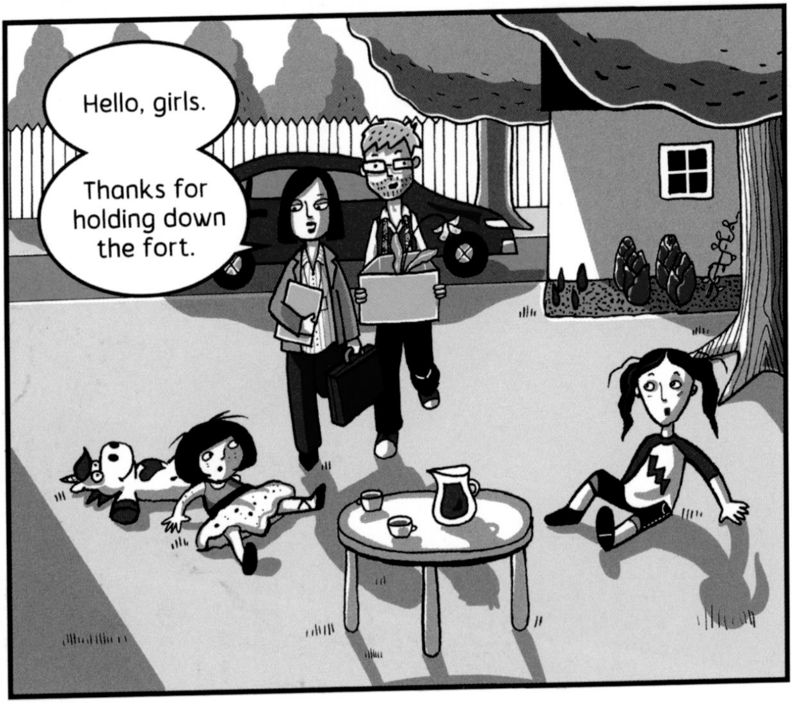
Hello, girls.
Thanks for holding down the fort.

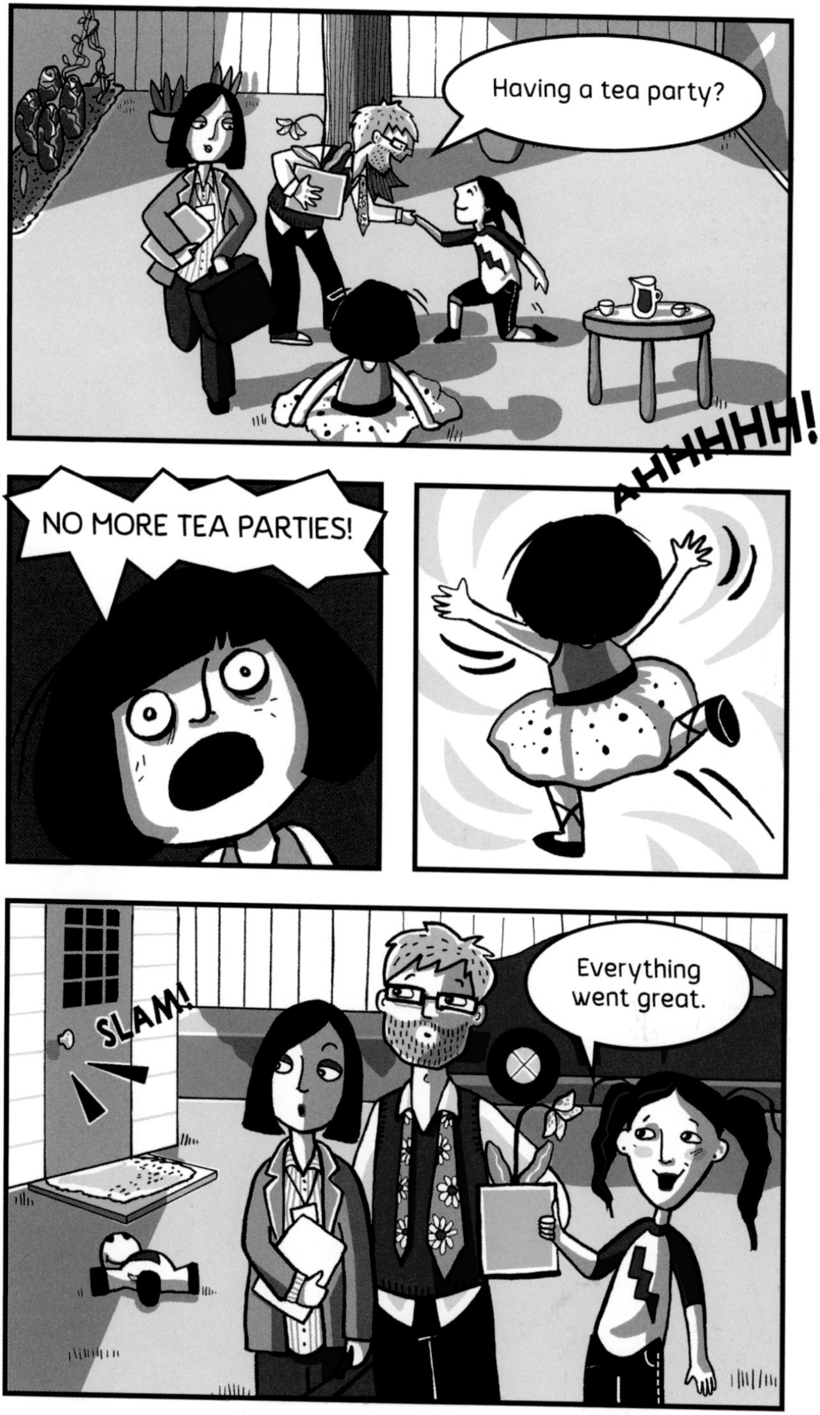
Having a tea party?
NO MORE TEA PARTIES!
AHHHHH!
SLAM!
Everything went great.

CHAPTER 12

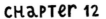

BEDTIME STORY

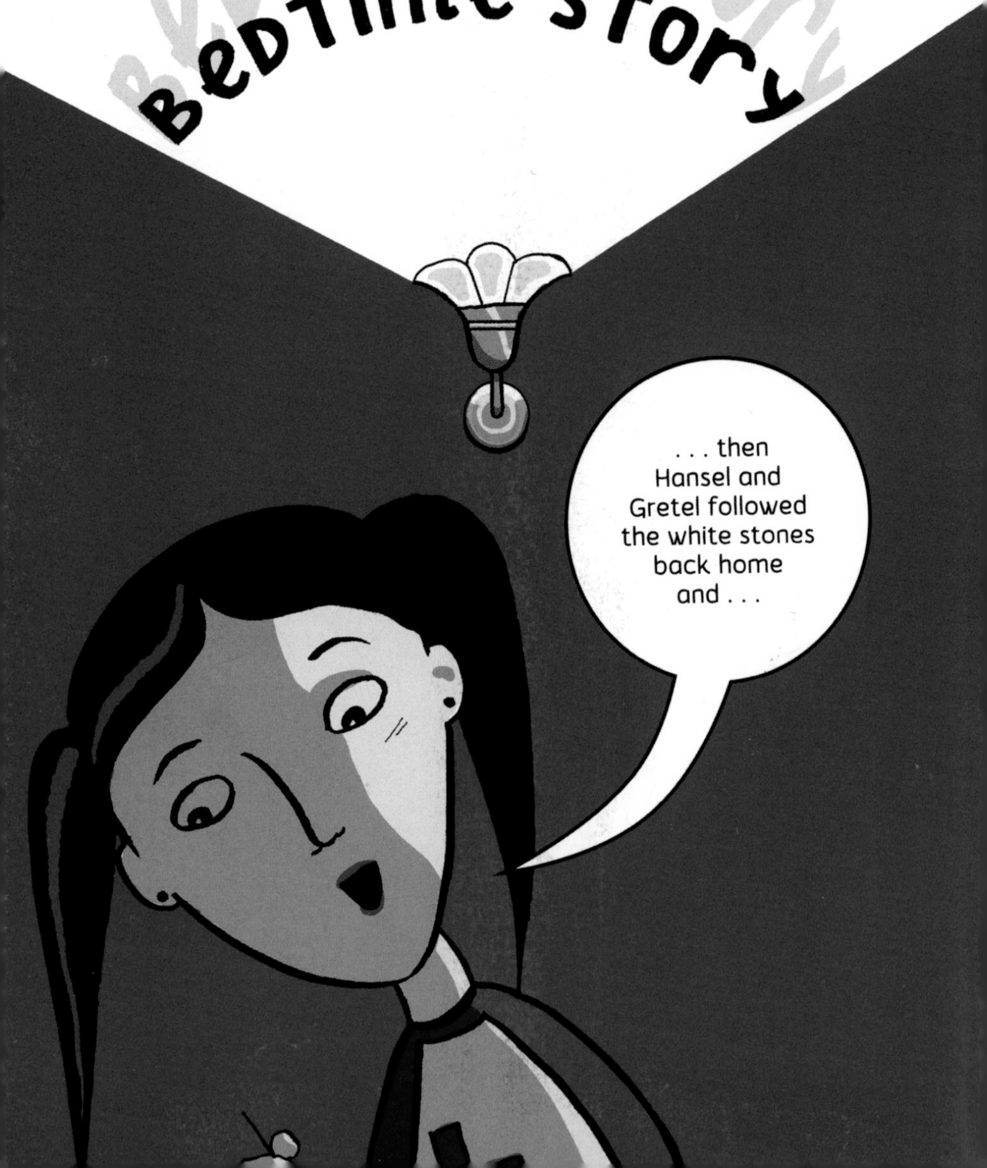
. . . then Hansel and Gretel followed the white stones back home and . . .

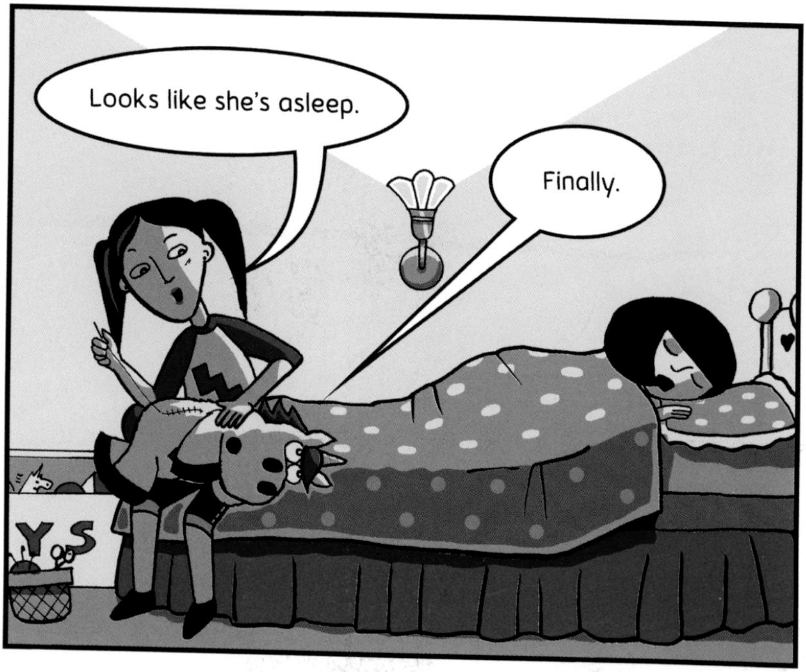
Looks like she's asleep.
Finally.

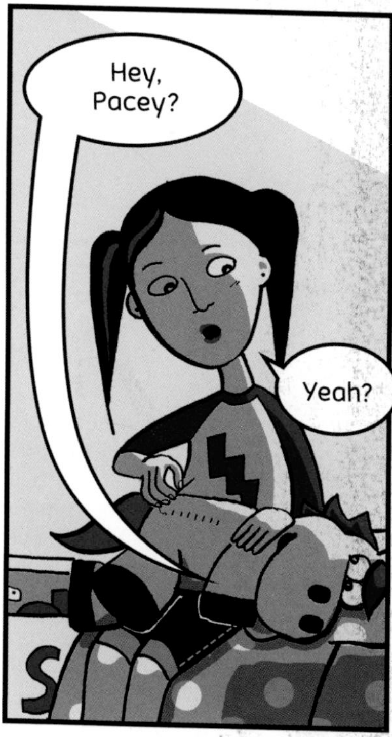
Hey,
Pacey?
Yeah?

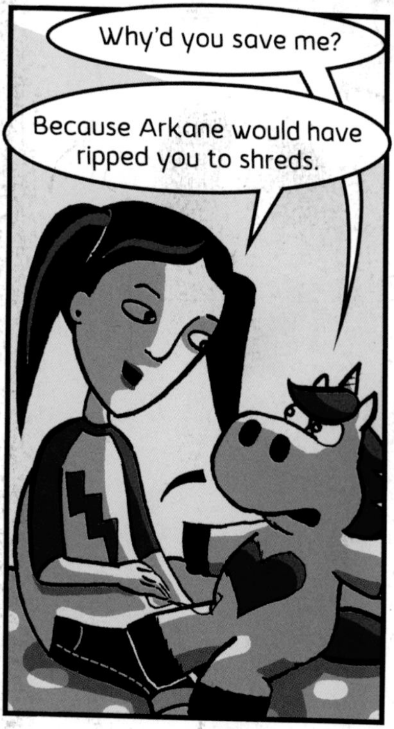
Why'd you save me?
Because Arkane would have
ripped you to shreds.

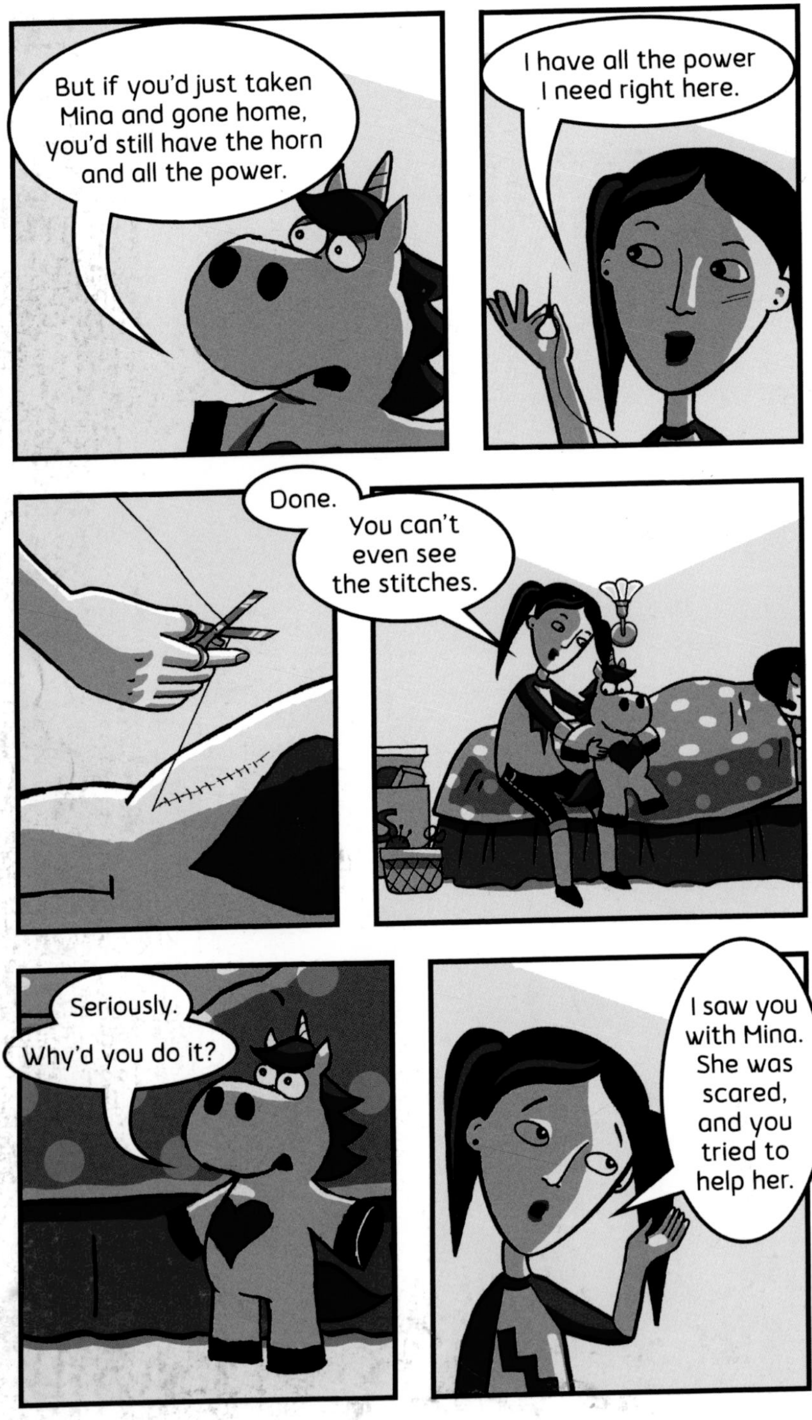
But if you'd just taken Mina and gone home, you'd still have the horn and all the power.
I have all the power I need right here.
Done.
You can't even see the stitches.
Seriously.
Why'd you do it?
I saw you with Mina. She was scared, and you tried to help her.

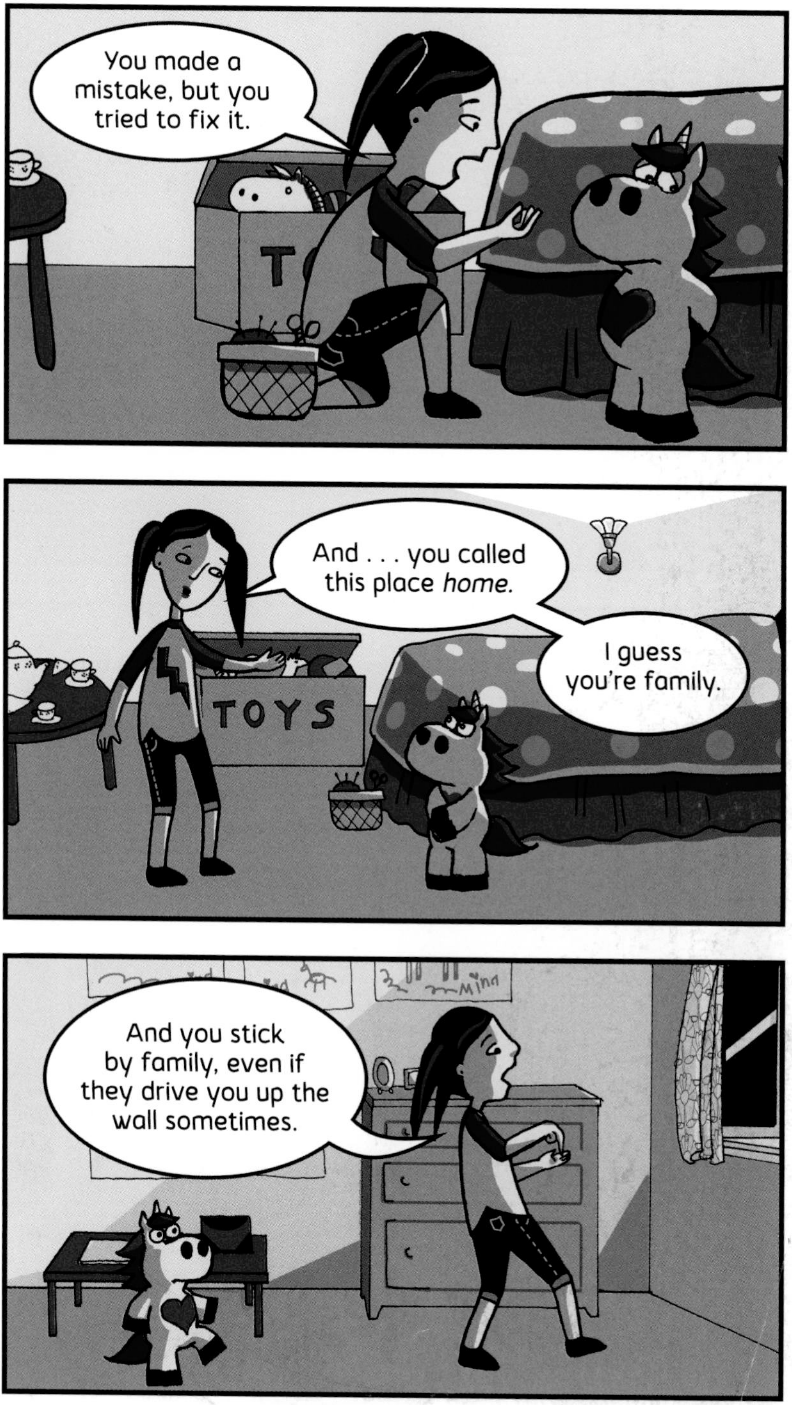
You made a mistake, but you tried to fix it.
TOYS
And . . . you called this place *home.*
I guess you're family.
And you stick by family, even if they drive you up the wall sometimes.

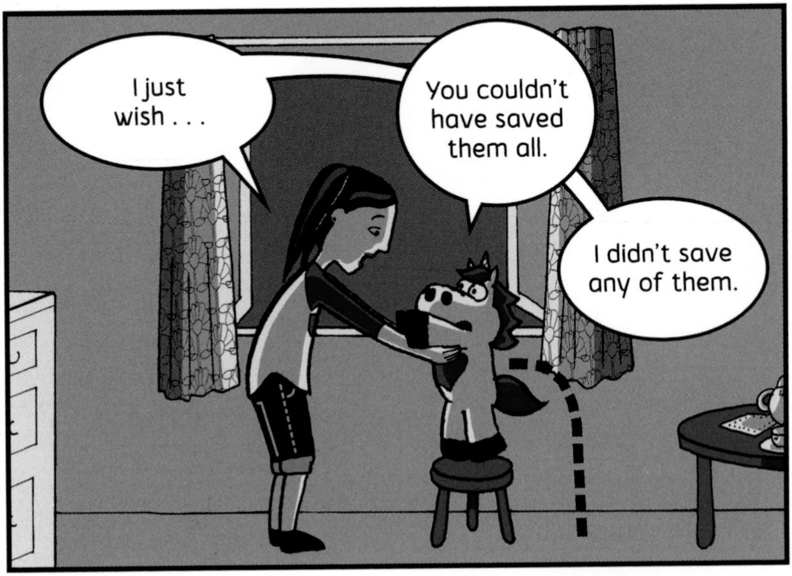
I just wish . . .
You couldn't have saved them all.
I didn't save any of them.

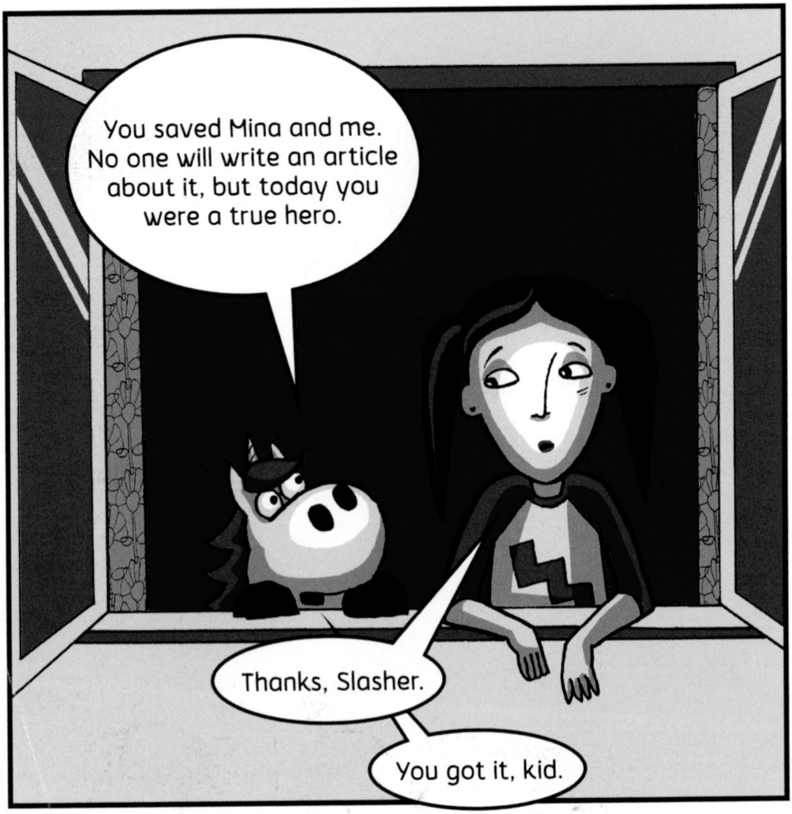
You saved Mina and me. No one will write an article about it, but today you were a true hero.
Thanks, Slasher.
You got it, kid.

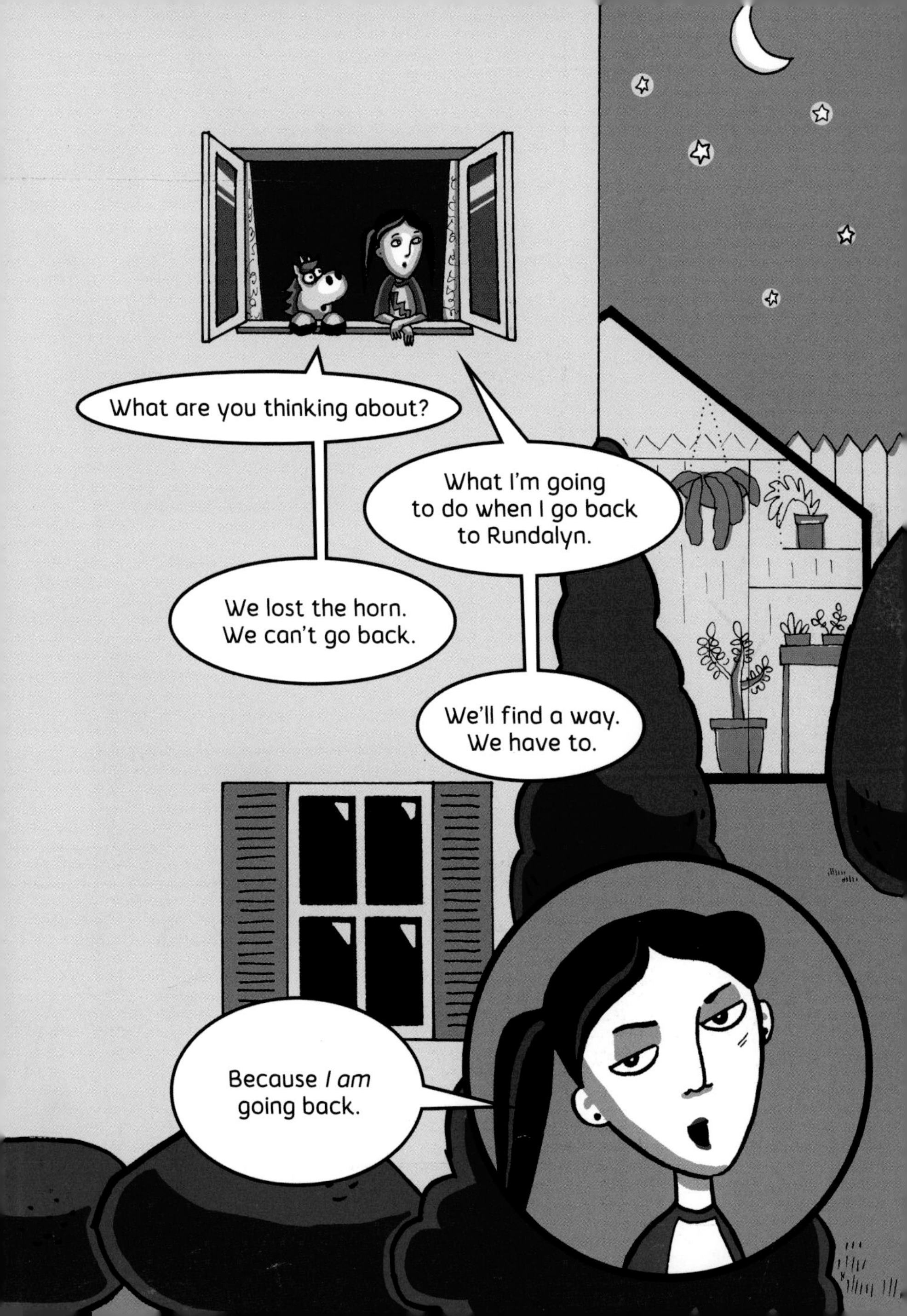
What are you thinking about?
What I'm going to do when I go back to Rundalyn.
We lost the horn. We can't go back.
We'll find a way. We have to.
Because *I am* going back.

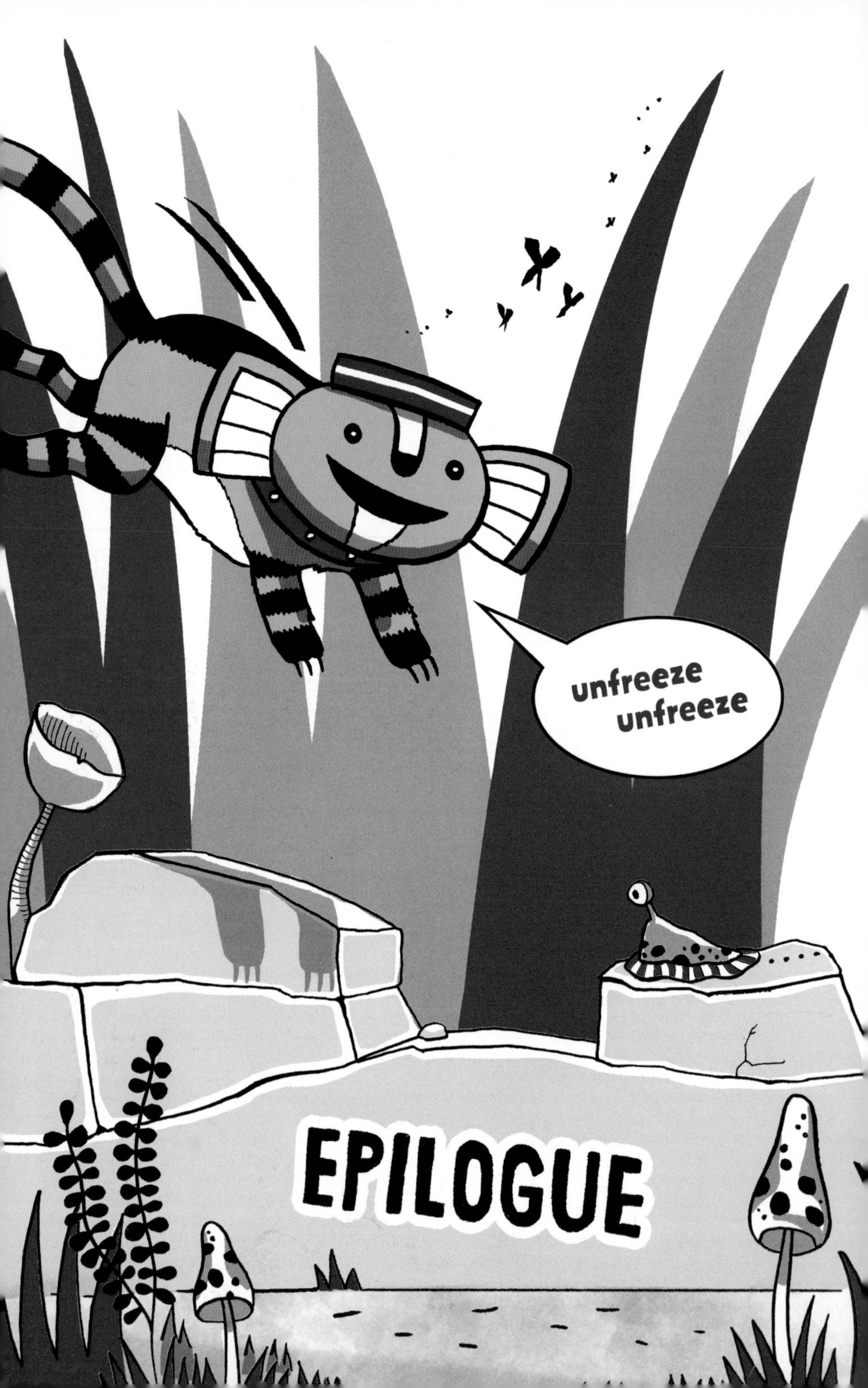
unfreeze
unfreeze
EPILOGUE

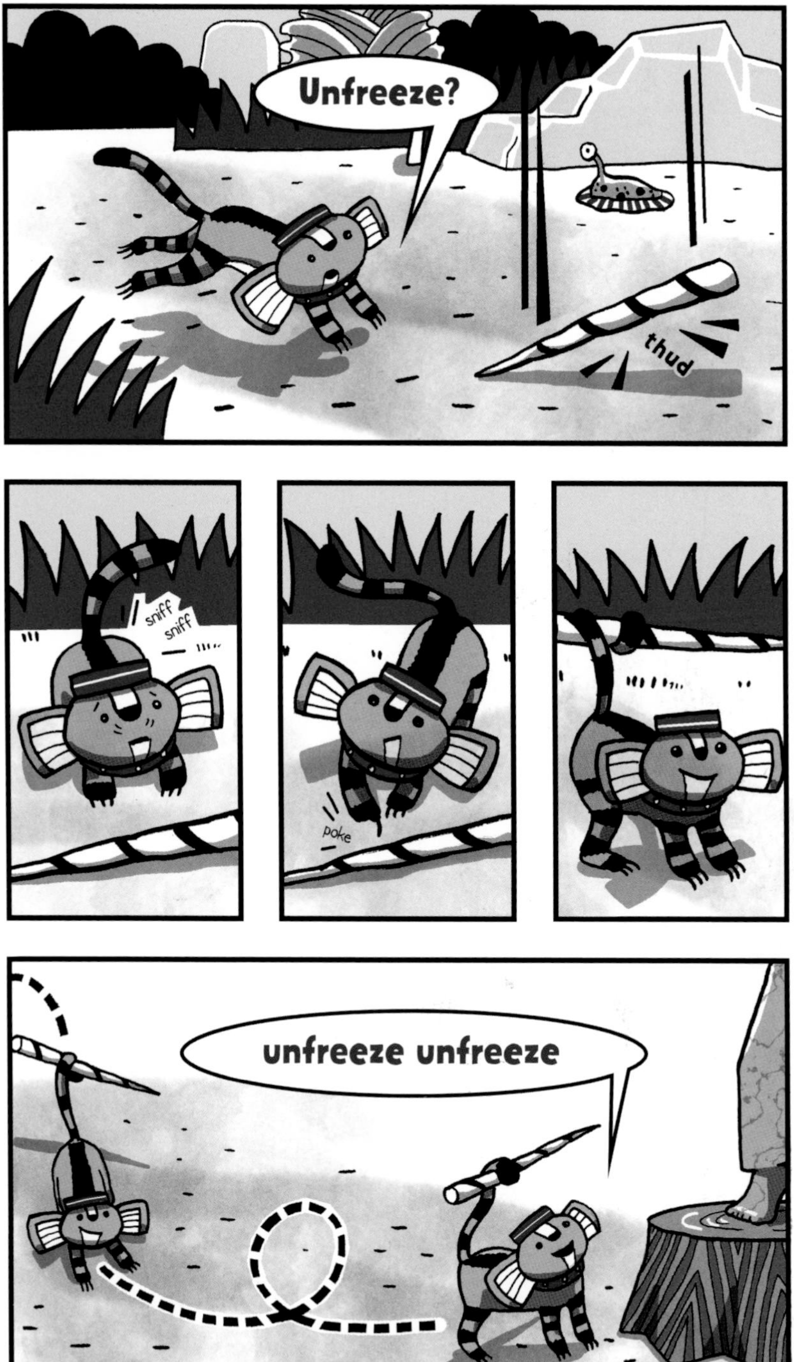
Unfreeze?
thud
sniff sniff
poke
unfreeze unfreeze

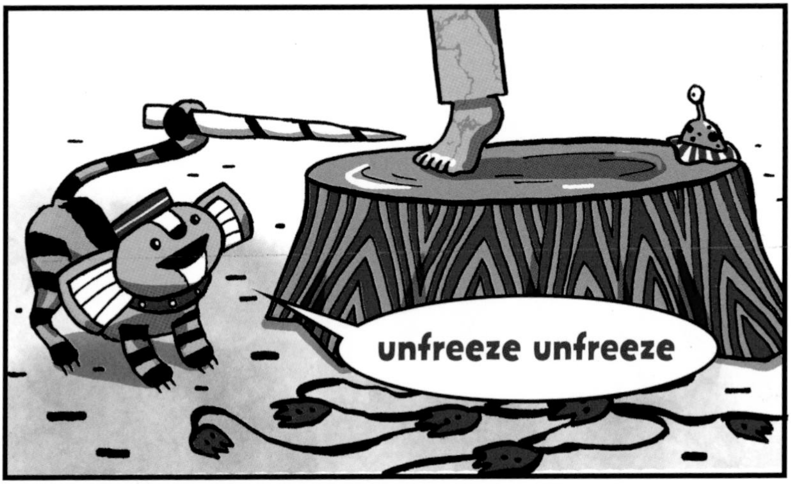
unfreeze unfreeze

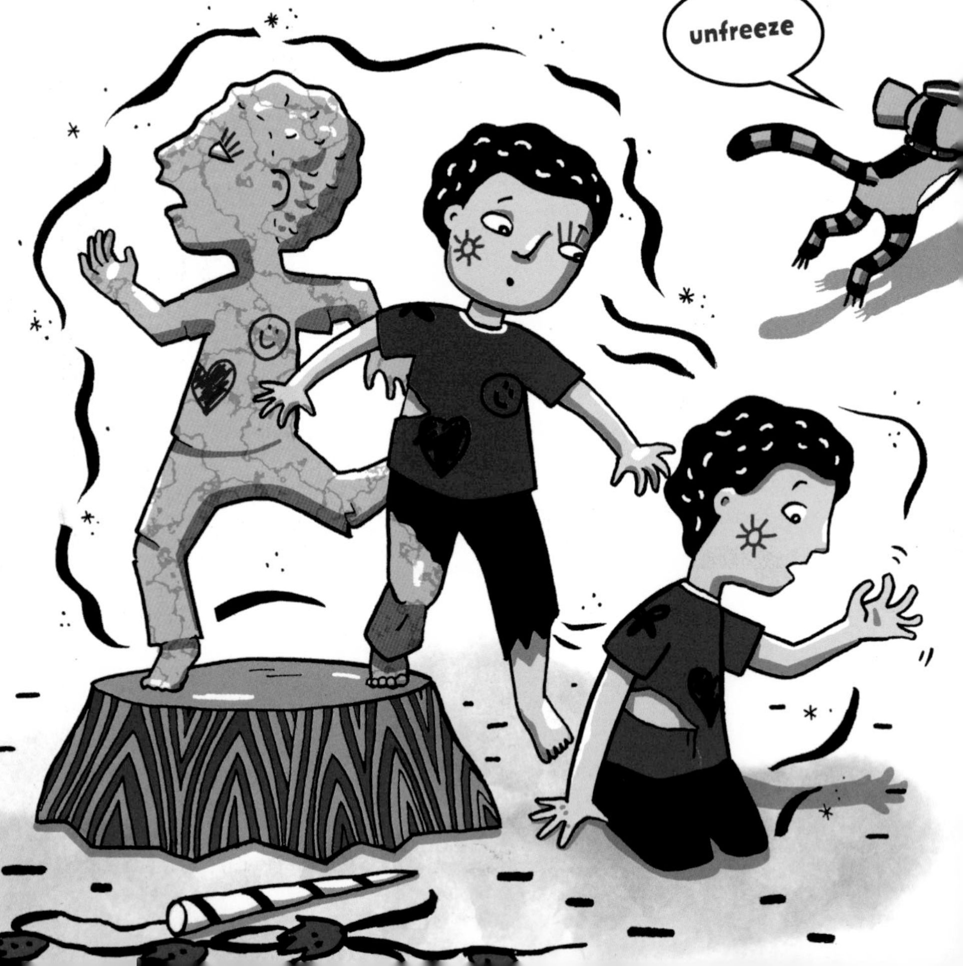
unfreeze

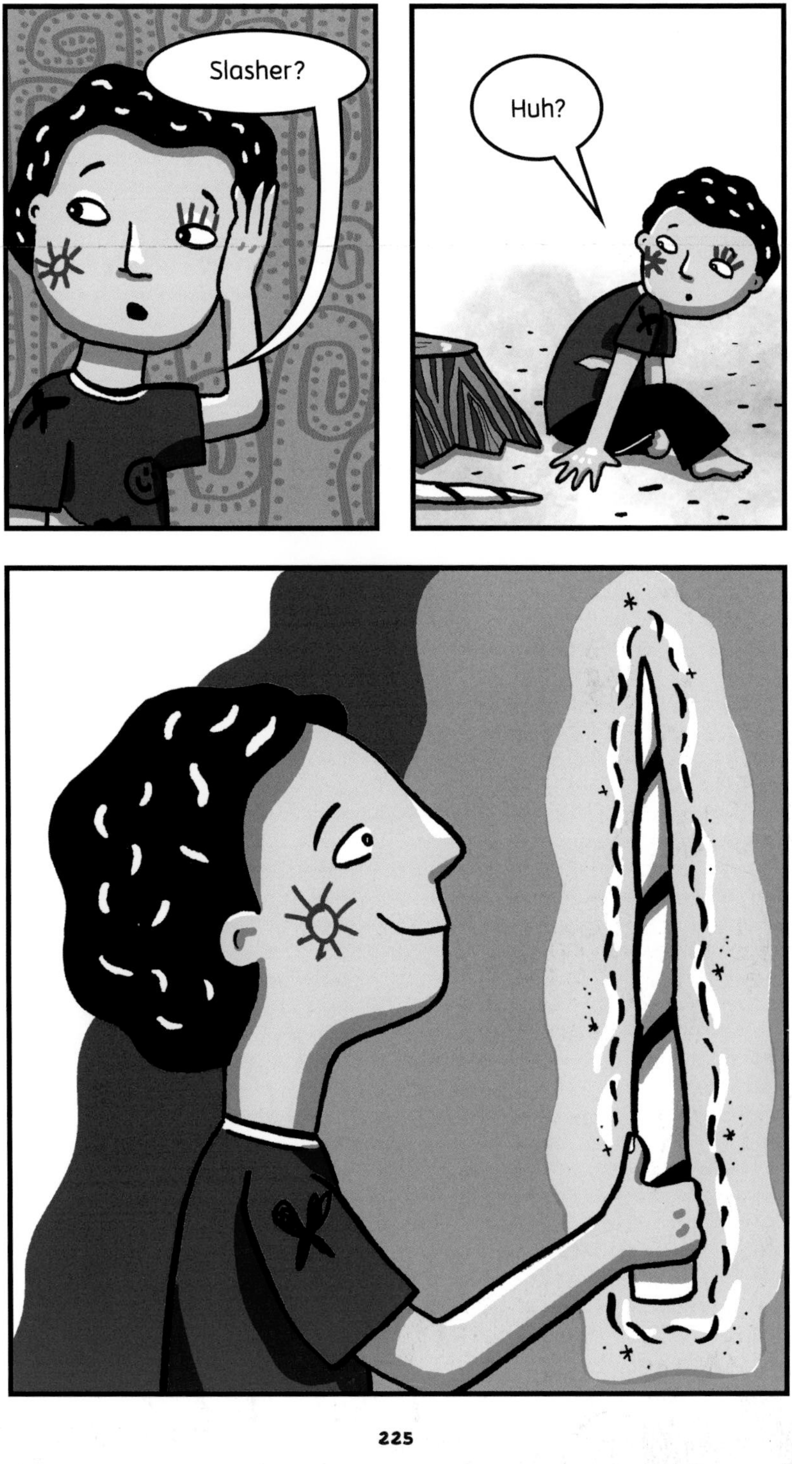
Slasher?
Huh?

The ~~End~~

BEGINNING

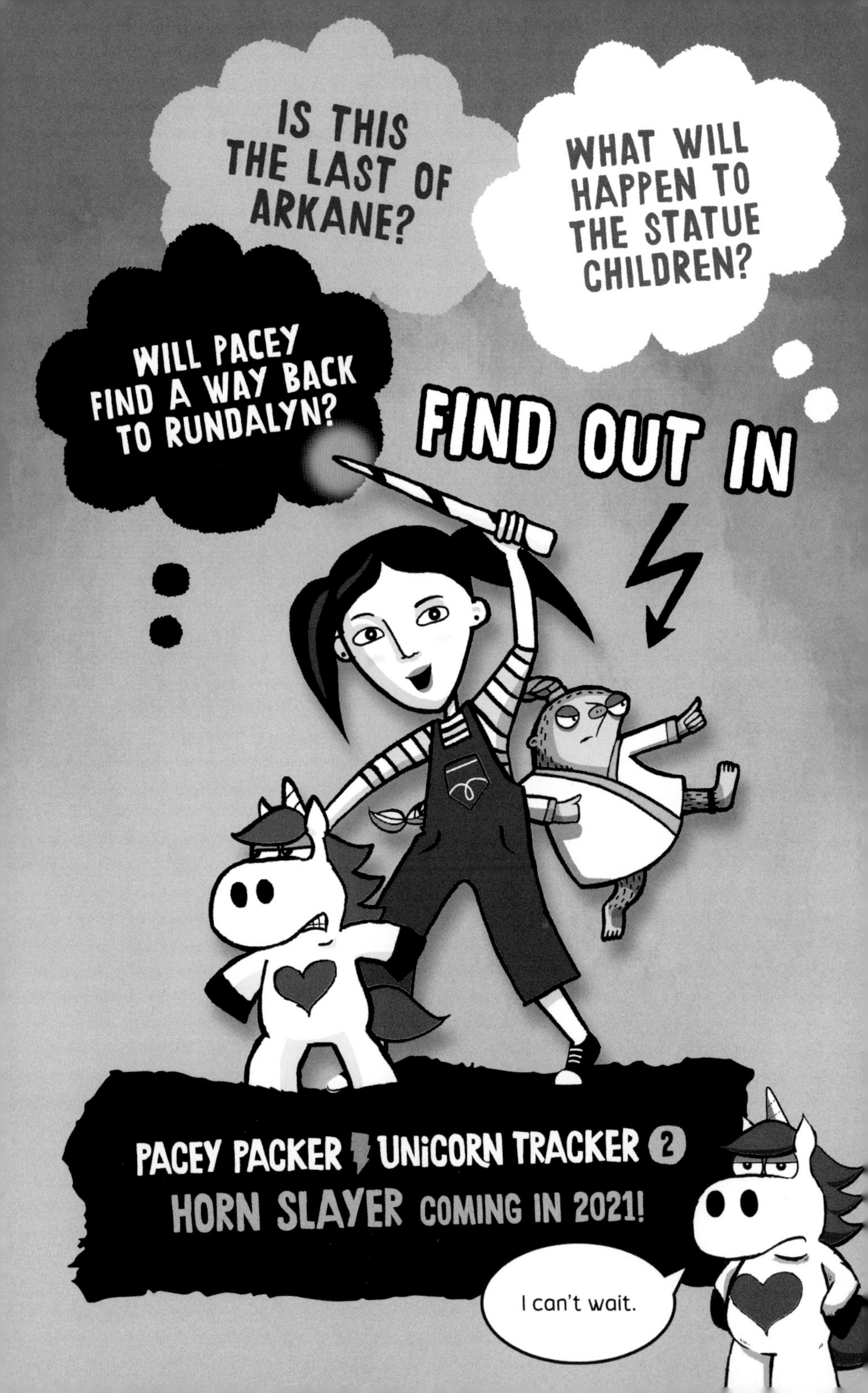
IS THIS THE LAST OF ARKANE?
WHAT WILL HAPPEN TO THE STATUE CHILDREN?
WILL PACEY FIND A WAY BACK TO RUNDALYN?
FIND OUT IN
PACEY PACKER UNICORN TRACKER 2
HORN SLAYER COMING IN 2021!
I can't wait.

DRAW IT! ⚡ SLASHER

1
Draw a wide oval.
Draw two circles on top.
(I sketch in pencil.)

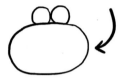

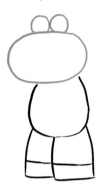

2
Draw a U
below the oval.
Draw two legs.

3
Draw an arm on
each side of the body.

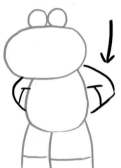

4
Draw the ear
on the right.
Then the front hair.
Then the back ear.
Add the horn.

5
Draw the back
hair and the tail.
Add details to
the eyes, nose,
and mouth.
Draw the belly
heart.

6
Ink over lines
you like and
erase lines you
don't need.

7
Color Slasher.
YOU DID IT!

PHYLLIS MEREDITH

J. C. PHILLIPPS is a picture book creator and longtime graphic novel reader, as well as the owner of a somewhat extensive (though mostly accidental) unicorn collection. Like Pacey, she has a slight bossy streak and occasionally has purple hair. Unlike Pacey, she hasn't met a real unicorn. Yet. J.C. lives in Connecticut with her husband, son, and two cats, Boris and Natasha. *Pacey Packer: Unicorn Tracker* is her graphic novel debut.

Visit her online at JCPHILLIPPS.COM and @JCPHILLIPPS.

And don't miss the next PACEY PACKER ⚡ UNICORN TRACKER, coming in 2021!

ACKNOWLEDGMENTS

This book has been in the works for a long time, and there are super, awesome people who have helped make it a reality.

A hundred high fives to my critique group, The Litwits. Ammi-Joan Paquette, Kip Wilson, and Natalie Dias Lorenzi, you have been with me from the start. Your continued support for this project helped keep it alive, and your fabulous advice helped shape the characters and tone.

Thanks so much to my agent, Michael Bourret, for your kindness, professionalism, and enthusiasm for my projects. And also, a hug to my friend Anna-Lisa Cox for sharing her agent with me.

Giant kisses to everyone on Team Pacey at Random House. My editor—Shana Corey—I am so lucky to have you on this project. You totally get me, Pacey, and Slasher, and you have the mad editing skills to make this book the best it can be. And to Michelle Cunningham, thank you so much for your fantastic creative insight and all those little sketches you've made. It has been a pleasure working with you both.

To my son, Cameron, thank you for reading through the manuscript, helping me with puns, and simply being the best kid ever. To my husband, Michael, thank you for buying me lots of unicorn stuff and allowing me to be the nerdy, dorky, creative weirdo that I am. You both fill my life with laughter and love. I am very lucky to have you.

To everyone who has asked me about this project, offered to look at some pages (Callie and Flynn), and given encouragement, from the bottom of my heart, I thank you.

3 1901 06210 0435